FIVE ELEMENTS. ONE REALM. ONE CHOICE.

FROM SPIRIT AND BINDING

NEW YORK TIMES BESTSELLING AUTHOR

CARRIE ANN RYAN

From Spirit and Binding: An Elements of Five Novel
Copyright © 2019 Carrie Ann Ryan

ISBN: 978-1-947007-88-8

Cover Art by Charity Hendry

FROM
SPIRIT
AND
BINDING

PRAISE FOR
CARRIE ANN RYAN...

"Carrie Ann Ryan knows how to pull your heartstrings and make your pulse pound! Her wonderful Redwood Pack series will draw you in and keep you reading long into the night. I can't wait to see what comes next with the new generation, the Talons. Keep them coming, Carrie Ann!"

—LARA ADRIAN
New York Times bestselling author of CRAVE THE NIGHT

"Carrie Ann Ryan never fails to draw readers in with passion, raw sensuality, and characters that pop off the page. Any book by Carrie Ann is an absolute treat."

—J. KENNER
New York Times Bestselling Author

"With snarky humor, sizzling love scenes, and brilliant, imaginative worldbuilding, The Dante's Circle series reads as if Carrie Ann Ryan peeked at my personal wish list!"

—LARISSA IONE
NYT Bestselling Author

To my readers. I know you've been waiting.

FROM SPIRIT AND BINDING

NYT Bestselling Author Carrie Ann Ryan continues Lyric's prophecy in this breathtaking sequel to *From Flame and Ash*.

In her quest to unlock four of her five elements, Lyric has watched those she loves fade into ash and ruin. Bearing the weight of much loss and heartache, she and her team try to regroup and journey back to the only home Lyric has left—the Obscurité Court.

With the future uncertain, and the one person who could help her control her new powers missing, Lyric has never felt more lost. But as the pieces begin to come together in an epic unveiling she wasn't prepared for, she'll have to remember why she was called upon to become the Spirit Priestess in the first place.

The King of Lumière wants revenge for his lost brother, but he also wants so much more. With a missing king, a lost prince, and a few unexpected allies, Lyric will have to battle more than one enemy, and face countless unanswered questions with regards to a prophecy previously lost to the Maisons.

LACE RUINS

ORY

FIRE ESTATE

OBSCURITE

RIT
RITORY

SPIRIT COURT RUINS

EARTH ESTATE

FROM
SPIRIT
AND
BINDING

CHAPTER 1

LYRIC

The world had ended, and still, I stood in silence. Others were screaming, shouting my name.

Yet.

Silence.

The world must have ended, because Rhodes was dead.

The world had clearly ceased, because Easton had disappeared right in front of me.

And if the world hadn't ended, then perhaps this was a dream.

It *had* to be a dream.

I knew my dreams, knew they came at me from all sides, from all edges of the world, and pulled at me until there was nothing left.

Yet this wasn't a dream.

I knew it in my soul.

"Lyric?"

I blinked at the voice, so soft when it was normally full of steel. I looked over at Aerwyna—Wyn—and swallowed. Her dark hair had come out of its braid, and she looked more disheveled than I'd ever seen her before. Between the two of us, it was usually me with my blonde hair out of sorts, my body covered in mud and blood. Wyn was a warrior and yet had more grace and poise than most people I knew.

Today, however, we both looked wrung-out—at least, she did. I felt as if I'd been beaten and bruised. And I felt lost.

And now…now…I had nothing. No thoughts, no breath, no…

"Lyric," Wyn snapped, putting her hands on my shoulders and forcing me to focus on her and not on the nothingness threatening to overtake me.

I shook myself out of my thoughts and looked at her. "I'm okay." I whispered the word and held back a curse at the weakness I heard from my lips. I was not weak. No one would allow me to be. "I'm okay," I repeated.

Wyn gave me a tight nod, even with her face pale and covered in cuts and ash. "Good. Because we need to figure out what to do next."

"Where did Easton go?" I asked, voicing the question that had been circling in my mind over the past five minutes as everyone around me moved to do other things.

It didn't make sense. Then again, nothing made sense anymore.

The battle of the Water Estate was over, and the Lord of Water was dead, as were so many of his people—and ours. My friends from the Obscurité Kingdom, as well as those in the Lumière, who had fought by my side, were mostly unharmed, though only mostly.

We had lost so much, and I wasn't sure what we were supposed to do next.

I had known when I came back to the Maison realm—the realm that was not of the human world but sat upon it—that things would be different. That *I* would be different.

I just hadn't known it would be like this.

When they told me I was a Spirit Priestess, the one that could unite the realm and help save everyone from impending doom, it hadn't felt like this. I had thought I would be able to do something. This didn't feel like anything. Instead, it felt as if I were two steps behind, trying to catch up with the world around me.

Because the Lumière and the Obscurité were enemies, two sides of the realm that had been fighting for centuries. They'd fought before the Fall, the great battle that had taken their first two kings, the monarchs that ruled during the great war and had fractured the realm into pieces.

Now, it was five hundred years later, and I was a Spirit Priestess, the one who was supposed to somehow glue those pieces back together. That's all they'd told me, everything I had seen. Except it didn't make any sense.

Because I was supposed to do this with the people who had helped me by my side.

And now, the two most important ones were gone.

Rhodes, the son of the Lord of Water, had died, sacrificing himself for me. Killed by his own father no less.

He was gone, thrown off a cliff by Air Wielding infused with bone magic—the taboo powers created by the sacrifice of death—and had sunk to the bottom of the sea, surrounded by everything that had ruined us.

He was gone, and I hadn't had time to grieve. Because I had been forced to use all I had to take out the Lord of Water and protect everyone else. To protect the realm itself.

And when I thought we were safe, when I'd thought to grieve while holding on to the one person I thought I could love more than anything else in the world, Easton had been taken away from me, as well.

Not killed, or stabbed through the heart like before, not thrown off a cliff like Rhodes. Just warped out of existence. I still didn't understand. The fact that I could even think the words that he'd been stabbed in the heart before just told me how much we'd gone through over the past year plus. Yet it had all been for naught. He was gone. And I had no idea why.

"Where is Easton?" I asked again, pulling myself from my convoluted thoughts. There would be time to go over what had happened here on the battlefield later, moments to count our missing and our dead. There would be opportunity to mourn. Though first, I had to try and understand what had happened right in front of me.

Because I had discovered just a few moments ago that Easton was my soulmate, the one person in the world who was meant for me. And I had thought he knew it, too. Then, something had come over his eyes, and he bluntly stated that I couldn't be his. That he would never love me.

And while it had hurt, had torn into my soul as if his words were a carving knife, I knew that something was wrong.

Then, suddenly, he was tugged away, a rope of shadow and smoke pulling him from me.

I had seen it. Had felt it course through my veins as the elements I Wielded pushed at me for control. But I had never seen magic such as that.

"I don't know where Easton is. We're going to figure it out. We need to get off this battlefield, and we have to make plans."

"I know. We need to go home." I whispered the last word, and Wyn's eyes widened as she nodded.

"Home."

"To the Obscurité Court. That's home."

I had been born in the human realm. I hadn't even known that the Maison realm existed for most of my life. Somehow, over the past months, the Obscurité Court had become home. Yes, those of the Lumière Kingdom had been the Maisons I met first. The ones who had drawn me close and befriended me. Rhodes and his sister, as well as a few others.

Though it was the Obscurité Court, the one I had thought was home to my enemies for so long, that had proven to be *my* home. Those there had trained me, and they seemed to understand what I had to accomplish. Or maybe they just understood that I needed time to figure out the prophecy.

That was where I belonged now, even if I wasn't sure it would always be the case.

We needed to gather our forces. And we needed to leave.

Rhodes sister came up to them then, her hair flowing in the wind, dirt covering her dress, though I'd never seen her dirty before in my life.

"Okay, we're going," Rosamond said as she raised her chin. She was Rhodes' sister, older by almost two centuries. It was odd to think that the Maisons could live for what felt like forever. And yet all of them that I'd met so far looked as if they were my age, either nineteen or in their twenties. Even their parents and the dead at our feet appeared young, as if no time had passed. Only those who lost their Wielding looked as if they aged.

I remembered an older woman from the caves, one who had been a Seer just like Rosamond. That woman had Seen herself saving me at the cost of her life many moons ago. She'd lost the rest of her Wielding thanks to the Fall and the two crystals that brought the realms together. The crystals were dying, and because of misuse by others, the realm was stripping the Wielding from its own people—their lives along with it. So, the woman had aged, and yet she had used her last bits of power, her remaining vestiges of life, to save me.

I would never forget her, even if I hadn't really known her.

She had been one of the first steps to me realizing who I was, even if it didn't feel like I had any answers anymore.

"We've already planned," Lanya, the Lady of Air said as she raised her chin. She was Rhodes' and Rosamond's grandmother, and stood next to the body of her fallen husband, the Lord of Air.

She looked so strong, so graceful. But I knew she was broken inside. Though not the same kind of shattered as I was because I didn't have centuries of love and connection, all of which she had just lost.

Nevertheless, she was strong, and if she could do this, then so could I.

"I will go back to the Air territory and do what I can to collect the necessary forces and get us prepared for battle. Because this is only the beginning. It seems it's always only the beginning."

"I will go with you," Rosamond said. "Even though I'm the last of my line…" Rosamond's voice broke as she said it, and Luken, an Air Wielder who had been best friends with Rhodes, reached out and gripped her hand.

She squeezed it in return and gave him a sad smile. "Since I am the last of my line, I suppose I am the new Lady of Water. However, with my uncle, I don't know if that's accurate. Regardless, I know I have to be with you. It's time for me to go with you."

Their uncle, the king of the Lumière, had been fighting against the Obscurité for as long as he'd been ruler. Longer, since his father had been the old king, who had died during the Fall when the realm fractured. None of us knew exactly what side he was on. We had a feeling it wasn't going to be on the side of good and fate, though.

Because that was the problem with being a Spirit Priestess. Not everybody *wanted* me to fix the realm. Some liked the power they had, or didn't believe I could do what the prophecy said. And while I had doubts in my own abilities, I had seen too much to believe that I didn't have at least something to do with bringing everyone back together again.

"And, of course, I'll be there, too," Luken put in. And I knew he wasn't just thinking about trying to protect Rosamond or even me. The love of his life had died in front of us only a year before. My best friend, Braelynn. She had come back as my Familiar, yet she wasn't the girl she'd once been. Braelynn was currently in the Obscurité Kingdom with Easton's uncles.

I swallowed hard, trying to push all those thoughts back. I didn't want to think about that. I just needed to put one foot in front of the other and get there. And then I'd figure out what to do next.

That was how I had been functioning for the past year or so. Longer if I thought about it. One step at a time, and then I would find my place.

"We're going back with you," Teagan added, putting his arm around Wyn's shoulders. Teagan was a Fire Wielder. In fact, he was the son of the Lord of Fire, a man I had met last year. He was Easton's best friend, and a fellow warrior, along with Wyn.

I looked down at the corpses and lost at our feet and noted that they had brought Arwin's corpse with them.

Arwin had died to protect me. A young Earth Wielder who was just learning, but such a strong warrior.

The plan was to bring his body back to the Obscurité Kingdom with us. There had been so much loss. But we would make it—we didn't have a choice.

"Okay, gather what you need…" I looked over and paused, my voice trailing off. I had forgotten that I'd burned everything to ash.

It was me. My powers had done that.

No one looked at me with disgust though, at least not among my friends.

I could still remember the horror on the faces of those who were either against us or those outside of our core group that had been fighting for us.

Because I could now Wield four elements. Air, Earth, Water, and now, Fire.

I'd found my fourth element. It had broken free from my soul deep down below the sea when Rhodes' father had tried to drown me, Easton, and Rhodes by chaining us to the bones of those the Lord of Water had murdered over time.

I had unlocked my fourth element under duress, and I couldn't control it.

Even now, I could feel all four of them competing for the top power—Water sometimes trickling from my fingertips with puffs of Air.

The earth occasionally rattled beneath the soles of my feet, and I hoped that no one noticed, but I knew they did.

And now, the Fire burned within me, hot spikes that licked at my skin from the inside. I knew if I weren't careful, it would all come forth at once and maybe hurt someone I loved.

It had already hurt so many people. I had been a living flame, and I hadn't been able to control it.

I was supposed to be the Spirit Priestess, the one to save the world, but I couldn't even save myself.

Instead, I had been forced to lean on Easton, the one person who could soothe me enough that I could control all four elements at once.

Now, he was gone. And I had no idea where he had been taken.

I knew it had to be connected to what had been pulling us apart before. Maybe Wyn and Teagan and Easton's uncles back in the Obscurité Kingdom would know. They had so much history between them that they *had* to at least have an inkling of what surrounded us every time we took a step toward victory.

Perhaps I would get answers. It was past the time of secrecy and trying to keep me in the dark. I needed to know.

I couldn't rely on Easton anymore. He was gone, and I had to figure out how to control my four elements by myself.

Eventually, I would unlock the fifth.

Spirit.

The one that nobody really knew about. Because there were no more Spirit Wielders.

They had all been murdered by the past kings or pulled from the realm. Some had run, and maybe that was how I came to be. Centuries ago, the old Spirit Wielders had come gone to the human realm and blended. The only Spirit Wielders I knew were the ones from my dreams, and an old man who lived in a cave and spoke in riddles.

How was I supposed to Wield five elements when I couldn't control four, and it felt as if I couldn't even handle one?

"Lyric?" Wyn spoke again. This time, Rosamond moved closer to me and put her hands on my face.

I looked into the Seer's eyes, irises so much like Rhodes' silver ones but just different enough.

The soft brown of her skin was currently dusted in ash, and I knew it was my fault.

When I broke, I had torn down the estate and the castle of the Water territory. No one had died. They had promised me that. Because Rosamond had Seen what I could do, Saw the destruction I would bring, and she had evacuated the building.

We were all still covered in the remnants of what had been lost because of me.

"Pull yourself together, Lyric. You can break, but not here. Not now. Soon, we will be with those we need. And we will find the answers. For now, we must leave. We can take the bodies of those we need to with us, and my grandmother will bury the rest. We will remember them. All of them." Her voice broke this time, and I reached out and hugged her close, her hands moving from my face to around my neck.

She had lost her mother, her brother, and her father all in a short period of time.

And while my own heart hurt, I knew I couldn't be selfish. It wasn't just my pain here. It was the grief and agony of everyone else.

We were broken, and yet we had survived the battle. We had won.

And though we had lost many close to us, I had to remember that we came out victorious.

As the others had said: we would fight, we would win—no matter the cost.

Now, we had to look at what we lost and tally the price paid.

"Okay, then. Let's go."

I didn't really know what else to do, I wasn't trained like they were, hadn't had centuries to gain the experience and the knowledge for cleaning up after a battle like this.

I did what Rosamond and Wyn told me to do and helped pack what was left. Soon, we had a group of people headed towards the Obscurité Court. It would be a long journey, mostly because we couldn't use the magic of either of the crystals to go from one place to the other quickly. First, because we weren't anywhere near the Obscurité Court and had no idea what the Lumière crystal even felt or looked like. Secondly, because the crystals themselves were dying, fading out of existence. Because of that, we couldn't use their magic to create a portal like we were able to before.

No, we would have to travel across the rest of the Water territory, through the northern Spirit territory, and then across the other side towards the Obscurité Court.

We had traveled the opposite way to get here, and we would make our way back. Minus Easton, Rhodes, and Arwin, but with a few Lumière survivors. And those of the Air territory that were coming at the Lady of Air's insistence.

"You need a healer, just in case. I'm giving you one. Take my people, even into the Obscurité Court. We aren't just light and dark anymore," she said. "We are those who want to save our realm, and those who don't want change. Who fear survival."

We would figure it out.

Everyone else had things to do, and though I did what I was supposed to and took orders, I still felt lost.

Where had Easton gone? Who had taken him?

How were we supposed to find him?

All of that spun through my mind, and my powers lurched, the Fire at my fingertips too much. No one was paying attention to me. Everyone was busy with what they needed to do so we could go home. So, I staggered away towards the cliff where Rhodes had fallen, and I let out the Fire. My hands were outstretched on either side of me, my elements seeping out of me as I tried to get myself under control. I knew others were probably watching, but that was fine.

They needed to see who I was, *what* I was. Because I certainly didn't have the answer.

And then I looked down into the rocky crevice just below and saw a bone, a little pebble that had once been part of a person, although it was now coated in bone magic.

I narrowed my eyes, wondering why it was floating on the surface, and then there was another, and another.

And then the answer flashed in my mind.

Rhodes had taken the full brunt of an Air Wielder's magic to the heart and had fallen off the cliff. *But* he had taken some of the magic-infused bones with him.

I looked down, hardly able to believe what I was seeing. And then I screamed.

Because the bones surrounded someone, and they had brought them to the surface. As I looked down, my scream ebbed, and I gasped, hope springing eternal even as I tried to temper its effect.

And then the eyes of the man below opened, and the silver stunned.

CHAPTER 2

EASTON

Claws dug at my chest as if their spindly fingers were no longer brittle, and instead strong, grasping without mercy.

I could feel the power of whatever lay beneath the shadow as it dug deep into my flesh and encircled my heart.

One squeeze, a single moment of time. I couldn't breathe.

I tried to move, attempted to pull at whatever tethered my body. It was no use.

This was my flesh, my destiny, my ending.

I had known there was something in the darkness waiting for me. I hadn't known it would be the darkness itself. The absence of light. It didn't matter that my kingdom had been named for the dark, while my enemy—or the one that should have been my enemy—for the light. This was new, a depth I hadn't known existed before now.

I tried to open my eyes. However, it was as if something were pressing down on me, forcing the life from my body even as it took control.

I couldn't allow this. I *wouldn't* allow this.

I was the King of Obscurité. I was Easton, the dual Wielder of Earth and Fire. I was perhaps one of the strongest Wielders of my time, and I would not allow anyone to control me.

Then, even as I thought the words that had been simultaneously the bane of my existence and the strength of my convictions, the fingers that weren't truly fingers squeezed my heart again. I tried to catch my breath, attempted to fist my hands at my sides. I gritted my teeth and tugged against my bonds.

Nothing happened. It was as if I were thinking all of these thoughts, trying to move, and yet nothing happened. My body was not my own. My mind was the only thing left, and still, those fingers were moving up my chest, across my jaw, and then burrowing into my brain. I could feel them slowly caressing my mind and squeezing, forcing their will upon me as I got lost in the darkness.

Perhaps I was even the darkness itself.

The cursed, the demented, the lost.

Maybe I was the hand of the puppeteer, the one controlling so much of what was happening in my realm. The one I'd thought had orchestrated so much beyond fulfilling a prophecy that I was destined to watch but not claim as my own.

I wasn't Easton anymore.

I was made of the dreams of the darkness, the darkness itself, and the claim of the master who held that hand, that shadow and smoke.

Then the hands or whatever they were left me, and I fell to my knees, the impact sending shocking pain rocketing through my kneecaps and into the rest of my body.

That agony opened my eyes, and I could finally see.

I wasn't just a thought, a mind, a hapless soul in the cosmos.

I was Easton again.

I wasn't lost, nor was I found.

I put my palms on the ground, trying to feel the earth beneath my skin. I had always been an Earth Wielder, just like I had always been a Fire Wielder. I had been able to feel the elements around me from the moment I was born. I'd been able to Wield, even if I hadn't known what I was doing. Like most children my age, I had been bound so I wouldn't harm myself or others until I learned control.

Some didn't come to their Wielding until maturity, but I was special. I was the son of the queen, grandson of the old king, who with the Lumière king had destroyed the realm during the Fall.

I had that power beneath my skin, running through my veins.

And all along, I had fought every ounce of pressure and torment that came with being who I was.

At least, I thought I had.

I'd never known what it would feel like to not have Wielding within me.

As I searched for my Earth Wielding to save myself as I tried to protect those under my care, I felt nothing.

The absence of power was suffocating.

There was no Earth. No Fire to call.

Though the power was within me, there was no element to reach out to in order to bond.

Because as I had taught Lyric, I knew that even though the power was within us, even trying to control us and overwhelm us at times, it was also what we called upon from around us to form that symbiotic relationship with the territories and the realm.

At the thought of Lyric's name, that shadowy hand clutched my heart again, and I fell to one elbow, gasping out a breath. I wanted to scream, needed to shout at something.

But I had no voice, no breath. I had nothing.

My eyes were open, though I could see only shadow, the purples and inkiness of whatever blackness was in front of me.

If I could feel the elements within me, surrounding me, yet see nothing in front of me, was I truly alive?

I had a feeling something had changed.

Before this, I had been standing on the edge of a cliff, looking down at Lyric after we had won the battle but lost so much in the process.

She had looked at me, seemingly seeing so much within me, even though I knew she couldn't see the truth.

Because I knew the truth. There was nothing there for her. There couldn't be.

I was cursed. Plagued to know that there was such a thing as hope and love and connection running through my body—but unable to feel it. To acknowledge it.

She had told me that she was my soulmate, and she knew I had to be hers, too.

My heart shattered again just thinking about it, that hand squeezing within me.

I sucked in another breath, trying to control my body, even as it shook on the ground, writhing in pain.

The curse had taken over the moment I wanted to tell her what I *wanted* to feel. That moment had proven that I would never be with my soulmate. That I could never love her. It wasn't that I didn't want to. No, it wasn't that easy.

I would know that she was there. She would stand in front of me and bear witness, bare her soul. That was my torment.

I was cursed to never have her.

To never truly love her. I could care for her, want her in my life, but never in the way that mattered.

Never soul to soul, body to body.

Because she was not mine.

I'd told Lyric that. I had said the words. And as she broke in front of me, clearly confused and unaware of what lay beneath my skin, something had taken me.

To where, was the question.

"I hope you're done overthinking exactly what's going on," a deep voice whispered from all around. I couldn't tell if the male was in front of me or behind. Or maybe within my mind.

It was if the clouds and the shadows themselves carried the voice, the whispers.

Yet it was deafening.

As the man spoke, it felt as if the sound were sucking all of the oxygen from the room, placing us in a tunnel so I couldn't hear anything but him. Yet I couldn't hear him at all. It made no sense. Still, I knew there had to be a reason for it.

Because I wasn't in the Maison realm anymore.

I couldn't be.

I looked at the shadows and knew the deafening silence could only mean one thing.

I was in the Shadow realm.

The realm that wasn't supposed to exist. The one among the others that had been a prison for so long. It should have been destroyed in the Fall.

Most people didn't even remember it had existed at all.

As I staggered to my feet, the shadows slid around my body as if snakes slithering along my skin.

Yes, this was the Shadow realm.

Whoever was around me had to be one of its prisoners.

One that had been banished long ago.

Suddenly, I knew who he was. Recognized that voice now. Knew it from the nightmares I'd survived as a child.

He was The Gray.

This, apparently, was my destiny.

"You're here because of your curse. And I figured it was finally time for the two of us to meet."

I could see in front of me now, and knew where the voice originated from even if it echoed.

The Gray stood before me in a large cloak, a cowl over his face and the rest of his body hidden so I couldn't tell exactly how broad his shoulders were or what he looked like.

He was just the disembodied voice of a man in a cape.

I knew the power within, though. I remembered the stories, even if I didn't know if all of them were true or not.

From the darkness surrounding me, and the fact that I was here at all, I had a feeling that everything that I had heard as a child, even the fairy tales and ghost stories of my past, had only been a hint of what this man was.

"You're The Gray," I said, trying to keep my voice strong even though I didn't feel that way.

"I am. The fact that you've heard of me bodes well. Although, I feel like this meeting of ours has been a long time coming. At least, where you could truly remember it. You never could remember the times with Lore at my side, could you? No matter. It's of no concern."

My eyes widened. "What are you talking about? Where are we? You need to let me go. I am the King of Obscurité. People will be looking for me."

"I know who you are, Easton. Son of Cameo and Zeke. Grandson of Singer, all kings and queens of the Obscurité. Much like you. But they will never find you here. No one remembers the Shadow realm. And maybe that is on them, or perhaps that is what I desire. You *have* heard of me. Yes, I am The Gray. And this time, now, we speak face-to-face. A time you'll remember me. Because the events in your realm have finally come to a point where I can have you brought here. For me. The Spirit Priestess is alive, and that means, it is time for the next phase."

I tried to take a step forward, but the shadows surrounding me wrapped around my wrists and my ankles as if chains held me in place.

"Don't you dare hurt Lyric." I gritted out the words, longing and pain sliding through me even as the emotions were doused by the curse threatening to take control of me.

"Is that love I hear in your voice?" The Gray asked, almost a laugh in the question. I could hear the smile, but I couldn't see it.

"Don't you dare touch her."

"No, it can't be love," The Gray answered himself, ignoring me. "Because you cannot love. You can never love your soulmate or be with her. I made sure of that long ago."

I froze, blinking. "No, it wasn't you." I swallowed hard, my tongue heavy. It couldn't have been The Gray. I couldn't be so important to him that he'd do something like this. Whatever this man was, there was one thing I knew. He was a myth. And to be within his line of sight meant death. "It was Lore who put the curse on me when I was younger. Lore, my mother's knight. He's dead."

"And the curse didn't break? Odd, isn't it? I would have assumed the curse would break upon his death."

I had assumed that, as well, but I had been wrong. It had been Lore.

He'd tried to torture me as a child. Did so much to me under the guise of trying to train me.

I hadn't truly known it was he who cursed me until his death when he used the crystal and tainted our realm. He killed my mother and so many others.

Lore had been my mother's second in command. He had also been the man who killed my father. Then again, I hadn't known that at the time. No one had known the depths of his cruelty, depravity, and power. And yet… The Gray had always been worse in my mind, even if he'd only been a legend.

Lore had wanted power, so he had used the crystal that held our realm together in a perverse way and stole the Wielding from the realm's people. It had killed some, created Danes out of the others—magic-less beings who were not human, but also not true Wielders anymore.

Lore was dead. Killed by Lyric after she had saved herself from a mortal blow.

A wound that I should have been able to heal. I frowned, looking down at my scar.

I remembered bleeding from the same spot where Lyric had bled. I'd thought maybe I had been hit by a rock or a piece of shrapnel or even gotten nicked by a sword. That wasn't the case. I had bled because of Lyric's mortal wound. In the same spot as mine.

It was said that between soulmates, a mortal wound on one showed up on the other, and that they were the only two who could heal each other.

The one without the original wound wouldn't die, and wouldn't suffer as deep a wound, but the original could only be saved by their soulmate.

Shock registered within me, and my hands clenched even as I fought my internal battle.

"Ah, I see you're coming to the realization you should have come to long ago. Yes, Lyric is your soulmate, but she will never be yours in truth. The curse will make sure of that. You'll never be able to truly recognize her, or want her or love her. She was able to save herself because of who she is. She doesn't need you. She never did. And she never will. The two of you together would be nothing. It will never happen."

I fought against my bonds, trying to push away the thoughts of what hurt and could never be, and tried to think of only freedom.

I couldn't. I couldn't do anything.

"Why?" I ground out, grasping at anything I could.

He ignored my question. "You were promised to me by Lore," The Gray continued. "Yes, he was one of mine. He got too greedy. So, in the end, he deserved what he got. He was weak. I am not. He was my third, but now you will be."

"I will never be yours." I couldn't be. Just like Lyric could never be mine. I didn't know why that thought came to me at that exact moment, but it was all connected within the boundaries of my mind. I might not love her, could *never* love her, but I'd do anything for her. And not just because she was the Spirit Priestess.

That phantom hand gripped my heart again, and I knew it was the curse, the one that would ultimately kill me and take everything from me, ounce by ounce, bit of soul by bit of soul.

The Gray smiled, and I could only see that because he moved his head ever so slightly so the lights coming from somewhere hit his face.

I couldn't see who he was, got only the impression that there must be beauty there, even with the beast.

"You will be my third. Not second, as you're not ready and will never be. But not lowest either, because I know what you can do for me with your connection to the Spirit Priestess and your realm." He paused. "I suppose you should meet your contemporaries. The ones who will help me go to the Maison realm and rule as I should have done long ago. That will come later. There are more chess pieces in play. You are but a pawn. Soon, you will be a knight. And the rook and the others on my board of the Maison realm will soon come into my shadows. And then I will rule. Alas, we're not there yet."

He snapped his fingers, and two shadows merged together and then split apart again before coming towards me.

They were shadows no more. Instead, they were two men with broad shoulders and dark hair. And wicked eyes.

The Gray gestured to his left. "This is Durlan, former Earth

Wielder, now a Dane because of your family. You cost him everything, and now he's mine. He is my second. He will teach you exactly what you will do as my third."

Durlan grinned at me, and though the man had once been an Earth Wielder, I could see the fire within his eyes. The pure hatred. The anger.

I fought against my bonds again, but there was nothing I could do. Nothing *yet.*

"And Garrik, my fourth." The Gray gestured towards the other man. "A former Air Wielder, and now a Dane. Yes, the Obscurité and the Lumière have finally come together, but under my rule. They are my court, my warriors, and you will be mine, as well. First, we have a few things to talk about."

I heard the smile in his voice again, and Durlan grinned while Garrik just looked at me blankly. I didn't know which expression scared me more.

"First, we shall play."

And at The Gray's words, the lightning came, and I screamed.

CHAPTER 3

LYRIC

S omeone shouted for a healer, while others screamed one thing or another, but I pushed their words and the sounds of their voices—anything and everything—from my mind.

I fell to my knees, the sharp sting of bone and rock digging into my skin painful, but I didn't care.

I couldn't care.

Not when Rhodes was in front of me, his eyes open, those silver pools pulling me in. He lay on the ground, his head in his grandmother's lap. Lanya knelt beside him, her dress covered in mud, dirt, and blood, but she was still graceful and beautiful. The Lady of Air bent her head over her grandson and wept, wiping his face with her fingertips as if she weren't sure he was real.

I wasn't either.

How could Rhodes be here? How could he be *alive*?

I'd seen him take the full power of the bone-magic-infused Air his father had sent toward his chest. And while the now-dead Lord of Water held two types of Wielding, Air and Water, he'd also used the stolen bone magic to increase his might. That meant Rhodes had taken the full impact of a blow of untold magics and Wielding, directly to his heart.

Yet, he lived.

"How?" I gasped, my heart beating so hard it echoed in my head. I hadn't even realized I'd said it aloud until Luken gave me a wide-eyed, watery look.

"We'll figure it out," Rosamond whispered as she sank down to the ground next to me. "First, we need a healer."

"Lyric," Rhodes gasped, and something squeezed my heart, a hand reaching in and not letting go. Tears pricked the backs of my eyes, but I couldn't cry. Not then. Not when we didn't know why he was back, how he'd survived, or if this was only a mere moment before reality crashed in and everything faded again.

A time when Rhodes would indeed be dead.

And Easton would still be missing.

No.

No, I couldn't think like that. Couldn't think at all.

I leaned closer, cupping his face. His skin was smooth, wet from the ocean I thought had taken him from us. How…? I still didn't know what had happened, but we didn't have a lot of time. We had to make sure Rhodes was safe, and then we needed to go home.

Rhodes…was he the Lord of Water now? Or even the Lord of Air, if lines of succession went to the next male heir rather than staying with a woman? I didn't know. It hadn't been in any of the books I'd read. And, once again, I felt as if I were falling behind in a world I hadn't been born in, yet had been tasked to protect.

"Rhodes," I whispered. "You're here."

"Lyric." His words came out on a breath. And then he closed his eyes, and my heart lurched.

Hands pulled me away, and I found myself leaning against Wyn as one of Lanya's healers hovered over Rhodes' prone form.

I sucked in deep breaths as Wyn held me, the two of us seemingly in the way of everyone who knew what they were doing. I felt so lost again, and I hated it. I hated all of this.

"I can heal," I said into the silence, trying to think. "I…I have healing powers." Not just with my soulmate, not only with Easton.

I winced at that thought, trying to ignore the ache and confusion I felt.

Wyn rubbed my arms, sending warmth through me. "Let them do what they were meant to do. We know you can heal, we've seen it, but you used so much power to protect us all. Recover a bit before we move out on our journey."

The others moved quickly, two healers working in tandem over Rhodes' body, and I shook myself out of my reverie, standing up with Wyn at my side.

I couldn't just hang back and watch, couldn't do nothing when we already had plans to move, to make our way to the Obscurité Kingdom.

I had questions. So many questions.

As if she knew exactly what I was thinking, Rosamond came to stand in front of me, her face pale, her eyes wide, and her hands clasped in front of her.

I didn't know her as well in reality as I felt I did in my heart.

We had spent so much time during my first trek to the Maison realm, searching for her because the Negs had captured her on the Obscurité knight's orders. She had been the main reason I'd first stepped foot into this realm, and yet I only knew her through our letters, and the time before I had known the truth of things. What magic was.

So, while I felt as if I knew her now, I didn't know all her tells. I didn't know if she would welcome my touch or my comfort.

I couldn't just stand there while she looked so lost. As the Seer who could divine the future grieved the fact that she wasn't able to See this because she couldn't See those that were close to her.

She couldn't See her brother, couldn't See what had been happening to her mother.

She hadn't been able to See exactly what her father had been up to when he killed so many in order to gain power.

All because she shared blood with them.

Now she was here, and Rhodes wasn't dead. We had to be grateful for that. I couldn't let myself feel anything more about it, though. Not when I couldn't really think at all.

Decision made, I took two steps forward and opened my arms.

"Rosamond?" I asked, my voice soft.

She blinked away tears, her light brown skin shining under the sun-light as it hit the tears she had let fall.

"I couldn't See…" Suddenly, she was there, in my arms, her head nestled on my shoulder as I hugged her tightly, trying to give her comfort, even though I wasn't sure I could give any at all.

"It's okay," I whispered, running my hands over her hair, the soft, dark curls skimming through my fingers. "It's going to be okay."

"I know. It has to be," she said, pulling back from me.

She wiped away her tears again and then rolled her shoulders back.

Rosamond was about four hundred years old from what I remembered. She had seen countless days pass, had seen so much more than I could ever imagine, and yet I was the one to comfort her. Or maybe I was the only one who could understand in that moment and had the time and comfort to give. After all, everyone else had something to do, getting ready for our move and what had to happen next.

My gaze traveled behind Rosamond for a moment, across the ashy and barren landscape that had once held a castle. A large estate that had housed the Lord and Lady of Water and their children. That had em-ployed servants and countless others who had served the lord and his small court.

Now, thanks to my Fire, the Water Estate was gone.

I had burned it down in my rage, in my need to protect my friends, the family of my own making that I was trying to build. Those I loved. The uncontrollable element within my veins had overpowered the other three, with the final one still locked within my soul. I hadn't been strong enough to hold it back.

I had destroyed the estate and the land surrounding it when the Fire within me became too much and almost cracked through my skin, trying to overtake everything.

I hadn't killed with my Fire—at least not the innocent.

Since I had first stepped foot in the Maison realm, I'd killed far more than I ever thought possible.

All to protect a realm that might not want me in the end.

Because not everybody wanted this change.

Some didn't want me to protect the realm and bring it together.

Yes, there was a prophecy, one that said I would be the one to save us all.

And yet I didn't know where I fell within that divination.

Not anymore.

"I still don't know what happens next," I said, rolling my shoulders back, much like Rosamond had earlier.

"I don't know as much as I should either," she said, pinching the bridge of her nose.

"Then you can be like the rest of us for once," Wyn said, but there was no sting to her words. She was just being practical. Because that was Wyn.

Rosamond nodded, her gaze far off in the distance. "I suppose you're right. I know I still need to go with you to the Obscurité Kingdom. I believe Rhodes needs to go, too. I didn't know what that feeling was inside me before. I felt I needed to be there. That if I followed this path, the next vision would come, I just didn't know anything else. Not until we saw him in the water." She paused. "I didn't See any of this, and I never want to *see* that image again in my mind."

My body shuddered, and I nodded. "Will he be okay to travel?" I asked, turning around to look on as the healers and Rhodes' grandmother worked.

"I believe so," she whispered. "Either way, he must come."

There were questions to be answered, though. "Is he the Lord of Water? Or the Lord of Air? How does this all work if you're taking him away from the Lumière Kingdom?"

"I think my uncle will make decisions for us," Rosamond said, looking into my eyes even though it didn't look as if she were truly seeing me. Maybe she was actually *Seeing.* "I said before that I don't believe it's Lumière versus Obscurité anymore. Not the way we thought for centuries. There are those pro change, and those against. One thing I do know, we must all be together so we can be as one and finish your training, unlock your final element, and figure out where the King of Obscurité has gone."

I swallowed hard, pain ratcheting up my body as my heart split in two once more, my hands shaking. "Where did he go?" I whispered.

"He's been taken before," Wyn said, her voice soft.

I whirled on her, my heart stuttering. Fire slicked up my sides, but I tamped it down, though not before Wyn's eyes widened. None of my friends stepped away, though. Not one. "Excuse me?"

"I thought it was Lore. But he's gone. I wasn't there when he died, we were on patrol, but I know Lore is dead."

I stepped forward, and Rosamond put her hand on my elbow so I wouldn't get closer to Wyn. She could likely sense the anger coursing through my veins.

"I know Lore is dead. I killed him myself." I snapped the words, but Wyn didn't pull back, she didn't even flinch. She was a warrior, after all. She could probably take me out with one hand movement, by just using her Wielding while I learned how to use my four. I was a weakling physically and in the magic department. They were all so much stronger than me.

"I don't know where Easton goes, and I don't even know if he's actually been taken before, or if maybe he just disappeared because he needed time to himself. A couple of times when we were younger, he was suddenly gone, and I thought perhaps it was training. But now that I look back on it, I just don't know. We will find him. He is my friend, my king, and he needs to be with his people. So, we will go to the Obscurité Kingdom, and hopefully, he will be there. I hope this is just a horrible dream, and he just disappeared to get ahead of us or something."

"It doesn't make any sense, Wyn."

"You don't think I know that? Nothing about this makes sense. But we can't just stand here and wallow. We need to *do* something."

"We do," I said. "We do. And I hate being lost, but it seems that's how I've been feeling for the past year."

"Well, our entire realm has been feeling that way for centuries because of the fighting. Now, we need to piece it together. And you're part of that. I hope to the gods that Rhodes is, too. That Easton is, as well."

"We will go to the Obscurité Kingdom like you said. We'll bring

Rhodes with us, we will bring Arwin's body. We will bring some of our own. Grandmother will go to the Air territory and ensure that we have allies there. But the Water territory? I don't believe it's ours anymore. Not the way we need it to be."

Rosamond visibly shuddered and then took a staggering step to the side as color leached from her face. "We need to go. We need to be quick. There won't be a lot of time."

Before I could say anything to that, the bracelet that Alura had given me when I was in the human realm burned on my wrist.

"Ouch." I gasped, looking down at the two symbols that glowed. Fire, and Earth.

The two elements of the Obscurité Kingdom. Easton's two. Representations of the place I now called home because I needed a *home*.

"This is Seer magic?" I asked, remembering what one of Easton's uncles had said back when we were in the Obscurité Court. Whenever something glowed on my wrist, it told me where I needed to go. Alura had been the one to give the jewelry to me, but she wasn't a Seer. Rosamond was.

I stared at the girl who was my friend, even if we weren't as connected as I was with Wyn or even the others I had traveled with before.

"I made that centuries ago and gave it to a girl named Alura when we were standing on the street, and you first came up to us. That time we went hiking. I gave it to her because I knew she needed to be the one to give it to you. I never knew why, only knew what I had to do. It's not easy Seeing parts of futures that don't make sense because they're a tangled web."

She took a breath.

"It's not my Seer magic glowing on your wrist. It is centuries of knowledge. The magics themselves pulling you towards where you need to go. We must begin our journey to the Obscurité Kingdom. We will go with your Teagan, my Rhodes, with Wyn, Luken, and a few others. We must go now. Rhodes is alive. I believe because of the bone magic."

I nodded, my whole body shaking. I had known that Seer magic was important, but the urgency in her voice worried me. "The bones went with him to the ocean, and they sang to us when we went through the sea towards the Air territory before. They opened that portal and saved us. Didn't they?" I asked, not knowing who might answer.

"That's what I felt," Wyn said, looking down at her hands. "I just didn't know it at the time. Not until we saw the bones and skulls on the sea floor. Their souls are crying out, they need closure."

"I am taking care of that," Lanya said as she walked towards us. "We are getting Rhodes set up on a cart so you can take him to the other kingdom. He will be safer there than here, I believe," she said. There was such sadness in her tone that I wanted to reach out and hold her, but I wasn't sure if that would be welcomed.

They had all lost so much, and I wasn't sure what I was supposed to feel.

Or if I should feel anything at all.

"I'll get the other things ready," Wyn said, hurrying off, leaving me alone with Rosamond and her grandmother. The others moved around us, and soon, we were ready to go, my body still shaking from the warring elements inside of me.

I couldn't control them, and that worried me. Because the one person that could help me center myself was gone, and that meant I needed to do it by myself.

I just didn't know how.

The ashes of the now-destroyed Water Estate stung my nose and left a mark on a landscape that had once been beautiful, even if it had concealed an evil that no one dared to name.

That was gone now, and we had to walk away. There would be re-percussions for what I did, for what we all did, but we would deal. *First,* we needed to get home.

So, we said goodbye to Lanya, to the others who had fought with us and would remain behind as our allies.

And then we journeyed east.

To the Obscurité Kingdom, to the place that I now called home. And, hopefully, one day, to Easton.

CHAPTER 4

LYRIC

I had wondered once what it felt like to live in a time that wasn't my own, back before there were cars and planes and different modes of transportation to get you from one side of the world to the other.

Then, I found myself in the Maison realm.

Technology didn't work the same here as it did back in the human realm, where I had been born and raised. Even though it had only been a little over a year since I learned about this new realm, it felt like eons. Maybe because once I had been taken away from all the comforts that made things easier to live and work and go to school, I realized they hadn't really mattered. Many of the Maisons had never even seen them before. They didn't venture to the human realm, so they didn't know what they were missing. They didn't know what it felt like to travel from one side of the Earth to the other in a steel tube flying at hundreds of miles per hour.

Rhodes, Easton, and some of the others in my circle had traveled to the human realm to find me.

Perhaps not *me* exactly. They had gone into the human realm to find the prophesied Spirit Priestess. The fact that it had been me, meant that their search had ended after hundreds of years.

It was still so odd to think that those surrounding me were centuries old, the youngest in their two hundreds or so.

Arwin had been younger. I let out a shuddering breath as I thought of him and looked back at the carriage that held his body.

He was the only dead we were bringing back with us. The others who had died for us and by our sides had been part of the Lumière Kingdom. We'd left Lanya behind, and she would take care of the Wielders there. She would bury them and make sure they had the services they deserved. Each of the territories had their own way of saying goodbye, of dealing with their dead.

One day, I would learn them, but for now, we had to move quickly through the northern Spirit territory to get to the Fire territory. To the Obscurité Court.

The Maison realm, while without technology, held magic.

Thousands of years ago, the territories had been split, along with its people. With the Water Wielders in the northwest, and the Air Wielders in the southwest. In the Obscurité Kingdom, the Fire Wielders occupied the northeast, and the Earth Wielders were far in the southeast. The Spirit Wielders had been the ones to split them, both up north and down south. In my head, the Spirit territories looked like two pieces of pie, their points gently touching, but I knew that wasn't technically the case. The borders were a little more ragged, not perfectly drawn, and along the lines themselves, the two territories blended. The first one I had seen had been Earth and Fire, where it looked like the red rocks of Colorado, the two elements combining to create the beauty. And the people within those areas sometimes had both Wieldings—or just one. Or, thanks to the dying crystals, none. They were Danes now, no more magic, beholden to those around them for protection.

"Sometimes, I really wish the old days were still here, the ones where we could just easily move from one part of the territory to another using the crystal and so much energy." Wyn came up to my side, and I looked over at her, giving her a small smile.

"I was just thinking that. I'm not exactly sure how you guys made it this long without cars."

"You know, I hear those are very helpful," she said, shaking her head. Wyn gripped my hand, giving it a squeeze, and I smiled at her a little more. We were both hurting, inside and out, all of us a little numb. But we were just trying to make it through, trying to get home so we could formulate a plan.

It was the time leading up to formulating the plan seemed like we were out of our depths. And I hated that.

I really wished there was a way to make everything better and sparkly and wonderful, though I knew it wasn't going to happen.

"You know, we did at least have our own invention of the wheel," Wyn said, shaking her head at me. "We have carts, as you can tell," she said, gesturing towards the two that held Rhodes and Arwin, as well as another larger cart that held some of the supplies that we'd been able to find for the journey. We hadn't taken much because we knew the Water Estate and those within it needed more supplies than we did. Or at least what was *left* of the Water Estate.

I rubbed at the spot over my heart again, trying to ignore the pain.

I wasn't going to think about that.

"And we have horses, though they aren't exactly like yours in the other realm."

I glanced over at the large beasts that looked almost like Clydesdales but were slightly different, their noses a little wider, their coloring not quite the same chestnut or white or gray that I was used to. There was almost something a little more magical about them, too, and they looked as if they could see into my soul with those deep, dark eyes. Then again, some people thought horses back in the human realm were the same way.

"I know we would have been able to find a few more to ride through the northern Spirit territory to make it easier for us, but we just didn't have that kind of time. And I wanted to make sure that the others had what they needed to get to the other territories," Wyn continued. I nodded along.

"Plus, do horses do well on boats?" I asked, pondering.

"They do okay. After all, the horses from the Water territory are used to traveling over water like that."

The Water territory was mostly seas and rivers with one large massive landmass in one corner where the Water Estate had once stood.

There was also a swatch of land that bisected the area with a river that ran through that.

There were smaller parcels of land around the seas, and even Water towns built directly on the water with mechanics and magics to create civilizations.

I hadn't seen those, mostly because the ships that we had been on when we were traveling through the Water territory hadn't gone in that direction.

It was something I thought I might want to see someday, but it was hard for me to focus on that now, to focus on anything really.

Because all I could do was think about what would come next, and the fact that I had no clue what to do about any of it.

We kept saying that we needed to go home. Because *home* would help us think.

What else was there? Where else could we go when it felt as if all hope was lost?

Rhodes was hurt, one of the Air healers in the cart with him, doing his best to help.

Easton was just...gone.

I sucked in a breath and rubbed a hand over my chest again as Wyn squeezed my other hand before letting go.

It was as if she knew what I was thinking about.

I didn't know what I was thinking about. Not really.

Easton might be dead. At the very least, he had been taken.

I couldn't get the vision out of my head: the rope made of smoke that had wrapped around his body and then pulled him through the shadows. Had ripped him from my arms.

No, that wasn't quite right. He hadn't actually been *in* my arms. He had held me, kept me from destroying myself and everything else with my lack of control, and then he had kissed me.

Followed by him telling me he could never love me. It was as if someone else had been saying it. As if something had come over him.

I hoped to the gods that I would eventually find out what he meant. What had happened.

It was hard to have hope and strength when, though we'd won some battles, it felt as if the war would be everlasting. And I'd only been in it for a short time. I couldn't imagine what the others were going through. After all, they had been dealing with this war and the aftereffects of the Fall for centuries.

I was just a babe.

It was hard to think about whether they would resent me for not being able to help, for not being able to save them all with a snap of my fingers.

"It'll be okay, Lyric," Wyn whispered before she walked away, going to the cart where Arwin's body lay. She jumped over the side in one graceful movement, looking like the warrior she was, and then spoke in soft tones over Arwin's corpse.

I turned away, giving her privacy.

It was hard to watch, not knowing what to say.

He had died in front of me, protecting me. And it had felt like he was younger than me, as if he were a young trainee, and I was in his class.

He had been older than me, at least in terms of age, though maybe not in everything else.

After all, the Maisons aged differently than humans did.

That reminded me that, once again, I didn't know which side of the line I was on anymore. Was I human? Was I a Maison? Would I grow old over time? Or would I have the lifespan of those in this realm?

Honestly, that didn't really matter at the moment, because I had to survive first. We all had to.

"Is Braelynn at the Obscurité Court?" Luken asked as he came up beside me, bringing me out of my thoughts.

I looked over at the blond warrior, his hair pulled back in a leather thong, his sword strapped to his back. He looked so sad, his face set in weary lines, but there was hope in his eyes, too, an expression that worried me.

"She is. I left her with Justise and Ridley, Easton's uncles."

"They're the ones running the court, then?" he asked.

I nodded. "Yes. Apparently, they did it before when Queen Cameo and even King Zeke left. From what I could tell, they've always been close to Easton."

"Justise? He's the weapons maker, right?"

I nodded. "He's a Fire Wielder. The weapons maker and blacksmith at court. His husband, Ridley, is their healer, but I don't know what his Wielding is."

"Most think he's a Dane," Teagan said, walking up on my other side.

Teagan reminded me a lot of Luken, the Obscurité half, rather than the Lumière. Teagan was Easton's best friend and had once been with Wyn.

Now, the Fire Wielder seemed as lost as the rest of us. He had been training Arwin, as well, and now that Easton was gone, none of us really knew what to say or do. There were plans to be made, and we had to keep moving forward.

It was hard not to look back when the path in front of us was so covered in shadow.

"A Dane can be a healer?" Luken asked, frowning.

"You have something against Danes?"

There was a rumble in Teagan's voice, and I almost stopped to try and pull them to the side and make them get along. Mostly because I didn't want to deal with in-fighting, yet I didn't really know what I could do to stop a fight between two hulking warriors. I might have more Wielding than they did, but I didn't have their control.

"I was only asking because I hadn't heard of that before." Luken narrowed his eyes as we continued walking. I looked nervously around, noticing that some of the Air and Water Wielders that Lanya had sent with us were slowly pulling away, giving the two warriors some space. Maybe I should do the same, but I wasn't going to.

"So, you don't have anything against Danes?" Teagan asked.

Luken raised his chin and then stopped. I almost tripped over my feet to stop, as well. Teagan was on my other side, glaring at the warrior.

"My soulmate was a Dane. We don't know how she ended up in the human realm." Luken let out a breath through his nose. "She died." The words were clipped. Harsh. And so full of aching sadness that my heart lodged in my throat.

"Luken," I whispered, not knowing what to say about Braelynn. She was alive now, only in Familiar form. A cat with bat wings, rather than the girl I knew, my best friend. And, yes, she had been Luken's soulmate. Maybe she still was.

Tears sprang to my eyes, and I wished there was something I could do. But, once again, I was helpless.

"I'm sorry," Teagan said, holding out his arm for a warrior shake. Luken gripped the other man's forearm, and they held each other, still glaring, but there was a sense of solidarity there, too. That was good, at least I hoped so. "I'm sorry for your loss, it's not fair to find the one that's meant for you, only to have them ripped from your grasp."

I looked away then, not wanting to hear more, not wanting to think about the fact that I didn't have my soulmate either. Mine didn't love me. What did it all mean?

Before I could wallow in my self-pity any longer, I froze, the shadow in the distance coming closer.

I didn't know what it was. It didn't look exactly like the Air monster we had fought, the Domovoi, which had been a dragon of sorts that was almost Spirit-like. This wasn't it. But it was something big. And it was moving fast.

When someone shouted behind me, I knew it wasn't just a figment of my imagination.

It was coming at us, and we were going to have to fight it.

CHAPTER 5

LYRIC

"Everybody, prepare yourselves for battle!" I shouted over the murmurs and yells of the others. The wind lifted my hair, and I ignored the heat from the sun shining down on my face.

I was still reasonably new at this, but I had been in enough skirmishes and fights to know what I needed to do. Hopefully, the others would know, as well.

Luken and Teagan took control of those fighting, those on our side, at least. They were warriors, those who had dealt with battle lines and plans for years. They had been on opposing sides more than once, something I would ask them about later, but they were working side by side now. Because we weren't Obscurité or Lumière.

We were fighting against whatever was coming at us. And it was big. Wyn was at my side, the wind blowing through her hair.

"What is it?" I asked, squinting in the blinding sun that covered the northern Spirit territory. It felt like night never fell when we were here. There was always a tone of sepia around us as if the sun had burnt everything to a crisp, and what was left, were the remnants of souls everlasting.

I knew at one time, the northern Spirit territory had housed cities, great civilizations with temples where the Spirit Wielders lived. Much like the southern Spirit territory. There had been people, cities, laughing children, and adults who had loved one another. That was all gone now. Because of the Fall. Because when the others had used the crystals and the Spirit Wielders to gain more power, they'd killed so much. And the war had brought devastation. It had truly been Obscurité versus Lumière then as the Spirit Wielders ran away, scared for their lives and not part of either court or kingdom.

They had died, and they had hidden, stashed away in the human realm.

Where I had been born. Where I'd lived.

And, one day, I would have that element, as well. Spirit. I would have all five.

For now, I was standing on a desert-like landscape with others shouting orders and getting into position. Someone would need to protect Rhodes, others were tasked with watching our supplies and Arwin's body.

I would have to stand up front because I had four elements. I only hoped I could control them. I had to.

I couldn't let them control me.

Wyn took my hand and grasped it tightly before letting go and spreading her fingers.

"It's a wyverin." She looked over at me, and my eyes widened.

"Is that like a dragon? Like the Domovoi? The ghost dragon thing?" There had been a Domovoi with its ghost rider when we last walked across the northern Spirit territory. It had only been solid when the rider was touching it, but when he jumped off to fight, the dragon had been ghostly and see-through again.

We had defeated it, but it had been close. And we'd needed Easton's Fire and Earth to prevail.

We didn't have Easton now.

I swallowed hard.

We may never have him again.

"Sort of. It's not like the Domovoi. It's solid. It has the head of a dragon, but can stand on two legs while it flaps its wings. They're almost leathery, like a Komodo Dragon you would see in your realm. Only it's far larger."

I licked my lips, my hands outstretched as my Wielding skated along my fingers.

"I can see that." I narrowed my eyes again, trying to focus on what I saw.

It was large and black, with blue and green scales gliding up its side as if a waterfall cascading.

That wasn't what I was staring at, though. And I wasn't looking at the sharp fangs and talons, either. Or its leathery wings as they beat a fast staccato, coming towards us as it moved in the air.

No, I was looking at the rider.

The one in the gray robes that billowed out behind him.

"There's a Creed Wielder riding him."

Wyn sighed. "Yes, it seems that the Creed of Wings is still alive. Though we should have guessed that. It wasn't as if we killed them all on that ship."

I shook my head, my Wielding scratching at my palms. The Fire licked at my fingertips, the Air gliding between the digits. Earth rumbled beneath my feet, and Water skimmed.

out of my eyes, my mouth. It was all too much, but it was *fine*. I would push it all out into the wyverin. Because if he were truly an enemy, then I needed to end him.

I need to end anything in our path.

End it all. Scorch the earth, drown the world. Become the power.

I pushed those thoughts from my mind.

No, those weren't my thoughts. That was the magic beckoning me. It had tried once before when things had been too much. I couldn't allow that to happen again.

It had been Easton's hold that had brought me back then, but he wasn't here anymore.

I would have to do this on my own. And I *would* do it.

Because I was strong. I had literally been born for this. Was meant for this.

And I would rely on no man, no Wielder to protect me.

I had to do this on my own.

Because, at the base of it all, I was alone.

All alone.

"Why is a Creed Wielder coming at us?"

"You know that not everybody wants you to succeed."

"Then who is his master?" I asked as others gathered around.

Luken was on my side, Teagan on Wyn's.

I looked over my shoulder at Rosamond, who stood by Rhodes' wagon, her hands outstretched. She was an Air Wielder as well as a Seer, and strong.

She would protect her brother, as would the healer. The other warriors would protect all of us. And I would do my best to do the same for them.

"Let's see what he wants first," Wyn suggested, and I nodded. "For all we know, he's a deserter. The Creed are supposed to protect the Air Wielders, right?" I asked, looking over at Luken.

He gave me a tight nod and pulled his sword from its sheath. He used his blade to project his Air Wielding, as well as to fight like a warrior. It was something that I had been training to do when I was in the Obscurité Court, training with Easton's uncle and Easton himself. However, I was nowhere near as good as Luken, and I wasn't sure I ever would be. He was just *that* good, as if he had been born with a sword in hand.

The only time I'd ever been good with a blade was when I'd almost died from being run through with one, and then used it to project power back towards Lore. I'd killed him after he basically killed me, as well as Cameo—Easton's mother and former Queen of Obscurité.

"They were meant for that at one point. I don't know what the king has in store for them now. We know that some of them were working with the Lord of Water, Rhodes and Rosamond's father. I honestly don't know what they want now. Their secrets, like the League's are that they are Water Wielders, as well. They hide themselves and do what they think is best. Or what those in power tell them to do. So much is unknown about them."

"I'm surprised you're not a Creed member yourself," Teagan taunted, his voice nonchalant.

I glared at him. "Do we really think this is the time?" I asked.

"I didn't mean any offense by it."

"Sounds like you did," Luken snarled.

"Guys, we do not have time for this." I was exhausted, emotionally and physically drained, and dealing with two posturing males fighting for whatever control or dominance they thought they deserved. It was far too much for me right then.

"All I'm saying is that he's a skilled warrior, and the Creed tends to pluck babes from their homes to raise them. And Luken would have had strong power before that."

"I'm a bastard." Luken breathed heavily. "And since we don't discuss the man who spawned me, I was never Creed material."

There was such vehemence in his tone that I looked over at him, my eyes going wide. I knew that Luken was a bastard, it was something he said often. And I also knew that nobody spoke about who his father was. I didn't even know if Luken actually knew who he was. At least, I couldn't really tell if he did. I only knew that it was something no one talked about.

Apparently, on a battlefield with a wyverin coming at us seemed to be the perfect time.

"I'm glad you were never Creed. At the moment, however, let's focus on what's in front of us."

Before we could say anything else, the wyverin opened his mouth, and fire sprayed us. Unlike the poison and ghost fire the Domovoi had, this was actual fire.

And fire I could deal with.

"I guess that answers that question," Wyn called out over the flames.

I put my hands up in the air, my fingers outspread. The wyverin's fire dissipated, splitting in two directions.

I couldn't actually make it go away, but I could do my best to redirect it.

The dragon screamed, spewing more flames.

Wyn went to one knee, slamming her hand down to the ground, and a shock of Earth flew into the air, a wave of soil and dirt and sand and remnants of whatever had once been here slamming into the wyverin.

It screeched again, but then there was another shot, and another. And another.

The wyverin wasn't alone.

No, there were more, at least twenty.

Twenty dragons, each with a Creed warrior of their own.

"Dear gods," Luken whispered. "They don't seem friendly," he rumbled, and then we were fighting.

The wyverins came at us, each using their fire, with the Creed warriors using Air to direct the flames where they wanted.

Luken shot his sword towards one, used his Air Wielding to slam power into the side of one of the wyverins.

It shrieked, rolled in the air, and its warrior fell off and smacked into the ground, though not with the sickening splat I expected. He must have used his Air Wielding at the last second, so he didn't hit as hard.

After all, we had learned before that Air Wielders could fly. Much like the Water Wielders could use the tips of waves to make it look as if they were flying, as well.

No, these were highly trained warriors, far better at Air Wielding than I was.

The only person I knew of who was better was Rhodes, and he was currently passed out and healing in the wagon behind us.

"Circle the carriages," I called out. "Protect Rhodes and what we have. Watch each other." I shouted out commands, and the others moved into formation.

Wyn gave me a smile and nodded. "That's our Spirit Priestess. Be our leader."

"You guys do what you need to. You know more than I do."

"Stop doubting yourself," she shouted as she shot another wave of Earth towards one of the riders. "You're stronger than you think you are."

"Thanks for that." And then there was no more time for talking.

40

Wyn held up both hands and then slammed them together in front of her face, two towers of Earth coming together like a heart in the Air as the point slammed into one of the wyverins, pushing it to the ground. It made a horrible crying sound as it started to be buried, and I hoped that there was some way to save it later. I didn't know if the wyverins were bad, or if they had been forced into service by the Creed. I didn't want to hurt innocent creatures. I didn't want to hurt anyone.

And then my power leapt within me, and I just wanted to rage and burn them all. No, I couldn't. I had to find balance, I had to make peace. I hadn't been sent here to kill.

Though maybe I was.

"Once a wyverin is touched by evil, there's no going back. Those who can ride them, who take control of them, *they* are the ones who turn their souls. There *are* good wyverins out there. The souls of those who have been touched by the Creed and are against us are no longer bound to this realm. They're gone, Lyric." I looked over at Teagan, who had dirt on his face, and Fire licking at his hands.

"What do you mean?"

"They aren't truly alive," he said softly, though I could hear him over the din. "Once they are ridden in the way they are now, they are just shells. Pawns. You're not hurting innocents. You're protecting those you care about. And the Creed are the ones who killed them. They're the ones that hurt them. If we stop those who are against change, stop those who use innocents for their own gains, we can protect the other wyverins. These? We can't save them."

Another wyverin made a crying sound, and I flinched. "They're crying," I whispered.

"They were dead long before now," he said. "You're helping them find peace."

"Are you lying to me to make me feel better? To help me control my powers?"

Teagan shook his head, his dark hair falling in front of his face. "I don't lie to you, Lyric. Even when it might be easier to do so to make you feel better. Come on, we need to protect the others."

CARRIE ANN RYAN

I nodded, pulling away from him to keep fighting. Teagan shot out more Fire, burning through two wyverins at once. He was strong, but he was going to burn out quickly if I didn't help. There were other Wielders around us, but they were Air and Water, and since we only had the water in our pouches and in the air itself to use, they weren't as strong as Earth or Fire Wielders would be. The Air Wielders were helpful, but they were more like healers, less like warriors. That was fine, I had some of the strongest Wielders in the Maison realm at my side. And I had the strength of four elements within me. Something I would do well to remember.

And so, I moved forward and pushed out my hands, palms outstretched.

Air rushed from me, a shocking wave that slammed into two riders. They fell, and Luken was there with Teagan, both fighting the Wielders hand-to-hand, or sword-to-hand as it was in Luken's case.

Whenever a Creed Wielder fell, those two took them out. Wyn and the other warriors were helping eliminate the wyverin, while Rosamond and the rest protected the wagons. And I was taking out anything in our path.

There was some water in my pouch, so I pulled it out, using my palms to hold it like a globe. When I pushed my hands together, it created a vortex, a sphere of Water that grew and grew as it collected the Air molecules around it. This was something that Rhodes had taught me, or at least had begun to teach me.

When the sphere grew large enough for me to handle, I tossed it into the air and used my Air Wielding to shoot it forward. It slammed into two of the riders, spiraling with them so it was almost a tornado of Water in the air that suddenly crashed down, hitting the ground with such force that it created a mud bath that pulled the enemy in, sucking them in so they would be crushed by the weight of the dirt itself.

There were shouts and screams, but only from those against us.

I didn't want them to die slowly. I didn't want torture, I didn't want pain. So, I used my right hand and shot out another wave of Fire, scorching those in my path. They screamed no more. It was just the

42

burnt shells of what they had once been, remaining embers of fate and loss.

I used my Air Wielding again, and then my Water Wielding, mixing them together to pull them out of the air. And then my Earth Wielding caught them and crushed them, while the Fire Wielding put an end to them quickly.

I did it over and over again, taking out each wyverin and Creed pair as they came at us. Soon, the others on my side came to me, watching me with horror in their gazes.

Horror or something else I couldn't grasp.

And then there was a scream, one that didn't come from a wyverin, didn't come from a Creed. I looked up and to my left as one of the Air Wielders fell to the ground, a talon sliding through his chest.

I screamed, Fire erupting from my body, from my face and hands. It slammed into the wyverin and burned it to a crisp, screaming as the Creed warrior tried to leap off. I sent my Earth towards him, slamming him to the ground. Then, he was moving no more.

I hadn't been fast enough.

I hadn't been strong enough.

Blood splashed onto the dirt as the fallen Air Wielder fell, dying as he did. His life's blood draining as if it were nothing.

People came to him, tried to help him, but I couldn't control anything. Fire licked at my elbows, the Air within my body trying to push out. I had no more water in my pouch to use with my Water Wielding, but Earth rumbled beneath me. I took a step, and the ground cracked. With another step, another crack.

I had to shut it down, I had to protect those around me. I couldn't do it. I didn't know how to control four elements. No one had before. I was supposed to have had a trainer, a road map.

I didn't have any of that anymore. I looked at the face of the nameless soldiers as they stared at me and tried to say I was sorry. Attempted to say I would stop next time. That I wouldn't let this happen again. But I couldn't lie.

I saw the blame on their faces, saw the fear.

And I knew it was directed at me. They were scared of me. And I was terrified of myself.

I closed my fists, forcing all of the Wielding back into myself. I knew I was shaking, but I was in control.

I didn't have Easton to hold onto, didn't have anyone.

The wyverins were dead. The Creed, at least the ones in front of us, were taken care of.

And we had only lost one.

Was that good enough? Was the math acceptable?

Suddenly, there were hands on my face, and I looked over at Wyn, who held me, her eyes wide.

"You're fine, Lyric. You took out the rest of them. You took out so many. Now, just breathe, hold in your Wielding."

"He's dead because of me."

"Yes, Pod is dead. And we will mourn him. We will carry him home to bury him. But it is not your fault. It was the wyverin, and the Creed who controlled them."

"I should have been stronger," I whispered, though I wasn't crying. I wasn't really doing anything. I needed to be stronger, I needed to protect everybody. I couldn't even protect those near me. We only had a few on our side, and I had lost one. Arwin's body was in one of the wagons, and he was dead because of me. Rhodes had almost died because of me.

I didn't know what to do.

And then Wyn's lips were on mine, and my eyes widened. There was heat there, though not what I had with Easton. No, she almost reminded me of Rhodes. Someone close…but not who I needed her to be.

She pulled back and grinned, while Teagan and Luken each coughed into their fists.

"What was that for?" I asked, pulling away and putting my fingers on my lips. They stung from her touch, and I wondered what the hell had just happened.

Wyn just shrugged, tossing her hair over her shoulder. "What? I figured Easton's kiss helped you before, why not mine?" she asked, and I knew she had only done it to bring me out of my shock, to anchor me to the present. It had worked. Then I was laughing, and then I was crying.

I knew this wasn't over. We had to keep going.

And I knew it couldn't all be my fault.

Easton was gone, and he couldn't help me.

That meant I had to help myself. No matter the cost.

CHAPTER 6

EASTON

I knew pain.

Pain and I went way back.

It wasn't something I was unfamiliar with. After all, I had been training to be who I was, and what I needed to *be* within my power, my entire life. And I wasn't human. So, I had over two full centuries of figuring out exactly how to survive in a world that was breaking. One that had slowly shattered after the Fall and hadn't been put back together correctly. One where the secrets of those around me had pushed their tendrils of agony beneath my skin as I fought to become who I was.

I had walked in my family's shoes, knowing that an end would come, that I wouldn't be able to save them all.

I hadn't known it was Lore, who was speeding up the destruction of our people. I hadn't known he was the one who'd killed my father. I hadn't known he wanted my mother to the point where he would try to kill so many.

And he *had* killed many.

I didn't know why I hadn't seen any of that. I'd only seen a man with a thirst for power. I hadn't known the power he had within his grasp.

I had fought alongside my people, did my best to save them from the Negs—the absence of light and dark. The monsters that roamed the streets and could be controlled by those with darkness within them.

Lore had controlled them.

Now, I knew they were actually controlled by The Gray.

By the monster that now controlled me.

Pain? Yes, pain had been part of all of that.

And now…it was back. I had to deal. Somehow.

I tried to ignore my surroundings, attempted to ignore the slicing of my skin and the way the cold leached any warmth from my body, from my bones themselves.

I didn't know how long I'd been trussed up with chains and hung from the ceiling, my toes barely able to touch the ground. I had been stripped of my shirt, and divested of my shoes. I only wore my pants, though there were holes in them now from where the whip had dug in. Where it had bloodied my skin and ripped parts of my soul from me.

That was the problem, wasn't it? Did I truly have any light within me? Did I have a soul?

Or did The Gray own it?

He had cursed me from the beginning. It hadn't been Lore, like I thought.

I had been wrong about so many things.

Because if it had been Lore, then the curse should have broken when the man died. When Lyric took his life.

Lyric, the Spirit Priestess.

The one I could not love.

She loved me. She thought I was her soulmate, and maybe I was.

Because I remembered the wound on my stomach when she'd had that mortal blow from the sword Lore had thrust into her belly. I remembered the shocking pain and the mirrored image of her wound.

But I couldn't be her soulmate.

Because I was cursed. Destined to never hold her as mine.

I needed to break the hex.

I had to get out of here.

It was imperative that I get back to Lyric and save my people.

While I might not love her since I couldn't hold that emotion within me, there was a hollowness deep inside me that needed to be filled with... something.

And maybe that was my people.

It made sense. I had left the legend of the Spirit Priestess to destiny in fate and that of the Lumière Kingdom. I'd turned my back on it for good reason, but I'd still done it nonetheless. I had left Rhodes and the others to search for the Priestess while I stayed in the Maison realm, trying to keep the Obscurité Kingdom from shattering into a million pieces.

Maybe I had given up far more than that. Maybe The Gray had been orchestrating things long before that just to curse my soul and my heart and my body.

I didn't know anything anymore.

What did I know? That everything hurt. I didn't want to feel the pain anymore. Didn't want to acknowledge it. Because if I did, I would also feel something I hadn't felt in longer than I could remember.

Fear.

A true terror that called to me like a siren's song. I had to be stronger than that.

I bet Rhodes was.

Something lurched inside me, and I tried to suck in a breath.

Because Rhodes was dead.

That damned Lumière prince was dead. Thrown off a cliff and drowned, killed by his own father. He was gone, and I had been taken here, to the Shadow realm. One of smoke and mirrors and...nothingness. And that left Lyric all alone.

I had to get out of here. I had to go back to the Obscurité Kingdom and protect my people against the King of Lumière. Because he would be coming. I knew it. He would want revenge for what had happened to his brother. He would want vengeance for so much. Because while I was still the king of the Obscurité Kingdom, I wasn't sure I had the power to do what was needed. Not with The Gray hovering over me. I still had to protect my people, though. Somehow, I needed to find the power to do that.

I had to protect Lyric.

Because if I didn't, then what was the point of anything?

There were reasons for fate and destinies and prophecies. They held our kingdoms together in a way. Because without that hope, what was the point of putting one foot in front of the other? Without people having faith that there was a Spirit Priestess out there who would bring them all together, we would falter.

Before we found Lyric, I had been the one to try and protect them.

The Lumière disparaged us. They called us the ruination, the darkness. The Obscurité were *evil* because darkness had to be. Even my last name, Scuro, had later been adopted by the Italians as their word for dark. It wasn't lost on me that Rhodes' last name, Luce, was also Italian for light in the human realm.

It seemed we would forever be put into our respective shiny boxes, unable to step out.

It was wrong. Because Rhodes wasn't good. He wasn't bad.

I sure as hell wasn't good.

But I wasn't evil either.

The curse that surrounded my heart like chains wrapped in amber as they tugged and squeezed? That was evil.

I needed to find her. I needed to save Lyric.

No, that wasn't right. She could save herself. She had proven time and again that she didn't need me. I needed to protect my people and somehow find a way to save her so she could figure out how to get all five elements and put them together.

We were so close.

In the end, we hadn't been close at all.

"Are you done thinking all those hard thoughts?" Durlan asked as he stalked around me.

I looked up at the Dane, the former Earth Wielder, and spat blood at his feet.

"I'm fine. Really just getting ready for whatever you think you can come at me with." I winked and grinned at the asshole.

"Oh? You think you're such a bad boy. That you can handle it all? Your skin is flayed open by *my* whip. Your blood is on the ground, and you're not even fighting back. What kind of king are you? You're nothing. All you do is stand there while your people die, and everyone lays prostrate at your feet. Who's in charge now? You're in chains. And I'm at our liege's side. The Gray believes in me. And you? You are nothing."

Durlan put his arm out to the side, the odd purplish light from the room glinting off the leather whip.

"Are you ready for your next question?"

"Not really teaching me anything, are you?" I needed to get out of here. I had to get out of my bonds and find a way back to the Maison realm. Once I got there, I could break the curse. I would find a way. Because all curses had to be broken. There were rules about that. Once I did, I would no longer be at the mercy of The Gray. And I wouldn't be a liability for my kingdom.

And maybe I could love. Perhaps that soulmate thing would actually work out.

I pushed those latent thoughts from my mind. There was no need for them. I didn't need Lyric. She sure as hell didn't need me. Everything would be just fine. But, first, I needed to get out of these chains.

Only, it was a little hard when Durlan kept looking at me like I was a big, juicy steak. I mean, he clearly had a nice appetite.

Ugh, this is going to suck.

The first flick of his wrist sent shocking pain down my back, and I instinctively tried to get away from it. I couldn't. It hurt. Then again, I had to remember, I'd been through worse. Even in this room.

He flicked again, and this time, I stayed still, a little more prepared for it. I hated showing weakness, and this man didn't deserve my yield. The Gray had left us alone long before this, going off to work on whatever scheme or plan needed his attention. I tried to listen, attempted to figure out precisely what would happen next so I could warn the others. But they were all being careful around me, and I gleaned nothing.

The Gray wanted something. He wanted everything to either shatter within the Maison realm so he could put it back together, or he wanted to bring us to the brink so we ran to him for protection, and he could rule us.

I was the King of Obscurité, and if I were out of the picture completely, he could position himself right in. I had a feeling he wanted more than that. He wanted *both* kingdoms.

And that meant the King of Lumière was either in danger or already working for him.

I needed to figure it out, and I had to get out of here.

Another crack, and I felt liquid trail down my back, warm blood pooling at the waistband of my pants.

I was done with this, though I couldn't get out.

Garrik, The Gray's fourth, walked into the room, a bowl of water in his hands.

"What do you think you're doing?" Durlan asked.

"The Gray asked me to wash his back and make sure he had some water."

"So now you're going to baby him?" Durlan asked, a snap in his voice.

"No. The more I help, the longer he'll last for you. And that's all that matters, right? That he'll last longer?"

"I can last all day, boys. I just didn't realize you guys were so bored that you needed me for this."

"Bored now," Durlan said, mimicking one of my favorite shows from the human realm, and then I sighed. Durlan snapped the whip at Garrik. The Dane, the former Air Wielder, took a step back, the bowl hitting the ground at his feet and splashing water on all of us.

Well, I would have liked some of that. I *was* a tad parched.

They had shackled me in ropes of smoke and chains, which drained my elements. I couldn't even Wield a single little piece of dirt currently. Let alone a flicker of flame.

I would find a way out.

There was no way I would let The Gray take over my realm.

I wouldn't let Lyric walk alone.

I might not love her—I might not be able to *ever* love her—nevertheless, she was mine.

CHAPTER 7

LYRIC

I was pretty sure I had begun to lose track of the days. While traveling through the Spirit territory, it was actually a little difficult to figure out what was day and what was night. There weren't sunrises and sunsets. Just that sepia tone that seemed to drip down and saturate every ounce of the land, sinking into every pore of our skin.

We were getting closer.

Rhodes was now able to sit up in the cart, his brown skin pale, but he at least was whole.

He hadn't spoken to me, not in the days since we started our trek, and he fully woke up. I hadn't really given him an option, though.

I walked alongside Wyn and Teagan, just trying to make it through the territory. We weren't moving at the fast speed we had when we made our way in the opposite direction towards the Water territory. This time, we had carts and people who needed us to go slower.

So, things took time.

It made me sort of wish for the days of airplanes and cars and everything that I had taken for granted when I lived in the human realm. It wasn't like I could ever go back, though. Because when this was all over? When the prophecy was fulfilled and if somehow I survived it all? There

There wasn't anything for me there. And it always felt like I was out of sync with the rest of the world anyway, even though I hadn't really realized what that anxiety and sense of loss meant at the time.

I hadn't been able to pick my major or do anything for myself in college. I'd just gone through the motions. I was average. Somehow sliding through life amongst the others and just going about my business without making any true choices.

I now knew that was because I was supposed to be here.

I was no longer running from that fact. It wasn't the idea that I had to try and tell myself who I was now. Because I knew. I could feel the elements coursing through my veins, the power that called to me underneath the world's dying breath.

I was no longer the Lyric that had first walked through the mountains into that crevice that served as the portal between the human and Maison realms. I was no longer the girl who was afraid of what she didn't know, scared of the divine.

No. Now, I had to scrape for everything I could see, had to fight for even those I didn't know.

It was hard to contemplate what it all could mean.

But I had to figure it out. I had to find the Spirit element. I needed to work with all five elements somehow and blend them together.

It was my responsibility to unravel the prophecy and find the truth. Uncover more, if there was any more to it.

I had to stop whoever was orchestrating this. I had to maintain peace within the realms. We needed to make sure that the King of Lumière and the Obscurité Kingdom were able to work together. Because if they didn't, the Maison realm would fall.

There was only so much power in the world, and with so much of it having been leached away, broken into fragments, there wouldn't *be* a Maison realm left to fight for if we didn't figure it out.

"You're growling under your breath again," Wyn said, reaching out to squeeze my hand. I gave her hand a squeeze back and then sighed. "I'm just trying to go through the checklist of everything we need to do. And it's not just, buy milk or feed the cat. No, it's things like save the world. Find the lost king. And make sure the prince back there is okay. You know, the little things."

"Well, at least you still have your sense of humor." Wyn just shook her head, using a leather tie to pull her hair back from her face. It kept coming undone, the waves spiraling out of control. I noticed some of the Lumière healers and soldiers looking at her, each of them unable to keep their gaze off her. I didn't really blame them. She was beautiful. Strong, a warrior, and she had a commanding presence.

I was grateful that she was my friend.

"It's hard to keep a sense of humor when I feel so lost. And I hate that I feel that way because it's stupid. People are going through things so much worse."

"We'll find Easton. After all, we found one of your men, we'll find the other."

I gave her a sharp look. "Seriously, Wyn?"

"What? It's how I decided to label them. It's easier than actually being serious about anything. Because if I am, I might start crying, or freak out and chop something into little bitty pieces. Anyway...we're almost there. I noticed you haven't talked to a certain Romeo prince. Other than looking over at him to make sure he's okay, you haven't really acknowledged his presence. Do you want to talk about it?"

I cast her a look before letting my gaze roam around the group of others. We were indeed close to the Obscurité border wards. Though I didn't really know how thick the wards would be, or how much magic might be running through them at the moment. Hopefully, Easton's uncles were keeping them up. With Easton missing like he was? I had no idea how the magic truly worked.

It was one more thing I needed to figure out. I would add it to my list.

However, even as I let all of that run through my mind, I tried not to stand out, to act as if my problems were more important than the rest. While some of the others had looked at Wyn with hunger in their eyes, they were still paying attention to their duties. Luken and Teagan were talking to one another, pulling the cart with Rhodes inside it. And

I knew Rhodes was probably chomping at the bit to get up soon. He hadn't been allowed to walk yet, though I knew it was going to happen at any moment. And that meant I had to talk to him.

"I don't know what to say to him. I thought he was dead."

Wyn reached out, seeming to want to grip my hand, but she let it fall before she made contact. "I was there. I know what you saw."

I shook my head, looking down at my palms. Hands that held so much power, elements I wasn't ready to control. Water slid out of my pores, dancing along my skin before seeping back in.

Air flitted between the tips of my fingers, as if a little Air sprite—if that was even a thing—did a dance along my skin.

"I thought he was mine. I thought he was my soulmate, but I was wrong. We weren't meant to be together. He couldn't heal me when the worst happened. And I wasn't able to save him at all."

"We're not always meant to save each other. We're meant to try. And he tried for you. Much like you tried for him."

"What if trying isn't enough?" I asked, the question lingering between us a far too heavy presence.

"You can ask that all you want, but we may never have a real answer. Because all we can do is try. That's our motivation, our goal. To try. And if we think that we're not good enough…that's fine. Because, in the end, someone has to believe we're good enough. Enough to protect our people and the others.

"It's not easy. It's never been easy. You're strong, Lyric. You always have been, even if you didn't think so. It's okay if we fail, if we make mistakes. We just keep getting back up."

"And if we fail at the worst moment?"

"I don't want to think like that. Because if I do, then it's harder to do what I was just telling you to do. Try."

I looked over at her then, my feet aching, my shoulders sore, the Wielding in me pressing against the inside of my skin as if it wanted to claw its way out. I was exhausted—mentally, physically, and emotionally.

Even as I tried to think of what to say, there weren't words. Because we had arrived.

The wards between the territories might have been opaque at one time. Now, you could see right through them, even though you could still see the magic from the crystal that kept the entire realm whole and healthy. The fact that the crystals were dying scared us all. Because that meant the wards would fall, as well. With the territories and kingdoms at war for so long, the wards had been necessary.

Now, I didn't even want to go through them. I just wanted to sleep.

Then I thought: *What if Easton is here?* What if whatever had taken him had brought him back to the court, and I'd be able to see him again?

Somehow, that energy flowed through me, and I was able to take the necessary steps through the wards. Unlike before, I didn't need to be invited in.

This court knew me. I wasn't only a guest, it was my new home. One that drew me in even when I hadn't known I needed it.

I turned, watching as Wyn and the others led the Lumière Wielders through the wards, as well as Rhodes on his cart.

He looked ready to bolt as he met my gaze.

I nodded, trying to give him a smile, but I knew it didn't reach my eyes.

His returning grin was much the same.

I didn't know what would happen next.

For everyone who wasn't an Obscurité member, they had to be personally invited and helped through the wards.

The first time I felt the wards of the Obscurité Kingdom, I had been walking through the southern Spirit territory into the Earth territory at the bottom edge of the kingdom. It had felt like gravity pushed down on me. As if I were walking through a thick and viscous material to get through. Pain had lashed at me, but we made it through. Mostly because we had made it through holes in the perimeter, rather than being invited in like we were before.

The fact that I hadn't needed an invite this time spoke to me.

Was I Obscurité? No, not really. Because those didn't actually exist anymore in my mind. Not when there were factions on both sides of the idea of change. Those who wanted change versus those who wanted to let those in power retain it—in both the Obscurité and Lumière.

We weren't fighting light and dark anymore. It wasn't Obscurité versus Lumière.

It was hope versus whatever the orchestrator of this mess wanted.

"You're back," Justise said as he walked out onto the path in front of us.

Justise was a large man, broad-shouldered, and looked like he worked with his hands. He came across as someone who could probably scare the crap out of you if you got on his bad side.

He was the official weapons maker and bBlacksmith of the Obscurité Court. He was also Queen Cameo's younger brother. I knew there was a story there, one that no one seemed to want to tell me. If it was important, and if I needed to know, they would tell me later.

Justise was Easton's uncle, and a good man, if a bit grumpy and standoffish. His husband Ridley stood beside him, a smile on his face.

I saw relief in both of their eyes, and I couldn't help but want to run towards them and just hug them, making sure that everyone was real and alive and okay.

I didn't see Easton beside them.

When they searched the group of us and frowned, I knew they were looking for their nephew, too.

Ridley was our healer, one who had helped me train my mental discipline so I could hold the elements that I'd had before I left.

Now, I had two more. Hopefully, he would be able to help me with those, too.

Because I knew I would need it. I couldn't do it alone.

And now, I didn't have Easton to hold onto. To lean on.

"We're back." I looked at them and then down at my hands, and then I was moving, without even knowing I was doing it, even though I knew I shouldn't. Ridley opened his arms, and I went to him. I looked up at Justise, who gave me a tight nod, then I noticed who was in his arms. Braelynn sat in the cradle of his elbow, her head tilted as she studied me. Her black bat wings were pressed against her sides so she could snuggle closer to Justise, and I had to hold back a snort.

The idea that this big man who said few words unless he was

growling was holding my cat, my best friend, Luken's soulmate, was kind of funny.

Then I remembered exactly why Luken couldn't hold his mate in the way he wanted to.

"Let's get everyone inside the castle, and then we'll talk. You came through the Spirit territory rather than through the Lumière Court, even though it's closer. I'm sure there's a reason for that," Ridley surmised, meeting my gaze.

I nodded. "Is he here?" I whispered, my voice so low I hoped only he and Justise and Braelynn could hear.

The men looked at me, their eyes widening ever so slightly as one. Even Braelynn's eyes got bigger.

When Justise shook his head, only a fraction of an inch, my heart broke.

My hands shook, and the ground shuddered beneath my feet. I locked down my element, pushing it away.

I was fine. Everything was fine. Why did this hurt so much? Why did it always feel this way? We didn't have time to introduce anyone, not when there were others around who could listen in, and maybe learn more than they should.

I knew that Lanya's people wouldn't say anything about what had happened, they had been sworn to secrecy even before we stepped foot into the Spirit territory. For that, I was grateful.

I didn't want to explain to the Obscurité Kingdom that their sovereign was missing.

Nor did I want to explain to them why we had so many members of the Lumière with us, or that one of their own had died.

Before we could get settled, Luken came to my side, his gaze on the cat in Justise's arms.

The last time Luken had seen his soulmate, she had been ash in the wind, killed by Lore.

Because of the magic and Wielding within her veins and the crystal that had been used, she'd somehow been transformed into the Familiar she was now.

I still didn't understand exactly how it had happened, but Rosamond hadn't been surprised.

She was the Seer, after all.

"May I?" Luken asked, his voice gruff. He held out his arms, and Braelynn jumped right into them. She nuzzled under his chin, and Luken's body rocked as if it had been dealt a blow. He closed his eyes, letting out a pained groan. Air circled around him, a gentle breeze that tickled at my skin and ruffled Braelynn's fur.

Braelynn licked his chin, and he grinned down at her. I had to force back tears.

Well, they had been reunited. It just wasn't in a way everybody wanted.

Braelynn looked at me and burped a ball of fire that made me narrow my eyes. Then she nuzzled into Luken.

"Would someone please explain the fire thing?"

"All in good time, Lyric," Rosamond said. "Now, I'm sure you have questions. We do, as well. I'll tell you what I know. All of it."

And for a Seer to say that, it meant something.

So we moved, all of us following Ridley and Justise inside.

Some of the Obscurité Court came up to us, but they didn't ask anything. I knew they were looking for Easton, but then again, so was I.

By the time we got some of the Lumière Wielders to their rooms, I was exhausted. This wasn't over. Not by a long shot.

I would rest later. First, there were things to do.

And one of them was going to hurt.

The keening cry that came from the older woman as she leaned into her husband slashed into me. I wanted to reach out and take away her pain. To somehow use the Wielding I had to make her stop. To make her not feel this agony anymore.

Her husband stood firm, his eyes dry as he stared off into the distance.

Wyn and Teagan were in front of them, both of their heads bowed.

These were Arwin's parents.

And now, they knew their son was dead.

I didn't know if I could say anything that would help. I couldn't just stand to the side and do nothing, though. So, I moved closer.

"Your son was brave. He fought well, and he protected me. He died saving my life. And I will be forever in your debt."

"Lyric," Wyn whispered, but I quickly shook my head. I didn't need for her to tell me it wasn't my fault. I didn't need any of them to say that. Because while the League and the Creed and the Lord of Water were the ones who did it, Arwin had been protecting me.

And I would never forget that sacrifice.

"They told us what happened," Arwin's mother said, reaching out to grab my hand. She had a firm grip for someone whose bones looked as if they could break at any moment.

She was a Dane, something I hadn't realized until she touched me. Someone who had been stripped of her magic—recently, it seemed. All because of Lore and his misuse and abuse of the crystal.

Damn it all. I needed to fix this. I had to save these people.

I needed to save *my* people.

Fire glided from between the fingers of my other hand, and I clenched my fist, but not before smoke tendrils slipped between my knuckles.

Arwin's father glanced down and then met my gaze.

"You are not in our debt, Spirit Priestess. You will not let Arwin's death be in vain. I know you killed those who murdered my son. I only wish I had been there to watch, to help. You will protect our kingdom, you will unite us so we can live. So our magic may come back."

He was a Fire Wielder, I could sense that much, but his wife was now a Dane.

I didn't know how to fix that. At least, not yet.

I would figure it out, though. I would.

"When you're free, when you have time, we will tell you about our son. About his smile and his laughter." Arwin's mother wiped tears from her face. "We will tell you the good so maybe it can overshadow the bad in your mind. He was our son. And he wanted to be a warrior."

"He *was* a warrior," I said, my voice stronger than I thought possible. "He was."

"Thank you."

I moved away then, letting Wyn and Teagan do what they needed to. They had done this countless times before, after all. They were leaders, ones who'd watched men and women fall in battle. They knew what to say and what to do.

I only had empty words, and what felt like emptier promises.

"You did good there," Rhodes said, coming to my side.

I froze, looking over at him. We were in the shadows now outside of the room, waiting for Justise and Ridley to meet with us. I just stared, wondering how he could be alive.

"I don't feel like I did," I said softly.

"Because of that, I know you'll do well no matter what comes at you. I'm sorry Easton's gone."

I looked over my shoulder, thankful that no one was around to hear that.

"We'll wait to talk with the others about that."

"I know we will. I will help you find him. He's your soulmate, Lyric. Together, you will be able to do so much. And I'll help you make that happen."

I studied his face, the strong lines of his jaw, noticed that his color was coming back, and then those silver eyes I had always been drawn to pulled me in.

He was my friend.

Maybe that's what I needed.

A friend.

"I don't understand you, Rhodes."

"I don't understand myself most days." He laughed. "I don't remember what happened under the water. I don't remember anything about bone magic or what might have been with me."

He shifted a little uncomfortably on his feet. "I only remember my father, and your face. Then I opened my eyes and saw you again, standing far above me as I came to the surface. So, yeah, I'm sure there are things to talk about. Let's figure out what happens next."

"Let's."

We moved to another room where Rosamond and Luken were already sitting. Braelynn was curled up on Luken's lap, purring, and I had to wonder if there was any way to bring her back. Because the look of longing on Luken's face told me that he missed his soulmate, but he would make do with the friendship of a cat. Much like I was doing.

"Where are the others?" I asked, and then I took a step to the side as Ridley and Justise walked in.

"We're here," Teagan said as he and Wyn walked inside behind them.

"Okay. Tell us what happened exactly," Justise began.

I raised a brow and then took a seat at the round table.

"The League and the Creed were working with the Lord of Water. He had been using bone magic. Killing thousands so he could gain more power and use his dual Wielding."

"Bone magic?" Ridley asked, his face going pale. "Dear gods."

"The bone magic saved me, though." Rhodes looked down at his hands. "I don't know what that means."

"In order for bone magic to save you, it must have deemed you worthy. Those souls are crying out for help, and they used what they had left to protect you." Ridley leaned forward and looked at Rhodes. "You did not hurt them for them to protect you. You gave them purpose. Remember that."

I stood still as Rhodes absorbed that information and gave Ridley a tight nod.

"I assume the bones were taken care of?"

"Yes, my grandmother and I took care of it."

"The Lady of Air?" Justise asked.

"Yes. She's on our side. Or, at least, whatever side this is. I don't know who is on the other side," I said quickly.

We explained about the battles and who we had lost, and relayed the fact that we didn't know what side the King of Lumière stood on. Because although some of our foes had been fighting under his banner, for all we knew, he could be on the side of good. We really didn't know, and that meant we couldn't wage a full-scale war to try and protect the crystals if he was trying to protect them, as well.

The idea that nobody knew the truth worried us, but we would figure it out. We had to.

"And you're saying a chain or rope of smoke took Easton away?" Justise asked and then met his husband's gaze.

"What?" I asked, "What was that look?"

"It's happened before," Justise said, his voice deep.

"Excuse me?" Teagan asked. "I thought he just disappeared every once in a while. You're saying this smoke thing took him before?"

"We thought it was Lore," Ridley said. "We thought it would stop with the knight's death. We were wrong."

"So, let me get this straight. The King of Obscurité is gone, and he's disappeared before, and because you thought it was the other bad guy, you didn't mention it to us? So now, this current unknown bad guy is the one who has him?" I asked, standing so quickly, my chair fell. The sound echoed throughout the chamber, and I started to pace.

No one stood up with me.

They seemed just as shocked as I was.

"Lore bastardized the crystal. We thought he was trying to torture Easton. We thought he was the one who put the curse on him."

Justise swore under his breath, and I looked at him.

"You mean the one that states he isn't mine? The one where he can never love his soulmate? Yeah, I know all about that. I guess we don't really have time for that though, do we? We need to find him. Before anyone figures out that the King of Obscurité is missing. We're at war here, they can never find out."

"We'll tell him he's in meetings. And he's not missing. We'll find him." Justise pinched the bridge of his nose. "He always comes back. Always."

"Under whose control?" I whispered, my voice steel. "We can't find him if we don't know where he went. We don't even have a trail. We have nothing. And, on top of that, we have to figure out exactly what's going on. We need to detail our next steps. And unravel the prophecy. And I need Easton for that." I sat and shuddered at the words. The elements inside me smashed together, trying to crawl out of my skin. I turned my back, not wanting everybody in the room to see my tears. I couldn't hold it back anymore, though. I was crying, my breaths coming in gasps. Strong hands wrapped around me, but I didn't lean into Rhodes' touch.

I heard the others talking, planning, and, inside, I was breaking. I wasn't handling this well. I needed to handle it.

"You need to breathe. As soon as you get some sleep, some rest, we can make plans, Lyric."

I ignored Rhodes' words.

"You're not doing this all on your own. We will always be here for you."

That was a lie, wasn't it? We had lost Rhodes once, and yet he was back. Now, Easton was gone.

And the prophecy said I would lose. Indicated I would lose others. That I would be alone.

I felt like I would always be alone.

CHAPTER 8

EASTON

They let me off the chains what felt like days later, but it could have been hours for all I knew.

The one who had tried to feed me, who attempted to give me water, had let me down. I didn't know what Garrik's plans were, but he didn't physically hurt me. He seemed to want me healthy. Whole.

I didn't know if I completely trusted him, but he was at least better than The Gray or Durlan.

The fact that I had a decent captor told me that there might be something else at play.

Or maybe he was just as much of a captive as I was.

Just as much a prisoner.

They put me in a cell with iron bars that stank of magic.

There was Wielding, and then there was other magic. I had always figured in my research that Wielding was a subset of magic itself. Not everybody could Wield spells and do actual magic that wasn't of the elements.

I had used a spell to ensure that nobody could see my face, so they wouldn't know who I was when I ventured into the Lumière Kingdom.

How long ago had that been? Years? Months?

I didn't know.

I had gone there to help Lyric, ventured to where the Seer magic had sent her so I could protect her.

And, honestly, to find out exactly what the Lumière were up to.

They had been my enemy for as long as I could remember, and just because the pretty-boy with the silver eyes might not be as bad as the others, I still couldn't trust them.

It was hard to trust when you had a thousand years of enemy history behind you.

I did trust the Seer, though. At least, as much as I could.

Rhodes' older sister, Rosamond, seemed good of a sort, even if she was a Lumière Seer.

Trusting a Seer meant that you had to believe in the visions, and that wasn't always easy. In fact, it could mean your death.

Because what they Saw wasn't set in stone. And, sometimes, they needed certain things to happen for the best outcome to occur.

Best for whom?

That was something I had always wondered, but not anything I'd been told.

I had to figure the best course of action for me was staying off the Seer's radar.

They wanted Lyric. They wanted her to save the world and all of that lovely stuff.

I wasn't part of that.

No, I was in a cell now, surrounded by magic, bleeding.

My whole body shaking from the cold.

I could usually withstand torture a bit more than I had this go-round.

It had to be the magic within this realm, the so-called Shadow realm.

I'd thought it a myth. Stories from when I had been a child and had read books about the time before the Fall. The age of my grandparents.

When the old King of Lumière fought hand-to-hand with the King of Obscurité, my grandfather.

I had never met my grandfather. I was born long after the Fall. I had heard stories, though.

Legends spoke of a tyrant, a cruel leader who used all his power to kill those who didn't supplicate themselves in front of him.

He wanted people beneath his shoe, for them to prostrate themselves.

I had seen the way my mother's eyes tightened at the retelling of those stories. And even the way Justise turned away, not wanting to hear about his father.

I knew why Justise didn't want to hear about him. After all, Justise was the secret-born, one that no one knew was alive until he just showed up one day.

At least, that's what the stories said. And I knew better than most that whatever the story said, usually meant it was true.

After all, the victors were the ones who wrote the history.

And my grandfather had died, right along with the King of Lumière when the Fall occurred, and the realm broke the first time.

That first fracture had split our realm in two, with more fissures going on each year as the magic tried to take hold, attempted to settle. Now, however, we were past that.

Without peace and understanding.

When I got back—not if—I would try to make that peace. Not because I trusted the Lumière but because my people were dying.

Lore had led us down a track that we couldn't turn back from. The crystal was still leaching Wielding and *life* from my people. Danes were being created daily because I hadn't been strong enough to see what was in front of us all along. My mother hadn't been able to see either.

Or maybe she did, but she wasn't able to stop it.

She had sacrificed herself to save Lyric. In the end, her death had helped us destroy Lore, the one who had started it all with The Gray pulling the strings.

Now, I was king.

And trapped in a cage

"I can't get you water," Garrik whispered through the iron bars.

I opened my eyes, my lips so dry they had cracked, blood seeping into my mouth.

The magical whips that Durlan had used had sucked the magic out of my body. And had injected something else into my bloodstream.

I didn't know exactly what it was, but I knew that it would kill me sooner rather than later if I didn't get out of here.

Why was Garrik trying to help me?

What did he want?

"The Gray is coming, but I can try to help you out."

I narrowed my eyes with the energy I had left. "Why?"

"Because no one deserves to die in a cage."

I studied his face, the paleness of his skin, the dark circles under his wide eyes.

Had he been in a cage before?

That would make sense. It seemed that Durlan had appetites, demons that he needed to exorcise, and in order to do that, maybe he needed someone in the cage. If Garrik was out, and I was in, perhaps that's exactly what Durlan wanted.

If Garrik let me out, what would that mean for him?

"And you're doing this out of the goodness of your heart?" I asked.

"If I let you out, you have to take me with you. Away from all of this." His voice shook, and the other man set the bowl of water down outside the cage, his hands shaking, as well.

"Take you where?"

"To…to your people. Your place. You're the king there. You can protect me from The Gray."

I couldn't even protect myself if the current state of things was any indication. Not sure why he thought I could protect him. Or that I would want to.

"I see." I didn't. But, beggars couldn't be choosers. And maybe if this wasn't a trap, he *could* get me out.

"Be back soon." He scurried away, and I tried to lean against the wall, blood pooling beneath me. My wounds hadn't closed, and they hadn't bothered to clean them this time. Apparently, they wanted me to die from malnutrition and/or an infection.

Oh, yes, that was a great way for the King of Obscurité to go out. In a pool of his own blood—and probably vomit at some point if my nausea didn't let up.

I still had the shackles around my wrists, unable to Wield.

If Garrik really wanted to get me out of here, he'd need to get rid of those. Because I had to use my Wielding. Being cut off from it like I was, felt like losing a limb. That foul taste in my mouth wasn't just from whatever toxins were being pumped into my body. No, it was what I missed. What I needed.

Before I could really focus on anything, robes billowed around, and The Gray was there. He stood outside of my cage and tilted his cowled head at me.

I would love to see exactly who this man is, and know why he holds so much power.

Shadow wasn't an element one could Wield. At least not that I knew of. There were only *five*, and Lyric was the only one who could Wield them all.

Was it shadow magic?

No, I didn't know any defense for that. If I got out of here, I would learn. Because this man was going after Lyric. And I would be damned if I let him get her.

Not that I loved her. I couldn't. I felt nothing when it came to her. But she was our salvation. She was important. And I *would* save her. Even if it meant the end of me. Of course, that time seemed a bit closer than it should at the moment. And that was fine. I would be okay.

"I see that Durlan had his fun while I was away," The Gray said, his voice smooth and dark.

If I were tempted by power, I might have been drawn in.

I had my own, even if it was shackled at the moment.

"Well, you know what they say, when the cat's away, the mouse will play."

"Ah, but *you* seem to be the mouse, the one in a cage. Who is the cat's master? That is the important thing."

I tried to raise a brow, but I didn't really have the energy for it. This was not going to end well.

"Have you thought about your curse in the time I've been gone?" The Gray asked, his voice a purr.

"No."

Lie. It was the only thing I kept thinking about, wondering if I could be closer to Lyric if I broke it. Pondering if I could help her. If I did, that would mean I could help my kingdom, too.

That's what mattered. My kingdom. Not whatever was missing between Lyric and me.

She was a weapon. One that I would Wield.

"Well, I know that was a lie, but I'm going to tell you anyway. The curse was to bring you to me. And, soon, I will use you for what I need. I'm going to give you a hint. Mostly because I enjoy watching you fight. Because you try so hard, and then you fail, which brings you right back to me."

I just stared at him, letting him go on. Maybe if he kept talking, I would get something out of him. I needed to get out of here. I had to get to my people. I didn't even know where they were. Had they made it back to the Obscurité Kingdom? Or had the light king wiped them all out? I didn't think it was the latter because The Gray would have taunted me with it. He hadn't, so I still had hope that everyone I cared about was alive.

At least, everyone that had been left when I was taken.

"In order to break the curse, there will be death and change. You need to change within, find the essence of who you are and who you could be, and kill what was not meant to be there."

Riddles. Of course, there would be riddles that didn't make any sense.

Because it couldn't just be a potion or a scenario where I found a key to suddenly unlock my curse. No, it had to be something that made no sense.

Just like the prophecy that surrounded Lyric.

There was a reason I didn't work in the shadows like some of the others. There was a reason I had become king and tried to protect my people without a façade.

I hated riddles and prophecies and innuendos.

I might have to work with them occasionally, but I despised them.

"Are you done?" I asked, trying to sound bored. I knew I just sounded weak.

And I was starting to get lightheaded. I knew if I didn't staunch the blood on my back soon, I wouldn't be around long enough to stop the curse and whatever else The Gray had planned.

"I look forward to seeing you again. First, however, I have other plans."

And then he was gone. A cold chill whipped over me.

Other plans? That didn't sound good.

I slept, not wanting to, but my body needed it.

If I weren't careful, I would die here, alone in a cage, unable to help anyone. What would become of my kingdom if I were gone?

I didn't have a successor, but maybe the uncles could take over.

Or maybe they would allow Lyric to rule.

Not that she was my consort or my queen. She *was* the one with power, though.

Perhaps Wyn or Teagan could do it. After all, each of them was connected to the lords and ladies.

There needed to be a clear line of succession, something I would do in writing once I got out of here.

Because I would get out.

As if he had been drawn in by my thoughts, Garrik arrived, a key in his shaking hands.

"We have to be quick."

"I didn't promise you anything," I said quickly, trying to summon any strength I could.

"I know. But we don't have much time. Durlan and The Gray are away, leaving me in charge."

"They'll know it was you."

"They would have always known. That's why I have to go with you."

"If you say so," I said, trying to sit up.

The cage snapped open, and I attempted to straighten, but I was too weak to do so. Garrik was suddenly there, undoing my shackles.

My Wielding slammed into me once they fell away, the Fire within my veins pushing out and licking at my fingers.

I grinned down at them. I'd missed my precious babies.

But before I could say anything, Garrik was shoving something into my mouth, and I tried to spit it out.

"It's a potion to help you heal. It's going to take out the toxins, just takes a while. But it'll at least help your back so we can get out of here."

"Really?" I mumbled over the foul-tasting concoction.

"Trust me."

I didn't trust him, but the brew tasted familiar. Something that my uncle had given me in the past. So, I swallowed, hoping it wouldn't kill me. However, everything was probably about to kill me, so I might as well just go with it.

It worked immediately, at least giving me enough energy to sit up.

My foot slid in my blood, and I cursed under my breath when Garrik reached out to help me.

His lack of magic stung me, and I shook my head, pulling away. It wasn't that I didn't like humans or Danes. Far from it. But the absence of magic within him seemed so hollow, far more extreme than a usual Dane. And that worried me.

Nevertheless, I didn't have a choice. He was getting me out. Maybe to take me to another cage where I'd be tortured more, but I at least had an inkling of hope.

One that whispered Lyric's name in my ear, and that meant I had to be quick.

"There's a tunnel out of here, and then we can make it to the portal to your kingdom. At least on the edge of the territory. We have to go."

"A portal, huh?" I'd have to figure out exactly where that was so I could close it later. But it didn't really matter in the end, did it? Because The Gray still held my curse, and he could apparently snatch me anytime he wanted.

I'd have to end it.

Change and death.

Well, considering we were at war, I was pretty sure that could mean anything.

We scrambled through the hallways, and I tried to ignore the cages on either side of me. They stank of death, but I couldn't hear anything within. Whoever had been there before was long gone. I couldn't help.

Damn this man, this orchestrator, this puppet master.

I would find out who he was. And I would kill him.

We were nearing the end of the tunnel when a familiar foot tread hit my ears. I turned and growled.

"I should have known not to trust you," Durlan said, leaning against the wall as if he didn't have a care in the world.

He was broad, muscular, and far stronger than me at the moment.

I might have a healing potion running through my veins, but I wasn't whole yet. I was sick, and I would have to be sneaky to get out of here.

Given how Garrik had frozen and tried to look small, he wasn't going to be any help.

Good. Apparently, Garrik was the mouse, not me.

Well, this was about to get interesting.

"I was kind of annoyed with the accommodations, so I'm going to find my own. Hope that's okay."

"I'm sorry it wasn't to your liking. I'll have to find you something darker and a little colder next time."

Durlan stood up, a knife in his hand.

I had my Wielding. That would have to help me at some point.

I reached for my power, but as soon as I searched for it, the magic in the walls pulsated. I cursed.

Great. I couldn't actually *use* my Wielding, I could only feel it. Damn, the Shadow realm.

I'd need to get that blade, then.

Hopefully, I could still fight, even if I wasn't a hundred percent yet.

Durlan came at me, blade in hand, a snarl on his face. Garrik shivered and huddled to the side. I ignored him.

He was at my back, so if he was going to turn on me, this was his best opportunity. I didn't have time to worry about him, though. I had to deal with the behemoth in front of me with the knife.

I ducked out of the way of Durlan's first swing and elbowed him in the gut. He let out an *oof* and sliced at my arm.

More blood ran, and I knew this needed to end quickly. I didn't have a lot of energy as it was, and I really didn't think I could lose any more blood and stay standing. Or alive.

Durlan slashed at me again. I gripped his elbow and twisted.

He let out a sound of rage and pain, and I reached for his wrist. The knife bit into me, slicing into my skin, but I ignored the fiery burst of pain.

My Wielding pulsated again, wanting to come out. It couldn't.

This was why I trained with others. Well, not this exact situation, but I couldn't rely on only my Wielding.

That's why I trained. That's why I was a soldier first.

I was also the King of Obscurité.

And I would not die in this tunnel.

I squeezed Durlan's wrist hard enough that I heard a bone snap, and then I grinned.

The knife fell out of his grip, and I grabbed it with my left hand before it fell too far. It might not be my dominant hand, but I had fought with both. I slid the blade between his ribs, right into his heart.

The soft sound of flesh tearing and muscles rending filled my ears. I ignored it.

I didn't like to kill. I didn't enjoy being that person.

Though I would do it. For my people. For Lyric. And for myself.

I twisted the blade, and Durlan made a shocked gasp, blood trickling from his mouth.

I pulled the blade out, and Durlan fell to his knees, looking at me, opening his mouth like a fish but not saying anything. I had pierced his lung, and he was having trouble breathing.

Good.

I kicked him in the chest, watched him fall, and then I turned.

Durlan wouldn't be coming after me. However, The Gray could be here at any moment.

I didn't know where the portal was, so Garrik would have to lead. I pulled at his arm, thankfully shaking him out of his stupor. And then we were off.

I needed to get to Lyric. Had to get to the Obscurité Kingdom. I didn't know if we were going to make it. It didn't matter. We were fighting. We were trying.

And I had a curse to break.

CHAPTER 9

LYRIC

"Hold onto the power and try to keep it at bay." I nodded at Teagan's orders and clenched my fists at my sides. My Fire Wielding was so strong that I sometimes couldn't hold it back. Okay, most of the time I had trouble doing so. And I needed to control it so I didn't let another innocent Wielder die because of me like they had on the battlefield.

Plus, I didn't want to burn down another castle if I could help it.

Rhodes stood in front of me, studying my face as he held himself back from trying to physically help me.

So far, we'd been able to delay the curiosity when it came to Easton's whereabouts. Still, it was getting harder to hold them off.

People needed to see their king.

And I did too if I were honest with myself.

Justise and Ridley were doing their best to stand in for Easton as they had the entire time we'd been gone. Soon, it would be apparent that their king wasn't here. And the uncles, as well as Wyn and Teagan, were trying to devise a plan for that. The lords and ladies hadn't been told yet, but I knew that was only a matter of time. In the two days we'd been back, we'd only put out some fires, not all of them.

I, on the other hand, had to train and get ready to take the next steps. I wasn't truly part of the court, so I wasn't much help there.

We were out in the courtyard in front of the Obscurité Court, training as a group. Wyn and Luken were sparring against one another, their Earth and Air Wieldings creating intriguing matchups of soil and wind. It was so fascinating, that I sometimes forgot I was also supposed to be training.

Of course, having them near meant I usually ended up on my butt instead of doing what I was supposed to do.

I couldn't help it, though. Watching the two of them spar was like watching power and grace come at each other in awed silence.

Luken used his sword to direct his Air Wielding with such precision that I was envious. Wyn was the graceful one. She didn't have the grounded power that I thought most Earth Wielders had.

Instead, she was light on her feet as she pushed her hands up into the air and then pulled them down, creating cascades of dirt and rock and soil as she moved towards Luken. Luken directed the Earth away using his Air, and I couldn't help but want to stop and watch.

Of course, considering that I was supposed to be training on how to use all of my Wielding, it wasn't easy.

My distractions led to a few bruises, a couple of cuts, and one slightly severe burn that Ridley was able to heal quickly. He had come out of nowhere. I'd thought he was working with Justise on the court issues, but he had shown up immediately to heal the burn Teagan had given me.

Teagan, ever the warrior, hadn't even looked apologetic.

After all, if I had been paying attention like I should have been instead of watching Wyn and Luken, I wouldn't have been burned like I was.

It didn't help that Braelynn was with us, using her little bat wings to flap around and hover about three inches off the ground as she watched Luken and Wyn, as well.

There was something weird about it all. I shouldn't have been paying attention to them. I really should have been paying attention to Rhodes and Teagan.

Rhodes stood in front of me now, his arms outstretched as spirals of Water and Air danced in front of him, a little smirk on his face.

And that expression reminded me of Easton, sending pain straight to my heart. I ignored it.

Because this was Rhodes, not Easton.

This was my friend. The one who had helped me find my way at first, who'd almost died to protect me. I had to be okay with this, as well. Because while we were training, we didn't have a lot of time to worry about anything except what was after us and the power within our realm.

I had to work on my elements, on my control. That way, we could continue on our journeys.

"Keep going, hold in that Fire," Teagan ordered, and I nodded. Teagan was trying to teach me how to use my Fire Wielding, and while it wasn't going super well, I was at least learning some technique. It wasn't all about throwing fireballs at my opponent.

No, there had to be precision and control when it came to Fire Wielding. So much that it exhausted me more than using any of my other elements.

I closed my eyes and focused on the power within me, knowing that if I weren't careful, I'd burn from the inside out. Or worse, hurt someone. I knew I had to figure out how to handle all four at once, but I knew the answer would tear me apart. Because the only person who could calm me was gone. Taken.

And never mine.

I would focus on what *I* could do. I would rely on myself and *only* myself.

As I put my hands out to my sides, my fingers spread wide, my Air Wielding burst from my fingertips, and Fire slid along the path that Air made.

I held back a curse and clenched my fist, but it was too late. My Wielding spun out from me, and Teagan and Rhodes both ducked out of the way, their hands outstretched towards the elements that I had conjured.

I fell back on my butt and shook my head, trying to bring my Wielding under control, but it shook me, and despair spread through me. I didn't have time for any of those feelings. Instead, I helped the others soothe my elements, that way, I didn't end up hurting anyone. I knew I had to be done for a little bit.

"I'm just not getting it," I roared, slamming my fist into the ground.

"It takes time," Teagan said. "We've had years, decades really, to figure out our Wielding. And a lot of us only have one or two."

"I'm supposed to end up with five." I didn't have my Spirit Wielding yet, and I didn't know what it would take to unlock that one. Considering that every other element had taken a part of myself, or me being forced to watch my friends getting hurt or almost dying to unlock, I was not looking forward to what might happen or what it would take to unlock Spirit.

"It's just going to take time," Rhodes said, his voice placating. Or maybe I was thinking too hard. Everyone was trying to help me, and here I was, complaining about it. I hated that I wasn't Wielding the way I needed to. I knew that I was missing something. Or someone.

Because before, the only way I could control everything and hold it all back, was when Easton was there.

He wasn't here anymore. And I couldn't rely on him. I had to figure things out myself. So, that meant more training.

It also meant something else.

"We're going to have to travel soon to figure out the rest of the prophecy," I said, sighing into my hands. I shook that off and stood up, ignoring Rhodes' outstretched hands. I was so tired of relying on others, of leaning on them. I should be able to do this on my own. I should be able to fix things. I didn't want anyone else to get hurt because of me. And Rhodes had already almost died. It had been sheer luck that he had lived. I didn't want him to get hurt again. Not because of me.

"We will. We're leaving in two days' time to try and figure out the rest of the prophecy." I looked at Rhodes and tried to smile, but nothing came. I felt so empty, yet full of rage and confusion at the same time. It didn't make any sense.

"Yes, you and Luken and Rhodes will search for more of the prophecy. While Wyn and I will search for the other thing we're currently missing," Teagan said.

I looked at Teagan and nodded. The plan was for him and Wyn to go out and search for Easton. I wanted to go, too. I wanted to find him. I needed to. But we had to split up. We had to find Easton *and* unravel the rest of the prophecy.

There was no use staying here anymore. And while we also needed the training, we needed Easton and my powers more.

Because we couldn't keep up with the lie of Easton's disappearance for long. Soon, people would start asking more questions, and we'd have to find those answers.

"We're going to do this." I knew my voice sounded a little desperate, but all of them nodded at me. I was grateful for that. Because I was a bit stressed out. Okay, I was a lot stressed.

"We're going to figure this out. Because that's what we do." Luken sounded so sure, and as he went down to his knee to rub the top of Braelynn's head, I wondered how he could be so certain. His soulmate was dead. At least, part of her was. The fact that he now had to pet her in some weird way didn't exactly make up for that.

My best friend was gone, and I had to remember that I had important things to do. Or so they told me. I needed to figure out the prophecy, had to unlock my final element, we needed to find Easton, and I had to make sure Emory was okay.

I hadn't forgotten that my ex-girlfriend was currently chained somewhere in the Fire territory. I hadn't really known what to do about it when I first saw her, wholly altered by some unknown force. Now, though...*now*, I knew I had to save her. Because I didn't want anyone else getting hurt because of me. I couldn't let it happen.

"Okay, one more round, and then we can call it a day. We have papers and scrolls to read through anyway." Rhodes dusted off his hands.

"Well, that sounds boring," Teagan said, and Wyn came up to his side.

"Hey, you used to help me study all the time," Wyn said.

"Yeah, because I used to be able to make out with you in the stacks while we did."

Wyn just rolled her eyes, and Teagan grinned.

Rhodes looked between them, confused, and I really didn't have the energy to explain Teagan and Wyn's weird relationship. Not that I knew everything about it. It wasn't my place.

"Okay, time to go again."

I put out my hands and let my Air Wielding through. Maybe it was because it had been my first element, or perhaps it was because Rhodes was in front of me calling for that element itself, but it came easily. And I felt like I had more control over Air than I did the others.

Rhodes gave me a small smile and nodded, and I let my Air flow.

It danced around us, ran through my hair, and then through Rhodes'.

I had to pull back on my other elements so they didn't come out, not when we were trying to use one at a time before slowly adding in a second and maybe a third. The power bubbled within me, and I did my best not to ignore it but to acknowledge its presence. To be the one in control.

"Okay, now let out your Earth Wielding," Teagan whispered.

I nodded, my eyes closed as I focused within. I had to learn how to do this with my eyes open, as well. But, first things first.

Try not to destroy this castle, too.

As I embraced Earth, the earth buckled in front of me, beneath my feet, and under everyone around me as well, if their startled shouts were any indication.

I tried to rein it in. Yet everything was out of sync. I wasn't doing this right. I opened my eyes, and Rhodes' silver eyes widened, as well.

I tried to suck my Wielding back in. It was too late. My Earth created a wave beneath our feet, and I stumbled forward, right into Rhodes. Considering that he was falling forward, as well, he ended up on top of me as we hit the ground.

My breath was knocked from my lungs, and I gripped onto Rhodes' shoulders, his body sliding between my legs as I kept my head from slamming into the ground. He had his hands braced on either side of my shoulders, his mouth a bare inch from mine as we looked at each other before breaking out into laughter.

"Well, that's one way to get things done," Teagan said, and I blushed, my face so hot, I was pretty sure everyone knew how awkward this was.

Rhodes cleared his throat and tried to get up off me, and then froze.

"So, it seems you also used some of your Water Wielding, because mud is trapping my feet."

"That's something I'm going to have to learn," Luken said, laughing. "Okay, let's get you out of this," the Air Wielder said, a smile on his face.

"Oh, great, I'm so glad that I can be the life of the party," I said, sheer mortification making me want to slide deeper into the soil and hide from everyone.

I knew given the position we were in, everybody was likely taking mental snapshots. I was really glad that phones and cameras didn't work in this realm. There was no way I wanted to see how we looked just then.

"What did I miss?"

I froze, wondering if maybe I had hit my head when I hit the ground.

Because I had to be dreaming.

I turned my head, my cheek brushing along Rhodes' lips as I tried to see who was speaking. Because I knew that voice. I had trained to that voice.

"Easton," I whispered, not knowing I actually said the words out loud until Rhodes stiffened above me.

"Easton!" Wyn said and ran towards him, jumping into his arms.

He hugged her tightly before letting go, his gaze on mine.

I saw the darkness in his eyes, those same shadows I had seen when I first met him. The ones that spoke of the unknown.

I didn't know who this man was. Who this Easton was. Or, maybe I did.

"Are you going to get off her anytime soon?" Easton asked, his voice a growl.

"Working on it," Rhodes said, his tone far too light. Whatever had been holding our feet together melted back, and Rhodes hopped up and then grinned down at me, those silver eyes sparkling with something I couldn't quite name.

He held out his hand for me, and I took it, wanting to get up as quickly as possible to reach Easton. When I looked over at him, all I could see was Easton watching us, his gaze on the fact that I was touching Rhodes.

I didn't have time for this.

"So, where the hell were you?" Rhodes asked, pulling me out of my daze.

"I thought you were dead," Easton snapped.

I couldn't say anything, not when the two of them were looking at each other like they wanted to kill one another. And, I feared that I knew why.

And I didn't want to be any part of that.

They stalked towards each other, Easton not even looking at me. I didn't know how he was here, how he had gotten away, or if whoever had taken him was still controlling him. I needed to make sure he was okay. Because he was here. And that had to mean something.

Easton wasn't paying attention to me. No, he was only paying attention to Rhodes.

"So, you didn't die?" Easton asked. "Pity."

"Yeah, I could probably say the same about you," Rhodes spat.

They were facing each other now, only a few inches separating them, and neither of them was looking my way.

Everyone else's gazes were darting between the two of them as if they were spoiling for a fight. No one was breaking them up.

I was done with this.

Easton was back, but I couldn't deal with everything running through me. My elements reached out towards him, begging for his touch, and I didn't want that.

I wanted my own control.

I wanted to make sure he was indeed alive.

Apparently, antagonizing Rhodes was the only thing that mattered.

So, I put my hands forward, let my Air Wielding slide to my fingertips, and shoved the two of them apart.

They slammed into the walls on opposite sides of the courtyard, their eyes wide.

It would have been comical if I weren't so angry.

"Are you done yet?" I asked, my voice sharp.

Before I let either of them answer, I turned on my heel and stalked away.

The others could come after me if they wanted. I needed answers. And I wasn't going to get them if they kept fighting like they were.

I needed to make sure Easton was okay.

And I hated that I felt like that was the only thing that mattered.

CHAPTER 10

LYRIC

My feet slapped against the pavers of the walkway as I ran across the other side of the courtyard and toward my room within the castle.

I couldn't get my thoughts in order, and it was getting harder to breathe, so I pushed all of that away and kept moving.

How could this be possible?

How was Easton back?

And was it really him?

Because if something…no, *something had* taken him before. Why had they let him go?

I didn't want to look at him. Because if I did, and it turned out to be an illusion or something worse, I didn't know if I'd be able to handle it.

Visions of that chain of smoke from before filled my mind, and I tried to push them out. I didn't want to imagine Easton being taken away from me. Not when I saw it happen over and over again every time I closed my eyes. That and Rhodes falling off the cliff, his wide, silver eyes filled with nothingness.

It didn't matter to my subconscious that Rhodes was alive and back to his normal self. At least, as normal as he could be since I wasn't sure if he remembered much of anything after his father's attack.

I kept moving, though, knowing someone was following me. And I knew exactly who it had to be.

There was only one person who could make the hairs on the back of my neck stand on end. Could make me shake—and not in the ways the darkness had.

I could feel him in every ounce of my being. He might not be my soulmate in the ways that mattered, might not be able to actually love me, but I knew who he was. I could feel his energy touching my skin as he drew closer. The hairs on the back of my neck stood up even more, and my skin pebbled.

Yes, I knew who he was. This was Easton.

I couldn't face him. Because what if it wasn't him? What if everything had changed.

"Lyric."

I moved faster. I was running now. I hated running. Oh, I used to love it. It used to be the one thing that I did when I was in the human realm.

Now I could fight. I could use my Wielding.

I hated running away. But I just couldn't face him. Not now. Maybe not ever.

I turned to the right, a little confused about exactly where I was, and cursed under my breath. I'd taken a wrong turn somewhere, and now I was at a dead end. There was nowhere to go.

I fisted my hands at my sides, my chest heaving, my Wielding spiraling inside me, begging to come out.

It didn't, it wouldn't.

Not when he was there.

Strong arms wrapped around me, a hand sliding through my hair, the other wrapped around my waist.

"*Lyric.*" A warm breath hushed against my neck, and that voice went straight through my body, all the way to my toes.

"It can't be you."

"Don't run. Please, don't run from me."

"How are you back?" I whispered, the words tearing from me.

I closed my eyes, willing myself not to lean into him, not to do anything to indicate that I thought this was real. Because this couldn't be real. I had lost him. I had lost him long before the smoke took him.

And I didn't know what to do about that.

Because I had so much in my life that I had no idea how to fix. And I honestly didn't want to face anything. I wanted to hide and cower and pretend that everything was okay.

I knew I couldn't. And I shouldn't.

"Lyric," Easton whispered and then let go of my hair before putting both hands on my hips and turning me in his hold.

When he cupped my face, I opened my eyes and looked into those dark irises of his, trying to catch my breath.

"I'm here."

"You can't be."

"Why were you running?"

"I lost you. How are you here?"

I didn't answer. Suddenly, his mouth was on mine, his tongue parting my lips. My body shook.

I kissed him back, closing my eyes and wishing that this wasn't a dream. Because Easton couldn't be here. He had been taken. He was gone. He didn't love me. He never could. So how was this Easton kissing me? How was he with me?

It didn't make any sense. And I was afraid it never would.

His fingers traced along my brow, and then moved down my cheek and along my jaw. His other hand ran through my hair, tugging at my messy braid that I had put in earlier, even though it had slowly unraveled during my training with the others.

I didn't know if anyone else was around, but in this moment in time, it was just the two of us.

I didn't think that Rhodes and the others would really leave me alone with Easton. Not now. Not knowing exactly where he had been and what he had been doing.

Easton had been taken. I saw it happen. It didn't make sense that he was here right now.

I pulled away, putting my hands on his chest.

That's when I realized that he was shirtless. He wore only pants, not even shoes. And there was blood. *So much blood on him.*

He had cuts and scrapes all over his body, down his back.

"What happened to you?" I hadn't actually meant to say the words. I was afraid that he would tell me and then turn away. Because something had to have changed him. Right? He couldn't have been taken like that only to come back out of nowhere just fine—injuries notwithstanding. Yes, it looked as if he had fought, but I could tell that something was wrong. What was going on?

"I'm back. I made it back."

To me?

No. Not to me. Because even as he looked at me, even as he touched me, there was something missing in his eyes. Something that I knew should've been there. He didn't feel like my soulmate, not like he should. He felt like he had before. I could feel the connection. Only it wasn't what it needed to be. He was the King of Obscurité, Easton, son of Cameo, lord of all within this kingdom. And he wasn't mine.

I pulled away, my hands shaking.

"Why won't you tell me what happened?"

"I'm back."

"And you're covered in blood. You look like you were tortured. What happened?"

Why can't you love me?

I pushed those thoughts from my mind, annoyed with myself. I didn't need to act like a downtrodden, sad little teenager who couldn't find the boy she loved. It didn't matter that he couldn't love me. There were more important things to worry about. It didn't matter that my feelings were pulsating inside me and clawing at me just like my Wielding did.

The Air around me spiraled, lifting his hair from his face. I frowned, the darkness in his eyes encroaching.

"What's wrong with you?" I asked, my voice soft.

"I don't know."

"Where were you, Easton?"

"I'd like to know that, too," Justise said from the other end of the walkway, Ridley and the others who were aware Easton had been gone with him.

I looked over Easton's shoulder, my eyes widening as I noticed that Luken and Teagan were holding another person between them. The man appeared to be around Easton's age, young, but definitely a Maison.

I couldn't feel any magic wafting off him, so perhaps he was a Dane.

He wore a similar expression to Easton's—shielded, and dark.

He had cuts and blood on him, as well. Though he still had shoes as well as his shirt.

"Who is that?"

"That's the man who saved me." There was something in Easton's tone. Something that said that wasn't the whole answer.

I looked at Easton again and frowned. "Saved you from whom?"

Easton opened his mouth, and it looked as if he were trying to say something, but no words came out. Instead, he clutched at his throat, his eyes wide, and dropped to his knees.

I called out, kneeling before him, trying to catch him.

"What's wrong? What's happening?"

The others surrounded us then, Ridley coming closer to try and use his healing.

"It looks like a curse is preventing him from saying the words."

"If you heal him, he'll be strong enough to remember this time."

I looked up at the unfamiliar man, narrowing my eyes at him.

"What do you know?"

"I know more than I should. And I'm here to help. I just need your promise that you'll help me."

I looked down at Easton as he clawed at his throat, and then I stood up, walking slowly towards the other man.

People were dying within this realm, and I didn't trust him.

Easton had been taken, and there were more foes than friends these days.

Who was this guy?

Had he actually saved Easton?

I guess we'd find out.

"What do you know?" I repeated, my Wielding swirling around me. I could feel the power pulsing within me, almost too much to bear. I had to rein it in. Because if I hurt anyone here, I would never forgive myself.

"Help me. And I'll help you."

I tilted my head up to him, studying his face. He looked sweet, a little scared, and young.

So young.

He might be a century or four older than I was, and yet, I felt far more mature.

He reminded me of Arwin. And that sent another shot of pain through my heart.

Arwin had died because of me.

I wasn't going to let anyone else perish.

"Help us help Easton, and then we'll see," I gritted out the words. He nodded.

The others looked at me as if I were the one who was supposed to make these choices. Was I?

I didn't know. Easton was the king here, and even though he couldn't speak, he should be ordering people around.

I only had the power in my veins, and I didn't know if I could control it.

I looked at Easton, and then at the stranger, and I hoped we were making the right choices.

After all, I felt as if I weren't making many of those these days.

CHAPTER 11

EASTON

I hadn't been gone long enough for the world to miss me, or at least, that's how it felt. I had been gone from the estate for longer periods of time in the past. I'd been on missions to help my people, times where I had hidden amongst them, so no one had known that I was the prince of the Obscurité.

I had never been gone for this long as the king, however. And I knew that I shouldn't have let that time pass, even if part of it had been against my will. My people needed me. And I hadn't been here.

No, first I had left to go with Lyric, to protect her, to figure out exactly what we needed to do to bring the realm together—because if we didn't, it would fracture beyond measure, and we would all die.

I would never be able to forgive myself for not being strong enough. For not being able to fight off my attackers and save who I needed to.

I'd never be able to forgive myself for being under The Gray's control for as long as I had been. For still being under his control.

Because I didn't know when or if he would take me back, or if he could do something with my memories or change things.

Was I even myself anymore? Did I have the ability to make my own decisions, to engage in my own actions? What would happen if The Gray took me again?

What would happen if he took me in front of my people?

What would happen if he showed up and changed everything?

He had already changed things, and maybe had done it before.

Just maybe we'd be able to fix this. I knew we had to. And as I looked into Lyric's eyes, I tried to remember why I had come back. For the kingdom. For my people. For the family I had made, and for her.

Lyric.

I looked into those wide eyes of hers, at the long braid that had come partially undone as it tumbled down her back, and tried to dig down deep and feel what I should. But I couldn't feel anything.

I looked at her and I *wanted*. Only something shrouded that need, buried it beneath shadow and my curse. She was my soulmate. The one who could heal me, the one who *had* healed me. If we each had mortal wounds, the other would have a mirror image of it on their body, and then we'd be able to heal one another.

We had missed the signs before, yet they were there. She had been able to save herself with her power, only the magic running through her veins.

I hadn't been able to do anything for her.

Just like I wasn't able to do anything now. Because I couldn't feel anything. I wanted to.

I knew my curse. I knew that I would never be able to love. Never be able to have my soulmate. Part of me felt like I should be able to. Why did it feel as if I were missing something? Shouldn't I feel the hollowness inside? None of it made any sense.

"You need to tell us where you were," Lyric said softly. Her words might have been soft, but there was steel beneath them. I was enjoying finding out exactly who this woman was. This girl. She was so unlike the Lyric I first met at the Fire and Earth border. She hadn't known how to use any of the power within her then, and I knew she was still learning. She was so strong. Not just in her inherent ability or the way she learned to use it. No, there was additional strength beneath that veneer of hers, and I wanted to learn more about it. Even though I knew I shouldn't. Because she could never be mine. I would never be able to love her. Ever.

That was my curse. Maybe I should tell her. Make it easier for us both. Or perhaps that would only make things harder.

"I don't know if I can." I rubbed my chest, then I looked down at my hands and shook my head.

"You're going to have to," Teagan barked. "Because you just showed up out of nowhere with this guy." He pointed at Garrik over his shoulder, then I nodded.

"That's Garrik. He helped save my life." At least, I thought he had. I still didn't trust him completely. Then again, I didn't know if I trusted anyone anymore. It was hard to trust when everyone kept betraying you, even yourself and your own actions.

"And how did he do that?" Wyn asked from Garrik's side. She had used her Earth Wielding to create manacles around the guy's ankles. It cemented him to the floor, and since Garrik was a Dane, he held no magic to get himself out. I didn't blame Teagan or Wyn for their suspiciousness. I was just as apprehensive.

From the look on Garrik's face, I knew that he figured he might die. He looked defeated, and he had no power of his own. And though he had gotten me out, I still didn't know why. What was the reason?

Was it because I was stronger? Because I sure as hell hadn't been when I was locked in that cage.

I didn't know when The Gray would come back. And I didn't know if Durlan was still alive.

All of it worried me. However, my worries just kept adding up these days, so I planned to ignore them. Or at least, prioritize.

"How did he save you?" Lyric asked, her voice soft.

I looked at her then, aware that the others were between us. Did they know she was my soulmate?

Because she couldn't be. Not really. Soulmates needed a connection, love. There had to be a magical pull between them. We didn't have that. Because of the curse.

"I guess I need to explain. I don't know everything."

"Well, you're going to do your best to figure it out," my uncle growled. "Because right now, you're not even acting like yourself. I don't even know if this is you in front of us, or just a trick orchestrated by the ones who sent you. Are you *you*? Or are you under their control?"

"Justise," Ridley whispered, but my uncle shook his head.

"No, we need to know the answers. He's our king. At least the boy we watched grow into a young man that was one day supposed to be our king. I don't know who this is in front of us. I don't know if this is really him. Or if everything's changed. So, he's going to explain. Or he's going into the dungeon right next to this stranger."

"I am your nephew. The King of Obscurité. I don't know how the hell I ended up here, how everything came to this, but I am. And I am going to do everything in my power to make sure I remain him."

"That wasn't cryptic at all," Rhodes mumbled, then looked over at Luken. I noticed that Luken was carrying Braelynn, the little polydactyl cat, who glared at me through slitted eyes.

Apparently, this was going to be a large family affair.

No one else was around, there weren't courtiers or other Wielders or even guards in this area. Not when so many of us could take care of ourselves.

Anything I said would be in secret. We would be safe. Or, as safe as we could be when I was the one who could be the betrayer. The one who could tell all the secrets to The Gray.

I hoped to hell that wasn't the case.

"Garrik saved me from The Gray."

Anyone who had heard the stories as children took a step back or gasped or widened their eyes.

Justise and Ridley looked at one another, seeming to have some kind of silent discussion or come to an understanding I wasn't privy to. Had they known? No, however, they obviously had suspected something. It was only Lyric who looked confused. Well, Lyric and Braelynn.

If a cat could really look confused.

Rosamond, however, just looked at me, those wide Seer eyes unseeing.

I didn't know what she could See with her magic. Or was it just with those eyes of hers? When I looked closer at her, I realized she was using her gift as Seer at that exact moment. And I wanted to know what she Saw.

"The Gray is the one who will come. The one who has always been here. He's the one who will end us. Not the one who will survive us. It's all so murky."

She shook her head, rubbing her temples as her brother came to her side and put his arm around her shoulders. She leaned into him, letting out a little sigh. It was odd to see any of the people in front of me leaning on someone else. Everyone was so strong and tended to do things on their own. The fact that Rosamond was even leaning on her brother at all, told me that whatever visions she had been trying to See, or even the ones that were coming at her without her control, were hard on her.

And there was nothing I could do for her.

I looked at Lyric again, her gaze uncertain. There was nothing I could do for her, either.

"What does that mean?" Lyric asked. "Who is The Gray? Why did it just spark a prophecy or vision from Rosamond? You're going to have to explain it better to me. I might've learned a lot over these past couple of months...*years*. But it's not enough. You have centuries on me. And I need to know. It wasn't in the books." She looked at Rosamond then. "Why wasn't it in the books? Shouldn't it have been if all of you seem to know the name?

"It's a fairy tale," Rhodes answered.

I wanted to punch him just then. I didn't know why. There was something inherent in me that wanted to get him away from Lyric. I made sure that Rhodes wasn't the one explaining things. He couldn't be the perfect one that had somehow survived thanks to the bone magic and would always be there for her. The one who had a clear future and who wasn't perhaps working for the enemy. I didn't want him to be.

I hated this. I hated it all. And I hated myself.

"A fairy tale?" Lyric asked, drawing out the words.

Rhodes nodded. "The Gray was supposed to be of the darkness. The one who was there at the beginning of time when the Maison realm was first created. Not much is known about him other than he should be a myth. Like the boogeyman of your realm."

"Something you told children to scare them into going to bed early or to coax them into not breaking the rules? That The Gray would get them?" Lyric asked.

This time, I answered. "Exactly. The Gray wasn't supposed to be real." I looked down at my hands, at the blood still on them, and shook my head. "He's real." I looked at Lyric, at her wide eyes. "Yeah. Really damn real. And he's the one who's been taking me. I don't know what it means. I don't know how many times he's done it. I'd thought it was Lore. Apparently, it was The Gray all along. I thought it was over. I thought whatever Lore had been trying to do to me, the magic he was attempting to siphon from me, I thought it would stop. I thought all of that was over. It's not. Instead, it's The Gray. And he's the one that put the curse on me."

"I need you to explain exactly what the curse is," Lyric said, her voice wooden. Her tone indicated that she had heard of the curse before. Maybe the others were talking.

That didn't bother me. I was a king. Everybody talked about me. It had been the case when I was the prince and was even more so now. I just had to get used to it. I didn't want her to hear things secondhand, though. I wanted her to hear the truth from my lips. That didn't really matter, did it? Because she wasn't mine. I needed to get that through my head.

She couldn't be mine if I couldn't feel anything for her. The conflicting emotions running through me confused me and pissed me off. It was like talons digging through my flesh from the inside. One scraping for knowledge, the other pushing things away and trying to hide from it all.

It didn't make any sense. The fact that I couldn't figure it out, meant I wasn't truly myself. And that worried me. Because if I weren't myself when it came to Lyric, who was I with anybody or anything else?

What other powers did The Gray have?

What other things did he control?

That was what we needed to figure out. That and breaking the curse. Because I'd be damned if I let someone else control my destiny. I already had the world trying to control things when it came to my future. I refused to let anyone else try and do the same.

"The Gray put a curse on me, one that has to be broken, though I don't know how."

"What is the curse?" No one else spoke when Lyric did. They all knew the answer, but I needed to say it. I didn't move forward. I didn't reach out for her. Part of me longed to, but the other part pushed that thought away. Because, after all, she wasn't mine. I didn't love her.

"I will never have a soulmate. I will forever walk in the darkness. I will never be able to love that person the way I should. So, it doesn't matter what fate has decided for me, I'll never love her."

I'll never love you.

I didn't say that part. Not aloud. After all, I'd already told her that to her face. And then, The Gray took me.

I really was an asshole.

"Okay," Lyric said softly. "That aside, if he put that curse on you, did he put any others?"

She was so strong. *So* strong. She constantly surprised me. She'd brushed over the fact that I was never going to love her, never going to be hers, and moved on to more pressing matters. It didn't matter what she felt for me. Didn't matter that she had a mythical pull trying to reel me in, something beyond her control. It didn't matter that she was going to break inside when all was said and done, and I'd be left empty.

She pushed it all aside and worried about the others. And maybe that was a good defense mechanism. I wouldn't want to feel that either.

Though maybe I wanted to feel something.

I didn't know anymore.

"I don't know. We need to figure it out."

"Yes. Yes, we do," Justise snapped. "We're going to break this curse, any curse he has on you. We're going to break his hold. You know that Lore had to be either working for him or was part of this in some way. He was too close to you for so long. And none of us was able to see it. I'll never forgive myself."

"I should have seen it," Ridley whispered. "I'm the healer. I should have seen it."

"Don't blame yourselves. The Gray has power. He was within the Shadow realm, and he has those who work for him." I looked at Garrik. "There's another, Durlan, who is his second. The Gray called me his third. I don't believe it. I would know if I had done something for him."

That was a lie. One that rocked me to my soul. I ignored it. I had to.

"Okay, we're going to fix this," Rhodes said, surprising me.

"And you want to help?" I asked, a little sarcastically.

"Of course, I do. You saw what my father did. What my uncle is doing. I refuse to let our realm continue to die because of these petty things. We are all Wielders. And we're going to figure out exactly what The Gray wants. The Gray's goal can't just be what's happened so far. There's an endgame here. You've always said, and it's something I agree with, that someone else is orchestrating all of this. Is it him?"

"I feel like it is," I answered.

"Then we'll figure it out. Just like we're going to figure out what Lyric's role in all of this is."

"We already have half the prophecy. We need to find the rest of it. Because I can't figure it out on my own."

I looked over at Lyric and tried to study her face for what was on her mind, but it was blank just then. I couldn't read it. Usually, her eyes were so expressive that I could figure out exactly what she was thinking or feeling. There was nothing. I felt nothing. Was that the curse? Or was she closing me out?

It was probably what I deserved, something that needed to be done. Why did it hurt? It shouldn't hurt.

"We already know where we need to go," I said, looking at all of them. "We need to go to the ruins in the southern Spirit territory, just like we went to the northern Spirit territory to find the first part of the prophecy. We need to figure out the rest down there."

"Can you leave so soon?" Wyn asked, studying my face. "You need to make an appearance and make sure everyone knows that you're alive and safe and that everything's fine. Then, we can go."

I nodded at her. "We all do. Because this isn't about me. It isn't about any of you either."

"It's not even about me," Lyric quickly added.

"It's *all* about you," I corrected.

"You're the one with the curse."

"Yeah, and you're the one with the prophecy. It looks like we're a pair."

I could've kicked myself just then, but something was pushing at me, and I couldn't help it.

"No, we really aren't," Lyric said, giving me a sad smile. One that I never wanted to see again.

"We'll leave soon," I said, looking away from her, forcing myself not to look at her.

"We'll all go with you," Teagan added.

"Not all of us," Justise grumbled.

"Do you mind us leaving? Will you watch the court again?" I asked.

He glared. "Of course. After you make an appearance and let the kingdom know that you're safe and sound."

"And we'll watch this one here," Ridley added, nodding at Garrik, surprising me. There was a little menace in his voice, something I didn't hear often.

"Yes, we'll watch Garrik," Justise confirmed. My two uncles shared a look, and I had to wonder what that was about. But there wasn't time to find out. There wasn't time for anything these days it seemed.

I forced myself not to look at Lyric, to wonder what went on inside her. Because there was a deadness inside me that couldn't reach out to her—that told me not to try.

We would figure out what she needed to do with everything. Discover how she could save us.

And after that, if I was lucky, I'd figure out how to save myself.

CHAPTER 12

LYRIC

"Are we sure it's okay to bring Braelynn?" I asked Rhodes as we finished filling our packs.

He nodded at me, looking down at his own bag, and I just shrugged.

"You don't think it's weird?"

"Any weirder than actually having a cat who's a friend that happens to also have bat wings and occasionally spews fire?"

"The fire. So, I didn't just imagine the smoke and flames that show up every once in a while when she burps?" I asked, wincing. "Because I didn't know cats could do that."

"She's not a cat. She's a Familiar." He tied up his rucksack and put it over his back. "She'll be fine. Luken won't let anything happen to her."

The words, *of course*, lingered unsaid in the air between us. She'd already been hurt before. Now, Luken would be there to protect her above all else. Maybe even above his king and kingdom. None of us wanted anything to happen to *any* of us. Though we especially didn't want anything to happen to Braelynn again.

After all, she had already died once. Somehow, the magic within her blood and the crystal had transformed her into what she currently was. Not that it made much sense to me. Though I wouldn't trade it. Because she was here. Alive. I'd just have to deal with this new reality. Like I had dealt with so many of them recently.

"Okay, then. So, Luken has Braelynn. And we're going to make sure we get to the southern Spirit territory.

"It'll be fine. We're going to use some of the crystal to get us there."

"Are you sure that's wise? I didn't think we could do that," I asked.

"Yes. With the combined power of all of us, we can make it work," Easton said as he came in, his bag over his shoulder. There was a darkness in his eyes, and my belly clenched at the sight of him. He was here. Alive. And he, at least, looked to be whole.

I hated the fact that we didn't know exactly what would happen next with him, let alone us. I couldn't think about that, though. He was cursed, and that meant we would have to deal. We would break that curse and figure out what was going on with me, as well. Everything would be fine.

And if I kept telling myself that, maybe it would actually be true.

"Like we talked about in private before, you're sure using part of the inner power is going to help the crystal?" Rhodes asked, leaning against the wall. He had crossed his arms over his chest, and I couldn't help but look between him and Easton. They were always at odds, but I knew it wasn't about me. After all, Rhodes wasn't my soulmate, and Easton might not ever be. And I wasn't self-centered enough to think it could be about me. They had a long history, one that went back to way before I was even born.

They did seem to like to puff up their chests when they were around me, though. That was getting a little old. After all, we had the end of the world to deal with.

"I'm not sure of anything, but I thought we already said it's no longer Lumière versus Obscurité when it comes to us," Easton said, his tone casual, even though he was anything but.

He leaned against the doorway, his arms also folded over his chest. I wasn't even sure the two realized they were mimicking each other. No, they were just standing casual-like, as if they weren't a prince and a king and fellow warriors. They were just each other's sworn enemy. Rivals that no longer had to fight each other, a battle where no one knew what was coming next.

Namely, The Gray.

I had a feeling we would have more to fight before long.

After all, we didn't know where Rhodes' uncle stood on the line of that battle. He hadn't contacted us yet, hadn't sent emissaries or anything to discover where his nephew and niece were. Hadn't offered condolences over their father's death. Hadn't done anything. He had to know that the Lord of Water was dead, as well as the Lord of Air. And yet, he had done nothing.

And that in itself was troubling.

But that was a problem for another time. Or for a little bit later, at least. First, we had to get to the southern Spirit territory so we could find the ruins. Maybe then I'd be able to figure out what the rest of the prophecy was and actually determine how I was supposed to piece this realm together.

"So, how do we keep that promise?" I asked, putting my bag on my shoulder. I was getting stronger with all of this traveling, but even with the magic coursing through my veins and my own Wielding, I was still the weakest link of the bunch. I didn't want to be, though. So, I was training as much as I could.

My Wielding training would have to continue while on the road. The others would help, and I didn't know what I would do without them.

And since I didn't want to actually think about that, I didn't. We weren't going to lose anybody else. I refused to let it happen. We had already lost so many, nameless faces I had never met, those on the trail, and those during the fight with the Water Lord. We lost Arwin. We lost Easton's mother. I had lost Braelynn in her human form. And I was afraid that I was going to lose everybody else. Maybe even myself.

"We're going to the crystal room. We'll use that to create a portal. If we rely on our own strength rather than only the crystal, we'll push our Wieldings through it rather than pulling Wielding from others. Lore messed up the crystal, cursed it in a way, but we're going to get it back. We're going to fix this."

There was such strength and finality to his tone, I wanted to believe him. Listening to him talk made me feel like everything was going to be okay, and I could rely on him.

I knew that wasn't really the case. We didn't know what kind of hold The Gray had on him or what could happen next. We didn't know much of anything right now. We would, though. Because we had to.

"Then let's get there."

I nodded, tightened my rucksack, and followed the boys to the crystal room. Luken was already there, his sword on his back with Braelynn on his shoulder. She was perched there like a parrot, and I couldn't help but snort.

That made me remember Slavik and the pirates. Those Earth-Wielding pirates had been against the crown, and against all who entered what they considered their territory. I knew his second in command was gone, no longer a problem, someone who tortured others and had even tried to kill me.

I wondered where Slavik was. And what side of the fight he would fall on when it came. Because it would. There would always be a battle when it came to this. It was inevitable.

Wyn and Teagan were arguing with one another in the corner, but it was just par for the course with them, so it didn't really worry me.

Rosamond came up to us when we walked into the room.

"We must go soon. If we don't, we'll miss the time."

"Another vision?" Rhodes asked as he went to rub his sister's shoulder. "They've been happening more often than not lately."

"Don't worry about me, little brother. I've been at this for four centuries now. I've gotten the hang of it."

"You may think so, and I know you're stronger than most people give you credit for, probably even me, but I'm always going to worry about you."

"Perhaps. But I'm the older sibling. I should be worrying about you." She put her hand on his cheek, and the two of them rested their foreheads together, showing themselves as a unit in every way that mattered.

I was so relieved that Rhodes was alive, that he had survived the fall off that cliff. I didn't know what Rosamond would have done if she had lost her entire family in one fell swoop.

I honestly didn't know what *I* would've done if I'd lost Rhodes and Easton.

Now, they were both back—one in light, one in darkness. Just like before.

And now our purpose in the grand scheme of things was to somehow mix the two kingdoms, the light and the dark, together to build something new.

"Your uncle is securing the prisoner," Ridley said as he strode into the room, worry lines marring his face.

Although everybody generally looked around the same age, considering that everyone stopped aging once they hit their peaks in their late twenties or early thirties, Ridley look far older right now. Maybe it was the weight on his shoulders.

"Prisoner?" Easton asked, and I turned back to Ridley, clearing my mind of far-off thoughts.

"He's not exactly welcome since we don't know his intentions, do we?"

"You're not usually the callous one," Easton said, his voice soft.

"No, and look what happened when I wasn't. The Gray got you. The thing of our nightmares took you, and we didn't know. So, maybe I need to be a little harsher. Perhaps I need to be a little bit more like my husband."

"That's not Justise speaking, he would never say that to you."

"No, he didn't have to. I can read his face. And I know he blames himself, just as I blame myself."

"My mother didn't even know about Lore or The Gray, Ridley. *I* didn't know."

"Well, we should have. And we're going to beat this. We're going to beat all of this. Because I'll be damned if I'll lose you. You might as well be my son."

I took a few steps back to stand near Rhodes and Rosamond as Easton moved forward, putting his hands on either side of Ridley's face.

"You and Justise raised me. Just like my mother. My dad was long gone, thanks to Lore. You were always there. And you're always going to be here. Just like I'll be here for you. Don't blame yourself for what happened with The Gray. We can blame The Gray himself. Now, don't let Garrik feel too much like a prisoner. Maybe we should let him think we believe him. That he's truly our friend."

My brows rose.

"Trick him?" I asked.

Easton shrugged. Then he moved back from his uncle. "Maybe. That might be the best. Because I don't believe for a minute that The Gray would just let him walk out like that. I also don't think that Garrik is The Gray's favorite. Something's going on there. And while I want to think the best of people, I haven't in a long time. And with good reason, considering everything that's happened so far."

"So, what's the plan?" I asked.

"You go to the Spirit territory and figure out the prophecy," Ridley said. "We will take care of the kingdom."

"And if our emissaries and scouts don't come up with anything from the King of Lumière, we'll know something's up. Well, something's *always* up. We'll be back as soon as we can. Because *Uncle Brokk* isn't going to stand by for too long after losing his brother. We all know that he's up to something. He always is."

"Uncle Brokk?" Rhodes asked, his brow raised. "I thought he was *my* uncle."

Easton shrugged. "I enjoy telling calling him that, makes him sound like he's an old man without a clear connection to reality."

"Maybe. He knows more than he lets on. He's far more conniving than my father ever was."

"That just means we have to get back as quick as we can." I shook my head as I moved towards the crystal. "Let's get there. Figure it out. And come back."

"We will," Easton said. He came up to me and tucked a piece of hair that had fallen out of my braid behind my ear.

I looked into his dark eyes and swallowed hard. I was scared.

So afraid that I was going to break in the end. And not just from my Wielding.

Even as I thought that, Fire licked at my fingertips, and I sucked in a breath, clenching my fist.

Easton looked down and then into my eyes before making a shushing noise as if trying to soothe me. My Wielding listened to him when it wouldn't listen to me.

It was hard not to resent him a little for that.

That I needed him when I wanted to do it on my own.

There wasn't time for that, though.

We made our way to the crystal and got ready for our journey.

"We'll link hands," Easton said, arching a brow at Rhodes as he glared at him.

Easton took one of my hands, and then Wyn slid deftly in between Rhodes and me and took the other.

She met my gaze and rolled her eyes, and I held back a smile, my lips twitching. No, we did not have time for the chest pounding the guys usually gave when they felt like acting that particular way in front of me. At least Wyn and I could find the humor in it.

Rhodes took her hand, and she smiled sweetly at him, but there was nothing *sweet* about it. It was more snarky. The baffled expression on Rhodes' face let me breathe a bit easier.

The others made their way around the circle, grasping hands, and then Easton mumbled something under his breath, his Wielding reaching out to mine. My Fire slid around my right hand and wrapped in a spiral around his, meeting his own. Earth rumbled beneath my feet. Water and Air rolled around me like a tunnel. The others' Wieldings were doing the same, and then they arched over our heads and into the crystal. Warmth spread through my chest, then moved down my arms and into my fingertips before arrowing down again through my legs and into my toes. It also shot up to the top of my head and settled in the tips of my hair.

I let out a shocked gasp, and the magic sucked in again. Suddenly, we were no longer where we were. Instead, we stood on the edge of the

Spirit territory, a place I had seen before. In fact, it was the exact spot where I had camped with Rhodes and Luken and Emory and Braelynn. We had stayed here before we entered the Obscurité Kingdom the first time. This had been the last place where I had seen Emory as herself before she walked away, following the trail back to the human realm portal and ignoring all of us and what power lay beneath the ground at our feet.

Then she had been taken. By whom or what, we still didn't know. And now, she was different.

I knew once we got back, I needed to find her. Had to help fix her. I owed her that. Even if she had been cruel to me, she had been changed because of my power. Because of my destiny.

I wouldn't let her get hurt any more.

"Okay, now what?" Teagan said, rolling his shoulders back. "That felt different."

"I don't think the crystal's been used like that before," Easton said, looking down at his hands before shaking it off. "At least not with all four elements in play like that. Regardless, it got us here."

"And, like you guys said, maybe the crystal will be better for it," I said, trying to contemplate the whys of that thought. "I mean, the Spirit Priestess is supposed to use all five elements to bring the realm together. Maybe using four elements with the crystal will help bring some stability to it."

"That's a nice thought, and one we can look into more later," Easton said quickly.

"Maybe, or maybe it'll take that fifth element," Rhodes added.

"We'll figure out Spirit when we can. Though I worry, at what cost?" I asked and pushed that thought away.

"Let's go, the ruins are to the west. I couldn't get us all the way there, but I did at least get us to this border."

I looked at Braelynn on Luken's shoulder, and she twitched her ear at me. She knew where we were, as well. There was nothing we could do now. Emory was gone, at least for the moment, and so was part of Braelynn. And maybe even a part of myself. We weren't the same people who had come to this realm to try and find Rosamond. We were far from it.

We walked towards the ruins, my endurance level clearly not what it needed to be since my legs were already hurting. Easton handed me some water, and I took the pouch gratefully before handing it back. He just gave me a tight nod and continued walking by my side, not saying a word.

The silence hurt, even though it shouldn't. Because the issue between him and me wasn't the important thing. Then again, maybe everything needed to be a little bit important. Something that hurt this much ought to be.

A rumble in the distance made my blood run cold, and I stopped dead. Easton stopped, as well. As did the others.

"What was that?" I asked, my voice a whisper.

"Something I really don't want to see. Okay, boys and girls, time to use that Wielding of yours. We've got ourselves a salamander."

"A salamander?" I asked, thinking of the little lizard. "Like what kind of salamander?"

"Oh, it's an Earth monster," Wyn said, shaking her head. "One made of rocks and flesh. And it usually has wings. I don't generally see them this far into the Spirit territory, but with the unrest and the magic on all sides of the wards, sometimes they get through. This guy traveled a little farther than most."

I swallowed hard, my hands outstretched as I pulled on my Wielding. The elements tugged back and slapped at me, and I cursed under my breath. Of course, it wasn't going to work right. Despite my training, my Wielding clearly didn't like me. Not when I had four elements running through my veins. They were always fighting one another.

I needed to figure this out. If I didn't, then what was the point of the prophecy?

"How do we kill it?" Luken asked, drawing his sword. Braelynn still sat perched on his shoulder, her claws digging into the leather of the strap there. He had put it there for her, and I couldn't help but wonder how he had thought of it.

"It's coming," Rhodes said under his breath, and then his hands were outstretched, Air and Water spiraling around him. The precision of the power within him was stunning, and something I needed to work on with my own elements. Only no one else had four, let alone five. And I wasn't exactly sure how I was going to learn to control them all.

The salamander was indeed made of rock and flesh, as if it had armor that split as it moved at angles so you could see the red skin beneath.

It shot fire from its mouth as it flew at us, its leathery wings tipped with rocks beating against its body.

It was a grotesque representation of Earth. And the fact that it had Fire also, told me that maybe one day at some point in its life, it had been part of the Fire territory, as well. After all, everything had been one big kingdom long, long ago when some of these monsters were first created.

Then, there was no more time to think of history and creation. Only the monster in front of us.

"Let's go!" Easton shouted, and then we were off. Luken and Rhodes worked together, using Air to push the salamander up and then down, strangling it as much as they could with Water. It shot fire towards them, and they ducked out of the way. Braelynn tucked tightly into Luken's arms as he got back to his feet. Wyn and Teagan worked as a pair as well, using their Earth and Fire to try and bring down the salamander. Fire wouldn't penetrate its flesh, but Earth could slam into it. Rosamond stood by herself, her arms outstretched as she created a wall of Water from the moisture in the air, something I couldn't yet master, and used Air to push the Water towards the salamander. The creature rolled to its back, screeching so loudly it practically pierced my eardrums, but I ignored the pain and kept my hands outstretched, my Wielding ready. Easton looked at me, gave me a tight nod, and we both pushed out, Fire licking at the thing. It may not be able to pierce its flesh, but it could get at its eyes and mouth. I had seen that much from Teagan's Fire.

I used my Earth along with Easton's, the two of us fighting side by side as if we had for eons rather than the short time we had known each other. Something tugged at me, an effervescence within my soul that begged me to reach out for Easton, but I pushed it away. Because there was no way he could do the same for me, it would only distract and hurt me in the end.

The salamander shot fire at us again, singeing Rhodes as he pushed Luken and Braelynn out of the way. Rosamond screamed and then rolled herself into a ball of Water as the salamander came at them. Teagan and Wyn were brushed off their feet, both yelling as the salamander beat its wings harder, creating a burst of wind that pushed my hair from my face, and knocked the others off their feet.

My Water and Air slid out of my hands, dousing the Fire and the Earth, and I cursed.

"It's not working!" I shouted over the screams of the salamander and my friends.

"Then make it work," Easton snapped. "You are stronger than this. You don't need me. You don't need the others. You just need to believe in the power and get your Wielding under control. Handle it."

I looked at him askance and growled. "If I knew how to handle it, I would."

"Well, you're not doing it. So, do better," he lashed out and then put his hands out to the sides as he used the Fire Wielding to move everything aside.

I screamed, all four elements rushing out of me in a whoosh. I couldn't handle it, I couldn't control it, but I needed to. So much relied on me, and I wasn't strong enough. The elements slammed into the salamander's mouth, filling him up. His eyes widened, his screams getting louder, and then he blew up like a balloon and burst.

Blood and guts spewed everywhere, landing all over the ground and us.

I spit out whatever had ended up in my mouth, gagging, and pushed some of the blood from my face as I looked over at Easton, who casually flipped some of the salamander's flesh from his forehead.

"Well, that was one way to handle it."

I held back a glare at Easton's tone, knowing I'd messed up, even if I'd saved us.

"Shut up."

CHAPTER 13

LYRIC

It took three more days to make it to the Spirit ruins. I had never traversed this section before as the portal from the human realm had been located to the east. I'd been in the Air territory before, but never so close to the southern border as to witness the Spirit territory from this vantage point.

It took longer than I'd thought to get here, but as these lands hadn't been traveled in what could be eons, we were making our own paths through the desert rather than following a man-made road or even a stream like in any of the other territories.

We'd had to fight two more salamanders along the way, the others taking care of them before I'd been forced to use my Wielding.

I tried not to be resentful, but the idea that I couldn't control my powers just proved that I wasn't ready for this.

I didn't feel like I was ready for anything.

I could only hope that perhaps what lay within these ruins would provide some answers. Because I was all out of them. Only questions remained, and even those seemed murky.

"I don't think I've ever seen these ruins," Wyn said, the awe in her voice surprising. I'd assumed that I was the only one who hadn't been here. After all, my friends, the people who were by my side, who had helped to aid me through these waters and paths, had already been through so much in their lives. They were warriors, travelers, seekers. They were protectors.

Apparently, they were learning something new, as well.

It was good to know that I wasn't always alone—even if that was just in my mind.

Something I had to continually remind myself if I was going to be okay.

The ruins were made of some white stone that had been dulled with age and neglect—brown and yellow and even a few red clay stains on them. It looked as if it had once been a great and large castle, like the estates the other territories had on their lands.

It was large, yet it seemed more like home than any of the others I had seen—other than the Air territory.

That one had felt like home to me, even on the tall cliffs where it seemed as if only birds and angels could reach.

This, though, even with its neglect and dereliction, felt as if there could be children running in the streets, families with big smiles and hearts all around.

I was probably just kidding myself, though. Wanting to see something that wasn't there.

I was doing that more often these days. But I couldn't help it.

I wanted to know more about the blood running through my veins. The only Spirit Wielder I had met, other than in my dreams, had been the one up in the northern Spirit territory. And he seemed more out of his mind than rooted in the present.

In fact, I didn't know if the Spirit Wielders who had come into my dreams, who'd saved me and tried to teach me even though they hadn't been very clear with their lessons, were even alive.

"So, there's supposed to be something in these ruins?" I asked, coming to stand beside Easton.

He reached out, brushing his hand against mine. I froze just a bare instant before he turned away, looking out across the distance.

Had he done that on purpose?

Or had it only been a reflex?

Why was he so confusing? Why couldn't I focus on the here and now and not on what could be?

"I hope so. There has to be something etched on these walls or hidden away in a cupboard or something. Somewhere obscure. That's what all the texts have said up 'til now, that there's something here. It's just hard to get out here, so not everyone can make it."

I thought of the salamanders and the countless other monsters we had hidden or run from or walked past.

I had several of the strongest Wielders in the entire realm at my side, and even though I was the one who held some of the greatest powers, they had more training.

I knew that we had survived because of each other, and mostly because of their experience. Maybe not everyone could survive like that and weren't willing to take the risk. I knew I wouldn't have made it without them.

"Then I guess we'd better go inside," I said, taking the first step.

"Sounds like a plan to me," Wyn said, rolling her shoulders back.

"A few of us should stay outside just in case there's an attack. We don't know whose forces are against us. Those who are working for The Gray, or those who are perhaps even working for my uncle."

I looked at Rhodes and frowned.

"Have you sensed them at all?"

"No, and that worries me," Easton said, his eyes narrowing as he studied the place. "If I can't sense it, and if Rhodes can't either, that means either they're cloaked, or they're waiting for us to do something."

"I'm going to ignore the fact that you didn't mention the rest of us," Wyn said, shaking her head. "But they're right." She let out a sigh and looked at Teagan. "Let's take first watch. Sound like a plan?"

Teagan shrugged, his stance one of readiness. "Makes sense to me."

"I can stay, too," Luken said, and Rosamond shook her head quickly. "No, I think Braelynn needs to be with Lyric. I don't know why, it's not a vision, just a gut feeling. I'm learning to pay attention to those more than I used to."

"I can carry her in," I said, and Braelynn nuzzled Luken's neck.

Okay, then. Maybe I wouldn't.

I just turned away, wondering exactly what would happen to Luken's heart if we never found a way to either bring Brae back or figure out exactly what to do with a cat who could apparently spew fire but couldn't quite fly all that great yet.

"Stay by our sides," Easton ordered, looking at Rhodes.

"Was that an order for me?"

"It's a good one," Rhodes agreed, and I narrowed my eyes at him.

"Really? You're both going to act as my protector?"

The two shared an unreadable look, and I held back a growl. Okay, then. Two against one.

The fact that they were right and I knew I couldn't protect myself from everything didn't make it any easier to swallow.

I would just have to get used to it. And grow stronger so I didn't have to lean on anyone anymore. I refused to let anyone else get hurt because of me. I wasn't going to let anyone else die.

We made our way through the tall archways, and I gazed at everything surrounding us.

It was hard to imagine exactly what we were looking for. Something etched into stone? A piece of paper floating on the wind that had somehow survived what felt like eons of disuse?

I wasn't sure. I had to hope that when I saw it, I would know.

Luken, with Braelynn on his shoulder, and Rosamond followed us. Luken's sword was out, and Rosamond looked off far into the distance every time I glanced behind me. I knew Luken would protect her, and Rhodes was keeping an eye on her, as well. Rhodes and Easton were mostly paying attention to me, though. As if they were afraid that I couldn't handle whatever we might see. Either that, or they were afraid that something was going to jump out of the darkness and attack me. Considering that things kept doing that, I really didn't have a leg to stand on with regards to denying that.

We walked through hallways of dusty stone, the cobwebs in the corners the only sign of life.

A gentle breeze flew through the open windows and the holes in the wall where either an attack had taken the building down, or gravity and age and time itself had taken its toll.

I wanted to ask what had happened. I wanted to know the real reason it looked like a storm had wrought destruction here, instead of the Spirit Wielders fleeing for their lives during the Fall.

I couldn't. It felt like walking on someone's grave, as if I would be hurting those around me, even their ghosts, by speaking when I shouldn't.

We turned a corner, and the others went still, their hands outspread, their Wielding ready. I didn't move, though, because I knew this woman. I knew the ghost that stood in front of me. Not that she was actually a ghost. I really didn't know if that was the case or not. Regardless, I knew this soul—living or dead. I'd heard her voice. Had met her in my dreams. She was who I called Seven. Because each of the twelve Spirit Wielders from my dreams had stood around me like the numbers on a clock.

She had stood at the seventh position, had warned me. Had prodded me.

And now, she was here, though I didn't know if she was actually here at all.

"It's you," I said, my voice a whisper.

"I knew you would come. You're a tad late. Only you've come exactly when you needed to."

Rosamond took a few steps forward so she was standing right next to my left shoulder, with Luken on my right.

"Are you the one who sent us here?" Rosamond asked, her voice breathy.

"Perhaps. Maybe it's the bracelet on your wrist, Lyric. Or perhaps it's all of us. Everything. That's just the way of the Spirits."

Oh, good, it looked as if we were going to be talking in riddles again. Just what we needed.

"Can you help?" I asked. I took a step forward, my knees shaking. "Can you tell us what we need to know? Explain what we need to do?"

"Perhaps."

"Perhaps, what?" Easton asked, his voice a growl.

Seven didn't look at him, but I saw the tightening of her eyes.

"The shadow's son is close."

"What do you mean by that?" I asked, taking another step forward.

"The shadow's son, his blood. He's close. It's merely those on his strings that you must worry about. The shadows will find who they need, but those against him are strong. They must come together for you to realize what side you stand on."

"Are you saying we can win?" I asked.

"Or are you calling me the shadow's son?" Easton asked.

"The shadow's son does not know who he is. You, King of Darkness, are not of his blood. Of the blood of the forefathers, the bearers of stains and blood and Obscurité. You must find your path if you're to help her. To keep her alive. For she must keep the world alive, and those surrounding her must support her. If not, you will all crumble because the weight of those who carry the shadows in their veins will be far too much for any one Priestess to bear."

"So, I can't do this on my own?" I asked, my throat dry.

"You were never meant to, Lyric."

"Then why do you call me the Spirit Priestess? Why is there a prophecy that says I'm supposed to save the world?"

"You are the beacon. Not the only. Do you not remember the personal prophecy?"

"It doesn't make any sense."

"It will."

"What do we do?" Rhodes asked, coming to my side as Easton did, as well.

"You must gather your forces. You must train. You must look at the connections you already have. And remember.

"*The Spirit Priestess will come of five, yet of none at all.*

She will be strength of light, of darkness, and choice.

You will lose what you had.

You will lose what you want.

You will lose what you will.
You will lose what you sow.
Then you will find the will.
Find the fortune.
And then you will make a choice.
A choice above all.
A sacrifice above will.
A fate left denied.
And a loss meant to soothe."

I wanted to scream, wanted her to dissect each line for me like I had tried to do. I knew she wouldn't. That wasn't her job. The fates or gods or whoever pulled the strings were not going to give me answers.

We needed to find those for ourselves. And in doing so, I was afraid we would never come out of the darkness, or even the light. Because there wasn't merely light or darkness anymore. There was both. There always had been.

"We know that part," I said, shaking my head. "I don't know what we're supposed to do."

"You will make the choice. You will fight your fate.
And once you find the one you choose, you will have more to lose.
When the crystals fall, the end is near.
When the crystals shatter, you will fear.
Then you will fade, you will choose, and the crystal will shine.
Though the world cries, and the one you love is in shadow,
The world will burn.
The world will live.
And you will know the end.
The end of all, the end of nowhere.
But the end."

And then Seven smiled at me, her voice still echoing in my ears as light shined through her. And then, she was gone, fading into the mist as if she hadn't been there at all. But her words shocked me.

My mouth went dry, my body shook, my knees went weak. Her voice echoed the second half of the prophecy again, but just for my ears, as if the mist of herself surrounded me, choking me, cloying. I fought not to lean to the side, attempted to keep steady. But it wasn't enough.

Easton grabbed me, holding me close as my legs went out from under me, and I tried to make sense of what she'd said.

What could it mean?

What did all of this mean?

CHAPTER 14

LYRIC

Seven appeared again in front of us, and I pulled away from Easton, my body shaky. I *had* to be strong. There wasn't another option, and I honestly didn't want there to be one. My knees shook, my palms were damp. I ignored it all. I didn't know why I'd almost passed out, other than that it was too much, and I had been overwhelmed.

I couldn't *let* it be too much.

"What did you mean by all of that? By everything you just said. Can you explain it?" I asked Seven. I knew she wouldn't answer. Because nothing was ever that easy.

The others around us didn't say anything, as if they knew that this had to be me. After all, it was all coming down to me. Easton stood by my side, his hand brushing mine. I didn't reach out and grab it. I knew I could if I needed to. He wouldn't push me away, wouldn't do anything to hurt me. Other than what had already been done, of course. Easton wasn't cruel. He was cursed.

"I have been here for so long, sent here so long ago, that sometimes it feels as if I've always been here. And yet it's as if I haven't been here at all." Seven looked off into the distance before staring at me, her eyes so intense, I had to swallow hard, my mouth going dry.

"You are the daughter of the daughter of the daughter of the daughter of the first Spirit Wielder, who had a lust for power but had a good heart. She was the mate of the first Dane. She left, holding her daughter to her breast as the Fall began, and our realm started to crumble and shatter. When we were no longer Maisons, but Wielders who were forced to fight against one another rather than coming together as we should."

Seven took a breath and continued. "You have always been of both, though never within this realm. You were sent to the human realm because of the blood within you. You were born there, as was your mother, and her mother before, and all the other mothers going back to the original Spirit Wielder."

She tilted her head, looking at me so intently, I could feel her gazing into my soul. "That Spirit Wielder had such shallow powers, she could barely hold a wisp of a soul in her palms. She couldn't dream walk, she could do nothing except be who she was. As I mentioned, that kind heart loved another. The first Dane. The one who had his powers stripped because the crystals were abused."

She took another deep breath as if she'd been waiting to unload all of this forever. Yet I couldn't keep up.

"When the great kings of old—Easton's grandfather, and Rhodes' grandfather, as well—when they died, the first Dane was born. And that was of your line also. No one knew beyond those two who would come. That Spirit Wielder knew you would be the one to save us all. That you would come. They knew that they would die in the human realm. They had to live as humans, even though there could have been other paths laid before them. They chose to live for their young."

My breaths came in shallow pants as I tried to comprehend it all. That was where my blood came from. That was why I was the person I was today. Why I was the chosen one. Because it had been destined long ago. During the Fall.

I didn't know how this woman knew. She did, though, and everything she said sounded like the truth.

"Why couldn't we find her bloodlines, then?" Rhodes asked. "We looked. That's how we searched for so long. Until we found her," Rhodes said.

"The lines were erased," Seven said, not looking at Rhodes but directly at me. It was eerie, a little unnerving. In that moment, I had a feeling that all Spirit Wielders were a little weird.

Seven had talked about holding a soul within someone's palm.

I didn't understand it. I was a little afraid of what would happen when I gained that fifth element. I didn't even know if I would still be me. Because look at what Spirit Wielding had done to the person in front of me. To the man we'd met before.

"You found her because it was your destiny. Because it was a Seer's wish. Nobody knew of the bloodline. They couldn't."

I swallowed hard, listening.

"Your parents didn't know. They do not know of this realm. Nor should they ever. Their parents before them and so on couldn't know either. Because your line was sent there for a reason. They were sent to live, to learn, to be pure of heart and mind. For without that, the Spirit Priestess would never have been born."

I shook my head, so confused. Pure of heart and mind? I wasn't pure, not in any way. I'd made mistakes, I'd made so many. And yet I was supposed to protect us all? I didn't even know how to save myself.

"What am I supposed to do?" I asked again. I needed a map. Something. All I had were words that made no sense.

"When the time comes, you will know."

I fisted my hands at my sides, my Fire Wielding licking at my fingertips as Air blew through my hair, and Earth rocked beneath my feet. Water slid out of my pores, dousing the flame for a mere moment before it flared again.

"No, I will not." My voice was firm, almost a shout. I couldn't hold back. The others looked at me. I ignored them, my focus on Seven.

"Calm down. Be calm, Lyric," Easton said into my ear. I risked a glance at him and glared.

"Let me do this," I snapped before looking at Seven again.

"You will be the Spirit Priestess," she reiterated. "You *are* the Spirit Priestess. Nothing worth fighting for is easy, Lyric," she repeated from my dreams.

"You always say that."

Seven just tilted her head, giving me a sad look. "And you never listen."

"I don't know how. How do you expect me to do this when I can't even control my powers? When people are dying beside me, and I can't do anything for them. Why can't you just tell me what to do? If you do, I will do it. I promise. You only need to tell me."

Seven just gave me a small smile as tears slid down my cheeks. The others gathered around me, Braelynn pushing against my shins. I leaned down to pick her up, rubbing my chin on her forehead as she cuddled into me.

My best friend had died and then came back as this. Something I didn't understand. And yet, no one would tell me what I needed to know.

"We cannot help you," Seven said. "We are not of this time, or of this place."

"What do you mean?"

"I am only here because the power wills it, but I am not here forever. When the time comes, you will learn to find the others, the ones who will help. The ones you seek. The ones that are no longer."

"They're dead? You're saying they're all dead? The ones in my dreams? Even the man I met in the northern Spirit territory?"

Seven reached out and scratched behind Braelynn's ears. The cat leaned in, purring, and I had to wonder if this was a dream. "He was gone for longer than I. He came back to help. We all did." She looked down at Braelynn. "You're such a strong one. I cannot wait to see what becomes of you. You know, though, don't you, little one? You've always known."

I looked down at Braelynn and then met Rhodes' gaze. He just gave me a slight shake of his head.

It seemed they were all as confused as I was.

"You can do this, Lyric," Seven continued. "When the time comes, you will find the final element. You will discover a way to piece the world back together." She looked at me, the sound of silence so loud in my ears, it was nearly deafening. "For if you don't, the end will not just be for us, but for all."

Before I could say anything, before the others could speak, she drifted away once more, her body going indistinct before she was nothing but mist.

I just stared at where she had stood, holding Braelynn to my chest as Easton leaned into my side. I had to wonder: *What on earth just happened?*

What were we supposed to do next?

CHAPTER 15

LYRIC

As soon as Seven disappeared, a storm blew in, sand and high winds shaking the ruined city.

We hadn't been able to stay long, there was no place safe for us to hunker down, so we left the ruins and headed back towards the Obscurité Kingdom.

We didn't have the crystal with us, or any way to easily travel with the magic so depleted within the realm itself, so we moved along the path we had taken to the ruins and headed towards the Earth and Spirit border.

We passed the portal where I'd first come into the Maison realm when I was with Rhodes and the others, looking for Rosamond, so unsure of what we would see.

And then I came through there again when I was on the hunt for my destiny.

It was odd to think that it hadn't been that long ago, though it seemed like eons.

We didn't speak much on the journey, our faces covered with cloths and linens so we didn't swallow sand.

It was a hard trip, my body aching from it. Nevertheless, we pushed on until we made it to the camping site that was very close to where I had stayed that first night with Rhodes and Luken and Braelynn and Emory

We had stayed here, trying to figure out our next step before we slid through the wards into the Earth territory.

Emory had left us here, and that was the last time I saw her in her normal state.

I still didn't know how she was, or what I could do to help her. We had been so focused on everything else that I had put Emory on the back burner.

When we got back to court, I would figure out what to do. Because I couldn't leave her to rot in that cell. If she was even still there.

It wasn't fair to her. It wasn't fair to anyone.

"We'll take first watch," Wyn said, gesturing towards Teagan.

"Why are we always first watch?" Teagan asked, grumbling as he slid Fire Wielding through his fingertips.

Fire, the one thing I wasn't good at. He was so casual about it, just like Easton was. And it showed the strength of his Wielding. I could do that with Air. The others were a bit harder.

I needed to learn though, because I had to be proficient. *Beyond* proficient if I were honest with myself.

"Because I don't trust anyone else to make sure that we at least get the lay of the land."

She looked over at us, shrugging. "No offense."

"None taken. I like throwing you out into the line of fire," Easton said, smiling, though it didn't quite reach his eyes. I wasn't sure any emotion reached his eyes these days. Either that, or he shielded from me so well I could never tell.

"Now I feel like I should go with you," Rhodes grumbled.

"Don't worry, princey, I wasn't talking about you. I'm sure you can take care of the big bads, and everything will be fine."

Wyn fluttered off, Teagan grumbling as he tromped behind her, even as he grinned.

Rosamond pulled Rhodes away to speak with her brother, even as he started to mumble.

Wyn sure loved antagonizing him. I didn't blame her. He had been the symbol of the enemy for so long, and now we were all trying to work together. It had to be weird.

And it seemed hard to believe. Though, of course, most things these days were hard to swallow.

"I'm going to go get us some water, and I'll take Braelynn with me." Luken gestured towards the cat on his shoulders as she licked her paws, her bat wings fluttering. I nodded, watching the two of them go. They seemed content, even though I didn't think either of them knew exactly what they were doing. Braelynn wasn't Braelynn anymore. She would never be. And Luken understood that, at least as far as I could tell. It was like he had a friend now, maybe not the relationship he once hoped to have, but it was something. It was better than what I had.

I held back a groan at that thought, hating the self-pitying tone even in my head.

As everyone dispersed, I was left alone with Easton. We hadn't really talked. There wasn't much to say. He was cursed, and The Gray could possibly take him at any moment. We didn't know what to do.

Yes, Rosamond was doing her best to See into the future and try to figure out when that might happen. But we just didn't know.

Not to mention what Seven had told Easton about his prophecy. It was all convoluted, and I didn't like that I still didn't know if I could trust him. I didn't know if I could trust him with the prophecy, or with my heart.

Leaving him back at the Obscurité Court hadn't been an option. Not when he knew the best ways to get to the Spirit territories, and he had the power to do so. He would have just followed us if we had tried to leave him behind anyway. And I knew he was already hurting enough, I didn't want to hurt his soul any more. His feelings. Not that I knew if any of that mattered since the world was going to end.

Great, now I was lamenting about everything that *could* happen, rather than what was actually happening in front of us.

"Rosamond said she was taking Rhodes to get us some extra food. We have enough in our packs, but it's always good to be careful."

I looked over at Easton, startled that he was speaking to me. He'd done a very good job of not doing that since his return.

"And if a Seer tells you we might need food?"

He snorted, his eyes brightening just a little. That was good. I had missed his smile. I missed seeing something in his eyes other than confusion and darkness.

"I don't think it was that. I think she just wanted Rhodes to get away from the others. Usually, she gets a little more deep and poetic when she talks about an actual vision."

"Ah. Yeah, sometimes it's hard to follow what she says. Much like Seven."

His brows rose. "Seven? Was that her name?"

I shook my head as I reached down to get my tent out of my pack. He knelt down next to me, his fingers brushing mine, and I involuntarily sucked in a breath.

I hated that he could do that to me. That I knew he was my soulmate, the one person who was supposed to be by my side to help me traverse this new world. He couldn't be.

So, I pulled my hand back without looking at his eyes.

I didn't want him to see my pain. I didn't want to *be* in pain.

"No, she was one of the twelve from my dreams. She stood where the seven would be on a clock. That's how I thought of them. Like hours on a clock. They never told me their names, so I just named them after their position numbers."

"That makes sense," Easton said, helping me with the rest of the supplies. We set up the first tent, then went to erect the others. He didn't say anything to me for a long while, and I was afraid that he wasn't going to. I hated that I wanted him to.

I loathed this feeling, the thought that I wasn't good enough. That he couldn't even fight against whatever was pulling him away. Even as I thought that, though, I remembered that I couldn't be the center of everything.

We had more important things to worry about than my heart.

Like the fact that The Gray was out there. Watching.

That he could be orchestrating everything even now.

And we didn't know what the King of Lumière was doing.

We knew nothing.

All we had was a bunch of words that together formed a prophecy that was supposed to help me save the realm. It all sounded like it was going to take something from me, something I didn't even know I had, and leave us all broken in the end.

So, yeah, it didn't sound as if my heart breaking over a boy should be the most important thing.

"What's wrong?" Easton asked as we set up the final tent.

I looked at him and just blinked.

"Where should I start?"

He laughed then, and I shook my head.

"That really was an asinine question."

"Maybe. Or perhaps there're so many things wrong, it's kind of hard to keep up these days. But to answer your question, I was just trying to think of the prophecy."

"I hate when things don't make sense. You would think after all these years they would give us a nice roadmap."

"I don't think there's ever going to be that."

He looked at me then, and I wanted to reach out and brush that lock of hair from his forehead. I didn't.

It wasn't my right anymore. Not that it ever was.

"We should only have to camp here one night, and then we'll make our way through the Earth territory. It'll probably take us a few days, but not as long as it would have if we had to cut any corners." He pointed up, smiling at me. "The Obscurité Court is just north. I would rather be on our side of the wards before we start traveling that way."

"Is there a reason we didn't go through the wards today?" I asked, sitting down on a log as he joined me.

I tried to ignore the heat of him next to me, the way his skin felt as his forearm brushed mine.

I hated it.

And I craved it.

"Because I don't really know what's on the other side right now. I never do these days, not with Slavik and his pirates doing their thing, and the Lord and Lady of Earth acting like they are."

"You do know that Rhodes and I owe them a boon, right?" I asked, looking down at my hands.

"I do. You told me before. They kept you alive. Mostly, I think they were trying to use Rhodes for that boon. After all, he is the enemy."

"He's not anymore. We've all said that. It's not Lumière versus Obscurité any longer."

"I know. But I've had centuries of hating him and everything he stands for. I don't think it's going to take just a snap of the fingers for me to like him."

I looked over at him then, followed the line of his jaw, the way his nose tilted up regally, just slightly.

"You two knew each other before, and not just while searching for me?"

He looked over at me then, his eyes meeting mine. I swallowed hard.

"We did. This war has gone on for centuries. It hasn't only been us trying to keep our people alive despite the misuse of the crystals. We've had actual battles and skirmishes, much like there was against the Lord of Water recently. We traveled through the Spirit territories many times to fight on either side, though most of the fighting happened on our end."

My brows rose. "What do you mean?"

"Although Lore tried, my mother wasn't really keen on traveling to fight a king that she knew would never fight face-to-face. Brokk was never on the battlefield, though my mother and I were. The King of Lumière would send out his brother and his nephew. Never his son. I don't really know Eitri, or how he fights."

"The true prince of the Lumière?"

"Yep. Rhodes was never a true prince, though it's what others called him because he was the figurehead of the battles. I fought him with my Wielding, Luken with his sword.

"And usually on our own soil. The actual battles where we fought face-to-face have become few and far between. Most of our fighting became insular as we tried to protect our own." He looked at me then, his gaze intent. "And in our search for you."

I looked away then, letting out a shuddering breath.

"You quit looking. You gave up on the prophecy."

He reached out, sliding his fingers through mine.

I froze, looking down at our clasped hands. I wanted to touch him. Wanted to hold him. I was so afraid.

"I didn't stop searching because I didn't believe. I stopped because I knew that Rhodes was out there. And someone needed to stay back for the people. Rhodes had his grandmother and his sister helping. He had others trying to keep his kingdom together. His territories didn't have Lore. Mine did."

I looked up at Easton, the growl in his tone warning me.

"No, they didn't have Lore. They had Rhodes' father, who ultimately killed his mother. And they have Brokk. The King of Lumière. And we don't know where his allegiances lay."

"Well, I'd like to say he's going to be on the wrong side of destiny, mostly because he's tried to kill me my entire life. Maybe he'll get his head out of his ass and want to protect us, though. Save us. And actually want to be on your side."

"That would make things easier—if we were all fighting as one."

"You mean against The Gray? If we were all fighting against him and trying to fix your prophecy so you could protect us all?"

I didn't slide my hand into his, even though I wanted to.

"That would be good, wouldn't it? If we could work together to save the realm."

He didn't remove his hand from mine. Instead, he gave my fingers a squeeze. I licked my lips, wanting this touch to mean something more than it did.

"I don't know, Lyric. I don't know what I can believe anymore. It's hard to want to believe something when I don't even have full control over what I am allowed to feel."

We looked at each other then, and I tried to swallow what was in my heart, attempted to just breathe.

"What are we going to do, Easton?"

"I don't know. And it's killing me." And then he leaned forward, and his mouth was on mine. I sucked in a breath, my lips parting.

I closed my eyes, moaning as he took his free hand to cup my face, deepening the kiss. My tongue tangled with his, my breath coming in choppy pants as my heart sped up.

And then he pulled away, resting his forehead on mine.

I opened my eyes, wanting to see something that I knew couldn't be there.

Because there was nothing between us, there couldn't be.

"I hate this curse," he growled. "I can't have you. I can't love you. But I still want you."

I was the one who pulled away fully then, just looking at him.

Something broke inside of me—if I had anything left to break.

"We'll fix this." I whispered the words, not knowing where they came from. They seemed like the right thing to say.

"The realm? Or what I can't have?" Easton asked.

I didn't have an answer for that.

I wanted it to be both. I *needed* it to be both.

Though I had a horrible feeling it wouldn't be. We would have to choose.

And there was only one answer.

It had to be everything that wasn't what my heart wanted.

It couldn't be the curse.

It had to be everyone else.

And, honestly, I knew we wouldn't choose any other way.

No matter what it did to my soul in the end.

CHAPTER 16

LYRIC

"We're almost there," Wyn said from my side as we made our way through the Earth territory and toward the Obscurité Court.

There had been no pirates this time, no attacks from unseen forces. I didn't know if it was because we were traveling with the King of Obscurité, or if we just hadn't been seen. Maybe it was because everyone else was dealing with their own issues. Their own battles and skirmishes. Because I could feel it in the air, the magic. I hadn't really noticed it when I was here before. However, as soon as I left the Obscurité kingdom and then came back, I could feel the difference in the air. It was as if the magic were being siphoned away, and there was nothing we could do to stop it. I knew it was the crystal. I realized that if we didn't figure out how to revive it or patch some of its shattered pieces, there wouldn't be a people left to save. The way to save the realm and the crystal had to be untangled within that prophecy. There *had* to be an answer.

"It'll be good to sleep in a bed for a day," I said wryly, pushing away thoughts of what couldn't be. I had been doing that enough lately, though I knew it likely wasn't going to stop anytime soon.

Wyn nodded. "That will be nice. Even though camping is nothing new to me since that's sort of what I do almost all the time these days. Still, there's nothing like the feel of my bed."

Teagan came over, leaning down and winking, and Wyn just rolled her eyes. "Okay, do you need me to make *the feel of my bed* jokes, will that make you feel better?"

Wyn shrugged and Teagan kissed her temple before going back over to Luken to sit with him. They were in a deep conversation about something or other. I wasn't really paying attention. The two had a lot in common, so it was nice that they were becoming friends even though they were on different sides of a war. Or, at least, they had been.

"There's so much history between everybody," I whispered. "Lately, I feel like I'm always behind," I said, looking over at Wyn.

She just shrugged. "You're not behind when it comes to me and Teagan. We're just friends now. We have the ability to live countless centuries and that counts for too many years to remain alone. And I would rather not be alone all the time. Teagan and I are good friends, and we comfort each other sometimes when we need to. Though that hasn't been the case in a while. We're much better as friends."

"So, he's not your soulmate?" I asked, ignoring the little clutch in my belly at the thought. Because I knew who my soulmate was, though that didn't mean I was actually going to have him in my life. At least not in the way I wanted.

"No. I knew that going in. You can just tell." She gave me a look that spoke loads. I didn't take the bait. Because we all knew who my soulmate was, and we also knew that wasn't going to happen. I didn't want to talk about it. Not right then. I didn't think I could.

"Well, I'm glad you have someone to lean on because I have a feeling we're all going to need someone to rely on in the coming days."

"You're right about that." Wyn shook her head. "It's getting scary out there, and the fact that we're still trying to figure out exactly what this prophecy means isn't helping."

"I hate when things are in riddles. Why can't they just tell us?"

"Because then everybody would be able to do it. It would be easy. And, as the lady kept saying, nothing worth having would be worth it—or whatever the hell she said." Wyn blew her bangs from her eyes and glared. "I need to cut my hair."

I snorted at that non-sequitur, shaking my head.

"I like it."

"Well, it's getting annoying. I lost a few inches during that last battle, Teagan's Fire got a little too close, if you know what I mean."

My eyes widened. "He singed off part of your hair?" I asked, trying not to laugh.

Wyn glared. "Just a bit. And he apologized. I can't forgive him. Not entirely. It's the principle of the thing. My hair." She winked, and I didn't know if she was serious or not about the forgiveness.

I looked down at the Fire dancing along my fingers and winced, trying to rein it in.

"I hope I never do that. I really hope."

Wyn gave me a sad look. "I don't think you will. You're still having issues?" she asked, blunt as ever. That was why I liked Wyn. She was straightforward; though she was never cruel. Unlike Emory, who happened to be in my thoughts today, someone I needed to ensure was okay.

"I don't know. I've never really thought about what I was supposed to do with five elements. Four right now seems like too much."

"And they're all fighting inside you."

It wasn't a question. I nodded anyway. "Yeah, as if they're trying to talk to one another and see which one needs to be my main one."

"That's not how it's supposed to work," Easton said as he walked up beside me. I sighed.

I glared over at him. "I realize that." He raised a brow at my tone. "Just because that's not how it's supposed to work, doesn't mean I'm actually getting things done correctly. You don't have to deal with your Earth and Fire trying to see who can win inside you. I *am* dealing with that. And I have *four* of them. So, excuse me for a minute while I try to figure out how to fix that before I have to go and fix everything else."

Wyn whistled.

She took a couple of steps back so she was standing next to Rhodes and Rosamond, leaving me alone with Easton. Oh, good. Exactly what I needed.

Everyone else was trying really hard to look as if they weren't listening. They were. I had shouted. And it wasn't as if I weren't used to everyone looking at me to make sure I was okay. I was the weak one in this. And I knew it. Didn't mean I had to like it.

"It's not supposed to be easy," Easton whispered, and I looked over at him.

"I know it's not. I never expected it to be. I just wish I had more time to figure things out."

I had wasted a year of my life trying to get my thoughts in order and pretend I was normal. A whole year. And I didn't think I would ever forgive myself for that. Maybe if I had stayed in the realm after losing Braelynn and Emory and part of myself, I'd have been stronger at this point.

I couldn't go back in time and change that, though. So now, I had to figure things out on my own. I had to learn how to use my elements without losing control.

"I've had centuries to figure out how to control my Fire. My Earth is always steady," Easton said. "Sometimes, it wants to take over and rumble beneath my feet. It's always a force there, waiting to catch you if you fall."

I frowned.

"Really?"

"Yes. That's how it's always been. The Fire constantly churns, wanting to control, wanting to take over. Maybe not in the same way as yours because it's not fighting three other elements. But it still does that. I've just had more time to learn how to control it. And I bet Rhodes back there has issues with Air and Water. Just like everyone with a single element sometimes has issues. Yours is just complicated because you have more. Soon to be five. You'll figure it out, Lyric. You always do. You're far stronger than you think you are."

I just shook my head as he reached out and tucked a piece of hair behind my ear. I hated the fact that I wanted to move closer, to lean in to that touch. I loathed that confusion swept over his face as he touched me, as if he hadn't realized he was doing it and wasn't sure what to make of it.

I broke myself out of my thoughts and looked around. We were at the border between the Earth territory and the Obscurité Court, and I knew we had at least another hour of walking ahead of us. I wanted to sleep, to pretend that my powers were working like they were supposed to. I wasn't sure that was ever going to happen.

"Lyric, look," Easton whispered, reaching out to grip my hand. I froze as the others came to a stop around us. I ignored the feeling of his warm fingers on mine and looked to where he pointed.

"Is that a…? What is it?" I looked at the little ball of Fire dancing along the ground.

"It's a firedrake. A young one."

It bounced around on the ground just a little bit, flames wisping off its body as if it were hopping like a little bunny rabbit. I had seen two firedrakes before when Rhodes and I walked through the borderlands between the Fire and Earth territories.

They had been adorable, dancing and playing. And then they had left us. Here was a single one, and it looked smaller than the other two I had seen before.

"Kneel down and hold your palm out. See what happens," Easton said, a smile in his voice. I gave him a weird look, though did as he asked, mostly because I wanted to see what happened. And somewhat because I felt like the drake was calling to me. My Fire licked out, dancing across my fingertips before it faded away. I held my breath. The firedrake moved closer, one bounce and then another, and then it almost sniffed at my hands, tickling my fingertips as it moved closer.

It gave one hesitant hop before nuzzling itself into my palm. I froze.

"What am I supposed to do?" I whispered, and everyone slowly moved around so they circled me completely.

"I think you're supposed to cuddle it," Wyn said. "It's so cute. Although, I've never really seen one out on its own before."

She looked off into the distance, maybe looking for another drake, and I moved my palm closer to my face. The firedrake nuzzled my cheek, tickling my skin, though not burning me. The Fire within me reached out as if to envelop it in a hug, and I sighed out a breath of relief. It felt as if it were the one time that my Fire Wielding actually did what I needed it to. Nurturing, protecting. As if it weren't dangerous.

Braelynn took that exact moment to hop off Luken's shoulder and come to my side. I looked down at my friend who was now a cat with bat wings, as she purred at the drake. The drake froze for just a moment before leaning forward and nuzzling its head against Braelynn's. The fire didn't burn her fur. Instead, the two just purred at one another, the firedrake making little purping sounds. I froze, transfixed.

"He was drawn to your Fire, to your power."

I looked up at Easton, swallowing hard. And then he continued.

"You can control so much, Lyric. You just have to take the time to believe in yourself. Little Drake here seems to like you. He trusts you."

"What am I supposed to do with him?"

"Make sure he has a home. Love him. Just like you do Braelynn. The two seem fast friends."

I looked down at my hands, at the fact that the two were now nuzzling each other, even as they brushed against my palm.

I didn't really understand what all of this meant, didn't know what I should be doing. I nodded at Easton, knowing we were close to home, so near to a bed where we could sleep and try to let some of our worries seep away. All I could think about was the little life in my hands, they were filled with magic and light and could be hurt so easily by those who were careless or didn't understand. I needed to protect him. Just like I needed to save all of those around me.

I would have to learn control. It was within me to do so. It had to be. And even as I thought that, I knew there were parts of me I needed to close off and resist before I could take that next step.

Things I had pushed to the side because it had been hard.

And the person I had ignored because I was scared.

I held the drake close as Braelynn hopped onto my lap. I sighed.

We were missing someone. And I knew it would hurt, but we had to go back for her. I had to fix things, even if I couldn't fix anything else, I needed to fix this.

I had to find Emory.

CHAPTER 17

LYRIC

We made it to the Obscurité Court without any issues. Ridley and Justise were waiting for us as we made our way towards the castle, each searching our faces for answers. I wasn't sure what we were supposed to say. It was hard to give someone answers when the words on your lips weren't truths, only more questions.

"Your friend Garrik is in his room," Justise said with no preamble.

Easton's brows rose as I looked between the two of them. I had no idea what Easton was thinking…not that I'd ever known.

"Locked in there then?" Easton asked, though it was more of a statement than a question.

"He's free to leave, if that's what he desires," Justise said, none too kindly.

Ridley shook his head. "If he does, then people follow him. I know he might've saved your life. But we don't know why, and we don't entirely trust him."

"No, we don't. I don't want him walking around alone." Easton frowned a bit, looking down at his hands. A single spark of flame touched his fingertips, and Drake bounced from my palm to his. Easton seemed surprised for a moment before a small smile played on his lips as he reached out to rub Drake's head.

Drake had been in my palm for the entire trip from where we first found him, all the way back to court. Braelynn had alternated from resting on my shoulder to Luken's.

It seemed the firedrake and Brae *had* become fast friends, even if I didn't understand it. Not that I understood much about Braelynn anymore.

However, Drake hadn't touched Easton once the entire trip. Now, it seemed as if they had become friends, as well.

"I don't want to be walking around alone either," Easton said, bringing me out of my reverie.

"What?" I asked sharply.

"We don't know what kind of hold The Gray still has on me. So, don't let me walk around alone. Bring guards, do whatever you need to."

"You know that none of your guards will be strong enough against you while at full strength," Teagan said casually.

"Fine, then one of you stay around me."

"None of us is as strong as you either." Teagan let out a sigh.

"Well, maybe prince boy over here," Wyn said, gesturing to Rhodes. "And, of course, Lyric."

Rhodes just glared at Wyn for a minute at the nickname she'd used and then shrugged.

"If you want me at your side, I'm there. Though I don't think you're going to allow anyone to control you. Now that you know the connection exists, you can fight back."

"Do you know that for sure?" Easton asked, glaring. "Because I sure as hell don't. And I'm not going to risk any of you and this kingdom with my ignorance. I already risked enough by leaving as I did and going on this journey for the prophecy."

"You weren't alone," I put in. "We were all there with you."

"Yeah, trying to protect *you*, and to make sure that I didn't mess anything up because we don't know who's controlling me. So, yeah, great job."

I just shook my head, letting him do what he needed for his temper. I'd already grumbled to the others. Apparently, it was his turn.

"We're going to figure it out," Ridley said calmly. "Speaking of figuring things out, how did the search go? Did you find anything else out about the prophecy?"

Everyone looked at me, and I rolled my shoulders back, trying not to look as defeated as I felt.

"We met a Spirit Wielder, one who told us the rest of the prophecy."

Ridley's eyes widened, and he and Justise just stared at me as I told him the rest of the prophecy, including the first part that we had heard in the northern Spirit territory.

It didn't make any more sense now than it had before. Maybe with all of us together, we would figure it out. I had a feeling that, no matter what, things were going to happen, and I would lose something or someone in the process. Maybe even myself like the prophecy stated.

"Okay, then, we have it. And not just the idea of the Spirit Priestess, we know what you need to do."

"In theory," Justise corrected his husband. "In theory."

"Let me get this straight, we have to watch Garrik, and apparently, our king," Teagan said, pointing at Easton and in the direction of the stairs. "We need to unravel the rest of the prophecy. We need to fix the crystal. Make sure that our people don't rise against us because they don't have answers, and they're all starting to stress out from the fact that we're still losing power. Anything else?"

"I need to fix Emory," I said. Everybody looked at me.

"Really?" Rhodes asked. This time, his voice was sharp. "After everything she did to you?"

"She said some cruel things. Now, she's in pain. The last time we saw her, she was writhing in agony after someone did something horrible to her. They made her a siphon."

"And she's currently in my parents' dungeon, right?" Teagan asked. I nodded. He was the son of the Lord and Lady of Fire. Technically, he could be considered a prince like Rhodes. Just like Wyn could be a princess of Earth. Not that any of them used those titles.

"I know we have a lot to do. We've been focusing on the prophecy, that and training, and we haven't come up with anything. We can try to help Emory, as well."

"We don't know that we can help her, Lyric," Easton said softly. I hated it when he spoke in that tone as if he were afraid to hurt my feelings.

I didn't really allow myself to have many feelings when it came to him, not that I would tell him that.

"We need to try. We need to figure out something. I don't know what to do about the other things. And, frankly, I don't know what to do about Emory's situation either. Putting it on the back burner just seems cruel. Emory didn't ask for this. None of us did. But she for sure didn't ask for what ultimately happened to her. If we can help her, we should try."

Everyone was silent for a moment as they listened to me, and I wondered if they were going to try and talk me out of it. Teagan gave me a tight nod before speaking. "Okay, looks like we're headed to the Fire territory."

"Just what we wanted, more traveling," Teagan said wryly. "This won't take that long, though. We can use Fire to get us there, now that we have so many strong Fire Wielders."

"It'll just be the three of us, then?" Easton asked, and I tried to catch up.

"We're going to get her?

Easton nodded, reaching out to touch my hair again before letting his hand fall away. The gesture did not go unnoticed. Everybody did their best not to say anything or overreact.

I hated the pity, the confusion in their expressions. It was par for the course these days, though. And if I could at least do something for Emory or *anyone*, then I would try. And that was why we needed to find Emory.

"Yes, just you, me, and Easton. We can use our powers and the crystal without taking too much from it. The connection between the Fire territory and the crystal is stronger than that between it and Earth."

I frowned. "Really?"

"Yes, though I don't know exactly why. It's always been that way."

"Because Fire is stronger, or at least more temperamental. And even though I'm a dual Wielder, just like the rest of my family, our Fire has always been a little stronger than our other elements. We won't hurt the crystal or our people by using it to transfer us there. And, hopefully, we'll be able to bring Emory back through."

Wyn folded her arms over her chest and nodded. "I'll make sure to keep an eye on Garrik. And get the place ready to hold a siphon." She looked over at Rhodes. "Want to help with that?"

Rhodes pinched the bridge of his nose but nodded. "Yes, though it'll be interesting to figure out *how* to do that. Siphons usually don't live long enough for captivity."

"Because you kill them?" I asked honestly, trying to keep the emotion out of my voice.

Rhodes winced. "Yes. And even if we could let them live, they have to learn how to control their powers, just like you do. Nobody knows how they're made or if they're born that way, and something just unlocks within them at some point. They can wipe out an entire army of Wielders if you're not careful. That's why Lord and Lady of Fire put the shackles on her. It nullifies her power."

"Is it hurting her?" I asked.

Rhodes gave me a look, and I knew that the answer was yes. It was hurting her. However, it was also keeping her alive.

I hated that.

"Okay, let's go."

Easton searched my face, and I didn't know what he was looking for, or if he found it. He just gave me a nod, and we headed towards the crystal room.

He handed Drake to Justise, and his uncle's eyes widened.

"You caught a firedrake?"

I shook my head. "He came to us. I keep calling him Drake in my head. Not very original, I know."

"Drake it is, then. Others without Fire Wielding will be able to hold him if he feels like allowing it, they'll be immune to him as long as he doesn't purposely try to reach out with his power. He's a young one yet, though. He should be fine."

"He's made friends with Braelynn," I said, probably unnecessarily.

Justise and Ridley shared a look, and I wondered what that meant.

"That makes sense," Ridley said, a little mysteriously. I didn't have time to question it. And, frankly, I wasn't really sure I wanted to know the answers to what was going on with Braelynn. Everything so far was enough for now.

We made our way to the crystal room after saying goodbye to Drake and Braelynn as Justise and Luken stayed behind to deal with them.

The crystal room looked as it had when I first walked in before everything almost shattered.

Where I'd died.

The walls were dark stone that shined in the light, the crystal itself black with jagged lines running through it. The lines looked deeper today, the gouges far more dramatic than they had before.

The crystal was dying, and that meant the realm was, too.

We needed to figure out how to seal the fissures.

Teagan held out his hands as he walked around the side of the crystal. "Ready?"

When Easton took one hand and held out his other for me, I slid my palms against both of theirs and nodded.

"Ready," I whispered.

And then Easton said something in a low tone, and the crystal glowed dark before Fire reached out and encircled us. The flames were hot, but they didn't burn. Instead, they slammed into our chests and then swirled around us like little cyclones before everything went dark, and we were no longer standing in the Obscurité Court. Instead, we were in the castle where I had been once before. It had been long enough ago now that it was hard to remember every detail of the estate.

"Son," Griffin, the Lord of Fire said as he walked forward, his battle leathers worn but elaborate. "It's good to see you." Griffin held Teagan in a warrior's hug before nodding at Easton. "My king." He looked at me. "Priestess."

He turned his attention to Teagan again. "Your mother is on her way. She was dealing with an issue regarding some of the landowners."

Easton's eyes narrowed. "Issues?"

"We have more Danes near us than ever before. The power is seeping from others at an alarming rate. We're dealing with the fallout, trying to help where we can. But it's not easy."

"Have you made a report?" Easton asked his lord. Griffin nodded.

"We were just about to send it. We can discuss it now if you'd like. Why are you here? Is something wrong?"

"They're here to see the siphon, of course," Shimmer said, her dark hair flowing behind her as she walked in. She wore court colors, red and black, and she looked like a princess of old walking through the archway.

"I knew you would come."

"Acting like a Seer now, Mother?" Teagan asked, coming forward to kiss her on the cheek. She patted his shoulder and smiled, real warmth infusing her eyes.

I had never been able to figure out the Lord and Lady of Fire. Were they on our side? Or were they simply too cunning for their own good?

"You're here without warning, and I can see the look in your Priestess's eyes. Your friend Emory is where you last saw her. Still in the dungeon. I'm sorry we couldn't move her, but it was the only safe place for her and our people."

I nodded, knowing it was the truth. "She tried to kill us, you know?" Griffin stated.

"She tried to siphon your powers, darling," Shimmer corrected. "But she didn't in the end. Instead, she allowed herself to be caught. I wonder what that means."

My eyes widened as I listened to the two of them. I looked over at Easton, who just shook his head.

"Will you be taking her back, then?" Shimmer asked.

"Yes," Easton answered for all of us. "The others are getting her room ready."

"No dungeon, then?" Griffin asked, snorting. A tendril of smoke escaped his nostril, and my eyes widened.

Interesting.

"No, our rooms are a little better warded because of the dual nature of the courts. Not that your rooms are anything shabby."

Griffin threw his head back and laughed.

"You were always a better warrior than you were a diplomat. But I understand. She's a siphon, it takes more than a single element to keep her safe and keep us safe from her."

"She's not going to be easy," Shimmer said, looking directly at me.

I blushed before I shrugged and cleared my throat. "She was never easy."

A smile twitched on the lady's lips, and she shook her head.

"We've done our best to take care of her. She was able to bathe, eat, read, and sleep in a bed. Yet, it's still a dungeon, and she has not been easy, like I said."

"Hopefully, we'll be able to take her through with just the magic of the crystal and our Wielding."

"We'll help," Griffin said. "You'll be able to pull on the crystal's magic if there are enough of us to replenish its reserves with our Wielding. We're strong enough not to succumb to the temptation of using too much—or giving too much."

I didn't quite understand the physics of it all, but since Easton and the others nodded, I assumed they did. I only wanted to make sure we could do something. At least help *someone*. If we did, then maybe I could sleep.

We followed the others to the dungeon, the heat coming off the walls radiating through me and stabbing into my skin. I would have thought most dungeons would be cold and dark and dank.

Not those of the Fire territory, it seemed.

"Prepare yourself," Shimmer whispered, reaching out to touch my forearm.

I looked down at her hand for just a moment before she pulled it away, and Griffin opened the door.

The bed was on its side, food splattered against the walls, and Emory sat on the floor, screaming obscenities and other things as she thrashed against her chains.

It looked as if they'd tried to make the place as comfortable as possible. Clearly, Emory hadn't wanted it. After all, she was still chained, a prisoner.

Even with all the power floating through her and me, I wasn't sure if I would have been able to react any differently than I had.

Of course, Emory had always had a temper, a cruel streak that I didn't understand before this. Though I hadn't known where it came from back then. Not truly. Her parents lack of love and attention might have been part of it, jealousy other parts. I just didn't know.

Emory noticed us and sat up, glaring at everybody.

"Look at what your family has done to me!" Emory screamed. Not at me, not at Easton.

But at Teagan.

"Excuse me?" Teagan asked, raising a brow. "You've done this to yourself."

"What?" Emory asked, shaking her head. Confusion slid over her face, and she shook her head violently. "You're not the light one. The bearer. Who are you?"

I looked at Easton, confused. "What is she talking about?"

Emory screamed. "Where is the precious prince? The one of light and air and all that crap? His family did this. Where is he? I thought you would be with both of them. Just like always. Leaning on those you think can help you," she snapped.

I could only look at her, shaking my head.

"That light bearer's precious king wanted me to be this. And now, look at me. Look at what they've done. Look where I am. And it's all their fault."

She glared at me. "It's your fault, too." She spat on the ground as waves of energy pulsated off her, sparking at the shackles on her wrists.

Easton cursed under his breath and then met my gaze.

"It seems the King of Lumière has some explaining to do."

I nodded tightly as the others spoke about how we were going to get Emory back, and what magic we needed to do it. But I could only half-listen.

Because someone had done this to my friend. And I had a feeling that everything surrounding what had happened was far bigger than Rhodes, his family, or even the king. Far bigger than any of us.

CHAPTER 18

LYRIC

I knew the screaming would live on in my nightmares until the end of my days.

Just like I knew so many other things would weave and tangle themselves into my dreams. Maybe to the point where they didn't feel like fear or sadness or anger anymore. Maybe this would just be my life, and I would become numb to it. Did I truly want to become numb to the fear?

I wasn't sure. Perhaps that was exactly what I needed.

Because every time I closed my eyes, I could see Arwin's face. I could see the slight edge of fear and panic slide across his eyes as he tried to defend me. As he attempted to save himself.

I closed my eyes, and I could see Braelynn. I saw her fall and turn to ash.

I saw her ashes blow away in the wind as Lore screamed and shouted and tried to kill us all.

I could see the sword slicing through my flesh as if through warm butter.

I could see the shock in Rhodes' eyes as he tried to heal me, as he realized that he did not bleed as I did. For I had been carrying a mortal wound, and he hadn't had one to match.

Therefore, we weren't soulmates. Instead, we were only connected in infinitesimal ways. The prince to the Priestess. Friends.

He hadn't been enough to save me. And Easton hadn't known what I was. He had sat by my side, trying to protect me and Rhodes and himself as the castle fell down around us. He had been bleeding from a wound in the exact same spot on the side of his stomach as mine. But he hadn't noticed. Or at least hadn't connected the dots.

Because he hadn't known I was his soulmate then. Why would he? The curse wouldn't let him feel what he should.

All of those things slid through my mind as I tried to sleep. Because those were the nightmares I had. They weren't what *could* happen. No, they were what had.

The Negs clawed at the edges of my mind, the absence of light and shadows, yet filled with magic all the same. Lore had been the one to send them into the human realm for me. And it wasn't until I had been healed by Rosamond and Rhodes after I fell off that mountain that I had been able to see them at all.

They were the monsters that haunted nightmares. The things under the beds of children if they didn't obey their parents.

And yet, they were real. And, yes, they haunted my dreams, but they weren't the true nightmares.

No, the screams of that old woman as she died in that cave. The shouts of the innocent as they tried to run away from the Lord of Water as he used bone magic to twist and penetrate the goodness of the Wielding.

Emory's screams as she sat in front of me, still chained to the walls in her room that was far closer to a dungeon than Easton had said.

Those were the things in my nightmares now.

As I rolled out of bed, sweat drenching my skin as I tried to calm my breathing, I knew that they would never go away. That there would be no more going home. This was my home now.

I would never see my parents again. They would forever walk through the human realm, their memories altered so they didn't even know that they had a daughter. Same as what had happened with Emory's and Braelynn's parents.

They couldn't miss their girls because their children had never existed to them.

I could never go back. And I wasn't even sure I wanted to.

I had never fit in there. Perhaps I could fit in in this realm.

And as the magic shuddered around me, the crystal flaring as it did more often than not these days, I closed my eyes, gritted my teeth.

The people here didn't trust me. They didn't know me. Some saw me as their savior because that's what the ancient texts said. Those tomes had only hinted at prophecy. They hadn't actually said what that foretelling was.

Only a handful of people, including myself, knew the words now. None of us knew the meaning.

We would figure it out. Because I didn't really know what I would do if we didn't. There wasn't a true answer. I suppose that's why fighting was worth it. Because we needed to unravel the prophecy to find answers.

Some people had more history, more brainpower and experience when it came to things like this. Perhaps *they* would find a way.

And then they could tell me what I needed to do.

And I would do it. No hesitation, no questions asked. These people had put their lives on the line for me. And I was far beyond the argument that I wasn't the Spirit Priestess.

I felt the four elements pulsating through my veins, fighting for control even as I slowly let them slide through my fingertips and out my pores.

I knew who I was, I just didn't know what that person was supposed to be in the grand scheme of things.

My shirt stuck to my skin, and I plucked at it, wincing. It was one of the Maison's shirts, not something from the human realm. Clothing and technology tended to implode here. Rhodes had said it was because of the magic in the air and how it was too much for conventional textiles and other things that came from the human realm. I just figured that the Maison realm was already in enough trouble, and it didn't want anything within its borders that could cause it more harm.

I quickly pulled off the tank as well as my shorts and walked to the washbasin so I could at least rinse off.

Not all of the rooms had showers and bathrooms in this castle, although Easton was working on the technology to make that happen. Everything wasn't medieval. It was more that some pieces of technology had moved faster than others, while some progressed in magical terms rather than industrial ones. And since the magic itself was fading and rotting thanks to the crystals slowly breaking down, it wasn't able to actually create new Wielders and inventions. It was too busy trying not to shatter.

Plus, Easton and his mother had been more focused on figuring out the actual rot within their borders. Namely, Lore. As well as trying to protect themselves in the war with the Lumière and process the fact that their people were dying. Because without the crystal feeding energy to its people, not only was the magic dying, the entire realm was. And once it folded in on itself, there was no coming back from that.

So, things like a shower in every household, even as high-tech as that seemed in this realm, wasn't the number one priority.

However, Easton had put me in the same set of rooms I had been in when I first entered the Obscurité Kingdom, the ones closest to his. So, I had a semblance of a shower.

Everything was still that same stone as before, the shiny, black obsidian that called out to me. I had seen the clear crystal stones, the white ones that shone in the marble parts of the Lumière castles as well. I loved them both.

They called to me, dual sides of a coin that reached out to my heart.

And that's why I knew I was made of both kingdoms, one realm.

It was hard to think that when I spent so much time in the Obscurité Kingdom and felt as if the Lumière Kingdom were the one on the other side of the enemy line, especially considering what Emory had said—even though we weren't sure we could trust her. And given the way the King of Lumière had acted, I just didn't know anymore.

I quickly showered and braided my hair back, knowing that I'd need to cut it soon. Long waves now reached the small of my back and were getting far too long for battle. Maybe I would cut it short like Wyn had always said she would do for me. I liked it long. Enjoyed being able to play with it and try different styles. At least, I used to.

Now, I always kept it back, a few pieces falling forward as I worked.

And I wouldn't lie to myself and say that I disliked when Easton reached out and tucked those pieces behind my ear. Even if he didn't realize he was doing it.

I was just finishing putting on my leathers when a knock sounded at the door, and Easton walked in.

I quickly turned, making sure my top was tucked in and my breasts were covered, concerned that I hadn't fully done so before Easton walked in.

"Thanks for actually waiting for me to say, 'come in,'" I growled, hating that my cheeks were red. I could feel the heat of my blush. Even more than the burn, I disliked the fact that I almost wished Easton had come in sooner to see.

I was a glutton for my own punishment. Since that wasn't stopping anytime soon, I just needed to get over it.

"I figured you would already be up and ready, sorry for intruding."

He didn't sound sorry at all. And as I turned to face him, I saw that cocky grin. The one that he always had, and that I had sort of fallen for. I said "*sort of*" because I wasn't going to actually admit it.

"Whatever you say. Are you here for a reason?" I asked, trying to put distance between us. It was hard when all I wanted to do was lean forward and hold him. To tell him that everything was going to be okay as he did the same for me.

I wasn't that little girl anymore. I didn't need that. I just needed to get things done. And I couldn't do that if I were pining.

"You said this morning that we would try to work on Emory. I was thinking all night, and I think I have a plan."

My brows rose, and I took a few steps forward. "What are you thinking?"

"A siphon pulls at the Wielding and the life energy of the Wielder in front of him or her."

"I know. At least, that's what you said."

"What if we were to use something that most siphons have never seen before."

"I don't know what you're talking about."

"A Spirit Wielder."

"I'm not one. It's the one element I don't have. And how is that supposed to work anyway?"

"A Spirit Wielder can see inside other Maisons. They can see all of the elements, the Wielder's soul. I don't really know what happens after that."

He stuffed his hands into the pockets of his light jacket, and I just shook my head. "I don't know what you mean."

"I don't really know either. But maybe it could help? I don't really know what to do, Lyric. Most siphons die because they don't know how to handle the power. And those that survive, usually end up on the other side of a sword because they're constantly trying to kill those in front of them. I don't want your friend to go through that."

"I don't know what to do."

"Justise is working on shackles that aren't so…physically restraining, as well."

My brows rose. "Your uncle's a weapons maker."

"He's a blacksmith," Easton corrected. "And he's the best there is. If we can tamp down her powers, maybe she'll be able to actually control what's going on inside her, and she won't scream all the time."

"She always had that attitude, though. What if it changed whatever's inside her, and not just the powers?"

"I don't know, Lyric. We'll do what can. What we have to."

I raised my chin. "I don't want her to die."

"Your ex-girlfriend is not going to die by my hand. Unless she hurts you. If she tries to kill you, then all bets are off."

"She wouldn't do that."

"You don't know that. So, let's figure this out. See if you can unlock Spirit Wielding or something to help her."

"If I knew how to do that, I would have done it already. I can't just unlock Spirit and make it happen. That's not how these things work."

"I know that. I've watched you unlock some of your other Wielding."

"People had to almost die for that to happen. I don't know what any of this means."

"Let's try and figure it out. It can't hurt." He paused and then shrugged. "Okay. It's probably going to hurt. We can spend the morning working on this. And then we have other things to do. The realm's in danger, and as much as I want to help your friend…your ex-girlfriend, that is, it's not the only thing on my plate."

"First, stop calling her that."

"What? It's true."

"You get all growly about it, and you're just doing it to needle me. I don't appreciate that. She harassed me enough. You don't get to do it, too."

A sober expression flowed over his face, and he gave me a tight nod. "Point taken. I'll stop."

"Good."

He held out his hand then, and I looked down at it, wondering if I should take it at all.

Then he gave me that mocking smirk again, and I slid my palm into his. See? Everything was fine. I wasn't breaking inside and overwhelmed.

He led me to the dungeon, slowly pulling his hand away as we entered the room where the others were.

Justise was there, three metal bands in his hands, two smaller, one larger as he glared at Emory.

Ridley and Rosamond stood on the other side of the room, talking to one another as Rhodes stood right in front of Emory, studying her face. Luken was in the corner, holding Braelynn as Drake danced around his feet. While Wyn and Teagan glared at each other, I noticed someone else in the room, as well.

Garrik.

I looked over at Easton, who leaned close. So close, only I would be able to hear his whisper against my ear. His warm breath sent shivers down my spine. I ignored it. "He's here because we're watching him. Don't worry, he won't learn our secrets."

I gave him a tight nod and tore my gaze from Garrik, who just looked timidly at me. He looked scared, as if he were afraid that we were going to murder him on the spot.

He'd worked for The Gray, maybe like Easton had, but Garrik had been free. Easton hadn't. Easton had been chained, while Garrik was able to walk around and do whatever he wanted.

I didn't really know who to trust at this point. But I knew it couldn't be Garrik.

"I didn't realize I was running late," I said quickly, and everyone turned to look at me, including Emory, who just glared.

"You don't sleep anymore, so I told them to let you rest," Rosamond said, her voice breathy.

I looked at her then, her eyes a bit glassy as if she were seeing far off into the distance.

"Are you okay?"

She nodded, rubbing her temple. "Just a slight headache. The visions are coming quicker these days. I hate them."

Ridley was suddenly there, lifting her chin to look into her eyes. "Tell me how you're feeling, Seer. Where are the headaches located? Any dizziness? Nausea?"

"I'm fine, Ridley. You're such a wonderful healer. But you can't fix this."

"You know healers get visions, too," he whispered, and I looked over at Easton.

He gave an almost infinitesimal shake of his head, and I went back to looking at the others. I hadn't known healers could have visions. Ridley was the one who could recognize Seer magic before. I looked down at my bracelet, the one thing that I always wore.

Alura had given it to me, and Rosamond had had it made. It told me what territory I needed to be in, at least that's what I thought it did. Each of the symbols that represented the territories and the elements would burn against my skin, and then I would know where I was needed most.

It lay inactive on my wrist now, and I figured that I was where the realm needed me. Or perhaps where I wished I needed to be.

"I'm fine, healer. Don't worry about me. Let's worry about Emory here." Rosamond's words were soft yet strong.

"I don't need your worries," Emory bit out.

"Emory. Let us help."

I moved forward, and the crowd parted so I could stand in front of her.

Her black hair was in disarray around her face, her normally trimmed blunt bangs no longer covered her forehead and were swept off to the side as if she had ripped her hands through them over and over again. Her bob wasn't above her shoulders anymore, this time touching her shoulder and even far past.

She hadn't had a haircut since we left the human realm. I hadn't either.

I wished there was something I could do. I knew there wasn't. I didn't think that me trying to unlock my Spirit Wielding would help her. Maybe once I actually had that element, I'd be able to help. Perhaps we could figure out what had happened and why she had such rage and anger.

"Why are you so angry?" I asked, not even aware that I was asking the question until it was already out.

"Because all of you did this to me. *I would've been fine.* I would've been okay alone out in the human world without this. Without knowing that realms existed. You had to fall for the pretty face and those silver eyes. Alura and Rosamond had to be there. And those monsters just had to attack us. I didn't want to be here. I came because I knew you couldn't do this by yourself." She laughed then. A chilling sound that slid down my spine and made me shiver. There was also something in her tone that told me that she didn't mean everything she was saying. She was scared, just like I would be, and that fear was coloring her tone.

"Emory. I'm so sorry."

"No, you're not. There's nothing for you to be sorry about. After all, I might be here because of you. However, it wasn't you. No, it was *them*. The ones who wanted to make me what I am. Whatever the hell I am. For whatever they wanted to use me for. Well, look at me now. I'm exactly where they wanted me. Bleeding inside and wanting to die. They wanted me to be the one to take you down. I couldn't. I couldn't even do that simple thing. I hate this. Why won't you just end me? Why won't you make this easier?"

She looked at Justise then, and I knew she had asked this of him before. She had asked him to kill her. I wanted to scream. I wanted to fall to my knees and try to make it okay. Fix this.

As the four elements within me merged, almost at peace for once as Easton stood by me, I knew I couldn't fix her.

I could possibly bind her or something.

At least, for the moment.

"You are in my kingdom," Easton said, his voice low.

Emory narrowed her eyes at him.

"The other prince. No, I guess it's king now, isn't it?"

"You seem to know a lot about our realm for someone who claims not to be part of it," he said casually.

"I listen. The guards talk. They all do. They forget that I'm here. I know you're the king. And I know that prince boy over there is related to the other king. The man who did this."

"He did this to you?" I confirmed, stepping forward. "Why? How?"

"*He* didn't do it. He had it done. Actually, I don't know."

Emory rubbed her temples, glaring. "I just remember them saying his name. Saying he was the king, and it was light. So, it can't be Easton over there because he's all darkness."

"What was the name they used?" Rhodes asked, his voice low.

"Brokk. Sounds like some football player who doesn't have a brain cell to his name."

She looked at me then, smirking. It didn't reach her eyes. No, this wasn't the same Emory I knew before. This one was in pain. And I couldn't fix her.

"Emory."

"Is it true. Is Braelynn really dead?"

I looked at her then, confused. "You don't know?"

"Nobody tells me anything."

Braelynn padded up next to me and looked over at Emory, tilting her furry little head.

I didn't have the heart to tell Emory what had happened. I didn't know that I could. What would make sense? Because the three of us had walked into this realm, not knowing where we were going or what would come for us. We still didn't. Everything had changed. Nothing was as it once was, and I didn't know how to explain that to Emory.

"Who's this?" Emory asked, looking down at Braelynn. "Never seen a cat with bat wings before."

She didn't reach out. Instead, she kept her chained hands close to her body as if afraid to touch anything. My heart broke for her. She might have said some cruel things in the past, might not have known how to deal with her pain and her temper. But she didn't deserve this. No one did.

"I'm sorry, Emory." And then I told her about myself, about Braelynn and the battle. I knelt down to pet Braelynn's head as Emory's eyes widened, and a tear slid down her cheek.

Emory and Braelynn had never been the best of friends. They had been friends, nonetheless. And there was no going back from this. No changing any of it.

And I still didn't know how to make it better. How to make it right.

Justise cleared his throat, and I looked up at him. The man who wasn't good with emotions unless it was with his husband, really seemed as if he had no idea what to say.

"I made these, with Rosamond's and Ridley's help. You should be able to wear them around your neck and your wrists to move more freely around the castle."

"You trust me?" Emory asked, her eyes on the bands in his hands rather than on his face.

"No," Easton said, his voice clipped. "But we can't trust most people these days, can we? You were a pawn in this, and we all know that. So, we're giving you some freedom. Not completely, however. You will still be watched. Though you aren't alone in being watched."

I resisted the urge to look over at Garrik.

Or even at Easton.

After all, Easton was never truly alone, although he had been when he came to see me in my bedroom. Perhaps others had been watching him, and I just hadn't noticed.

After all, I had been very much in my head at the time.

"What am I supposed to do?" Emory asked.

"Figure it out," I said, so tired now. "A war is coming. Or maybe it's already here. We need all the help we can get. And if the girl I knew is still inside you somewhere, find her and help us. I will do my best to return you to how you were. For now, this will help you. Right?" I looked at Justise.

He nodded. "This'll bind your powers and make it so you can't feel it. It might make you tired. You may not have the same energy you once had. But it won't hurt you. You can trust me on that."

"I don't know who to trust," she whispered, and my heart broke for her. I hated that she was going through this. There wasn't anything else I could do, though. It was either this or leave her in a dungeon. And I hated the thought of doing the latter.

"Let's figure this out together, one step at a time. Because this is only the beginning, Emory. I've already lost Braelynn, at least most of her. I can't lose you, too."

The others were silent as Emory looked at me. I didn't know what else there was to say.

When she nodded, relief flowed through me, and I knew that this moment was our break, a time where we could just breathe, the calm before the storm. I would take it.

I would accept this bit of freedom, this moment of peace. Because the darkness was coming, and he had a name.

The Gray.

Only he wasn't working alone, and it was those other members that I knew we had to be leery of.

Not only were we worried about Garrik and about Easton. But now we had to look at Emory, too. Because what if she worked for him? What if we were all wrong?

We would find that darkness, and we would try to bring it to the light. I just didn't know what would happen before then.

CHAPTER 19

EASTON

I draped my leg over the edge of the chair as I watched the others move around the room. I was exhausted. I didn't really want them to know. *Nobody* could know. Though I had a feeling my uncles did. And Lyric. I couldn't help but notice the way her eyes constantly met mine as if she knew exactly what I was thinking. The fact that, sometimes, even *I* didn't know what I was thinking, however, meant that she may know more than I did.

I purposely didn't look over to where Lyric stood with the others, instead choosing to focus on trying to remain upright in my chair. I was exhausted, but I wasn't allowed to show it. Not even to the family or to the people closest to me. Every single person in this room.

I had spent the day walking through the court, talking to as many people as I could. I met with the farmers, the butchers, the weavers. I met with the soldiers and the infantry. With the other minor healers and teachers. I tried to meet with everyone so they could see their king, attempted to reassure them that we were finding answers, that we were one step closer to figuring out exactly what to do to protect them and their families.

I both hated and loved that part of my job.

I loathed the lying because I knew we weren't any closer. Not really.

It didn't matter that we knew the prophecy. That Lyric was here as a beacon of hope.

We didn't know what the next step was. And for someone who prided themselves on figuring out exactly what needed to be done in order to protect their people, I wasn't doing okay with that.

However, the part of my job I *did* like was actually speaking to my people. They had watched me grow up as the queen's child, the *prodigal son*. We weren't light, we were of darkness—something that I never forgot. The world had cast its shadow upon us when we were in infancy. Said that our powers were of the dark, not the light. In reality, my people were the opposite. They brought the light; they brought purity to my kingdom. It wasn't me. It wasn't anyone in power. It was those who worked hard day in and day out to keep the crops alive, to teach their children and watch them grow into adults, into Wielders. Those hanging by the thread we were all dangling from as they tried to create new lives in a world where their powers could be taken from them at any moment as the crystal sparked its energy.

From the time I was a boy, I had watched my people start to deteriorate, even as they tried to stand firm and grow.

The Fall had occurred long before my birth, my mother's father having lost everything, including his life, during the war with the former King of Lumière.

I knew of the atrocities each side had committed, although, in reality, my grandfather hadn't been the worst.

No, it had been the King of Lumière, Rhodes' grandfather. Just like the king's second son, the late Lord of Water, Rhodes and Rosamond's father. They had bastardized their magics, killing and stripping the lives of the Spirit Wielders and Obscurité alike.

That had been their legacy. One that had been tarnished over time to where there now was pure evil and goodness on either side. And then again, the Obscurité *had* to be the dark, they *had* to be absolute evil. Without them as the enemy, as the darkness, then the light couldn't be just in their wars. Because that's what history had written, even if it might not be the truth.

Today, however, I had walked through the people, trying to help where I could. I hadn't slept the night before, too worried about what might come, of what might take me in my sleep and wrap its shadowy chains around me without me knowing.

The way we fought, the way we *won*, had to be different this time. It had to be.

I couldn't let The Gray take me. Because if I did, then all would be lost, and there would be no point in any of this.

I had helped to rebuild some of the buildings that were damaged. The battle with Lore wasn't the only thing that had caused destruction. Every time the crystal shattered a bit more and sent out the shockwave that stripped the magic from its people, it also destroyed anything in its path.

So, it was my job to ensure that everyone knew I would be around to help as much as I could. Then I wondered…*what if they find out who has had control of me this entire time?* What if they figured out that I was just a fake? That I wasn't who they thought I was.

"Why are you frowning and brooding like that?" Ridley asked, coming to stand closer to me.

I shook myself out of my reverie and looked over at my uncle, smiling. It helped to smile, to pretend that everything was fine. Even though nothing had been fine for a long time—longer than I cared to admit.

Ridley saw right through my façade. And as Justise came up to his side, slowly wrapping his arm around his husband's waist, I knew that he saw through my act, as well.

I looked at my two uncles and wished that I had what they had. They'd been mated for as long as I could remember. And they always had each other.

I didn't know the story of their courtship, they kept it private, something just for themselves. I knew they loved each other beyond measure. And they were always there for me. Even when I didn't know I needed them. Cameo had loved her younger brother with all of her heart, and she had made sure that the world knew that while she was queen. He was family and should be revered just as she was.

Justise had never liked the spotlight, though, and so he had shunned anything royal until I needed help. And now, anytime I had to leave, Justise and Ridley were there, assuming the mantle so I could do what I needed to for my people.

And they tried to keep me safe when no one else could. The fact that they knew I had disappeared for a time and they had thought it was Lore, reaffirmed my worries regarding what we'd all thought in the past. We'd been wrong, so wrong about everything we'd thought to be the truth. More than once.

Because the orchestrator hadn't been Lore. No, it had been The Gray.

And I didn't think any of us were strong enough to fight that shadow monster.

"I'm not brooding," I brooded.

"You are. It's sort of your trademark. That and the smirk," Ridley said, his eyes full of laughter.

"You know, I *am* your king. You should probably bow to me instead of treating me like a little kid."

"When you stop acting like a child as you sometimes do, then maybe I'll stop treating you like one," Justise said, and Ridley elbowed him in the gut.

"Be nice. If anyone broods, it's you, dear husband."

"I do not brood. I glower. There is a difference."

"Did someone say brooding?" Teagan asked as Wyn followed him, rolling her eyes.

"Please don't say that you brood," Wyn said, snorting at Teagan as he frowned.

"I brood."

"No, you really don't. You try, and then you snort and laugh and growl. You don't brood."

"Can we please stop using the word *brood?*" I asked, sliding my leg over my chair so I could get up. I hated when everybody stood around me while I was the only one sitting. The layout of my grandfather's court had made it that way, mostly because his throne had been a little bit higher.

My mother hadn't ruled from that pedestal. She had only required some of the reverence to keep people in line. She wasn't like dear old Grandpa.

Not that I had ever met the man. My grandfather had believed in fear and power to keep the uprisers out bay—or out of the picture altogether. My mother had done her best to keep the idea of purity and power within the kingdom so wrapped up in mystery that the members of the territories would never truly understand who she was. That's how they could love and her believe in her rule.

I needed to figure out what kind of king I wanted to be. However, I didn't really have time for that right now, because the king I needed to be was one who had to keep his people safe. And that meant keeping Lyric safe.

I looked at her where she stood, Rhodes and Rosamond on either side of her. She had a drink in her hand, and the three were talking to one another over the canapés that had been laid out. Tonight was family dinner, even though it really wasn't just family anymore. I risked a glance at Uncle Justise as he looked at me, and I knew that I didn't really have much family left. Just the two men at my side, who I knew would do anything to help me. "The darkness won't have you forever," Rosamond said, cutting through the other conversations as she and Lyric and Rhodes came towards me. Everyone quieted, and I looked over at her.

"What do you See, Seer?" I asked. Rhodes glared at me.

"Don't badger her," he snapped out, and Lyric put her hand on his arm and gave it a squeeze.

I wanted to reach out and tear her away from him, to punch Rhodes in the face so he'd never let her touch him again.

Then something inside of me slowly moved up, like an oil slick spreading through my body as it dug in its claws, and then I could feel nothing. Only numbness.

I rubbed at my chest, trying to catch my breath. I hated this. Why the hell had The Gray done this? Why did I have this curse?

I knew something was there. I could feel it aching beneath my skin. But every time I reached for it, every time something came through, even just a peek of feeling that might actually be real, the curse came back, and I could feel nothing. Nothing but what The Gray wanted me to feel.

And I hated myself for it.

"I don't know what I'm Seeing," Rosamond said, pulling me out of my dark thoughts. "Only that there has to be light. If that weren't the case, I wouldn't be Seeing it at all."

"So, you only see for the Lumière?" Teagan asked. I nodded—I had the same question.

"No, this group is not Lumière and Obscurité. We're the light, and the dark."

"As that's the literal translation of our names, it would be nice if you were more specific," I drawled.

"Light as in what is right, what keeps us whole. The darkness is of shadow, not the magic in your veins. The shadows that creep, that whisper lies, that probe secrets and unearth truths that were never meant to be aired. Light and dark might not be the words chosen. However, they are the words for now." Rosamond shook her head and rubbed at her temple. "I hate sounding like one of the Spirit Wielders," she said, flashing a self-deprecating smile.

This time, Lyric reached out and hugged the other woman.

"Well, I think that made a little more sense than the others. At least what you just said were almost complete sentences rather than riddles."

I wanted to reach out and pull Lyric close and tell her that we would figure this out. I just didn't know if that would be a lie or not. And I didn't want to lie to her. She had been through enough, and I wouldn't compound on that.

"I guess since we've had a vision from the Seer, that must be the dinner bell," I said, trying to sound jovial and as if nothing was wrong.

I knew nobody believed that. After all, we were all waiting for the next shoe to drop. To hear the next scream, join the next fight, feel more pain. Because that's what happened when you let your guard down.

I looked around the room at Rhodes and Rosamond, at my uncles, at Teagan and Wyn, and then at Lyric, and I knew that not all of us would survive this. We couldn't.

Not with a snake in our midst—and while I could be that serpent. Not with all the unknown, or the fact that we didn't know what the King of Lumière was planning. Or The Gray. The world was dying, turning to embers and ash, and I was afraid I wouldn't be enough to help save it. That the curse holding me back wouldn't allow me to protect the girl in front of me. The one I should love. The woman I could feel nothing for other than a desire I knew wasn't strong enough to surpass the magic that held me back.

There was a knock on the door, and the guards poked their heads in. I held up my hand and gestured for them to enter, and Garrik stood between them. The man who had been The Gray's fourth looked at me, and then at the others, and seemed to close in on himself, as if he were afraid of what the others might think.

I wanted to believe this act. I wanted him to be good and simply under The Gray's control, same as I was. However, if I didn't trust myself, I knew I couldn't trust him.

And even as I had that thought, as I thought of Lyric and what I wanted, a shadow slid around my heart, chaining it to a wall of smoke. I gasped out a breath, falling out of the chair to my knees.

Lyric was there first, her hands on my face as she said something I couldn't hear. There was white noise in my ears, as if all sound had been sucked away, and all I could hear was the vacuum of vastness. Ridley's hands were on my back, telling me to do something. What, I didn't know.

Garrik was there, as well, his eyes full of fear as he came forward. The guards held him back, Teagan glowering at the man, as well.

"I'm fine," I rasped out, knowing it was a lie. "I'm fine."

The others didn't believe me, and I didn't blame them. Because I *wasn't* fine. The Gray had control of me—or at least had a hold on me. And I couldn't break the tie.

I had a feeling the only way I could break that cord was something that would be the *final* end.

Because The Gray couldn't control me if I weren't alive for him to grasp on to.

And to save Lyric, to save my people, I would sacrifice myself in a heartbeat.

I really hoped to hell that wasn't the answer, though.

CHAPTER 20

LYRIC

"Are you going to tell me what that was about?" I asked as I followed Easton into the courtyard after our dinner had been cut short.

Garrik had stood in front of us all as if wanting to reach out to help Easton. None of us let him touch him, though. We didn't trust Garrik, and we weren't sure we could trust Easton for long—not with The Gray coming for him. And that's what must have happened. It had to be. "It's fine. I'm fine." He spit out the words, and I wanted to reach out and tell him that it would be okay, just like he kept saying to me. Lies. But I couldn't. I just stood behind him as he looked off into the distance, the wind blowing through his hair.

"It wasn't nothing. You fell to the floor, clutching at your chest. Was it The Gray?"

He whirled on me, Fire dancing in his eyes as he glared. "Of course, it was. It's always going to be him now, isn't it?"

"Maybe. Though it doesn't have to be. We can figure this out."

He let out a bark of laughter that told me he didn't believe me. It wasn't like I actually believed it either.

"The Gray has always been the bogeyman. The myth told to keep us on the side of good for fear of him getting us. He was the one who slept under our beds, who crept through our closets in the night before wrapping his spindly, smoky fingers around us, clutching at us until we could no longer breathe. Until we could no longer Wield."

"Those stories are a little darker than the ones I grew up with," I said, trying to come across as nonchalant. I attempted to sound as if I weren't scared to death that I would lose him, even though I didn't really have him.

"Your fairy tales, at least the ones I remember seeing when I was in that realm, are based on far darker ones than mine. They're about death and dismemberment and horror. Then they add a little smiling elf or bird and, suddenly, it's cute."

"Okay, you may have a point there."

"At least, yours aren't real," he said, his voice bleak again. Fire slid across his fingertips, and I didn't even know if he realized he was doing it. It was as if it were a game to him, the way he didn't even care about how I felt.

"We have to be able to win at something," I said, my voice low. I hadn't even realized I was going to say the words until they were out. And when they were, they seemed so trivial, as if I were reaching for something that might not ever come. It wasn't like I could actually do anything. All I could do was pray and wait. And learn. And train. And help others while I tried to figure out what to do for myself.

"I wish I could say I had your optimism or even your enthusiasm to think we could win. I can tell you're lying to me just like you're lying to yourself."

He turned again, this time so I could see his profile. His dark hair slid over his forehead as the breeze blew it this way and that. The sun had set, and now, only the lamplight from the courtyard walls illuminated his dark brown skin.

He was stunning, and with that chiseled jawline and smirk he always wore, he was wicked in every way.

And I had fallen for him.

Mainly because of the way he picked others up as they fell. The way he threw himself into everything he did—even into pretending he didn't care. How he did his best to act as if everything were fine. As if the world around him could crumble and he would find a way to survive along with his people and that would be all that mattered.

I knew that was a lie just as much as he did. Or perhaps, *more* than he did.

That was why I had fallen for him. And not just because my soul reached out to him as if there were a cord tying us together.

"We'll break the curse," I said, my voice a whisper.

He turned to me then, his eyes shrewd. "That would be nice. Because I don't want him tainting my life. I don't want him doing anything that could break us."

I knew he wasn't talking about *us* in terms of him and me. No, he meant the group of us, and I understood that. Loving me would only be a fraction of what mattered, and I understood that. I felt the same.

As he moved forward, his hand outstretched, I froze, wanting it to be so much more than I knew it was.

His fingertips traced the line of my cheek, and I closed my eyes, wanting to savor the moment.

Because if I closed my eyes, maybe I could pretend that there was love there. That there was something more than curiosity about what he couldn't have.

I wanted to believe that the aching breaths between us meant that I wasn't alone in my needs or wants.

"You have so much power within you, Lyric. And so much more to come. I'm in awe of you."

My eyes shot open, and I stared into his dark orbs, wanting to understand what he meant by that.

Before I could say anything, there were footsteps behind us, and then we were no longer alone.

Easton's eyes widened fractionally, and I turned on my heel, aware that his hand was still on my hip as if ready to push me to the side or pull me back at any moment.

"Garrik, what are you doing out here?"

Garrik stood there, his eyes hollow, his shoulders hunched as he looked at us.

"Where are his guards?" I whispered, and Easton's hand gripped my hip harder.

"I have a present for you," Garrik whispered, his voice deeper than usual.

And then the transformation in front of me forced me to take a step back so my body pressed against Easton's, his hand squeezed my hip with bruising force.

Garrik rolled his shoulders back, his eyes narrowing as they filled with anger.

"When I tell you to go, run," Easton whispered into my ear. Garrik clucked his tongue.

"No, that's not how this works." Garrik looked at us, and I swallowed hard.

"How what works? What present?" My voice was far steadier than I thought it could be. I was afraid. Terrified. Something was coming, I could feel it in my bones, and I didn't think I would be strong enough to beat it back.

We had known not to trust Garrik, so we had put guards on him. We'd wanted to see what he would do. Apparently, it hadn't been enough.

Once again, we hadn't been enough.

"You know, it's quite sad that you never trusted me. You should have. *Poor, feeble little Garrik*, he saved you, and yet you couldn't leave him alone for even a moment so he could just be. No, you had to have guards on him at all times. And not only your friends. The little guards with their little Wielding."

"What have you done to my people?" Easton asked, his voice low. He took a step to the side so we were standing side by side, though he was a bit in front of me, just enough that I knew Garrik noticed, as made evident by the tightening of the skin around his eyes.

"You know, it's your fault they're gone. But that's fine." He waved that comment off as if he hadn't just hinted at killing them. "If you had trusted me, they would still be alive."

Nausea clutched at me, my heart skipping a beat. Who had been watching him? Wyn? Teagan? Rhodes? No, after dinner, they had gone down to make sure Emory was okay, to see if there was something they could do with her cuffs. I didn't think anyone that I knew personally had been on Garrik's detail.

Oh my God. Oh my God.

Easton moved his hands from his side, from my hip, and Fire encircled his palms.

"Don't think to use your Wielding on me, King."

"Why shouldn't I? You're a Dane, someone with no magic. Yet, somehow, you killed two of my guards easily. Who are you, Garrik?"

"That's always the question, isn't it? You see, The Gray knew who I was. Knew that though my magic had been stripped from me, it was only the Wielding that was gone. Not everything."

I wanted to look at Easton, to see what he was thinking. But I couldn't take my eyes off Garrik. My hands were out, my Wielding pulsating inside me, ready to break free, to fight. When I was by Easton's side, I felt in control, like I could use all four if I needed to. I just didn't know what we would do in these close quarters. And though I could hear the footsteps of the others coming, and I knew that Teagan and Wyn and Rhodes and even Rosamond would be there soon, I didn't know if it'd be quick enough. Because there was something different about Garrik, and not just in the way he stood, or how he spoke.

This man felt dangerous, and I didn't want Easton to get hurt.

Especially not when The Gray still had hold of him—just like it seemed he had a firm grip on Garrik.

"What are you?" Easton asked again.

"I'm a *Whisperer*," Garrik said, a smile on his face. And while I could feel Easton start ever so slightly next to me, I had no idea what a Whisperer was.

Garrik looked at me, a glare on his face even as he smirked. It wasn't like Easton's, and I hated it.

"They never told you what a Whisperer was? Tut tut. I thought you were supposed to read all the books and know everything. Aren't you the Spirit Priestess, the one who's supposed to save us from the big bad? Well, it seems as if they kept you in the dark. Maybe you're not on the right side of history, after all. Perhaps *you're* the big bad. Ever think of that, little girl?"

"Enough," Easton snapped. "She's new to all of this. She's learning. I've beaten The Gray's second, I can beat you, too."

"You beat him because I let you. You know nothing, *King*." Garrik sneered the last word, and I let my Fire slip across my hands, mixing with the Air within my Wielding.

I was stronger than Garrik. *I knew this.* I didn't know what his plans were, what he had put into place around us and *between us.* And that worried me. I couldn't let innocents get hurt because I didn't understand the situation.

What was a Whisperer?

As if he had heard me, Garrik answered. "A Whisperer is more than a mere Wielder. I hear things. Oh, not everything. But enough. I can hear the lies and the truths among those who think to deceive. That's why I'm here. To figure out exactly what your soon-to-be dead king knows. Too bad it doesn't seem like much. However, I learned one thing."

I didn't move, didn't react. Garrik continued. "You see, you have weaknesses. You all do. Yet you, Spirit Priestess, have two huge weaknesses. So big, I'm surprised the others didn't keep them safe for you."

I'd already lost Braelynn, Emory, and at one point, I had lost Rhodes and Easton. Who was he talking about?

And then I knew. Before he even snapped his fingers and purple smoke slithered into the courtyard between Garrik and us…I knew.

I knew who my weaknesses were. Who I had thought we had hidden away in the open without memories of who I was. We hadn't done a good enough job.

Garrik snapped his fingers again, and the shadows slid back, whispering themselves. Suddenly, my parents were there, kneeling on the stones, confusion in their gazes and blood trickling down their faces from small wounds on their heads. Their hands were tied behind their backs, and the fear that permeated off them curdled my stomach and made me want to throw up. I wanted to scream, I wanted to run to them and make sure they were okay.

How were they here?

My parents. The ones who had loved me forever. Who might've wanted to push me in a direction I wasn't sure of, but they had only done it because they didn't want me to feel left behind. They wanted me to succeed. These were the people that loved me no matter what choices I made. The ones I had run from because I wanted to keep them safe.

Alura had put a spell on them so they wouldn't remember me. Same as Easton had done when I left for that first trip.

We had worked magic on their minds so they didn't remember they had a daughter.

As they looked at me, shock and fear in their gazes, I knew that spell was no longer there.

They remembered me.

And they were so scared.

I didn't know how to save them.

Not when my Wielding could hurt them, and I didn't know what else Garrik or The Gray had up their sleeves.

"Lyric?" my father whispered. His voice was so steady, not a single ounce of fear in it. He was trying to be so strong. For me. I hated Garrik for this. I loathed The Gray.

Fire licked up my body, and I knew it surrounded me like an aura. My mother's eyes widened, a tear trickling down her cheek as she watched me.

I was no longer their little girl. I was the Spirit Priestess. And I had lied to them for so long as I tried to keep them safe. It hadn't been enough.

"What's happening, Lyric?" my mother asked. "Baby? Who is this man? Are you okay?"

"Mom." My voice cracked. I needed to be stronger than this.

Of course, they would ask if I was okay. They were bleeding and hurt, and I wanted to scream and shout and just do…something. They were worried about me.

As Garrik smiled, I screamed, taking two steps forward, trying to get closer. He just tilted his head and pushed out his palm. Smoke and shadow poured from his body and plowed into my parents. I screamed, my Fire breaking loose, slamming into the sides of the courtyard as the others shouted my name. Easton grabbed me around the waist, pulling me back as his Fire and Earth escaped to try and stop the smoke from coming towards my parents.

We weren't fast enough.

Because this wasn't Garrik's magic. This wasn't his Whispering or whatever you called it. This was The Gray.

And he had worked through Garrik as a vessel.

The smoke wrapped around my parents' necks in an instant. As I pushed my fingers and hands towards them, trying to create a shield with Air, another line of smoke and shadow slammed into my chest, and I hit the ground, my body stinging from the impact with the pavement. Easton was thrown back, blood spurting from his mouth as he slammed his head into the wall. Then we were both up again, trying to reach my parents, Water sloshing out of the pools to our side to aid us as I threw it towards Garrik. The smoke blocked it. I moved my hand again, trying to break the ground beneath Garrik's feet with Earth, but the smoke slapped at that, as well. I moved Air and Fire, but it wasn't enough. I wasn't fast enough.

My parents looked at me, tears sliding down their cheeks, and the smoke tightened. The snap in the air was like the crack of a bullet.

Their eyes went vacant, their heads lolling to the side as The Gray snapped their necks.

And then Garrik waved, a grin on his face that I never wanted to see again, and then the shadows enveloped him, swallowing him whole.

Suddenly, no one was there, just a ghost in the shadows as the smoke dissipated, leaving the bodies of my parents on the ground. The others ran towards us as they finally pushed through whatever smoky barricade had blocked their path before.

I could do nothing. I could only look at my parents, the people who had raised me, who I loved with every ounce of my being. And then I screamed.

I screamed.

CHAPTER 21

LYRIC

I stood on the connection point of five elements, where twelve points of a clock struck and began. I stood at the space of four directions.

Only I was the fifth of all, the thirteenth from all.

I stood where I had for so many dreams, countless hours in sleep where I thrashed and screamed and felt the Air in my hair, the Water on my face, the Fire on my skin, and the Earth beneath my feet. I stood in the place I remembered before the world turned dark. When I had thought I was only human.

I stood somewhere that haunted my life—my waking dreams, and the nightmares of sleep.

I stood where I had wished for more and had been given so much, even as more had been taken away.

I stood in the place that screamed my destiny, yet begged for forgiveness.

"Lyric, come to us." One of the numbers on the clock spoke, but I didn't want to listen.

I knew that voice, it was one who always spoke to me. A Spirit Wielder.

I didn't want to look at them. I refused to see, refused to look beneath the cloaks of those who said they wanted to help. Did they? No, they just wanted me for my powers, the magic I supposedly had, the destiny that was purportedly mine.

They didn't want to help, they just wanted to use me. Like everybody else.

Because I wasn't enough. I had never been enough.

I had been given these powers, had unlocked them, one by one, and now I was a force that no one could hold.

Yet, I was nothing.

They were gone, taken from me, and I had done nothing to stop it.

I hadn't been strong enough and I hadn't been able to see the deception that had been right in front of me. I couldn't see it.

My lungs seized within my chest, and I clawed at my clothes, the garments that weren't mine. Given to me by those who thought I was the Spirit Priestess. They clothed me, fed me, and kept me warm as I trained. Because they thought I was worthy. Because they thought I could do something for them.

It wasn't enough. *I* wasn't enough.

"Lyric, pull yourself together, you can do this."

I knew these voices. They weren't my friends, though. It wasn't Easton, wasn't Braelynn, wasn't Rhodes.

It was the numbers of the clock, the Spirit Wielders. Those here, yet not.

The ones who haunted my dreams, just like the Negs that had brought me to this realm and to this destiny to begin with.

"Why?" I screamed, my voice ragged.

It wasn't until right then that I realized I had been screaming the entire time. Wails and calls as I tried to wake up. As I attempted to figure out exactly what had happened.

"Why are they dead? I thought they were supposed to be safe. Why weren't they safe?"

"No one is truly safe, my darling," one of the Spirit Wielders whispered, and I turned my head towards her, Fire licking at my fingertips.

I knew this was a dream, I knew this wasn't real, even though it had to be somewhat real because I could feel it.

Maybe it was happening even as it wasn't.

"Why are they dead? They had nothing to do with this. We wiped their memories. They were supposed to be free. Was it all fake? They couldn't really be there. They couldn't be there."

I screamed again, tears sliding down my cheeks as my knees buckled. I fell, my hands digging into the floor beneath my skin even as my Earth Wielding shook.

"It was real. I'm so sorry, my darling. Perhaps it was supposed to be this way. It shouldn't have been, and I'm sorry they were taken. But you have to be strong. You have to fight through this. So many are counting on you. *You* are counting on yourself. Be strong, my darling."

I was no one's *darling*. The only people who could call me that were now gone. I had seen their necks twist, heard the crack of vertebrae echo in the air and my ears as that monster killed them. He had used smoke and magic and things I didn't understand, and he had taken my parents from me.

I couldn't breathe. I couldn't take in oxygen, and as the dots overtook my vision, I tried to suck in a breath. It wasn't working. I couldn't breathe. Why was this happening?

They couldn't be gone.

Flashbacks from when I was a child, little smiles from my mother as she looked at my father, assaulted me. The put-on frown as my dad was forced to eat peas because I needed to eat them. He never liked peas.

Images of Christmases when we opened gifts and smiled and laughed and ignored the dangers out in the world because they didn't affect us directly. Weren't anything that could touch us.

Memories of my mother dancing with my father in the kitchen late at night when I was supposed to be sleeping.

When my mom yelled at me for breaking a dish when I shouldn't have been playing with her expensive wedding china. I'd wanted a tea party with my friends, even if they were imaginary.

She had yelled, and then she had held me, crying. And I'd cried with her because I was so afraid. So scared that she wouldn't love me anymore because I wanted to play a game and broke her dish.

She'd helped me clean up the pieces and wiped my tears, and then she held me as we read. The next time I wanted to play tea, she was there with a plastic tea set. She had always been there.

I remembered the time my father gave me the keys to his car so he could teach me to drive. How he'd had a white-knuckled grip on the dash the entire time. He never raised his voice. Was so good, so calm.

They always saw the best in me, even when I didn't. They always wanted the best for me, even when I didn't know what that was.

And I had walked away from them the first time in anger because I'd known they didn't understand. They had tried to push me into what they thought was best for me, even though I knew they would have accepted any decision I made in the end. I hadn't actually made one.

Because I hadn't known what I needed, what was meant for me.

Not then. And maybe not even now.

However, there was no going back. I would never make memories like those again.

And I would never be able to tell them everything that had happened after I left. I would never be able to tell them what had happened with Braelynn or Emory. Or the boy I met, Rhodes. About Rosamond. I'd never be able to tell them that I had fallen for a dark-haired boy with Fire at his fingertips and Earth beneath his feet. That he was the King of Obscurité, and I was the Spirit Priestess.

I couldn't explain to them that I could never be his queen, and not just because of the title and formality. Because the world had pulled us apart. He was cursed, and he could never love me. Though I knew something else was coming. Maybe love wasn't the answer. But I would never be able to tell them any of that. Because they were gone. Dead. And I couldn't reach them ever again. Damn it, I was the Spirit Priestess. What was the point of all of this pain and sacrifice if I couldn't fix this? If I couldn't save them?

What was the point of any of this?

"They're gone, they're really gone," I whispered, and yet it sounded as if it were a shout in the heavens. It echoed through the walls of my own mind, and I wanted to scream yet again, but I had no voice. I had nothing.

My parents were dead.

And it was all my fault.

It was Garrik's fault. He killed them. I had known he wasn't trustworthy. Sure, he had saved Easton, but for a purpose. Was it for this? To break me? Or would there be more?

I couldn't think, couldn't breathe, couldn't really form sentences. I needed to get through this. I had to figure out why I was here. Why was I in these dreams again?

"Am I dying, too?" I asked, pulling on the last ounces of strength within me so I could speak.

"No, you're here for another reason. This isn't a dream, not really. It's not death either. You know what this is. Feel your Wielding, know what's breaking inside of you."

That was Seven speaking. I knew her. She was the one who had called me *darling*. Honestly, I didn't think anyone else would dare.

Easton, perhaps, though I would likely never see him again. Because I would die here. There wouldn't be more after this. There couldn't be.

And then I looked up, and the Wielding within me reached out. I shouted.

"Mom!"

"Dad!"

This wasn't a dream. This wasn't like the others I'd had before.

These were the Spirit Wielders, and now, I was one of them.

Warmth spread through my body, moving down to my fingertips and along my skin. It crawled up my arms and over my shoulders, then slithered down my back and over my legs until it reached my ankles, touching the tips of my toes. It came up my legs again, over my stomach, over the tips of my breasts and then up to my neck once more. It wrapped around my throat just like the smoke had done with my parents. Instead of breaking my neck, it cocooned me before caressing my face. My whole body felt as if it were swathed in that golden rope of warmth, and I knew.

My fifth element had been unlocked. The cost had been steep.

Sacrifices were to be made. I knew that.

I knew the lines of the prophecy. Knew I was going to lose those I love the most. It shouldn't have been them, though. They were innocent in all of this. It shouldn't have been them.

I looked ahead and saw the souls in front of me. The gray wisps of matter that had once been people, had once been the essence of the humans and the Maisons that lived within our world. Maybe there were even more worlds, I didn't know. There were so many colors here, even as some of it was a faded gray.

If I focused on one thing too long, the colors faded. Out of the corners of my eyes, I saw a rainbow. Like a cacophony of light and sound and essence all at once.

It was everything and nothing, and I could barely hold it in my grasp.

There were two souls I was most focused on. "Mom, Dad. Don't go. I can see you. Maybe I can save you." I didn't even realize I was standing again until my knees shook once more, and my hands flew out, reaching for my parents' souls.

They looked at me, their eyes sad. They didn't reach out. Instead, they wobbled in front of me, small smiles on their faces as they looked at me.

They knew. I knew they knew everything now. As if in death, they realized exactly what they had brought into the world. Me. And I was the reason for their ending.

Then there were hands on me, so many arms holding me back and whispering my name as they tugged me away from the center of the circle.

The Spirit Wielders had moved. I didn't realize they were able to do that. My parents nodded at me and then faded away.

They were nothing again, an endless void of what had once been mine. Their essences were gone, their lives extinguished in a matter of moments, their souls evaporating into nothingness.

I could barely breathe. Scarcely understand what I was looking at.

They were gone, and the Spirit Wielders holding me back hadn't let me reach out to them.

"Why?" I asked again. This time, my voice was stronger. "Why can't I touch them? Why did you pull me away? I could see them. Maybe I could have saved them. Why did you do that? I feel like I killed them all over again."

Tears flowed down my cheeks again, and this time, Seven leaned forward so she faced me, running her hands through my hair.

"Dearest Lyric. You can't. You can't bring back the dead. You can't touch death. Not in the way you might want."

"Then what good am I?" I whispered, pain wracking my body. My soul hurt, everything hurt. Blood seeped out of my fingernails, ran down my chin, out of my ears and my eyes. I could feel the warm tendrils as they slid down my face, and I knew my body was breaking. There was too much power inside me, and I couldn't hold it all. Maybe the prophecy had been wrong. Or perhaps it was right, but I wasn't the person meant for this. "Why can't I save them? Why do I have all five? It's too much. It hurts." I had whispered the last part, my voice cracking.

The twelve Wielders held me close, even as they lay on the floor near me.

I didn't know if they were dead or alive, if they were out in the human world or hiding in the Maison realm. I didn't really understand any of it. All I knew was that they were here for me, and yet they had held me back from saving my parents.

I couldn't touch death? Then what *was* a Spirit Wielder?

What *was* Spirit?

And what was I going to do with five elements that were breaking me from the inside?

"You will be fine. Your body can handle this. Just let it equalize, and you will figure it out." It was One speaking, his voice matter-of-fact, as if he dealt with this kind of thing every day.

I had a feeling that this had never happened before. After all, I was one in a million. One in a trillion.

And I felt like I was dying.

"As soon as your body deals with holding five elements, you will wake, and everything will be fine."

"Nothing will be *fine* again," I snapped. "My parents are dead."

"They are," One said matter-of-factly.

"Stop it," Seven snarled. "That's enough. This is not the time for math or science or physics."

"No, this is a time for *Spirit Wielding*. And we don't have the option of going slow or easing her into this," One said.

"Into what?" I asked, reaching my hand up to my face to wipe the blood from my chin.

"Your body will handle this. Even now, I can see the fissures in your skin healing. As will the others who are watching your corporeal form rather than your ethereal form as we are."

"So I'm bleeding in real life, too?" I asked.

"Yes. But you will heal. First, though, know that you couldn't have touched your parents. You could not have brought them back. It's not only not done, it could also unravel the entire fabric of the universe. You can hold the spirits of the living. The dreams of those who are with us. And the future of those who look upon us. That is what being a Spirit Wielder means. You will figure it out, Lyric. You hold so much promise within you. So much strength. Just believe in yourself and trust those who have always been in your corner. You can do this. And not just because the world needs you or because you have to. Because we believe in you. We're the Spirit Wielders, the last of our kind. You are one of us now. You are the truth, the passion, the future. Just breathe."

As I looked over at Seven, her eyes warmed, even with the fear I saw there. I opened my mouth and screamed.

My eyes opened, and I found myself on the ground in the courtyard where we had been, where I knew the bodies of my parents were.

I didn't know why I knew that not a lot of time had passed. Maybe a blink of an eye in normal time. Within my dreams, with what had just happened with the Spirit Wielders, that hadn't been just a blink. I didn't know why I knew that, no matter how much time passed when I slept in those dreams, when I fought and I realized what was happening, when I felt all of those elements within me, no time had passed here.

Maybe that's how it had always been, even when I was in the human realm and didn't know what those dreams were.

I couldn't think about any of that right now, though.

My body shook, all five elements now within me fighting for control and dominance. I knew Easton's hands were on me, as were the others'. I couldn't look at them. Instead, I pushed my hands out, and the Water and Air Wielding within me slammed into the ground. That rocketed the Earth Wielding, and everyone that had been hovering near me was flung away from me.

I had been lying on my back, prone. Now, I found myself standing. However, my feet weren't touching the ground. I hovered, the toes of my boots trailing along the ground as the Air Wielding around me made my hair stand on end, floating in a breeze that wasn't really there. The earth rocked beneath me, and flames danced within my eyes and across my fingertips. Then there was Water. Water spigots and spirals from the ponds around us flew through the air, creating a cascading waterfall effect that I knew the others were observing out of the corner of their eyes.

Their full attention was on me.

The air was static around me, and I knew with the flame and the raw power within me, I could burn buildings. Just like before, I could turn all of this to ash, to dust, to Spirit, to...nothing. I could use the power within me and break them all. I could hurt anyone in my path for daring to touch what was mine. I looked at the bodies in front of me, the ones my friends hadn't moved because there had been no time.

I stared at the corpses that had been my parents.

I didn't scream, didn't shout. I didn't say a word. I just looked at them and knew there was no going back. I would remember this moment until the end of my days, even if those were numbered. They would pay for what they had done. The Gray would die by my hands, as would the monster who had killed them. The traitor. Garrik.

They would all die, and I would rise. I shook that thought out of my head, trying to control the powers. All five at once was too much. And I didn't like the voice in my head. Didn't like the fact that it didn't sound like me. I needed to be Lyric. I needed to remember the girl I was. Because if I didn't, then I would be the worst kind of monster of all. I would be the one who ended them by losing control. I would be worse than The Gray.

As people shouted my name and reached out to me, I looked down and saw Easton. His dark eyes took me in, and his hands were outstretched. I knew I saw trust there. Not worry. Nothing but pure unadulterated trust.

He might not love me—but he trusted me.

I couldn't fail him. I couldn't fail anyone. Not anymore. I wouldn't let it happen.

As I pulled the Wielding within me as if I were locking it in a sphere within my soul, I screamed again and fell to the ground with a thud.

The others came to me, yet it was Easton who got to me first. He held me as Braelynn hopped onto my lap, curling into me. Rhodes had his hands on my shoulders. Rosamond was near, as well. There were others around, those who wanted to help. I could only close my eyes and let the tears fall.

Because my parents were dead. But...I had unlocked the fifth element.

I was now the Spirit Priestess in truth.

The reckoning would come.

Now, I knew the price. Sacrifice. Sadly, I hadn't been the one to pay it.

CHAPTER 22

EASTON

I'd put Lyric in my rooms, not hers. And at the moment, I didn't really care what anybody thought about that particular decision. I might be a bastard, but I was a royal one, the king. Everyone would just have to deal with my edicts.

I couldn't stand not knowing where Lyric was, even if every time I thought about her, it was as if something twisted inside of me, an icy block that didn't let me get too close.

I was fine. She was going to be okay.

And, once again, I kept telling myself that, hoping it would make it the case.

"Rosamond's with her," Rhodes said, coming up to my side. "I don't really like the idea of my sister in your bedroom," the Lumière prince rumbled.

I looked over at him, raising my brow. I didn't really have the heart to do so in earnest. I knew I would never get the sound of Lyric's screams out of my head. Not until the end of my days, even if that end came quickly. Just like I'd never get the sight of the blood rushing from her eyes and nose and even what looked like her skin as her body cracked and she shuddered out of my memories.

It was hard to be a complete asshole, the king I was so good at playing, when all I wanted to do was make sure she was okay.

Something glided into my heart, a shadowy fist that clenched around the organ. I held back a shuddering breath. I couldn't look weak, especially not in front of Rhodes. Hell, I knew that The Gray still had a hold on me. And if I weren't careful, he would take everything from me just like he had with Lyric.

"Your sister's safe from me. You don't have to worry about that."

"Do I have to worry about Lyric?" Rhodes asked, his voice low, and I knew he wasn't teasing, wasn't prostrating. He was worried.

Hell, I was worried, too.

Did he still want her? Should I care? She couldn't be mine. Maybe I had to let her go. Let her be his.

No.

No, that wasn't right. She couldn't be.

Once again, I ignored the oily, slick ice in the cavity where my heart should be. The curse had taken care of the organ long ago.

"You know I don't have the answer to that," I said, surprising myself with my honesty. I did not like the look in his silver eyes, the fact that Rhodes seemed to take that as truth. I'd spent my entire life thinking he was my rival. After all, we were two sides of the same coin.

Both sons with the powers of each of our kingdoms.

I was constantly trying to outmaneuver him on the battlefield, at least that's how it'd been in our youth. And then he left to search for Lyric, our Spirit Priestess. And I stayed behind to save my people.

This was the man I was supposed to hate. The one I had thought Lyric loved. It turned out they weren't soulmates.

No, Lyric was supposed to be mine. Just like everything else I touched, I had screwed that up, too. Maybe, like my rivalry, it had been set in stone at birth.

"Did you know that Garrik was going to do that?" Rhodes asked. Rage was a familiar friend as it slid over me, and I fisted my hands at my sides.

"Of course, I didn't know what he was planning. What the hell do you take me for?"

Rhodes took a step forward so we were nose to nose, his eyes narrowed as he huffed out breaths, his hands fisted just like mine.

"I don't know what I take you for anymore, Easton."

He sneered the words, and I wanted to punch his face. I wanted to take that silver out of his eyes and just beat the pulp out of him until everything within me stopped hurting. Until I could make things better. I knew that wouldn't happen. It was never going to fricking happen.

"I didn't know," I ground out.

"You say that, *King*, but what if you did? What if The Gray is controlling you? Why don't we have you locked up or in chains like we do Emory?"

I met his gaze, saw the intensity there, and I didn't have a damn answer.

Instead, I looked away. I didn't lower my shoulders or my head. Didn't do a damn thing to show him that I was giving in. But I did look away.

And then I turned towards the crystal room and looked in where Lyric had been killed, where my mother had died. Where Lyric's friend had died. Where all the hope I had in actually having some semblance of control within this kingdom fell away.

The crystal sputtered before brightening again, feeding its magic and Wielding into the kingdom.

I knew we were all in our last months, maybe even days. I knew, in my bones, that we didn't have even a year. How could we? The crystal was dying. And our hope was the girl currently lying in my bed, passed out from the powers overwhelming her body and the grief echoing in her heart.

"We don't know anything," I said, my voice wooden. "The others are watching me come and go. Watching me lead my people. Acting as if they are guarding me for the sake of those who don't know the truth." A pause. "I can feel you watching me."

"I am." There was nothing apologetic in that phrase or in Rhodes' tone. "And that's why I don't think you had anything to do with Garrik. Besides him using you to get in here."

I stiffened and then turned to look at the other man. "So, you're just trying to get a rise out of me?"

"Maybe. The fact that your control is like it is? Yeah, that tells me it's not The Gray, it's all you. You haven't used your Wielding once on me, and I've been a complete asshole to you. Condemning you, threatening you right in your own court. And you haven't done a damn thing to me in response. So, yeah, I know it's you. And I honestly think you're stronger than you were before because you *know* what The Gray can do."

"He cursed me."

Rhodes nodded, his silver gaze still on mine. "I know."

"Well, good." It was good to know that everyone in our circle knew that I could never love Lyric. Maybe she and Rhodes could find their way to each other and discover their own love, where I didn't have to be part of it. Anger burned through me at the thought, right before it was dampened by that same gray ice that I always felt where Lyric was concerned.

I couldn't even feel jealous. The damn curse wouldn't let me.

I was a mess and worrying about things that didn't matter.

"Wyn and Luken took care of the bodies?" I asked, knowing that Rhodes would know the answer.

"Yeah, your uncles went with them."

"We'll have to have a funeral. One that's small enough so the rest of the court doesn't find out what happened. They can't know everything. There's already enough fear and distrust within our ranks. We don't need to add the knowledge that two humans, parents of our precious savior, were killed on our watch while we did nothing."

"We tried to do something, Easton. We all know it. The Gray employed enough power to stop the Spirit Priestess and the King of Obscurité in their tracks."

I turned on him. "You don't think I know that? But I did nothing against him. And it wasn't even the true Gray. It was his pawn. The one we let into our ranks as he learned all about us. And what secrets did he unearth? We know his power now. This…Whisperer. But we likely don't know all of it. On the flip side, he could know all of our plans."

Rhodes fisted his hands at his sides, his Air Wielding skimming between his fingers even as my Fire did the same on my hands. They were our dominant elements and were what came out even when we weren't thinking about it. "No, the only thing he could possibly know is part of the prophecy, if he overheard us talking. We haven't finished our plans. Meaning, we need to talk with my uncle and figure out what the hell is going on. Try to make peace with him. Maybe form an alliance if he's on the right side of things."

I sputtered, even though I knew that was our deal.

"I'm right, and you know it."

"I know. I hate your uncle with a passion, though."

"You're not alone there." Rhodes sighed, pushing his hand through his hair, looking as if he belonged on one of those human magazines or hung up on a wall as drawn by the artists in our realm for girls to titter at, and boys to pretend they weren't staring at. No wonder Lyric had a crush on him.

Again, no jealousy. Just anger sheathed in gray ice.

"We'll have the funeral. For Lyric. If that's what she needs. I don't know what we're going to do about the human realm. I don't think that's within our power anymore."

"Maybe we can get word out to Alura," Rhodes put in.

"If you can get word to that mysterious woman, go for it. We all know that she dances to her own tune and never really listens to us."

"I know. She was with Lyric for that year, where none of us could be."

"So I was told." And Lyric hadn't asked for help.

The entire time she'd been gone, she hadn't asked for help. Would she have even asked *me*? And would The Gray have let me help her? That was the question. The one I really didn't want to know the answer to.

"We'll deal with the strategy in the morning. It can wait for now." I said the words, yet I knew they were a lie. We didn't have time, and all of us knew it.

The one person we needed beyond all others was passed out cold because of the power within her…and her grief. I knew that it surrounded her, sucked her down, and it would always be with her. I didn't know how to fix it.

"I'm going to go check on her."

"Are you sure that's wise?" Rhodes asked.

I glared at him. "I know my own mind when it comes to Lyric," I lied.

"We both know that's a lie," he whispered. "Don't hurt her, Easton."

"You already know that I hurt her just by breathing. By existing."

"Then figure your crap out."

"What do you think I'm trying to do? It seems that's all we're doing these days. We're always one step behind The Gray, beyond this prophecy. I don't really think that me trying to figure out what's going on or *not* going on between us will help anything."

"You never know. Don't hurt her. Any more than you already have..."

"You say that like I have a choice," I said, my voice soft.

"Maybe you do. And perhaps that's the whole point of this. Because I know that we keep saying that none of us really have choices, futures of our own making, not these days with this war and this prophecy. But maybe that's what the Fall was all about. Reminding us to make the choices our forebearers didn't or couldn't."

"Or at least make some decisions that are the complete opposite of what they did. Considering that they brought us to this moment with their greed."

"And their hate. And their distrust. And their anger. Their feuding. All of it."

"I want to fix it, Rhodes. I always have. It's just easier said than done."

"You know it. Now, go and talk with Lyric. Make sure she's okay. Because even though it pains me to say this, she needs to pull through quickly so we can get to the next phase."

"Just like you had to get through watching your parents die?" I asked.

"Yeah, same as you. It seems that's our lot in life. To ignore the fact that everyone we thought would always be here gets turned to dust and fades away. Hopefully, not from our memories though as we focus on the hell burning around us."

"Well, we have to focus on all of it. Because if we don't, who else is going to clean up this mess?"

"I don't think there is ever going to be an answer we like to that question."

At that incredibly true statement, I walked away and headed toward my bedroom. There was a woman in my bed, a woman I wanted even though I didn't know why. It couldn't be fate, I wasn't allowed to feel that because of the curse. But I still wanted her. And I hated that there was nothing I could do about it.

I walked into the room without bothering to knock—after all, it was my bedroom.

And I figured since a Seer was watching Lyric, I wasn't going to walk in on anything I shouldn't see.

Rosamond stood, her book closed in her hand as she looked down at Lyric and slid her fingers through Lyric's hair.

"She'll wake soon. And then we will take our next steps. We always do."

I reached out for Rosamond as she staggered ever so slightly into my arms.

"You should rest." I sat down, sounding far more brotherly than I ever had before in my life.

"You're a good man, Easton."

"No, I'm not. But I am the king. So, I need to protect those in my court."

She looked at me and shook her head. "You say those things. However, they're not completely true. You are a very good man. And one day, the world will see that. Or they will watch as we perish in the folds of our own darkness. For the Spirit Priestess is not of one but of five, and will fade into The Gray as the curse of the unknown shatters into the darkness of the obsolete."

She shook herself as I sat there, trying to keep her steady even as my blood ran cold.

"What was that?" I asked, my voice low so as not to wake Lyric. Not yet.

"Rosamond?"

"She wakes soon. Be good." Then she kissed my cheek before drifting out of the room as if her feet weren't even touching the floor. I knew that wasn't the case. Sometimes that woman was so damn eerie.

As the door closed, I tried to collect myself, wondering what the hell type of vision she had just had as Lyric shifted on the bed. I was at her side in a flash, my hand holding hers as I waited to see what she would say. I didn't want her to be alone when she woke.

I didn't know why I felt that way. Something pushed me away until I almost made to leave. She wasn't mine. I didn't need her. She was nothing to me. And even though it hurt, even though I wanted her more than I cared to admit, I told myself that it was just lust. Just need. And that was fine, but I had to push that out of my mind. Because it didn't matter.

"Easton?" Lyric asked, her voice shaky.

"I'm here." I listened to an ache in my voice, the jagged edge of the man I had once been.

"Do you want to talk about it?" I asked, not knowing what else to say.

"I'm fine. I don't want to talk."

I nodded, figuring that was exactly what I probably would have said, and then I wasn't thinking at all. Suddenly, she was sitting up, and her lips were on mine, and I could barely breathe. I parted my lips, tangling my tongue with hers as I slid my arms around her, fisting one hand in her hair and moving the other around to her waist as she kissed me hard and fast.

I needed to pull away.

I couldn't.

Not when she was moving, suddenly straddling me at the edge of the bed as she kept kissing—faster, harder, deeper.

There was an intensity to her that scared me, as if she were trying to taste life on my lips, to feel something that wasn't there.

She groped at me, tugging at my clothes, wanting more. And even though I wanted it, too; even though the evidence of exactly what I wanted was between us, I pushed her away just slightly. I cupped her face, searching her gaze. She panted, her brown eyes bright, her lips parted. I wanted to kiss her again, needed to touch and hold her.

It would be wrong. Wrong in so many ways. So I let her breathe, let her calm, and slid my thumb across her cheek.

"Not now, little girl. Not now, Priestess. Not now."

"Don't call me that. I can't be your Priestess. Not here. Not with you."

I nodded. "Just like you said I'm not your king."

"Like how I'm not your Priestess?" she asked, her voice broken.

"You are Lyric. And kissing me and doing whatever else we could have done just then isn't going to solve anything. It won't fix this. When and if we do something like that, it'll be because we're both ready, and it's the right time."

"There's never the right time. Or enough time." Tears filled her eyes, and I was thankful that I'd pushed her away when I did. I was already a bastard. I wasn't going to take advantage, too.

Though, because I had to, I leaned forward and brushed my lips against hers. And felt…nothing. My pulse didn't race, my heart didn't beat in time with hers. There was nothing. I hated her crying, though.

"They're gone," she whispered.

"I'm so sorry." And that was the truth. I could be sorry, even if I couldn't feel anything else. The hollowness within me echoed throughout my body, and I hated myself for it. Was that hate a feeling? Or just the truth.

"I'm going to kill him."

"I can do that for you. You don't have to kill, Lyric. You don't have to have that on your soul."

"I already have. I can do this. You don't have to do everything for me."

"And you don't have to do everything yourself."

She closed her eyes and slid off my lap. She paced to the other side of the room and faced the wall, folding her arms over her chest.

I sighed and stood up, pushing my hands through my hair. Anyone walking in would probably wonder what we had just done. It wasn't their business. I was the king, she was the Spirit Priestess, and they could all rot for all I cared.

"Lyric." She twisted on her heel and pulled up my shirt. I was so stunned that I didn't move fast enough. Her training was clearly going well if she'd moved that quickly. She didn't pull my shirt up any higher than my chest. Instead, she slid her fingers along the jagged scar on my stomach, and her eyes widened.

"This was from me," she whispered, her voice soft. "This is from when I died."

I swallowed hard. "Yes, I bled because you were dying. I didn't know it at the time. And I don't know why I even know now. I *shouldn't* be able to feel anything for that memory or understand the connection. Not with the curse."

"I don't know if I can fight this anymore," she whispered.

"Fight what?" I asked, worried. I was always worried.

"I have to fight so much. Who I need to be, the powers within me, the expectations of those who want so much out of me, and the fear that I can't do it. I've already failed at so much, and I don't want to fight anymore. So maybe...maybe I won't. And perhaps the curse will always be there, and you'll never be mine, and I'll never be yours. We'll never have that bond. I don't want to pretend that I'm not hurting. And I don't want to pretend that I don't want to reach out and touch you. Because that's always in the back of my mind. Even though I know it shouldn't be. If I just give in, perhaps if I just let myself touch you, if you let me, then I'll be able to focus on everything else."

I stood there stunned, my throat tight. "That's a half-life, Lyric."

"No, it's a human one. Humans don't have soulmates, they don't have promises beyond trust that is usually broken. You don't have to love me. I just need you to be here. Can you do that?"

I didn't shake my head, didn't nod, I just swallowed hard. "Will that be enough?"

She didn't answer, and I didn't say anything more.

Instead, I watched as she trailed her fingers along my scar. I stood there, letting her.

Because there were no easy answers for any of this. Then again, there never were.

If I could give her this, at least pretend that I could love her, that this was okay and would be our happily ever after, maybe she could focus on everything else.

Perhaps that was my lot. To be there so she could save the world, even when I was dead inside.

I stood there and watched. I didn't yearn. Didn't love.

Because I felt nothing. Just like always.

CHAPTER 23

LYRIC

The voices echoed as a cacophony of sound in my mind, and I rubbed my temples, wishing I had coffee or some other form of caffeine. I hadn't been a coffee drinker in the human realm, but now I missed it. Oh, there was coffee in the Maison realm. But it wasn't the same. Whatever it was, I really wanted it. Maybe I could ask Ridley for an elixir or something to help me wake up. Because even though I had passed out and slept hard in Easton's bed the night before, it hadn't been real rest. No, it had been my body fighting off whatever had come at it, trying to find its equilibrium again.

"We need to meet with the king and see what his plans are."

I looked at Rhodes as he spoke, as he tried to keep his voice calm. I knew there was anger just beneath the surface.

"And what help will that be?" Teagan asked. "Your bastard of an uncle has never helped us. Never listened to us. No, he just kills our people and tries to take our lands."

"We've been at war for centuries," Luken put in. "It's not just the Lumière who are at fault."

"Oh, I know that the Obscurité have their faults, as well," Wyn said. "We just don't torture and murder like the Lumière have done."

I stood, putting up my hands. Everyone quieted.

"Stop it. Almost every person in this room has said more than once that this isn't Lumière versus Obscurité anymore. And yet these arguments make it sound like that's exactly what this is."

"It's hard to go back on so much history, pet," Easton said, and I glared.

I didn't like his nicknames. But I guessed the posh "pet" was better than Priestess or little girl. Maybe.

"It's The Gray versus the rest of us. And we have to see what side the king is on."

Rhodes' jaw clenched. "We don't know that my uncle's working with him."

"No, we don't. We don't know that he isn't either. Maybe things will work out, and we'll be able to talk with him and come together. If we're united, perhaps we'll be too much for The Gray."

Even as I said it, I knew I didn't believe it. After all, I had five elements burning through my system, and they were there for a reason.

I had lost my family for this power, so I could unlock Spirit. That meant I had to use it. Or at least some amalgamation of the five. Talking with the king wasn't going to save us. I knew that. That wasn't part of the prophecy.

We had to take all paths.

And as I told them that, they shot me looks I didn't want to see. I hated the pity. There wasn't a *single person* in the room who hadn't lost someone.

The fact that Luken was holding his mate in his arms as she purred against him was evidence of that.

The fact that we didn't know who wore the mantle of Lord of Water because the one who had lived and ruled was dead. His children were still here, but we didn't know who would rule, or if the King of the Lumière would even allow them to try.

Easton was king because of death, we had lost Arwin, we had lost so much. Emory was in the corner, her hands bound as she looked at all of us, confused yet trying to be part of the group even if she didn't say anything.

All of us had lost something, someone. Even parts of ourselves.

And that meant we needed to figure out what our plan was. We had to meet with the king.

"So, we'll meet with the king."

"I'm sure he's already searching for us," Rhodes said, his voice deadpan.

"He is," Rosamond said, and we all looked at her.

She held up her hands. "That's not a vision. It's just our uncle. His brother is dead, and his niece and nephew are missing. Even though he should know exactly where we are. He'll search for us. That's the way of things. We'll make sure he knows that we weren't taken against our will." She rolled her eyes, looking as if we weren't talking about war and kidnapping. I knew she was as stressed as the rest of us. She had dark circles under her eyes, something I hadn't ever seen on her before. She was usually effervescent and a shining example of beauty and grace. I knew the visions were taking their toll.

Out of all people, it was Emory who moved forward and brought Rosamond a glass of water.

The action made me freeze, stunned me to my core.

Emory just met my gaze, shrugged, and then walked back to her chair next to where the pitchers of water and food were set up.

None of us had really touched them yet. Rosamond looked over at Emory, a small smile on her face before she shook her head and drank deeply from her glass.

"So, we'll send someone to see what he needs?" I asked, pushing through the tension in the room. We had more important things to worry about than personal feelings, even if we all buried them far too often. "I'm not really sure how that works."

"We can send an emissary," Easton said. "First, we need to make sure we know exactly what we're going to tell him."

"How about we start with the fact that I'm the Spirit Priestess, and we don't want to get everyone killed, and we really want to end this war? How about we tell him that if we don't, our world will literally crumble?"

It wasn't lost on me that I had said, "our." I had long since gotten past thinking I was part of the human realm. Maybe I'd never truly been.

"That's always a good place to start, pet," Easton said, and I resisted the urge to shove him.

"Let's make a plan," he added, and then everyone was talking again. My head throbbed, and the discomfort must have shown on my face, because Ridley gave me a curious look. I shook my head. Even though I had thought about a tonic, I didn't want to take anything that could mess up my Wielding. Not that I thought it could. It was more that I was still trying to deal with everything writhing inside me. It had been hard enough with only Air. Now, with the addition of Earth, Water, Fire, and Spirit, it was almost too much. However, I knew I could do this. Because there wasn't another option. I had to succeed. So, maybe if I believed in myself as much as possible, it would be enough.

The others continued to argue amongst themselves. I knew that they were trying to come up with a plan. I let them. I didn't know the history as well as they did. I didn't know all of the intricacies. So, I was no help here. I would be eventually, only not right then.

I walked past them towards the crystal. We had been meeting in the throne room and the crystal room. That way, we could see exactly what we were fighting for. Plus, theoretically, those areas had the best security. Sure, I might have died there once, but that hadn't been because of the guards and those in the room. That monster was gone. Long gone.

As I walked towards the crystal, it glowed, light emanating from each facet, and I froze.

Everyone stopped talking, all of them turned towards me.

"Easton?" I asked, my voice a whisper. He was at my side in an instant, and I was grateful. We had come to terms with each other the night before, in a desperate yet unsure truth of who we were to one another. He would be by my side, and I would be by his. Even if it didn't mean what it should.

"What's happening?" I asked, my voice breathy.

"Maybe the crystal's reacting to you? What does it feel like inside?"

It wasn't Easton that answered. It was Rhodes, and he came to my other side.

Easton stiffened. Rhodes ignored it, and I did my best to do so, as well.

"It's warm, like something's pulling at me, near my heart, reaching out. I don't really get that."

"I tend to have the opposite reaction. I don't think it's the crystal." I knew Easton was talking about The Gray. I couldn't say anything to that. There really wasn't anything *to* say.

I sucked in a breath as the crystal lit up again, the dark black and purple and gray tones of it shining brightly as if it were healthy and whole.

I knew that wasn't the case. I knew it was dying.

"Maybe if you touched it?" Easton asked. I looked over at him, and he shrugged.

"This is new territory for all of us," he continued. "Who knows. Maybe you can breathe life into it or something. After all, you do have Spirit Wielding now. And that's part of life and death and souls. Just like the crystal."

Seven had told me that I could hold a soul in my hands. Not take it. Not bring life from death. They had actually said I couldn't touch death. The crystal wasn't dead yet. Maybe this could work.

I took a few steps forward with everyone watching me and placed my palm right on the crystal. It warmed under my touch, searing my skin before it brightened, turned so bright, I almost closed my eyes.

Nothing. I could feel nothing within it, no magic or Wielding or power reaching out to me. It dimmed back to its cracked facade, and my shoulders slumped.

Easton's hand was on my lower back in the next moment. "It's okay. It was a stupid idea, anyway."

"No, it was a good idea. It'll never be that easy, though. Maybe I need to cut my hand and put blood on it or something."

"Let's not shed your blood so quickly," Ridley said from behind us, and I turned, putting my back to the crystal.

"I wasn't actually going to do it right now." I smiled as I said it, though I knew it didn't reach my eyes.

"You know, blood could work," Wyn said, tapping her chin. "Not that I want to bleed you dry or anything."

"Thanks for that," I said dryly. "Perhaps. Or maybe I need to figure out exactly what type of chant will work. Or maybe I can even speak the prophecy around the crystal. The problem is, there's not only one crystal."

The others looked at me, and I rolled my shoulders back. "None of us are from the same territory or kingdom. I'm not even technically from this realm."

"Neither am I. Or Braelynn," Emory added on, and I nodded at her.

"True. We're all from different places. That means I know that, no matter what happens, it's not just this crystal. It lit up for me just now, why? We have to figure that out. But it's not just that crystal."

"It's the Lumière's, as well," Rhodes said, his voice soft.

"Exactly. I think that, no matter what, we're going to have to bring the two crystals together. Because that's the whole point of this, isn't it? The Fall broke the realm in two, split the kingdoms. Now, there are two, and maybe you weren't fighting as much as you used to because you're too busy trying to hold together the stones of your foundations. Something is wrong. We all know that. The number of Danes is increasing day by day, and people have begun in-fighting because they're scared. Others want power they have no right to. No right to *take*, I should say."

"And putting the two crystals together may be the only way. After all, we never had two before—at least before our time," Easton said, looking at Rhodes.

"You're right. There was only one before the Fall. The one that served as the crystal for the Maisons. For all of our people. For the Wielders."

"So, we need to make that happen again. Bring them together. Though I have no idea how to put two magical geological crystals together without maybe that blood sacrifice I mentioned."

"We're not bleeding you," Easton growled, and I just shook my head.

"We might have to. But first, we need to figure out exactly how to get the two crystals in the same room when they reside in two separate courts that hate each other."

And as if the heavens had heard me, hell opened up and seized us all.

People screamed outside the castle, and the earth rocked beneath my feet.

I staggered to the side as Easton gripped my elbow before letting me go to run out onto the balcony that overlooked his court.

"What's going on?" I asked.

"It's part of the new Fall, but I've never seen it like this."

"What does that mean?" Emory asked, coming up to my side.

"I don't know," I whispered.

"It means that every time the crystal flares, it's not only Wielding that's stripped. The monsters that used to hide and were pushed back by magic are coming out. We saw that in the Spirit territories as well as in the Lumière Kingdom. Those monsters from the past and myths are coming out of hiding and their sleep. There are natural disasters that are rocked forth because of the crystal's magic."

"And that's what's happening now?"

"I don't know. Maybe."

I looked at Wyn and then closed my eyes as the brightness of the crystal got so intense that my corneas felt as if they were burning.

"What is that?" Emory screamed, and then Easton was at my side, shielding me from the blast.

All around us, people were shouting, and I knew that there were even more wails down below.

"We need to help the others!" I called out, and Easton nodded.

"Come with me. Justise, protect the crystal," Easton called out to his uncle.

"If we even have a crystal left after this," Justise growled. I looked over at it, finally able to see. It was no longer blindingly bright. Instead, it was a dull gray, so much of its color gone.

"Dear God."

Easton cursed under his breath. "If we don't hurry, we're going to be too late, and there won't be a crystal left to save."

I nodded and ran by his side as we stormed down the stairs with the others and headed out into the courtyard. People were on the ground, shaking from where they had fallen during the earthquake. Rain slammed into us, the drops large. Instinctively, I threw up a hand, using my Air and Water Wielding to keep it off of myself, even just a little bit so I could see. I didn't care about getting wet, it was more so it didn't affect my vision.

Rhodes did the same on my other side, and Easton slicked his hair back from his eyes, then gave me a nod of approval before going off to help the others. Lightning pierced the sky, one bolt after another—boom, boom, boom.

I pulled Emory out of the way, wondering why she was even here. But since she was, maybe she wanted to help. I didn't know. She couldn't siphon anyone, not with the cuffs she wore. But she was with us. Rosamond went to Emory's side and pulled her away, then the two of them went off into the distance, presumably to help. I followed Easton, knowing he would know what to do. Wyn and Teagan went one way, Rhodes and Luken the other. I could only hope we would be enough.

Hail struck us, icy pellets one after another slicing into skin.

I used my Water Wielding to push them out of the way, and then used Air to bracket and buffer as much as I could. I threw myself over a young child who had tripped in the rain and used my Wielding to protect him. Others used their Earth Wielding to bring up shields, some using Fire to burn off the hail before it hit them.

All I knew was that I needed to help others. I stood up and picked up the small child I had been protecting before putting him into his mother's arms. I did my best to make sure everyone was out of danger. The earth rumbled beneath us, and I instinctively knew that wasn't Wielding.

That was the crystal. We were in the middle of another Fall, just a small one. Regardless, it would be bad. There was more screaming, and I turned around as Wielders went to their knees, one after another, clutching at their hair and skin, trying to hold on to whatever power they had. I could see their Wielding being stripped from them in an instant—Fire, Earth, sometimes both, pulled from their bodies as if they were being suctioned off into the essence of nothingness.

"Damn it!" Easton called out, going to the people on their knees.

"Can you hold on? Can you fight?" he asked, keeping his people close. I went with him, trying to help. There was no use. We were watching Danes being made right in front of our eyes and the helplessness swelling within me was almost overwhelming. Their Wielding, part of their identity, was being stripped from them…and it seemed hopeless.

And then someone screamed from behind us, and I turned, knowing that voice. Wyn looked at us, her eyes wide, her hair flowing all around her as the earth rumbled. And then she paled.

"No!" I screamed and got to my feet. Easton was right beside me. There was nothing we could do. Teagan was there then, holding Wyn as her powers were stripped, as she became a Dane.

She had lost her Earth Wielding, lost part of her soul, what made Wyn…*Wyn.*

"Wyn!" Easton called out. We didn't move forward. I think we were unable. Others still fell all around us, and we couldn't help them.

Wyn just looked at us, her body shaking as she held on to Teagan before pushing away.

"Help the others. I'll be okay." There was so much in her voice, and yet nothing. I didn't think anything would be all right ever again.

I followed Easton towards other groups of people and used my Wielding to lift a fallen tree, my back straining as I pushed all of my Air and Earth Wielding into it, knowing that I needed to try and protect some of the homes and what was left of the court.

People were still shouting, calling for loved ones, crying.

And it hurt. It hurt so much.

As we went from person to person, trying to make sense of what we saw and what was left, what had happened, I knew we could make no sense from this.

So many people had lost their powers, some had lost their lives. And all from a crystal shining brightly and then fading.

Because of what had been done to the crystals in the past, we were now afraid there would be no future.

My body ached, my hands were smeared in blood, and there was no more rain to wash it away.

Instead, I stood by Easton as the wind blew through our hair, and the scent of burned oak and twisted metal filled my nose.

"What else can be done? I asked, coughing.

"I don't know. And that scares me most of all."

Before I could say anything else, before I could even think of what to say, Easton stiffened, and I followed his gaze, freezing.

A man stood on the other side of where we were, his bright blue and silver leathers feeling like an albatross in the darkness.

He was not of the Obscurité Kingdom, that much was clear. How had he made it through the wards?

Maybe there were no wards left.

"It's an emissary from the Lumière. They're allowed to come in as long as they don't have any weapons, and so long as it's not a Wielder. That's how he got through the wards."

I looked over at Easton, wondering if he had read my mind.

"My men will deal with him. It seems the King of Lumière wants to speak."

Easton walked off, going to help someone, and I followed. Because there were more people to help, others who needed us.

It seemed that, no matter what, we wouldn't have time to rest. The time for decision making was long since past. Now, we had to make those choices and carry out the actions.

Everyone had already lost so much. But I was afraid that it was only the beginning. We would lose more. Somehow, I just knew we would.

CHAPTER 24

LYRIC

"The king wants to meet with us," I said into the void, and everyone stood around the weakening crystal.

Well, not everyone. Wyn was back in her room, sleeping after Ridley had given her a tonic. Her whole body had shaken. She hadn't made a sound other than those first few cries she had let loose on the battlefield.

No, it hadn't been a battlefield. It was a courtyard. Where people had been walking and talking. Where children were playing. They'd been trying to find life in the darkness. They'd been attempting to move on and make do with what happiness they could find. And yet war had come for them nonetheless.

"We need to go soon," Easton said, grumbling to himself more than any of us. I only half-listened as the rest of them kept talking. I was thinking about everything that we had lost in such a short period of time.

It killed me that I was afraid there wouldn't be anything we could do for those we left behind. Wyn couldn't go. I didn't know when she would even be able to get out of bed. I had a feeling the warrior would find a way. She would fight with a sword, do something. It wasn't going to be the same, though. And I had to do everything in my power to make sure that we figured out exactly what we needed to do to bring Wyn's power back. To bring the Wielding back to so many.

"We can go to him today," Rosamond said, frowning. "Well, not all of us. We have a Spirit Wielder with us. That means, we can use the crystal to get us through the wards and to the other court."

I looked at Rosamond, frowning. The Lumière Court was the only major area I had never been to, and even as goosebumps dotted my skin, I knew I needed to go. There was only one thing troubling me. "A Spirit Wielder can use the crystal?" I asked.

She rubbed her temples, and once again, Emory was there with a glass of water. Maybe she was paying her penance? I didn't know. Emory didn't say anything, she just helped with the water. Considering that Rosamond trusted her and didn't See anyone poisoning her or anything like that, I counted that as a good thing. Maybe.

"They can. I don't know why."

"So, you Saw it?" Easton asked, emphasizing the word *saw*.

"Yes, a vision. They're coming in spurts now as if they're supposed to make sense. But, they don't. Of course, they never really have. I've been doing this for over four hundred years and, sometimes, I feel like I'm just starting out."

"Well, that gives the rest of us something to strive for then," I said, trying to lighten the mood. There was nothing light about it.

"We're going to head out and meet him, huh?"

"I don't know that we have a choice," Easton said.

"No, we don't," Rhodes added. "We need to meet with my uncle. If we can't plead with him to help us put the crystals together somehow and go up against The Gray, we can at least figure out what he plans to do with the Water territory."

"Are you the Lord of Water?" I asked bluntly.

Rhodes just shrugged. "Honestly, I don't know. It might go to Rosamond. Or even Eitri."

"I don't think a Seer can be a lord or lady," Rosamond said, looking off into the distance.

"Why the hell not?" Emory asked.

"Because, for centuries now, most people thought Seers were unstable and quite mad," Justise put in dryly, and everyone looked at him, even as Rosamond smiled.

Rosamond nodded. "He speaks true, don't get mad at him. I'm not mad. Sometimes, I feel like it would be better if I were."

"So, it could be your cousin, then. The prince of the Lumière?"

Rhodes nodded. "Yes. Although, he is the heir apparent to the throne. Not that my uncle will ever step down."

"Your uncle likes power, that's sort of his thing."

"Your mother was much the same in some respects."

Rhodes winced then opened his mouth to say something, Easton stepped in. "No, you're right. And that was because she didn't trust anybody. And because Lore was in the background making sure that his needs were met and everyone else suffered for it. If my mother had been able to trust those under her, maybe we would have been able to put a stop to it beforehand. That's not the way things rolled. And now I am the king, and I have to meet with the King of the Lumière. I must also present the Spirit Priestess."

"I cannot go as an emissary of the Obscurité Kingdom," I said, trying to phrase my words correctly.

"We never thought you were ours," Easton said, and I ignored the hurt. Because I knew he meant that in more ways than one. So did everyone else.

I raised my chin. "Good. Because the people of the Lumière can't think that the Spirit Priestess works for the Obscurité. If that's the case, then they won't come when we need them."

"And we will need them," Rosamond said softly. "If you are to defeat The Gray, you'll need more than just those in this room and those who follow you now. The prophecy is only the beginning. You must do more."

The Seer sagged against Luken, who held Braelynn, and Emory was once again there with a glass of water that nobody took. Well, at least my ex was trying.

I didn't like the sound of Rosamond's words. It wasn't as if we could fight what they meant at the moment.

"Okay, then. Who's all going?"

"I'm going," Ridley said, surprising us all.

"Are you sure, Uncle?" Easton asked.

"You know I need to. For more reasons than just wanting to be by your side to make sure you're okay. You'll need a healer."

"What do you mean?" I asked before I meant to. The others just shook their heads, and I knew there were more secrets in play. There always were. That's what happened when centuries of histories and misgivings were all tangled up into one. I didn't have time for that, though.

"Who else?"

"I'll go," Luken said. "Plus, I guess he's my king, so I should pay my respects," he said dryly.

Braelynn perked up in his arms, and I figured that meant she was going, as well. Well, wherever he went, she went. And I liked when she was around. I wanted to know more about what kind of powers she might have. Maybe, one day, we'd be able to bring her back.

"And, of course, I'm going," Rhodes said. "Rosamond?"

She nodded, looking pale.

"And since the king asked for the king, I suppose I'll go, as well."

"You're going to need someone by your side," Teagan said.

"I'll stay behind," Justise said, looking at all of us. "Emory shouldn't go, not only because we don't know what's running through her veins, but because we don't know what the King of Lumière will do."

"That's fine. I'll stay behind. Help you with Wyn, if that's okay."

It was if she were a completely different person. Maybe almost dying and having her veins flooded with power had done that. She was trying, and I would try, as well. And, no, she wasn't a completely different person. She reminded me of the girl I once thought I loved. And maybe that was okay. Perhaps she needed to figure out who she was as she had fought and lashed out along the way. I had buried myself, and she had done the exact opposite. We both ended up on similar paths regardless.

"Okay, good. When?" I said.

"Now works," Easton said, looking over at all of us. We'd each showered or at least bathed and changed into different leathers. I didn't own much in this realm, so I figured this was as good as I was going to get. My long, blond hair was coming down in waves since it had dried naturally, and I hadn't bothered to pull it back into a braid. I didn't look like a princess, didn't look like what a Priestess might, a least based on what I imagined in my head. I looked like me. And that was just fine.

"Okay, hold the fort," Easton said to Justise, and his uncle smiled even though it didn't reach his eyes.

"Always. We'll take care of Wyn and your court. And we'll do what we must."

I took a step back as Easton and Justise discussed the logistics of what needed to be done while he was gone and looked down at my hands, wishing that the power within my veins would calm down just a little bit. It rose to a crescendo every once in a while, and I found it hard to hear and harder to breathe when it did. As if all five were fighting for dominance and hadn't really figured out who was going to win.

I wasn't really sure what I was going to do about it because it wasn't like someone could train me. Oh, people were trying to teach me how to Wield each of the elements, but no one was around to help with Spirit. No one even knew what it did, exactly.

All I knew was that I couldn't bring my parents back from the dead.

I couldn't touch the Spirit Wielding. I knew it was there, in my pores, around my heart, within my veins. It was everywhere and nowhere, and yet I didn't really know what to do with it.

I only knew that the two people I had loved for my entire life were gone, sacrificed so I could have it.

I would never forgive myself for that.

I would never forgive The Gray.

I'd never forgive Garrik.

He would die by my hands, and for once, maybe I wouldn't mourn the loss or abhor who I was when I did so.

"Okay, let's go," Rosamond said, standing by the crystal now. I nodded, pulling down my leather tunic so it looked somewhat straight and not as if I had too hastily gotten ready.

I was exhausted, covered in the blood of those who had been hurt because of the crystal, and even though a lot of it had washed away, the stains of what had happened and what it meant still remained. I would always know that the stains were there for a reason. Because I wouldn't forget. I couldn't forget how Wyn had looked. I couldn't forget Arwin's face. Couldn't forget that lone soldier who had died on the battlefield.

I couldn't push away the looks of distress and fear on the faces of those who had thought that I wouldn't be able to hold or control my power. After all, they had been right.

Easton grabbed my hand, and I followed him around the room. Rhodes stood on my other side as always, and we circled the crystal. Everyone turned to me as if they thought I knew what I was supposed to do.

"I don't know what I'm doing."

I felt like I needed to get that tattooed on my body somewhere.

"Just look at the crystal and let yourself imagine it opening up and pulling us towards the next place."

"We'll do the chanting for you," Rhodes said, making clear the laughter in his voice.

"Good. And if someone could actually teach me that chant at some point, that would be great. Because I really hate feeling behind."

"You're doing just fine, pet," Easton muttered under his breath, and I blushed, hating myself for it. I focused my gaze on the crystal, and then I dug deep inside for that warmth.

Magic seeped into me, tangling in my veins and wrapping around my heart. And then the dark crystal glowed, and the others' chanting filled my ears. And then, it felt as if something tugged on me, pulling me. I had used transportation like this before, but this felt different. It was as if the crystal were moving through me as I moved through it. There was a shout, though. I looked to my right. Ridley was there for a moment and then gone the next. I tried to reach for him, but it was too late. He was gone, and then it was just Teagan, Luken, Braelynn, Rhodes, Easton, Rosamond, and me.

Ridley wasn't with us anymore.

We all landed in the courtyard, this one far different than anything

I'd ever seen. Even as I tried to take everything in, I looked around, searching for Ridley. He wasn't here.

I met Easton's gaze, and he gave a tight shake of his head.

"He's fine, I can still feel him."

I didn't realize that Easton could do that.

"He's my uncle. It's family. He didn't make it through, though. I have a feeling the king didn't want a healer here."

Before I could question that, the others surrounded me, and people in dark silver and gold robes moved towards us.

Some were in battle leathers, others in court attire as if they hadn't a care in the world other than looking their best.

And maybe they didn't. Maybe the Lumière Kingdom was safe because their crystal wasn't as fragmented as the Obscurité's crystal. Or maybe I was just seeing into things that weren't really there.

It was as if we were at the mirror image of the Obscurité Court. Everything was white and silver and shined under the bright sun. The castle in front of us had turrets and large, open spaces where people could gather to make merry and do everything that I would imagine doing at a Renaissance Faire.

Everything had gold plates and diamonds and resembled much of the Water Estate, not so much the Air Estate. After all, the King of Lumière and the late Lord of Water were siblings.

People milled about, smiling and laughing just as I had seen in the Obscurité Court.

Everybody looked different here, though, as if their happiness hung on something I didn't quite understand.

I didn't have time to think about that because the king was coming. Only the King of Lumière would be dressed in gold and diamonds. Would be seated upon a white horse as if it were his prized stallion. Though it wasn't actually a horse, it was one of the beasts that I had seen in the northern Spirit territory.

Brokk slid off, his arms outstretched, a wide smile on his face, his teeth straight and white and perfect.

Everything about him was perfect. From the chiseled jaw to the smoothness of his skin. All the way to the way his hair curled just right on his forehead.

He looked as if he'd been carved from stone. Rhodes and Luken took a step forward, as did Rosamond, a mere step behind the two men. Braelynn had jumped into Teagan's arms as if she didn't want to follow Luken towards the King of Lumière. I didn't blame her. Teagan took possession of the cat in stride and lifted her to his shoulder so she could watch. It was what she liked, and it kept his hands free in case there was a fight. For some reason, I had a feeling if this didn't end perfectly, we were going to be fighting our way out.

"Hello, well met. Welcome to the court of the Lumière. I'm honored that you listened to my emissary and have joined us in my court, in my kingdom."

He sounded just like his brother; I knew this was a mistake.

"Uncle," Rhodes whispered.

"Ah, Rhodes. My dear brother's son. It is good to see you are alive. The last I heard, you had fallen from a cliff and rose again as if a phoenix from the ashes. Or rather, from the water. For you are Lumière. I know that Water and Air run through your veins.

"And you have your trusty warrior beside you. Luken, it's good to see you." There were murmurs among those who watched, and I stiffened at Easton's side.

"I would ask about your family. Alas, you don't know who that is, do you?"

And there it was. I wanted to kill him already. I had the urge to kill him just for the way he put that tightness in Luken's shoulders. The way Braelynn's back arched as she held in a hiss.

I needed to end him.

I knew that part of that compulsion was the elements of Wielding within me, trying to push themselves out. The dark seduction of my power. However, if I didn't kill him, I at least wanted to smack that smug look off his face.

"And my darling Seer. You are a true beacon. Beautiful light. You look frail. Are they not taking care of you over there?" He growled out the last words, and I noticed that he did not say her name. She was "Seer" to him. Not even his niece, or her given name.

I didn't like it. I didn't like much of any of this.

"Now, let us meet the rest. As I'm sure you know, I am Brokk, King of Lumière. You've met my family." He pointed to the man near him. "This is Eitri, my prized son, prince of the Lumière, heir to the realm and to my throne."

To the realm. Not to the *kingdom*. That was telling.

I knew Easton had caught it, as well.

I looked over at Eitri, who looked like a much smaller version of Brokk. He had a pointed nose and an even pointier chin with weak shoulders and a narrow waist. He didn't look like a warrior or a future king. Maybe he would grow into that role. After all, I knew he was younger than Rhodes and Rosamond. Maybe he still had time. From the sneer on his face and the heated look in his eyes, though, I had a feeling his weakness had nothing to do with his body and everything to do with his soul.

How did I know that? How did I feel as if I could see inside the person and find the truth of the man?

My Wielding burst inside me just a bit, and I suddenly knew. It was the Spirit Wielding. Could I tell the state of a soul just by looking at a person? Maybe. Or perhaps I just really didn't like Eitri.

"And, my wife, my darling Delphine, the queen of the Lumière, mother of the future. She is beautiful, is she not?"

And she was. She looked so much like Rhodes, it was startling. She was gorgeous, a stunning queen with a regalness to the tilt of her chin, the way she held her shoulders, everything. Even the way she breathed and moved. I knew that she was a true queen. But she didn't have any power here. No, that was all Brokk, king of the Lumière Kingdom.

I was worried.

"I'm glad you're here. For we must discuss what has happened."

He had introduced himself but didn't seem to want to know who we were. *Well, that's nice.* Though maybe he already knew.

"King, we're here as you requested, what exactly was it you wished to discuss?" Easton asked, sounding bored as usual. I liked that because I really didn't like Brokk.

"Ah, pup, you're here." Brokk sneered.

I squared my shoulders. I really wanted to say something, but Easton took a small step forward, blocking me. I wasn't sure anyone else saw the move except for our group.

"I'm King of Obscurité. Thank you for welcoming me peacefully into your court so we can discuss the important matters at hand."

"Ah, yes, Easton. Welcome. You know we must discuss things having to do with our court first, though, of course. After all, my brother is gone. Killed." He looked at me then, and he didn't say anything. I could feel the death in his eyes and knew that if he had a chance, he would break my neck. Use his Water Wielding to pour down my throat and kill me. Fracture me into a thousand pieces.

I wasn't about to let that happen.

"My brother is dead, as is his wife. We must discuss who the new Lord and Lady of Water are. Could it be Rosamond? Can a Seer rule? That is the question."

So he *did* know her name.

"Or is it Rhodes? Well, it's a very troubling time indeed when I see that the lines of our courts are starting to blend so much. Those are all things we will discuss. In time. First, let us mourn and rejoice in the reclaiming of our children as they come into this court. For I have missed my blood, the power within my veins that holds true within those in front of me. And I know we are here together because of the one, the one of light that's in front of me, as well. Welcome, Spirit Priestess. You are our savior, are you not?"

He called me a light. I was not. I was of both kingdoms and yet none at all. Light *and* darkness. That was something others needed to know.

"Yes, let's discuss our Priestess first and how we'll bring our kingdoms through these new hard times. It seems as if the Fall is upon us once again."

Before I could say anything, before anyone could *do* anything, a cloud of green smoke slid around Luken. He coughed, clutching at his throat.

He fell to his knees and then onto his back as the others started shouting. I threw my hands out to the sides, ready for battle. Braelynn had flown over to Luken's prone body, arching her back once again, hissing and spitting fire as she did.

Someone had just attacked us, and they would pay.

The problem was, I had no idea where that green smoke had come from. Or if it was coming back.

CHAPTER 25

LYRIC

"What have you done?" Rhodes growled, and I moved forward with Easton, trying to get near Luken. The warrior was so still, I was afraid he was dead, and I couldn't get closer to Braelynn, couldn't help her. I had no idea what to do.

"How dare you claim I would do this!" King Brokk shouted, spittle flying from his lips. He no longer looked like the golden god and king that he had tried to show us. Instead, shadows crept around him and entered his eyes. I didn't see any light, I didn't see the Lumière king.

Instead, I saw who he worked for, who controlled him.

Like I now knew that Lore hadn't been his own man, neither was the king. The knight of the Obscurité had worked with The Gray, and it seemed the King of Lumière worked for him, as well.

And I would be damned if I let The Gray keep his talons in the King of Obscurité. That would come later. First, we needed to get to Luken, had to get Braelynn, and we needed to get the hell out of here.

"Luken is on the ground with poisonous gas around him, and you claim that you had nothing to do with this?" Rosamond asked as Rhodes slumped to the ground, his face covered in an Air and Water shield as he pulled Luken towards him.

There was no time for answers, though, and it was clear the king wasn't going to speak anyway. Instead, he used his Wielding, and I was thankful I was ready.

I threw my hands out to the sides, Water from the pools around us tunneling up to the sky in falls of light and Air and Water as I used them to push at the Lumière guards that came at us. They had swords in their hands, Air and Water Wielding at the ready as they slammed into us. Easton and Teagan used their Fire Wielding to create a flame barricade to protect us.

This was it, there would be no going back from this. There'd be no fighting alongside the king to defeat The Gray. Brokk was lost to us.

And that meant... "We need to get back," Easton growled, raising his hand to the sky as Fire erupted from his palm. He sliced his arm down, and a blade of Fire slashed across the flaming wall that they had made and into the fighters moving forward.

"How are we going to do that?" I asked, pushing my Air Wielding towards the others coming at us.

It was almost as if the poisoned Air that had surrounded Luken had rotted the king's mind. His guards were throwing all of their Wielding at us, and I knew that this had all been a trap. The emissary had been sent so those here could kill the King of Obscurité and the Spirit Priestess and anyone else who dared to harm the Gray's precious men.

The only way we could get out of this, was by using the light crystal like we had the dark one, or by finding our way out of the Lumière Court and going back to the Obscurité Court on foot.

The latter seemed like the only feasible option since there was no way we could use the Lumière crystal at this point. I could feel it pulsating behind the Wielding of those in front of us, but I couldn't see it, couldn't touch it. The King of Lumière clearly didn't want us to put the two crystals back together. He didn't want to protect the realm.

He wanted to rule it. Or, at least, have his puppet master rule it.

"If you would just bow before The Gray, you would not have this problem. Bow before me. I am the King of Lumière, I am the one who will rule us all. Throw down your arms and your Wielding and toss the King of Obscurité aside. He and his line have always been usurpers. Our lines, the ones of the light, have always been good, right. We are prosperous. While the Obscurité have faded into near extinction, we thrive. The dark kingdom does not deserve what we have. Come, Spirit Priestess. Be by our side and forget the Obscurité."

"Your uncle is delusional," Easton growled, slamming his Fire Wielding into another guard. I ran towards Teagan, using my Air Wielding to bolster his Fire Wielding. Our magics didn't meld as well as Easton's and mine did, but I had been trained enough that I could help.

Teagan gave me a tight nod before pushing at the wall of Water and Air again, his Fire Wielding strong. It wasn't going to last forever. We only had so many power reserves.

And if we weren't careful, we were going to lose this battle. And then the war.

"He'll have another battalion waiting for us," Rhodes said, shouting over the din of violence and Wielding. "This was a trap all along. Even though we might've seen it, we had no choice," Rhodes kept shouting as he tossed Luken's body over his shoulder. Braelynn's bat wings seemed to have grown, and she hovered on Rhodes' other side, spitting fire at anyone who dared to come too close to Luken or Rhodes.

"How do we get out of this?" I asked, slamming my Earth Wielding into the ground so it lifted up rocks and shoved them at the onslaught.

"We'll use the crystal," Easton said, a grin on his face that scared me.

Was it The Gray? Would this be another trap? Or was Easton genuinely losing his mind and thinking we could actually get through this?

"How on earth are we going to do that?"

Another slap of power, another fiery death as I slammed my Wielding into someone who tried to throw a dagger of Air at me.

It was as if the single moment of green gas around Luken had kicked off a war that we hadn't been prepared for. A battle that would only have one ending, a resolution not in our favor.

"You are the damn Spirit Priestess," Easton growled out. "Find the crystal and use it. Rhodes and Rosamond are strong enough to use their powers to get us back, but they need the Spirit Priestess for that. So, call it. Use it."

"I don't know how to do that. And even if I did, wouldn't that hurt the crystal? I don't want to strip anyone of their Wielding just to get us home." I rolled to the ground, and Easton held out a hand and lifted me to my feet. The Wielder with the sword in his hand fell, and Rosamond hovered over him before slamming Air Wielding down into him, punching it into the ground beneath him. I used my Earth Wielding to cover him, essentially killing him—at least, I hoped.

I didn't want to kill, I didn't want death. But there was no going back. This was our new normal.

We had to fight to live, for others who couldn't fight for themselves. I would deal with the ramifications of my actions later.

"Pull into yourself like you did with the dark crystal. The light crystal knows you're here. Call to it, and this will work."

I looked into the Seer's eyes, a bare kernel of hope popping within my soul.

"Are you sure? Is that a vision? Or a hope?"

"It is what it needs to be. Fight, Lyric. Pull on the crystal. We haven't much time." And then she hovered off, flying towards Rhodes' side. Braelynn landed on her shoulder, and the three of them, Luken over Rhodes' shoulder, fought against those who had once been their court, their family.

I hadn't seen where the queen and the prince had scurried off to. The king had disappeared with them after his speech. He'd left his own men, his cannon fodder, and we were just pawns in his game of chess. No longer. I refused to be that.

The Lumière Kingdom, at least his court, was firmly against us. And not us as Obscurité or those they thought might be traitors. No, those against The Gray.

And it scared me more than I cared to admit. But it didn't matter. We would fight. Because we had to.

"Close your eyes and focus," Easton snapped.

"If I close my eyes, I can't see what I'm fighting."

"Then let me protect you, and you can get us out of here. Trust me, Lyric. Please."

I looked into his eyes for just a moment, his pupils so wide that I saw the fear in them. I had never truly seen the expression on his face before, and seeing it now scared me. However, I would do as he asked. As they all requested. They were counting on me, and I trusted him. I didn't trust The Gray, but I trusted Easton to fight what bound him. To protect me with everything he had.

I nodded. The relief in his eyes was there for a bare instant before he slammed out his hands again, a wall of Earth protecting me from a stray blow of Water power.

Then I closed my eyes and reached out towards the crystal.

It was as if the Lumière crystal had been waiting for me. It was warm yet surrounded by a frozen chrysalis. As if somebody had been trying to steal its light and heat.

I knew it was the king. I knew he had used bone magic just like his brother. The king had been using this crystal for his own gains. His greed. Just like Lore had used the dark crystal.

We were running out of time. The crystals only had so much left to give. If I could give part of myself to them, part of this Spirit that swirled inside me without a purpose, maybe I wouldn't take too much from it or anyone else.

The crystal's energy wrapped its tendrils around me as if it had been waiting. As if it were a long-lost friend who wanted protection. Even as it tried to protect me.

"I won't fail you," I whispered to the crystal, though I knew it wasn't truly alive. It helped give life, though. Helped keep those in its grasp alive, and I would not let it fail.

"Help us, please."

The crystal's hold tightened before power shocked my body.

I threw my head back, and power erupted from my eyes, my mouth, my hands, everywhere.

Easton shouted, then there were no more sounds.

There was so much power within me, each of my elements fighting each other. But it didn't matter. I was meant for this. I was strong enough for this. "Don't give me too much, you need to be whole again."

I didn't know why I was talking to the crystal like it was a living being. It seemed to understand me and pulled back just slightly. I could hear the others of my group coming closer, and then I heard the screams and the shouts of those against us.

I must've been a sight. Maybe it would put the fear that they needed into them. Perhaps they would give us time to recover so we could formulate the plans we needed to.

Maybe this would be enough.

"Let's get home," I whispered.

I could feel the crystal as if it were breaking. As if it had emotions. I felt sadness from it.

"One day you'll be my home, too. For now, protect these people. Please. And then I will come back for you. I promise."

I hoped these words of assurance made sense. Even though I wasn't sure what they meant.

I pushed power into the crystal, and it flared to life. Rhodes mumbled words and chants next to me, and I knew we were going home. I reached out and brushed my Wielding along the crystal's facets, and it hugged me close before saying goodbye.

We arrived back at the Obscurité Court as tears slid down my cheeks. I hoped that this wouldn't be the last time I saw the light crystal. I hoped that I could keep my promise and go back to save it. And not just the crystal, but also its people. The crystal was dying, and it knew it. It had used some of its power to protect me.

Just like the dark crystal had.

They were clearly two halves of a whole, dying without each other.

I needed to bring them back together.

We stood in the crystal room, people moving around as Ridley came to Luken's side. Rhodes barked out orders, even though he had no orders to give. Rosamond was shaking, helping Braelynn and Luken as well as she could. Teagan and Easton were moving around, most likely making sure that the kingdom was safe.

I only had eyes for the crystal.

I could feel Justise's gaze on me as he watched. I didn't care. I moved forward and put my hands on the dark crystal. Power and light flared for just a moment, and its tendrils hugged me just like its brother's had.

"I'll find a way. I promise, I'll find a way. I'm sorry."

The tears continued to fall, and I knew the others were watching me with curiosity, their hushed voices worried.

"The king is a puppet of The Gray. Just like we feared. There will be no help from that corner. We left the crystal and people who need it behind. I will fight for them, just as we will fight for each other." I turned, my palms leaving the crystal even as it reached out to me. I turned my back to it, only so I could see the others. I could feel the heat of the crystal behind me, even its jagged shards, and I somehow knew that it understood. It got that I wouldn't be leaving it behind. No matter what.

"Brokk did not want a healer there," Ridley whispered.

"No. He wanted to kill everybody. He didn't want anyone healed. He didn't want you there to help Luken."

"He's always hated Luken," Rhodes whispered.

"Okay, then. I'm sorry for that. We need to figure out what to do next," Easton growled. "We need allies."

"Allies," I whispered. "Who is on our side? Who can we meet with to form our army? Because it's going to require more than the handful of people in this room. We need an army to protect these crystals. To bring them home."

Nobody questioned the way I was talking about the crystals. Or their people. There was no need to. They were as worried as I was, and now that I had felt the soul of each crystal, I knew that, no matter what, I would give my dying breath for them. Just as they were doing for their people.

"My parents might be able to help," Teagan whispered.

"The Lord and Lady of Fire would be strong allies," Easton said simply.

"I don't know about my parents. Maybe they'll be able to help," Wyn said from the doorway, and I turned to see the pale warrior standing tall in her leathers. She looked shaken, and I knew it probably felt as if she had lost a limb without her Wielding. Yet she stood there, ready to fight.

I hoped that the Lord and Lady of Earth would stand by our sides just as strongly as she was.

"My grandmother will help," Rhodes said.

"She is the one ally I know will always be on our side," Easton said, and the layer of trust in those words wrapped around my heart. I knew it was hope.

"Okay, then," I whispered.

"The lords and ladies. Those of power. That is who we meet with."

"We cannot allow the King of Lumière to act as he has," Easton said, regalness in his tone. In this moment, he was royalty.

"You're right. The King of Lumière cannot stand. And after this, hopefully, there won't be two kingdoms at all." I looked at Rhodes, and his silver eyes narrowed.

"It's time for our generation to step up, for our kingdoms to thrive."

"Then we'll meet. And we'll plan. And we'll protect our people." The others looked at me as I spoke, and I raised my chin, even as the Wielding within me shook.

"We must save them all, no matter the cost."

And I knew these weren't platitudes. I knew we were going to win.

Because, in the end, there wasn't any other option.

CHAPTER 26

EASTON

Perhaps in the eyes of those far older than me, I was still young, untried, a mere pup, hardly older than a teenager. I had lived centuries. I had fought, bled, had almost died.

And in all of my years, I had never had a meeting quite like this one.

Perhaps I had never even heard of one such as this. Oh, there might have been summits that contained these key players before the Fall... however, I hadn't heard of one since. I should ask Lanya. She would remember. Rhodes' grandmother, the Lady of Air, had felt so wise beyond her years. As if she had witnessed the Fall and had tried to stop it before. Her husband had been the same way, had died to protect those under his care, and even those who hadn't fallen directly under his umbrella.

I didn't know all of the histories; I wished I did. I knew the King of Obscurité hadn't been the dark creature portrayed. My grandfather hadn't been pure evil. Oh, he had killed thousands, but it had been to protect the world.

I knew he hadn't been the darkness that some thought. It had taken me too long to see beneath the layers to who he was, and I was only now figuring it out. However, people needed enemies. They needed figureheads for their darkness and untruths of history. So, they cast Easton in that light—no matter that he hadn't deserved it.

So, my grandfather would always be the hated one, the arrogant sovereign. The one who had gone head-to-head with the original King of Lumière because of power.

I knew deep down in my soul that it wasn't as it seemed. There was more to it. That just like now, the Lumière Kingdom had darkness along with its portrayed light. They were the ones with the tendrils of hate and deception and the shadows in their souls.

So now, we were meeting, a summit of the lords. Sadly, I did not think it would be enough.

The part of myself that pulled at my heart, that sank its tendrils of hate and fear inside, knew that this would only be a part of it. We would have to sacrifice more than our positions and our old loyalties and treaties in order for this to work.

I looked over at Lyric, who sat on my old throne not because she was in power but because she was exhausted.

I knew we would have to sacrifice more, and I think she knew it, too.

She looked at me then, her gaze weary as she gave me a small smile. Surprisingly, it reached her eyes. Then again, Lyric was always surprising me.

While we waited for the lords and ladies to enter the crystal room under the guise of secrecy, I ignored my uncle's pointed looks and went to Lyric's side.

"If you can't rest before the meeting, you at least need to eat."

I knew I sounded like an asshole, as if I were ordering her around. Then again, I was.

She sat up straighter, shaking her head. Her hair had long since fallen out of its braid, and it now tumbled over her shoulders. My hands itched to reach out and tangle my fingers in those strands. I held myself back. It was lust, nothing more. Every time I tried to think of something more, icy shards sliced through my body and wrapped their way around my heart before piercing a hole.

I was an angrier version of myself and if I thought about anything more, I'd break, so I wouldn't think at all.

"There's no time, I'll be okay." She must have seen the skepticism in my expression. "Really, I'm fine. It just took a lot out of me to open up the crystal like I did to bring us here."

"You do look nice on the throne, I'm just saying."

She shook her head, rolling her shoulders back as she stretched as if she were waking up from a nap. Rest she desperately needed. "No, I don't think the throne is for me."

No, a Spirit Priestess didn't get to be king or queen. I had figured that much out. So, it was a good thing that we weren't able to be soulmates. Because having her as my queen wouldn't be a good thing.

It would only lead to heartache and death. Something I was sadly getting better at.

"I don't want to be sitting here looking like I'm bored or thinking I'm queen when they get here. Help me up?" she asked, surprising me. I held out my hand, and she slid her smaller one into mine. My Wielding reached out to hers like a spark. Her eyes widened, and I gave her hand a squeeze before letting go as she stood up.

She stiffened ever so slightly, then I remembered our truce. I leaned forward to brush my lips against her brow. We could never be soulmates, but maybe we could be friends. Perhaps even lovers. And that would be enough. Because someone had to lean on another when the worst happened. If that's what Lyric wanted, I could make it happen.

"Are you ready for this?" I asked, looking at her face.

"As ready as I'll ever be. Though these days, I never feel like I'm ready for anything that comes at us."

"You still make it through. That has to count for something."

"Perhaps."

Before I could comment on that, I felt the others behind me stir. I turned.

Rhodes and a newly healed Luken stood on one side of the room, their faces grave. Luken was a little pale, Braelynn on his shoulder. My uncle Ridley had healed him as best he could. Apparently, the poison had been meant exclusively for Luken, one that clung to the pores attracted by his bloodline. I knew it had to do with his father, the one that nobody really knew anything about. It was the only explanation for Luken to be targeted over anyone else. Especially considering that most everyone else there was either a king, the son of a lord, or the Priestess herself.

Wyn and Teagan stood near Luken and Braelynn, a unit. Ridley stood on the other side of the room, not necessarily apart but enough that our group covered the whole area before we sat down at my table.

Emory was back in her room, though not because we had asked her to go there. She hadn't wanted to be the focus, hadn't wanted to stand out, and I was grateful for that. I didn't know what Emory's plans were, or if we could ever trust her. However, seeing Emory take strides to becoming a better person helped Lyric, and I was all for that.

Another icy shard flared in my chest, and I held back a grunt. Lyric gave me an odd look, and I answered with a barely perceptible shake of my head. No need for her to know that every time I thought of her, every time I got angry, it felt like my body was shattering into a thousand pieces.

Rosamond stood on Lyric's other side, her hair flowing in a wind that wasn't actually there. I had thought only Alura could do that. Clearly, Rosamond possessed the same skill.

We were waiting for our summit to begin, and now the lords and ladies were making their way in after resting from their journey.

Pulling people through this crystal as Lyric had without her actually being near them had taken a toll on everybody. It had taken some of their energy, and I knew we all regretted it, even if it had been necessary. It would have been easier for the others if Lyric had traveled back and forth, but we weren't sure the crystal had that type of energy, and I was damn well sure Lyric didn't.

So, we had done it this way, and now the lords and ladies would be in front of us, waiting to plan.

At least, I hoped.

The fact that they had answered the call at all had to count for something. Unless they were all treacherous men and women, and this was just a meeting for the King of Lumière and The Gray to figure out exactly what we were planning.

Lanya, the Lady of Air and Rhodes' and Rosamond's grandmother came in first. Rhodes went to her side at once, holding out his arm so she could put her hand on it. She ignored it and instead reached for a hug. Rhodes leaned down to his smaller grandmother and brushed his lips on the top of her head before holding her close. When she moved away, she patted his cheek, smiled like a grandmother would, even though she looked nearly the same age as Rhodes, and then finally took his arm before walking towards the others. She greeted them all, every single one, with hugs and warriors' holds before coming to where Rosamond, Lyric, and I stood. She hugged and kissed her granddaughter, resting her forehead against Rosamond's for just a moment before coming to Lyric.

"You must rest soon, my child. For we are here to take your burden. At least, part of it." She kissed Lyric on both cheeks and held her close. Lyric didn't say anything. She just gazed at the other woman in awe. I was right there with her. There was something about Lanya that went straight to the heart. As if she could see into your soul almost like a Spirit Wielder could.

Not that I knew exactly what a Spirit Wielder could do. I was trying to pick up things when it came to Lyric. No one could help her train that Wielding, not the way we were helping with her other four elements. Thought maybe we would all figure it out along the way.

I hated that she was so alone in this. Another jagged shard stabbed my heart, and I winced.

Lanya gave me a sharp look before holding out her arms. For some reason, I ducked my head and held her close just as she wanted. I felt as if I were a little boy again in my mother's arms. I had never met my grandmother. She'd died long before I was born. I had never met any of my grandparents now that I thought about it. I'd had my mother, even as she grew colder in her years.

I knew now that it was to keep me safe from Lore, maybe even from The Gray himself. And while she might've thought she failed, I always knew that she was there for me. I would have done anything for her.

I didn't know why holding this woman not of my territory, this fierce warrior lady with the tender heart and soul made me think of that.

As she leaned back and cupped my cheek in her hand, all I wanted to do was hug her again and have her tell me stories and say that everything would be okay.

Those were not the thoughts of a king. They were the fantasies of a young boy who had long since perished.

I nodded my head, giving her the respect she had earned and deserved.

"You also need rest, my son."

I didn't correct her usage of the title: son. It was hard to do with Lanya.

I looked out of the corner of my eye and saw Rhodes staring at us, not glaring. No, he almost looked as if he were happy. At least pleased with what was going on. Not that I knew exactly what that was or what any of this meant. It was hard to understand when it came to that man.

The Lord and Lady of Fire walked in soon after Lanya went to Rosamond's side. They looked regal as always, and I grinned at Shimmer.

I had always liked Griffin and Shimmer, even if I didn't always agree with them. Then again, the lords and ladies of court were never supposed to always agree with those in power. There were meant to be confidants, advisors, and for courtiers to have opinions of their own. At least, that's how my mother had always liked it.

That's how I wanted it, and one day, if I had a chance to actually rule a court that wasn't crumbling around us, I wanted to keep it that way.

"My son," Shimmer said, holding out her arms. Teagan went to her and hugged her close, Griffin doing the same. They said hello to the others, though they only hugged Wyn.

Both the Lord and Lady of Fire gave each other looks, though they didn't say anything as they held Wyn close.

They could tell what had happened to her, but no one was going to say anything. At least, I hoped not. I had a feeling when Wyn's parents, the Lord and Lady of Earth, walked in, things would get tricky.

"My king," Griffin said, his voice gruff.

"Lord, Lady," I said, bowing my head slightly. It was out of respect, and I hoped the others realized that. These had been my elders for as long as I could remember. Having our new stations in life didn't mean that I had to forget who they were to me. Teagan was my best friend, and that meant they had been in my life as long as he had.

"Thank you for inviting us. We're interested to hear what you have to say," Shimmer said softly before going to Teagan's side.

When the Lord and Lady of Earth walked in, Rhodes, Luken, and even Lyric stiffened. My gaze moved to Wyn.

She looked at them, her eyes wide, resolute.

And when they walked past her, their own flesh and blood without even saying a word, I wanted to reach out and strangle them.

I couldn't. It wouldn't do anybody any good if I beat them down using my Wielding or even my fists.

They weren't going to acknowledge their daughter now because she was a Dane.

They had used her, even tried to marry her off to me, even though she was technically my cousin. All because they wanted power. And while they might be in this room now, I didn't know what side of the coin they would land on when the real battle came. We needed allies, but despite that, I wanted to kill them right here and now for what they were doing to Wyn.

Lyric let out a choking sound, and I reached for her, grasping her hand in mine.

She squeezed this time, and I held on.

I shook my head slightly, and she nodded, even though there was Fire in her eyes. And not just the metaphorical kind.

No, her powers were holding her back, and she wanted to hurt the Lord and Lady of Earth for daring to hurt her friend.

However, there was nothing we could say.

The Lord and Lady of Dirt—like Rhodes always called them—nodded at me but didn't come forward. I was their king. Though, clearly, they were still the same bastards they'd always been. Valor and Zia still didn't acknowledge their daughter, didn't acknowledge anyone other than issuing a slight nod, then went to stand on the opposite side of the wall near my uncles. The fact that Zia and Justise were siblings had not gone unnoticed by anyone in the room. Zia didn't say a word to her brother. She always chose to ignore Justise. Maybe because Zia only wanted power. She had always gone to Cameo to try and get it, not even Justise. Her brother had been nothing in her eyes, not even a steppingstone, so she ignored her sibling.

I didn't understand why they were still Lord and Lady of Earth, and that was on me. I needed to change that. Soon.

"Let's all take a seat," I said, dismissing the formalities. Everyone took their seats without another word, thankfully not fighting over who had to sit by whom. They'd already done that by separating to different sides of the room.

"Why are we all here?" Valor asked, the Lord of Dirt looking as if he'd rather be anywhere else.

Frankly, I wanted him somewhere else, too. Though I couldn't say anything.

"The King of Lumière is working with The Gray. We saw the shadows as he fought us. We need to stop him, using any means necessary."

Though I had said "any means," I knew in my heart and my soul, that I didn't actually mean that. I wanted to see what the others thought.

There was silence for a moment, and then everyone exploded at once, asking questions and explaining things. It hadn't mattered that half the people at the table were there for the battle, they all had questions about what to do.

I slammed my fist on the table even as something tugged at my chest. I knew that The Gray wanted me. I pushed him away, snipped those cords because I knew what was coming. Maybe he had always done this, perhaps that's why I had always felt pulled. Now I knew what it meant, and I ignored it. The Gray would not have me. No matter what happened, The Gray would not take me again.

"Silence," I rasped out.

"You're still an insolent pup," Valor sneered, and Wyn opened her mouth to speak. Lyric interrupted. Maybe to protect me, perhaps to protect Wyn. Either way, I was grateful.

I needed to work on making sure those cords couldn't wrap around me again, and that The Gray couldn't keep his hold on me. I might still have my curse, I may not be able to ever love, but I would not allow The Gray to tug me under his control.

I had at least that much power where I hadn't before. It could have been because I knew of the control The Gray had over me, even if he had been the one to unveil it himself. Or maybe it was because I was stronger. Perhaps it was because of the woman at my side—but I put that thought away.

I couldn't. Not if I wanted to keep her safe. And myself.

"He is your king, it would do you well to remember that," Lyric said. Before Valor could say anything else, she shook her head. "We are here because, like Easton said, we need to find a way to stop The Gray and the King of Lumière. You see the devastation and loss within your own people, I have talked with each of you about it. The realm is dying, and if we don't find a way to put the crystals back together, to reunite our people, we'll all lose."

"Our?" Zia asked, her pointed nose in the air.

"Oh, shut it," Shimmer snapped. "This is not the time for you to be thinking of courts and ladies and your betters. She is the Spirit Priestess. She is part of us all. The people in this room are of two kingdoms, two worlds. Now, we have to rise together."

"Thank you, Shimmer," I said, knowing I liked her for a reason. She might have a temper, but that came with Fire. In the past, I didn't always know where her loyalties lay. Now, however, I knew she would fight with us. Same as her husband, who had reached out to grab her hand, giving it a tight squeeze before kissing her brow.

Teagan just grinned, looking over at his parents as if he knew that they were completely badass. They would fight with us. Good.

"If we fight in a war right now, I'm afraid we will lose," Lanya said, looking at all of us.

She was the grandmother of a Seer, a Truth Seeker just like her grandson, and we all listened when she spoke. Well, not *all* of us. The Lord and Lady of Dirt seemed to have better plans. At least they didn't say anything.

"I don't want a full-scale war," I said softly.

"None of us do," Rhodes said. He paused. "Okay, maybe my uncle does, but we sure as hell don't."

"We need to know that we're all in each other's corners, and we need a plan."

I nodded at Lyric. "Then let's make one."

It took hours and a lot of screaming and yelling and discussing numbers of people on our side. The problem was, we didn't know. We knew that there were people who were sympathetic to our cause in each of the four territories. And we knew that perhaps the Spirit Wielders, the ones who walked in Lyric's dreams, could be counted on to help. However, we didn't know exactly how.

This was just the beginning, and it had to count for something.

"We will stand with you in this. However, I want it to be known that there is still a boon in play," Valor said, looking between Rhodes and Lyric.

Once again, I resisted the urge to strangle the Lord of Earth.

"I know we owe you a favor for letting us live," Lyric said.

"Which is ridiculous," I growled. Rhodes shook his head.

"No, there must be honor, even amidst all of this. There must be honor. We recognize that, but I don't know what bearing that has on this."

Valor only shrugged, though I knew he had something up his sleeve. He just wasn't ready to show it yet. "I wanted to make sure that everyone knew that. However, we will be there when you decide what your next step is," he said, looking at his wife. He didn't look at his daughter, though.

"I will always be by your side," Lanya said. "Always."

"We will be with you, too. However, first, we must try for peace," the Lord of Fire said.

"I agree," Lanya said before I could say anything else.

Rosamond clasped her hands in front of her. "I know you tried to meet with him, and it was a trap. But with all of us, with our combined powers, perhaps he will see reason, or we can make way for peace as a group. If the world sees us as we are, coming together, maybe it will do some good. I know that if we go in with our powers blazing and the world ready to burn at our fingertips, we will lose far more than just our lives. We will lose the war and our people."

Rosamond was the one speaking, yet it was Lanya who nodded along, holding her granddaughter's hand. "She speaks the truth. We must try for peace. We must attempt to use words first."

"They tried to kill us," Luken ground out. Braelynn nuzzled against him, and he reached up to scratch her neck.

"It'll be for the good of the realm to try. It's also the rules of war," Lanya put in.

I growled, though I nodded. They were right. And the truth burned.

"So, we will meet with the king, we will try once more for peace. If not, then we know we must fight. Gather your troops, train, protect your territories. No matter what, know that we may fight in the battle of our lives. Because The Gray is no ordinary puppet master. The King of Lumière is a puppet, but he has power."

The others agreed, though the Lord and Lady of Earth were slightly cagey at best.

I looked over at Lyric, who appeared just as—if not more—tired than before. Yet she nodded at me, and I knew we were making the only choice we could.

Perhaps words would help us find peace and reason.

I knew that the world would burn around us if this didn't work.

And I feared that time was coming sooner than any of us wished.

CHAPTER 27

EASTON

I knew this was going to end badly. Hence why, though we were coming for peace talks, trying to give the King of Lumière one last chance before a full-scale war broke out, we were also dressed in battle leathers, our Wielding reserves at full strength.

I'd spent the past day going over plans with my inner circle and the lords and ladies of their respective elements. And when I wasn't knee-deep in battle and peace plans—the latter something I knew wasn't going to work, though we had to try for our people's sake—I was meditating with Ridley and the others.

The Gray might still have his spindly fingers around my heart when it came to the curse, but I'd be damned if I let him wrap his smoky ropes around my body and pull me into his realm again. Now that I was aware of what he could do, I was shoring up my defenses as well as filling my wells of power.

Ridley was the best at this, and with good reason considering his past. I had watched him teach Lyric his form of training months ago, and because of that, I had gone to him again for similar training of the soul when the lights had been extinguished and Lyric had been asleep.

I had spent decades thinking I could do everything on my own, that I *had* to. No longer.

Now, all of us were going to end up bloody and beaten, so any extra power we could hold onto so we didn't end up spent husks of our former selves would be a boon.

"Are you ready to go?" Justise asked, giving me a solemn look. I didn't like that expression on his face. He was always the strong one and, yes, the broody one, even though that was a word he hated. I didn't want my uncle to have to fight at my side. I didn't want either of my uncles to be involved in this. However, they were going to be there, just like the rest of my blooded family.

I sometimes forgot that I had family other than Justise. "We're ready. We're heading towards the center area soon. As a group, though some will be staying behind to protect the court and those who can't fight."

"Plus, I don't think you really wanted to bring your entire army for this," Justise added.

I nodded. "You never know, this whole talking thing could actually work, and the king could suddenly not seem as if he's working for The Gray. Everything could be fine."

"You know I wish that could be the case," Justise said, his voice soft.

"I know. And I also know that someone might die today. I can only hope it's him."

I wasn't bloodthirsty. Okay, I was a little. I was also tired. So damn tired. I'd been in some form of war my entire life, and my realm was falling. People were dying, and one of my best friends had lost her Wielding because of the crystals. Because of what we had done to it over time.

There needed to be an end in sight, and that meant Lyric had to get close enough to pull the two crystals back together. I just hoped to hell we figured out how to do that before it was too late. Even though part of me thought it was already past that. With all the things that had happened thus far, maybe we were past the point of no return. Perhaps this was our apocalypse.

Justise studied me before pulling me into a hug that surprised us both. We weren't the touchy-feely types, and I wasn't a fan of hugs. After a moment of stiffness, I returned his embrace.

He didn't say anything, though I wasn't sure anything needed to be said.

He would fight alongside us, a Fire Wielder of immense strength, as well as a weapons master. I only hoped to hell that he didn't die.

I hoped no one did.

"Let's be off, then," I said, trying to put some cheer in my voice. We both knew it was fake. I supposed it was better than nothing.

We went down a hallway and through the courtyard to where we were meeting. A few dozen Wielders waited for us, bowing as I strode by. I nodded at them, grateful that they were coming with us. They would be our guard, our court. We had gone last time with so few, and we had almost lost because of it. Then again, we'd still won, and with only a handful of us. I had to count that as something to be proud of.

We had gone for a simple meeting with the king before Luken had almost died, and the King of Lumière had attacked us full force.

I wasn't going to risk Lyric or anyone else's life by not having the right backup this time. My other Wielders surrounded the court and were set up in strategic places within my kingdom, ready in case the king used this moment to invade. My words were as strong as they could be, considering the strength of the crystal, and I had to hope that would be enough.

The Lady of Air had sent word to her king that she wanted us to meet, and since she was his subject, it had seemed the right thing to do. The king had to know who would be arriving, and I only hoped to hell that this wouldn't be the end of us.

It'd be great if this were the end of it all, and we could find peace, though. Because my people needed it. As I looked at my Wielders, their bodies strong, their magics a force, I hoped to hell I wouldn't lose them. There were so few of us left compared to before, and considering that I had been at war my entire life, I didn't want my people to die because of my decisions.

Heavy was the head that wore the crown and all that.

I looked at the men and women around me, the Wielders who had come with us and I knew we needed to bring every single one of them back.

I moved past those I knew but were not part of my inner circle, and stopped in front of my people.

"Okay, better get this over with," Teagan grumbled, and Shimmer reached out and ruffled her son's hair.

The fact that Teagan was a fierce warrior and at least a head taller than her didn't seem to stop her in the slightest.

"Mother," he said out of tight lips. The Lord of Fire just smiled from where he stood next to his family.

"You shouldn't grumble," Shimmer said.

"Your mother is right. We're here to fight. And win."

"We're here to try and talk reason into that man," Shimmer corrected. She patted her leather-clad hips and gave her son and husband tight nods. "However, we will probably end up fighting because that's what he likes."

"Oh, believe me. I know," Lanya said as she came over. She wore camel tan leathers over her lithe body, her hair braided back. However, the pieces that had fallen forward over her face blew in a wind that only she could feel. I had seen some of the other Air Wielders do that in the past. And even Lyric. I wasn't sure if she knew she did it. Because I watched as she stood in transfixion as she looked at Lanya and then Rosamond at her grandmother's side. No, Lyric didn't realize that she had that same effervescent quality. It would be interesting to see what would happen when she realized the extent of her powers and abilities.

"This is a waste of time," the Lord of Dirt snarled. His wife patted her husband's arm, both of them still pointedly ignoring Wyn at their side.

Wyn had two swords strapped to her back, something I didn't see much from her. Sure, she was trained with them, as we all were, but they usually got in the way of her Earth Wielding. She didn't have her magic anymore, though. She was a Dane now, and I hated this. We had to find a way to bring these powers back to the people. Because Wyn without Wielding was like a sunny day without the sun. It just didn't make any sense.

"Are we just going to stand around and do nothing, then?" Wyn asked, trying to keep some lightness in her tone.

Her parents stiffened, but they still didn't look at her. Not even a glance. Didn't acknowledge her in any way. When this was over, I was going to kill them. First, I needed their help to kill the King of Lumière. Details and all that.

"We should get going. No doubt the king already has his spies waiting," Rhodes said, rolling his neck. Luken stood by him, his sword at the ready, and Braelynn on his shoulder. I wasn't quite sure why they thought bringing the Familiar would help. She was very protective of Luken. Lyric, as well. And I could tell she was growing in power, something I was grateful for. It would be interesting to see what happened when she came into herself.

Lyric had no idea what she was in for.

"You'll do the talking, then?" Lyric asked the lords and ladies. "Because we already tried talking, and he won't listen to us."

"We will," Lanya said, tucking a piece of hair behind Lyric's ear. Lyric had put her hair into two braids down her back, trying to keep it out of the way of any passing Wielder who wanted to use it as leverage. We knew we were going into battle, even through the farce of peace talks.

We would find a way. We had to.

"We will try to make the king see reason. However, we know he won't. He never does." Layna looked off into the distance as Shimmer nodded at her.

"As a young boy, he always wanted more. Even when we were all children of the courts, watching our parents make the same mistakes we seem to be making still." Shimmer turned to her husband, gripping his hand.

"The time has come. We must go, or we'll be late. And if we are, then we have resigned ourselves to our own fate," Rosamond said, shaking her head. "I hate when they come to me in rhymes."

"I think I would hate having them interrupt my speech at all," Emory said, looking at all of us.

I raised my brow and looked at my uncle. "We're bringing her?"

"*Her* is standing right here. And, no, I'm not going. I'm staying here. I just wanted to wish you all luck. Because I'd rather not have this be the last time I see you guys. Come back. Whole." She reached out and squeezed Lyric's hand before walking away, and Lyric just shook her head, confusion clear on her face. She wasn't the only one. But I knew we didn't have time for that.

"Let's get going, then," I said and went to stand by Lyric. She reached out and gripped my hand, and I tangled my fingers with hers. I knew the others were watching. I wasn't going to pull away. She needed me. As a friend and an ally. I could do this.

"Let's do this."

"Yes. Let's." And then we took a few steps, and I turned around suddenly, remembering that there was something else I needed to do. I was the king, after all.

"Maisons, we will try to find peace. I promise. If that cannot happen, fight for your people. Fight for those we have to leave behind. Fight for those who have already lost their lives and their powers." I refused to look at Wyn, I could feel her eyes burning into me.

"We have the Spirit Priestess, we have the lords and ladies of more than just our kingdom. We will be strong. We will find a way to make this work. This will not be our end of days. Fight for what is right. Use your brains, your Wielding, your skills, and each other. Lean on one another and work together."

There were murmurs as people nodded and shouted their agreement. Well, that was one way to get the morale up.

"Fight and come home." I said the last as an order, wishing to hell people would actually listen to it.

Other than the lords and ladies and those in my inner circle, everyone here was a Fire or Earth Wielder. I knew we'd have to have more than just this for the next battle. When we got through this, we would need Water and Air Wielders who believed in fighting for what was right and wanted out from under The Gray's control.

However, that was for another time.

For now, we needed to make our move.

Lyric squeezed my hand and then let me go. And we all moved towards the wards. They slithered along my skin as if trying to hold me back and yet saying goodbye at the same time. I knew that, one day, the wards would fall completely. With the way our crystal was running out, there would be no more power left for them to rise at all. It was inevitable.

Maybe that was a good thing. Because if we were going to fight with those on the Lumière side who agreed with us, then perhaps there shouldn't be wards separating us. I let those thoughts go away because, first, we had to win. We had to prevail before we took any next steps.

The King of Lumière stood on the other side of the clearing as soon as we passed through the wards. This was neutral ground. One where we'd had countless meetings over the years, and even some battles. It stood right at the southernmost tip of where the two courts met and was heavily guarded so no one could go in and out of either court without us knowing. My guards were already there, slowly moving into formation behind us.

As I looked at the battle leathers the king wore, and his immense army that he had gathered, I knew this was not the time for talking.

He wanted to end the Obscurité. Wanted to be the king of all, and he had come prepared.

Well, so had we.

"Lanya, Rhodes, Rosamond, come to my side. You are not with the Obscurité. You are the Lumière. You are of light and goodness and power. Not the scum of the realm that has forsaken all goodness. I am your king, and you will listen to me," the King of Lumière called out without preamble.

There had to be over four hundred Lumière Wielders behind him, all in their gold and silver armor that looked as if they'd just shined it that morning. So many Wielders…and yet, they couldn't see what their king was doing. I recognized a few from when we had fought the Lord of Air, and knew that there would be no reasoning with them. Not when they knew their lord had used bone magic to kill so many innocents.

The League and the Creed stood with Brokk, as well, though their ranks weren't as full as they had been when we fought the king's brother. Either they were not all here for one reason or another—perhaps in my territory or theirs being spies and assassins like always—or not all of them wanted to follow the king. I wasn't one hundred percent sure about that. I knew that they would be our fiercest competition. The king also had his own circle, the strongest of his Wielders. Unlike my mother and me, he did not like to keep powerful Wielders at his side. He preferred to rule from a place of power of his own making, rather than having knights and warriors like we did. So, he did not have someone like Wyn or Luken or Teagan. He did not have my uncles, who were healers and weapons makers and fighters. He had himself, and capable warriors. Mine were stronger. And though I had brought fewer people with me, we were a force to be reckoned with. We had all trained together, even Lyric. And we would prevail.

We had to.

"Come now, Brokk," Lanya began. "Don't you see we must discuss what's happening with our realm?"

"If you do not come to my side now, you will be labeled a traitor, and you will die by my hand."

"I am the Lady of Air. You cannot strip that title from me. It takes more than a decree from a mad king to do so," the Lady of Air spoke, her voice echoing throughout the land as Air slid over her, her tunic billowing ever so slightly over her leathers. She looked like a goddess, and I was really glad she was on our side.

"I will do whatever I need to do in order to protect my kingdom," Brokk snarled.

"You say that, and yet here you are, letting The Gray control you. We can see the shadows amongst your members. We can see them in your eyes," Rhodes spat.

I looked at Lyric, who gave me a tight nod. The two of us did not need to speak yet. No, we would let the family hash out what they needed to and make sure our side was ready. And then, we would fight.

"Lies! You speak lies. I know it's the taint of the Obscurité. They have the dark ones. They are the ones who must be in league with them. Come to us, Rosamond. Be our Seer in truth. Don't let their dark lies and seductions take you from your family. They've already killed your parents, don't let them kill you, too."

"I am on the right side of my destiny. It appears, Uncle, you never were."

"Just kill her, Father," Eitri snapped. "They've always been weird. You know that they must have been working with the Obscurité all this time. They're the reason your brother is dead. Come on now, let's get this over with."

Eitri folded his arms over his chest, and I resisted the urge to shake my head. This boy was not future-king material. He was not a warrior. His leathers fit him perfectly. They weren't worn, had probably never been used. Eitri was coddled by his father, and with the way his mother stood off to the side, I knew that the Queen of Lumière, Delphine, couldn't fight her husband or son. There was something off about her that I couldn't quite put my finger on. She wasn't going to fight today, that much was clear in what she wore, her long, flowing gown rather than battle leathers. She looked at Rhodes, at Lanya, at Rosamond, and Luken, and I saw yearning there.

When we got out of this, *if* we got out of this, we would have to use that. Figure out exactly what Delphine thought. Because there was something there. Something in my gut told me that.

"Enough," Brokk snapped. "You said you wanted to meet to talk, so...talk."

"The Gray has always been a thing of nightmares," the Lord of Earth began, and I let him speak.

"I do not care what the lords and ladies of the Obscurité to have to say." Brokk waved his hand. "They are the enemy. Don't you see this? They're just going to spew lies at us. They have spent so much of their lives in darkness, in horror, that they do not know what is happening to our realm. It is their fault that so many are losing power. And now, they stand against us. They are not us. Don't listen to what they have to say."

"Then listen to me," Lyric said, and I straightened, walking beside her as she moved forward just a bit from the ranks.

"What do you have to say, girl?" Brokk sneered.

"I am the Spirit Priestess. I hold the five elements." There were murmurs on both sides of the lines, and I remembered that not everyone knew who she was or how many elements she held. She was a thing of legend, just like The Gray was. Like the prophecies themselves.

And she was coming into her power. She had to be our beacon of hope, because I sure as hell knew I wasn't.

She was exactly what we needed, and as soon as she figured that out, there would be a reckoning.

"Lies."

"I'm not lying, Your Majesty," she said, and I held back a smirk. No one used "your majesty" in this realm. I liked it.

Brokk looked as if he weren't sure if she was serious or if it was meant as an offense, and I had a feeling she'd intended it to be a bit snide.

That's my girl.

The oil slick over my heart iced over, one pulse, then another, and suddenly I couldn't feel a damn thing anymore when it came to the power at my side.

"All of your childhood stories and prophecies were about this moment. About the moments that are coming. We need to come together, and I'm here to help that happen. You need to help, as well. We cannot do this without you, King Brokk. We need to use both territories to fight as one realm against the darkness."

"You're with the darkness, or don't you know what Obscurité means."

"Obscurité is the kingdom. It's The Gray who holds the darkness. We are not just light and dark. We're a mix, just like The Gray is. We need to figure out exactly how to defeat him. And if we keep fighting amongst ourselves, we won't survive. Help us. Stand with us. Don't waste time. He already has his claws in us. In all of us. We must win. Or the realm will crumble."

"Pretty words for a girl who can't even hold her own head up high with her powers. I mean, the King of Obscurité has already shunned you, why should I have you?"

I wanted to snap at something, wanted to throw my hand out and slice Fire along his body. I didn't. Though I only barely stopped myself. Someone had told him about my curse, was it Garrik? The Whisperer?

Or was it the many spies that I knew he had in my court. I had done the same with the spies within their court. Every noble did. It was how I tried to keep abreast of the situations within the court. Just like I looked for his weakness, he'd found mine. He killed my spies more often than not when I tried to show mercy.

Well, hell, this wasn't going to be pretty.

Lyric didn't falter, didn't do anything. Instead, she just tilted her head before shaking it.

"I see we're too late. I can see into your soul, into the darkness that creeps. I'm sorry that we're going to lose you. I'm sorry you were on the wrong side of fate. The Gray is coming, and we can't hold back any longer."

She sounded like Rosamond just then, and the hair on the back of my neck stood on end.

There was no time to do anything. Instead, Brokk threw up his hands.

And then, the battle was on. There would be no more talking.

"Lyric, at my side. Always." She looked over at me, her eyes full of flame, and her Air Wielding ready to go at her fingertips. "Okay. Just don't get hurt."

I smirked at her, feeling like we were right back to the first time I'd met her, when we were at the border between Fire and Earth. When we were at the red peaks, and I first touched her Air with my Fire.

"You can't get hurt either."

"Deal." Then, the fighting began.

Swords clashed as those who used them hit first. Wyn was already in the fray, a sword in each hand as she twirled them around, flipping into the air and using them as though she had been born with them in her hands. Luken was at her side, his sword at the ready as he slid his Air Wielding down the blade, blowing a group of Air Wielders back twenty feet. Braelynn flapped her bat wings and spewed fire at those who dared to come too close to him.

And...was it my imagination? Or was she twice the size she had been the day before? She was growing into her new self. Soon, we would know exactly what type of Familiar she was.

Teagan and his parents fought as a trio, looking as they had when we were younger, and his parents had first taught him how to use his newly discovered Fire Wielding. Griffin had his arms out, flames on either side. Then, without even moving his hands, the Fire licked at the others coming for his wife and child. They shouted and screamed as they burned, using their Air and Water Wielding to stop most of it. However, he got a few. Teagan fought like a blunt instrument, one round of Fire after another, not even sweating from the intense heat or exertion. He was angry, that much I knew. Angry about Wyn, at the fact that we had to deal with this now.

Wyn refused to fight next to him. Instead, she fought near Luken because of her swords.

Teagan fought alongside heartache, just like Wyn had been forced to.

Shimmer spun in circles, her flames dancing as if on air currents before they bounced into her husband's and her son's Fire, intensifying the flames and turning them blue.

They were so hot, they burned violet and blue and white. No crimson or orange in the mix. So hot, they seared through the Water Wielding of those coming after them, and Shimmer shouted in power.

Rhodes and Lanya and Rosamond fought together, as well, each of them using their Wielding in turn. Lanya once again looked like a goddess, Air flowing around her as she formed tornadoes to pull up the Wielders who came at her grandchildren.

Rosamond danced, just like Shimmer did—as if she hadn't a care in the world. And that's when I knew she Saw the others' moves before they made them. She darted out of the way, and pulled her brother out of the way, as well. Rhodes fought like a king, and one day, I hoped he would be the one to rule the Lumière Kingdom before we figured out the next phase.

Because the power within him had always made me a little jealous, even though I never cared to admit it. Rhodes lifted one hand, and twelve Lumière soldiers—ones he might have fought with and trained—levitated up before slamming to the ground. And then my other Wielders came, fighting hand-to-hand, power-to-power.

We were outnumbered four to one. Not great odds, but not the worst we'd faced either. We would make this happen. We were stronger. We were battling for a purpose. A reason. To protect both kingdoms and the realm as a whole, not just our homes.

This had never been about talking, never about simply finding peace. And though I had known the others had wanted that, the King of Lumière would never let that happen.

The Lord and Lady of Earth stood off to the side, fighting. They didn't really seem into it. They were only protecting themselves and some people around them. They weren't battling to their full abilities. I would have to deal with that later. I needed to make sure I survived this first. The King's League and Creed surrounded him, and nobody could get to him. That was what Lyric and I would do. My uncles were both fighting at our sides as our personal guard, at least according to Justise. We would make it to the king. That was our goal.

"Lyric, get down," I called out as a blade of Air came at her.

Instead of dropping, she levitated up, flying into the air and flipping before landing on her feet, her arms outstretched. Water flew from the pools on either side of us and slammed into the man who had tossed the deadly weapon directly at her chest.

I had never seen her do that before. In fact, I had only really seen Rhodes do something similar.

I had to remind myself that this was not the time to find it sexy as hell.

Oil slick again in my chest. I ignored it.

The Creed came at my uncles, their hands outstretched and in a formation of a dozen. They tried to throw their Wielding at Justise, and I screamed, knowing I would be too late. And not because it was just the Creed. No, the League had joined in. They had it out for Justise, and I didn't know why, other than the fact that he was my uncle and a trusted weapons maker and advisor. Maybe that was enough.

I wasn't close enough. I lashed out with my Fire, trying to flick at the edges of them with my flame. They shot it off, flipped it away as if it were a gnat. Lyric was at my side, her feet pounding on the ground as we ran toward my uncles.

I couldn't lose Justise. Not now. Not ever.

"We need to get closer," Lyric called, throwing out her arms and letting a wave of Water smash into the man who tried to get at me.

I hadn't even seen him, my gaze so focused on my uncle. I cursed at myself. I shook my head and kept running, grabbing Lyric's arm so we could move even faster.

The Creed and the League clung together, the Air Wielders puffing up the Water Wielders so they could surround my uncle.

That's when Ridley did the one thing I had hoped he wouldn't do.

He held out his arms, and using the Wielding everyone thought he didn't have, he shouted.

"Stay away from my husband!"

Ridley was not just a healer, wasn't a Dane.

No, Ridley was a Water Wielder.

As Water crept up from the ground below, from the reservoir that was the drinking water for this area, it slid up the legs of the Water and Air Wielders who had come after his husband. Like spindly fingers, it crawled and crept around their legs and tightened, sending screams out from the League and the Creed members who'd dared to come for Justise. It pulled them into the mud, and the Creed and the League clawed at the ground, trying to get up. It was no use. They were stuck, halfway in the earth, halfway in the air.

Either they would die there, or they would find a way out. I didn't have time to think about that. I had seen the way the king watched Ridley move, and I knew our secret was out. We'd had a secret Lumière this whole time.

The original spy for the Lumière, a once-trusted advisor for Brokk, and then the husband of the brother of Cameo.

The spy who had turned, switched sides to become one of us.

It was so long ago, that no one actually remembered. They'd all thought my uncle was a Dane.

He was not. Ridley was one of us, and yet not.

Justise cursed under his breath, slammed his mouth against his husband's lips, shouted at him, and then went back to fighting.

We were winning, each of us using our powers, one blow after another. Fire against Water, Earth against Air.

Lyric moved like a sprite, blending her elements as if she'd been born to do this. In a way, she had been.

I pushed out my Fire Wielding, and she merged her Air with it, creating a firestorm, flames that rained upon those who came after our friends.

As the first scream entered my ears, I knew I had been too confident.

Shimmer shrieked and looked down at her chest, blood seeping into her battle leathers. Griffin roared as Teagan burst into flames, Fire licking at his body as he burned alive the Air Wielder who had plunged that Air dagger into his mother's chest.

Blue Fire erupted all around them. I knew it was too late.

Shimmer fell into her husband's arms, and the Lady of Fire gasped her last strained breath.

She wasn't our first casualty. Wouldn't be our last.

One by one, my people fell as the sheer numbers overwhelmed us. Sweat covered my body, and Lyric tripped over her feet as her power cascaded over her body and the others began to fall back.

"We have to retreat," she whispered. "We won't be enough. We have to save our people."

I nodded, cupping her face for just an instant before turning around to pull the earth around the Water Wielder that had tried to sneak up from behind.

"We're so close," I whispered.

"Not close enough."

I nodded. Before I could shout out to retreat, gray smoke slithered around us, and my breath froze in my lungs.

This time, it wasn't the smoky ropes coming to pull me back. This smoke allowed a person to step out of it.

But it wasn't The Gray.

Instead, the King of Lumière slipped right behind Lyric. Before I could shout, before I could pull out my Wielding, before she could even turn, Lyric screamed.

I looked down at the tip of the metal dagger peeking out from her leathers. The king pulled the dagger back out from her where it had pierced her heart, and the shadow took him away again.

I coughed up blood and looked down at myself, at the cut on my chest as blood poured out of it.

Fated mates had mirrored wounds that would bleed just the same as the mortal wound on the original individual.

Lyric was dying, and the blood on my chest and pumping out of my body proved it. She fell into my arms, and I went to my knees as the Lumière's people began pulling back, and mine surrounded us.

I tried to cover her chest, to put pressure on the wound, except as I watched, blood seeped through my fingers. She looked at me, her wide eyes full of fear, blood dribbling from her lips. I knew this wasn't going to be enough.

And then I screamed.

CHAPTER 28

LYRIC

I knew if I lived past this, I would never forget the sound of Easton's scream. It was guttural, as if it had been ripped from his throat, and if I hadn't known the blood on his lips had already been there from before, I would've thought he'd hurt himself with that shout.

All of this had happened in an instant, and all I could do was try to clutch at his hand on my chest and attempt to stop the bleeding. To try and stop anything. It hurt. Everything hurt so much, and I couldn't breathe.

The king had stabbed me, and I only knew it was him because Easton has said his name.

I hadn't seen his face. Hadn't seen or heard him come up. I saw the smoke out of the corner of my eye, and then, suddenly, there was a blade in my chest. It didn't hurt at first, and then it burned and forged a fiery path through my flesh and into my organs.

I was dying.

Was this supposed to be what brought everybody together? My death?

What type of prophecy was that? One that called for my death and my end?

Maybe it was what needed to happen. Perhaps it was the only thing that would help.

"Don't you die, Lyric. You're not allowed to die," Easton said, blood dripping from his lips as he spoke. He coughed again, matching mine, and I could feel the warm blood pumping from the wound, draining from my body.

I looked down at his chest and tried to reach up, attempted to staunch the bleeding. I didn't have any energy. No strength.

He was dying. Just like I was.

His mortal wound matched mine, and I didn't know what to do. He was my soulmate. And we had everything but the bond of love that was supposed to bring us together. He was dying because I was. I knew if I faded into the darkness just like my parents had, like I had watched when the Spirit Wielders had held me back, Easton would die, as well. And I'd never forgive myself.

He wasn't supposed to die.

Others gathered around me, and I could feel Brae's fur on my cheek. And then she was gone, and I knew someone had likely moved her away. I didn't want her to see this. I didn't want *anyone* to see this. Ridley's hands were on my body, trying to heal me. I could only look into Easton's dark eyes.

"Don't die. Don't, I need you."

No words fell from my lips. I didn't have the strength to speak. I prayed he understood the words in my eyes, the ones I wanted to say.

My limbs were heavy as my lifeblood poured out of me.

I didn't want to die.

My death would bring others together. Shimmer had died, I'd heard her scream. She was gone. And I couldn't find Teagan, couldn't move my gaze away from Easton to make sure he was okay. I didn't know about Wyn or Rhodes or anyone else. Was this what the prophecy had wrought?

Had Rosamond Seen this?

Was this what had brought me here, all the way from that mountaintop in Colorado when I fell because the Neg had pulled me down?

And when Rosamond healed me because it hadn't been a mortal

blow, and I had been able to see what lay on the other side, was that all for this moment?

Easton had one hand on my chest, and then pulled my arm up so my hand rested on his wound.

"You can't die. Fight, Lyric. Fight."

I wanted to tell him that I was trying. It was all too much.

Yet wasn't enough.

The king was gone, as were the rest of the Lumière. Everyone was leaving, and I guessed I was going with them.

He was my soulmate, the one who held me, but The Gray had stolen him from me.

It seemed fitting that The Gray's puppet would be the one to steal me from him.

I wanted to fight, except metaphorical ice covered me. I felt so cold. Nothing even hurt anymore. I could no longer feel my blood leaking from my body.

Easton shouted at me, and I could hear the others moving around. I couldn't really process it, though, like I was three steps behind.

This was my end. My destiny.

I was going to die today, but maybe this meant a new beginning for others. I hoped so.

I didn't want to say goodbye.

However, in the end, I didn't even have the strength to try.

CHAPTER 29

EASTON

"No!"

I held my hand to her chest, the blood sliding through my fingers slowing.

"You must heal her, King," Ridley said, and my gaze shot to his. Ridley never called me *King*. I was always Easton or son. I was family. He looked so pale, so scared, that he reverted to being the healer to his king.

"I don't know what I'm doing. How the hell am I supposed to heal her? You're the healer. You do it."

Blood spurted from between my lips, and I used my free hand to wipe it from my face. There was still fighting going on around us, though the Lumière soldiers were retreating, going back to start on whatever else their king had planned.

What more could he do? He and The Gray had come together, and they were killing Lyric. My Lyric.

My heart pulsed, once, twice, and I tried to push out The Gray's ice.

She was dying in my hands. The hope for our world and so much more, fading.

She was Lyric. And she was mine. I would be damned if she died in my arms.

If she did, I would go right along with her. Because I might not be her soulmate, not in the ways that mattered, but I still had the wound on my chest.

I would pass with her. To the end. There would be no more living without her. No more hope. No more anything.

She was it. She was everything.

"I can't fix this. Why can't I fix this?"

I knew. Because I couldn't fix *anything*. My people were fading, my realm was faltering, and the woman I should love was dying in my arms. And I was perishing right along with her.

"You are her soulmate, damn it," Rhodes roared, pushing Teagan from my side. I hadn't even realized my best friend was kneeling next to me before I heard him cursing at Rhodes for daring to touch him. It didn't matter. Nothing mattered.

"I can't. I'm cursed." I tried to reach into my heart. Attempted to find something to tug on, to make this whole soulmate thing work. It wasn't happening. She wasn't mine in truth. She could never be.

"I watched her die before. I will not do it again."

I looked at Rhodes, gazed into those silver eyes, and I wanted to hate him. I wanted to make him pay for making me think any of this could be real. For letting me have hope.

"You couldn't feel it either. You aren't hers."

I snapped out the words, and Rhodes flinched as if I had struck him. Good. He should hurt like I did.

I knew my body was fading along with Lyric's. I knew I should be in pain, but I couldn't feel anything. I was numb, and I would be forever emotionless unless I could save her.

The damn Gray had taken everything from me. And now, he was going to take her from me, too. And when he did, he would rip away our realm, as well. I couldn't even think that far ahead. Not when all I wanted to do was think about Lyric and her smile. Her persistence. Her strength. Everything. She wasn't mine in all the ways that mattered, and she never would be. And it hurt.

"You're right, she wasn't mine. But she is yours. That wound is evidence of that. You are the king of the damn Obscurité. You have power.

So many people behind you. Use it. Use our strength. Break the curse. It's the only way to save her. It's the only way to save our realm. Do it. Do what I couldn't."

Rhodes' volume increased with each word, and by the end, he was yelling at me, his nose pressed almost to mine as he screamed.

I didn't know how to fix this.

However, I couldn't wallow either. Lyric deserved more than that. She was lying pale in my arms, no longer moving, her heartbeat so slow I could barely detect it.

"Save her, King," Rosamond said, standing behind Rhodes. She put her hand on his shoulder and pulled him back.

"You can do this," Wyn said, her face covered in blood. Thankfully, it wasn't hers. She stood near Teagan, who shook with rage.

Luken held Braelynn tightly as the little cat mewed and cried.

My uncles knelt beside me. And I could still barely feel anything.

I knew that Lanya was around, most likely helping our troops, and the Lord of Fire was doing something, probably grieving his wife. Teagan was by my side, even though his mother had died. He was *here*.

He was stronger than I was. I needed to do this. Not for myself, but for Lyric. For all of these people who needed us to be strong.

"I'm going to break the curse. I don't know how, though. The Gray had me in his clutches for so long, and I didn't even know."

"I can see the way you look at her," Wyn said softly.

"It couldn't mean anything before," I growled out.

"You love her," Rhodes whispered. "You will love her with everything you have, so pull on that. Use it. Screw what The Gray says. He doesn't get to win in this. He doesn't get to take her. Not now, not ever. The prophecy hasn't come to pass. She has to survive this. Meaning, you need to figure out how to break the curse and bring her back. She is your goddamn soulmate. Figure it out."

"I'm trying."

"Not hard enough. She wasn't mine. I wasn't good enough for her. Apparently, you are. Fate gave her to you. So, earn that gift. Do this."

I closed my eyes and focused on her. Concentrated on everything that she was to me, or what I needed her to be for me. What she was for everyone else.

I focused on what she deserved. While I might not think that was me, she deserved to live. And I would spend the rest of my days making sure she understood that. That she was worthy of so much more than the life she had been given. I refused to let her fall into the abyss of death. And even as I thought that, the oil slick feeling came over my heart again and started to ice. I growled, anger pulsing through me.

I closed my eyes, my hand still on Lyric's chest even as Ridley began to work again. There was only so much a healer could do in this situation, and I knew he wouldn't be enough. Not alone. Not when he had used so much of his power to save his husband. He had shown the world his true powers, and there would definitely be a price to pay for that. And if I survived this, if we all survived this, I would make sure nobody looked down on him for his birth. He had chosen Justise, just like I was choosing Lyric.

She deserved more than a half-life, she deserved so much more. So, I focused on that oil slick, and then I let the Fire within me burn. I used my Earth Wielding to ground me as I slid Fire Wielding through my body. I screamed, my skin glowing red-hot as people murmured and shouted around me.

Everyone scrambled away, and I knew the Fire had encircled us. It didn't matter.

Lyric would survive this, and with any luck, I would get to watch her shine.

I used my Fire Wielding to burn away that oil slick, heated it up so it could slide away and never come back.

And then I pulsed my Wielding through my hand and through her chest.

She gasped in my arms, her back arching, and I shouted, the pain so intense that tears slid from my eyes. I knew I would have a scar on my chest, just like the one on my side.

I would kill the king for this. I would murder him, and I would enjoy it.

Before I could do any of that, though, Lyric needed to breathe.

I did what I knew was natural, even if I didn't know why. I healed.

The first gasp of her breath shocked me to my core, and I shook, the flames brightening around us as Earth trembled beneath us.

She was healing. I could feel her cells warming, her skin knitting itself back together even as I felt my wound painfully closing, as well.

She would live, she would be whole, and she would survive.

Even as the oil slick burned away, sending ash out my nostrils and my pores, I knew I wasn't done.

She needed to be whole, had to heal. The King of Lumière had struck her through the heart, severing arteries and doing so much damage, I didn't know if I would be enough.

This was what soulmates were all about, though. They could heal mortal wounds.

I screamed, Fire erupting from my pores, something it had never done before. It didn't hurt, it didn't burn. Instead, I felt like I was being tugged and ripped open from the inside.

And, just like that, something snapped.

The curse was gone. I knew it. I felt it to the deepest part of my soul.

As I looked down at Lyric, her brown eyes wide, and her mouth open on an endless scream, I felt it.

The bond clicked into place as if it had always been there, just waiting for The Gray to be purged from my body.

I heard a scream in the distance as if covered in shadow, and I knew it was *him*. He knew, and I was glad. He knew he had lost this round. I could love. I could feel. I could *be*.

Good.

Lyric's eyes widened even more, and I leaned down, pressing my forehead to hers as a cord wrapped around my heart and connected with hers, tugging tightly. An irrevocable bond that could never be broken, not even by the worst treachery, magic, or soullessness.

Lyric was mine, forever.

I would burn the world to save her.

Everything that had been hidden within me burst inside, slamming into my mind, my ribcage...everywhere.

I loved her.

Lyric.

The girl who could save the world.

The girl who had saved *me*.

I. Loved. Her.

She was my forever, more so than even this realm, more so than the throne I sat upon.

She was mine.

And she was healed.

The others murmured, saying things that might have been important. I couldn't care. I didn't notice.

I only had eyes for Lyric, and she was breathing. She was whole, and she was mine.

Forever.

CHAPTER 30

LYRIC

Had we won? No, I didn't think we had. Could you call it winning when the world felt as if it had crumbled? When people had died? When *I* had nearly died?

No, I didn't think we could call it a victory. However, we could call it life. And the fact that we were here, those who had survived anyway, and we would live to fight another day was something to celebrate.

It was still hard to think of this as a true victory even though those that I loved and cared about were alive—at least most of them.

I sat in one of the chairs in the throne room, tired and yet energized. I knew that it came from the magic swirling inside me, thanks to Easton. I would think more on that later.

First, I needed to look at those around me and see what I could do.

There was pain, so much of it, and I wasn't sure we would be able to truly heal until we defeated the king.

Perhaps even The Gray.

And after what I had just witnessed, I wasn't sure we could do it. Not yet. I had five elements, and I still hadn't been enough.

I had almost died, and it had taken Easton to save me.

I didn't like that.

I needed to be able to save myself. I had to protect those I loved. That was just one more thing we needed to work on.

One more thing.

I turned to the right and looked at Teagan, who paced the room, looking down at his hands, not talking to anyone.

I wasn't sure anyone would be able to break through his barriers at the moment and speak to him.

He looked to be in so much pain, and yet he was stoic at the same time. As if he had nothing to say. Because what was there to say?

His mother had fought for all of us, had used her Fire Wielding in a way I had never witnessed before. I wasn't even sure I could do it, even with enough practice and training. Then, she had died. Because of the king. Because we hadn't been strong enough to save her.

Teagan's father had retired to his room to heal in more ways than one. I knew the man must be grieving terribly after losing his wife, his soulmate. Teagan had mentioned once that they had been together for hundreds of years, had weathered war and famine and betrayal by others. Through it all, they had each other.

It killed me that there was nothing I could do. Nothing would make this better for them or bring her back.

Shimmer had died to protect this realm, to save her son, to help all of us. There was no coming back from that.

I turned away from Teagan, knowing he needed privacy, even in a room with no corners to hide in. Instead, I looked at Wyn, who just stared at Teagan, her gaze distant.

Wyn had changed out of her battle clothes just like the rest of us had, though no one had really taken a full shower or bath. Instead, we simply wiped off the blood, healed our bruises as much as we could, and then came to talk about what we needed to do.

Wyn's wet hair had been braided back from her face, and she finally pulled her gaze from Teagan, looking down at the sword in her hand.

I wanted to reach out and tell her that we would fix this. That we would find her Wielding again and that everything would be okay. But that was a lie, at least right now, and I didn't want to promise things we couldn't deliver.

I didn't know how to bring back her Wielding. All I had been doing so far was making sure we didn't let the crystals fail any more than they already had.

If they didn't fade any more, that meant that no one else would lose their Wielding.

What would happen to those who had already lost everything, though?

I didn't know. And that's why I couldn't talk to Wyn. I would be here for her if she needed me, but I didn't think she did. I didn't know what she needed or what Teagan needed to pull himself together...I didn't believe any of us knew what the next steps would be.

"I can hear them out there," Easton said, pacing in front of me.

He looked at me then, his dark eyes boring into mine before he turned away. We needed to talk, had to discuss what had happened. But not right now.

The kingdom needed us. Later, we would deal with the fact that the curse was gone, and I could feel the bond pulsing between us even now.

"They want answers," I said, and Easton gave me a sharp look. It wasn't anger, though. Maybe it was helplessness. That's what I felt, after all: helpless.

"I don't have any answers to give them. They're going to revolt because they don't know who to trust. They're dying, and our court is losing, and it's hard to want to follow a king that can't win."

"That's bullshit, and you know it," Justise snapped from his chair on the other side of the room. He had one leg elevated, and a bandage on his head. Ridley sat next to his husband, not speaking.

Ridley had done his best to heal everybody. We all knew that he wasn't just a healer. Wasn't a Dane.

No, he was a former Lumière member, a Water Wielder. He had been hidden in plain sight for so long that nobody remembered he hadn't been born here.

I didn't know what would happen to him. In the end, it wouldn't really matter.

We kept telling each other that it wasn't Lumière versus Obscurité anymore. It was those against The Gray, and those who didn't want the realm to heal all the way.

Honestly, I didn't think a single person in this room would judge Ridley for the choices he made. Actually, it almost seemed like a perfect love story.

I didn't know what anyone else thought, though. All I knew was that Ridley had sacrificed everything for Justise. And, most likely, Justise had done the same for his husband.

I was honored to know Ridley. And the fact that we had such a strong Water Wielder on our side could only mean good things.

"What do you mean?" Easton asked, his voice a growl.

"They know the power that you Wield. And everything that you have done for them. They're scared, yes. You go out there day after day to make sure that they can see your face. Just like the rest of us."

I still had a hard time knowing what to say. I hadn't been here long enough to truly feel like I could be of help. I was just a vessel, even though I didn't know what I'd be used for in the end.

Justise continued. "Add the fact that you and Lyric are together? It will help. It would also help bring other people on the Lumière's side, scared of what their king has become, to want to come over here."

My gaze shot up, my eyes going wide. "Excuse me?" I didn't care that Justise was speaking to Easton at the moment. I didn't like where this conversation was headed.

"We all felt it, the bond between you. The curse is broken."

Silence. Utter silence. It glided over my skin, and I held my breath.

"Yes," Easton growled out. "However, that's something that Lyric and I need to talk about in private later. First, we have to discuss the war."

"Your bonding is part of that," Justise countered.

"How?" I asked.

Easton stood near the side of my chair, but we didn't touch. I could feel him. He was mine, and I would do anything to protect him.

I didn't know how I felt about that yet.

"You have always been the symbol," Rosamond answered instead. "And now, with the two of you together, you will be stronger than ever."

"It'll help," Rhodes put in, and I held back a wince.

"It'll help what?" I asked.

Rhodes just looked at me, those silver eyes narrowing on me. "You're not Obscurité, not Lumière. Now, you are bonded to the King of Obscurité. It will help those who have always believed in the prophecy. Those who want The Gray gone, even if they don't know that The Gray exists. Those who want to realign the crystals and help our dying factions. I'm not saying they'll become Obscurité. They will see reason. And you being Easton's mate and the future queen will help that."

There was no bitterness to his tone, no anger there. I was grateful. Rhodes had never loved me, and I had never loved him. We had just thought there was a connection between us until we realized that there hadn't been.

"I'm not the Queen of Obscurité," I said, and Easton reached out and squeezed my shoulder. I didn't want to hurt him. It just needed to be said.

"You're with the king, it sort of makes sense," Emory said. I looked over, having forgotten she was even there.

She stood by Rosamond and Rhodes, her hands clasped in front of her.

She had nowhere else to go, so she was with us.

She had helped bandage and clean wounds. She hadn't been on the battlefield. But she had been there for the aftermath.

And that was healing. At least I hoped it was.

"No, I can't be the queen of a kingdom when I'm also the Spirit Priestess."

There was silence, and Easton squeezed my arm again. I reached out to grip his fingers. He didn't pull away, and I breathed out a sigh of relief.

"She's right. And we'll deal with titles and all of that crap later. First, we need to have a realm or even a kingdom to rule."

I didn't know what that meant. Would he step down? Abdicate? I didn't know. It didn't matter then. And, he was right.

First, we needed to protect our people. And to do that, we needed a plan.

We needed rest.

"We'll regroup after we rest. After we sleep and try to figure out what to do. We healed who we could, and next, we'll formulate a plan." I looked over at Teagan. "With your father, if he can."

"He'll want revenge, will want to tear out the throat of anyone who dared to hurt his wife. To take her from us." Teagan swallowed hard.

It was Luken who came over with Braelynn on his shoulder. Teagan leaned into the other man, and Braelynn hopped over onto Teagan's shoulder, nuzzling his cheek.

I didn't say anything because there wasn't really anything to say.

So much damage. And I didn't know if we had anything to show for our losses.

It didn't matter that the longing for Easton pulsed inside of me.

Didn't matter that I was finally bonded to the one person I could love more than anything—except perhaps my purpose. I'd never been given the chance to wonder.

We had lost too much.

And I didn't know what to do or say.

Instead, we said our goodbyes, promised we would meet in the morning, that we'd have another summit with the lords and ladies who were left, and then we would go and try to win.

I followed Easton to his room, not even bothering to go to mine.

I didn't know what would happen. I just needed to think, and even though it was sometimes hard to think with him around, I knew that wasn't going to be the case tonight.

Easton closed the door behind me as we walked into his room, and suddenly, I was nervous. I didn't know why. I had slept in this room before. I had slept near him before.

I had touched him and held him. Kissed him. But now, it was different.

There wasn't anything pulling him back. He was here. I could feel him in my heart, in my soul, with every breath I took, and in all that I was.

And I was nervous.

"I should have said this before…but I didn't know how." I turned to look at Easton and swallowed hard. He looked so different. As if a weight had been lifted off his shoulders, even though I knew the literal weight of the world rested on them just as it rested on mine.

It didn't matter, because he was mine. And I didn't know what I would do if I lost him. Just like he had almost lost me.

"What? What should you have said?"

He took two steps forward, and then he was there, his heat against me as he cupped my face.

He slowly lowered his head, his nose brushing along mine as he exhaled a breath that sent shockwaves through my body. As if he had so much riding on him, that he couldn't even formulate words. Now we could rest. Just *be*.

Because, in this room, right now, he wasn't the King of Obscurité, and I wasn't the Spirit Priestess.

We were just Easton and Lyric.

"I love you, Lyric. And I'm sorry I couldn't say it before. I'm sorry that it took so long for me to say the words. I couldn't feel them. I knew it was there, but I couldn't reconcile it. I love you, Lyric. And I will fight to the end of the world to keep you happy, to keep you whole. I don't know what I did in my life to deserve you. But I will make sure that no matter what, no matter who comes at us, I will prove myself to you. Through the depths of the world and even to the end of it. Even if that may never be the case."

I blinked through my tears, wondering if this was all a dream. Maybe I had died on that battlefield, and he wasn't really here, saying these words. When he slid his thumb under my eye, wiping the tears away, I let out a shuddering breath.

"You're real," I whispered, my voice shaky. He smirked at me, and then I knew this was real. Because that smirk did funny things to me. I could only smile back at him. I didn't want this to end, I didn't want to go back to the real world and have to think about what we needed to do to save it. I wanted to make this moment last forever. And even though I knew it couldn't, I could at least pretend. For a little while. And Easton would let me pretend. He would give me this moment. And I would do everything in my power to make sure he shared this moment.

"I love you," I whispered. "I didn't think I would ever actually be able to say that to you," I said, a watery smile on my face.

Easton lowered his head and brushed his lips against mine. Before I could deepen the kiss, he pulled away.

"I could kill The Gray for not letting me have this moment before now. For making me wait."

I shook my head.

"No. You can want to kill him for many things...but this moment? Let's just keep it between us. Okay?"

He nodded, and then he kissed me again, this time a little deeper, a bit sweeter, and then harder before he pulled away again.

"We don't have to do anything tonight, Lyric. We can just sleep and rest like we need to."

I opened my mouth to say something when he spoke again.

"Although, of course, I wouldn't mind doing something more."

There it was again, that smirk. I loved it so much.

"Oh?"

"It's just you and me. And I'm okay. I'm ready."

"Are you sure?"

"For you? Always."

And then there were no words. He kissed me, and I sank into him, wanting more. His hands cupped my face and then slid down my shoulders. When I leaned into him, craving him, knowing that this was us, our future—even if we only had a few more days left—I knew I would never regret this.

He made me feel wanted, loved, needed. And when we held each other in the aftermath, I clutched him tightly, never wanting to let him go.

He just kept whispering my name, saying that he loved me, and I wiped the tears from his cheeks.

Because what we were doing, what we were feeling, wasn't only about this moment or what we had just done.

No, it was about the fact that The Gray had taken something from him. Yet, somehow, we had found it. Together.

And even if I died tomorrow to protect the realm I loved, I knew I would never regret this moment. I'd never forget it.

Because life was short. And while the world tried to take everything, they couldn't take this. Not again. No matter what. Because Easton was mine, and I was his, and we would face the horrors of the world together.

And the worth of what we could lose was one thing I had learned about the pain and the heartache and loss that we both shared.

The one thing I would never forget.

CHAPTER 31

LYRIC

Even though it felt like my whole life had changed, I couldn't dwell on it. Because now I had to sit through another meeting and formulate more plans.

I'd never thought to be involved in battles or part of battle strategy. It wasn't something I had studied in school or was even taught by tutors like everyone else in the room.

Emory hadn't been taught either, but we were on a crash course to learn.

Even Brae looked confused with her little furry face, and I hoped that we could play catch-up.

Because everyone else had decades' worth of experience in fighting the Lumière, and I was just trying to keep up.

I did not appreciate the fact that everyone kept looking to me for answers. All I knew was that I somehow needed to use all five elements to fuse the crystals together. That meant I had to get them in the same room. Right?

In order to do that, we had to get the king on our side.

Or kill him.

I hated that that thought came so quickly to my mind. As if killing someone, taking their soul straight from their body, was something normal. Maybe it was for everybody else. It surely wasn't for me.

"Are you okay?" Easton murmured out of the side of his mouth, and I looked at him and nodded.

I knew a blush stained my cheeks when I looked at him and hated the fact that it did.

Not that I blushed at the thought of him, more that everyone else could see it. They would know what we had done last night. Not that I was ashamed of it. Not in the slightest. However, I needed time to process it and wonder if we would actually have a future together. Because while I knew that we might be soulmates, I didn't know if there was a future there.

And that was why we needed this meeting. We had to ensure that we would survive.

"We'll have to meet him on the battlefield again. This time, we'll have more Water and Air Wielders with us," Lanya said, looking down at the map of the two kingdoms that someone had spread over the long table where we had eaten the night before.

I could see the divisions of the territories, the mountain ranges, even the red rocks that we had gone to when I first met Easton.

All of it was on a map, with little toy pieces on top to represent the armies.

It wouldn't be as easy as taking out a little symbols, knocking it over.

No, we would have to use our strength and what numbers we had to kill him.

To take the shards and destroy them.

In reality, that would mean lives, not just wood.

"There are already defectors crossing the border," Justise said, moving more pieces around.

Easton crossed his arms over his chest, nodding as he studied the map, and I did the same.

I needed to memorize every inch of this map, and I was exhausted already trying to do it. Because not only was I attempting to learn every single bit of terrain, I was reading the histories of the people that Rosamond had given me, trying to catch up and understand all of the underlying tensions between the factions, who might be our allies, and who would forever be lost.

Slavik was in the back of my mind. I had hoped that the pirate king would be on our side if we called to him. We couldn't find him at the moment. I just hoped to hell that he wasn't already on our opposing side.

With his second in command out of the way, he would be a good ally if we could secure him. Even if he didn't always follow the rules and thought of himself as a ruler in his own right, he had the strength of numbers, and power that was quite startling. We already had feelers out, people searching for him.

I just didn't know if we would find him in time.

Didn't know if it would be enough.

"That means that there's probably people on our side going to their side, too, right?" Emory asked, and we all looked at her. She shrugged, her head down. "I'm just saying. There's probably Fire and Earth Wielders, and even Danes who would prefer The Gray in power. Maybe he promised them something? Like their own power if they fought with him."

"You're right," Easton said, surprisingly. He didn't like Emory, for many reasons. And not only because she was my ex. She hadn't been a good person. But she had suffered enough. And she was learning. Kind of even helping.

I was trying to do the same.

"We have men and women out there searching for the defectors. Both sides?" Easton asked, and Justise nodded.

"Yes, we're bringing in those who were formerly Lumière."

"Good," I added. "And we'll make sure that they're actually going to fight with us and that they're not spies?"

Ridley winced, and I covered my face with my hands. "Sorry. I didn't mean it like that."

"No, it's fine. We all know that I used to be a spy. Things didn't work out well for the Lumière king."

It was the first time that Ridley had ever announced openly that he had been a spy. I wasn't sure what more there was to say about that. Every single person in this room had fought with him over the years.

They trusted him. And so did I.

Love changed a lot of things, even though I'd never thought that was possible. I used to think it was a myth, a ruse. I had been wrong.

So wrong.

"Yes, we're checking for that," Lanya said. "As much as we can anyway. They won't be in the inner circle. They are people that I know and trust. And those that I don't, the ones I'm not quite sure of, we'll have those who we *do* trust watching over them. It's not an ideal situation with so many borders being crossed, but it's the best that we have at the moment."

"Well, our numbers are increasing, even though some are leaving."

I looked at Easton. "People will follow you. You don't want total control. You just want to save the kingdoms."

"And that's what the King of Lumière is promising. That if you give him full control, he'll bring the kingdoms back together."

"And he says that the answer is slaughtering this entire side," Rhodes snapped. And then he pinched the bridge of his nose, letting out a breath. "Sorry. I'm a little pissed off right now."

"We all are," Easton said, not sounding worried in the least. "You're welcome to go punch something or go use your Air Wielding and make something break if you'd like. There's a whole courtyard out there that we use for temper tantrums."

"A temper tantrum?"

"Boys," Lanya said, her voice stern and sounding more like a mother or even a grandmother than I'd heard from her before. "Not now."

"Sorry," the King of Obscurité and the former Lumière prince said at the same time.

My lips threatened to quirk, only Wyn shook her head, her lips twitching, as well.

No, now would not be a good time to laugh. Though there wasn't much levity these days, so maybe that's exactly what we needed.

"Is your father going to join us?" Easton asked Teagan, who nodded tightly.

"He's mourning. He'll be out of his room soon and will help with strategy. He just needs a moment or two."

"I won't hold that against him," Easton said.

"I wouldn't hold it against him if he needed time away from the battle," I said, frowning. "Though I really hope he doesn't need that much time."

"He wants revenge. Wants the king's head on a platter. So, no, he won't stand back. He's just so angry right now, he could burn down this whole throne room. So, he's meditating with some techniques that Ridley taught him."

"I'll go check on him soon and make sure he's okay," Ridley added, then we all started talking battle strategy again.

Every single person in the room was trying to help us win. It was apparent that one couple was not here. One who had vowed to fight with us. They had left the battlefield mid-skirmish.

And when the door opened, I hoped it would be them, finally coming in to help us with battle plans, and to fight on our side. It wasn't.

Instead, it was a courier with a note in hand. Dread filled my belly.

"Sire, I have a note for Rhodes."

Rhodes' brow shot up, and Easton looked at the other man.

"Well, open it," Easton said.

Rhodes went to the courier, nodded in thanks, and took the note.

Then he crumpled it in his hands. His Air Wielding spiraled around his hair, the water in the goblets in front of us moving in their cups.

"Tone it down," Luken whispered, taking the note from the other man's hand.

"They're gone," Rhodes barked. "The Lord and Lady of Dirt have left. They didn't say where." A pause. "But, they called in their favor."

He looked directly at me, and my hopes sank.

"Their boon? They called it in? What does that mean?"

"That we can't outright kill them. They're leaving. And I have a feeling they're not going back to their estate."

Wyn let out a pained sound and then turned, her arms folded over her chest as she faced the window. Teagan moved forward and put his hand on her shoulder. She shrugged it off.

Her parents were now traitors, and we all knew it.

And Rhodes and I couldn't be the ones to take vengeance on them because of what we'd promised them.

"Fine," Easton snapped. "There's more than just the two of you in this room. We'll take care of it when we see them next." He looked over at Wyn for a moment and then turned back to the map in front of us.

There was no use trying to console Wyn then.

Everything had been taken from her—her Wielding, and now her family.

She was with us, and she was fighting.

And that counted for so much.

It had to.

The door opened again, and that same courier came in, his eyes wide. "Sire, there's someone here to see you. We didn't know exactly who she was until it was too late."

Everyone went on alert, my Wielding at the ready as I looked at the door. I gasped as I saw who walked through.

Delphine, Queen of Lumière, strode in, her chin high. I could see the pain and unsteadiness beneath the mask. This woman was moving on fumes and pretense.

"I know I'm the last person you expected to see," she paused. A small smile played on her face, even though it didn't reach her eyes. "Okay, perhaps not the last, but likely close."

"Aunt Delphine, what are you doing here?" Rhodes asked. It was Rosamond who answered.

"You defected. I didn't see that coming."

"No, you wouldn't. Because I didn't know if I was really going to make the decision until I was already making it. I'm sorry I couldn't give you a heads up. My heart barely let me know."

I stood there, transfixed. "Defected. You've left the Lumière?"

She nodded tightly. "Yes. I can't watch what my husband is doing. What he's already done. I know I haven't been the best queen—he stripped my power within the kingdom long ago. I only had my Wielding. Even then, I could never Wield with him near me." She held up her hands and pulled back her sleeves. Bruises shone on her wrists. She had always worn long sleeves. Now, I knew why.

"He bound your powers," Easton growled. "The queen?"

"Yes, I took the shackles off. It weakened me. I need a couple of days. Hopefully, we have that much time. I'll be able to fight. I can't stand what he's doing to the kingdom, and I'm sorry I wasn't strong enough to help before." She looked at Lanya. "I'm sorry I wasn't there to help your daughter." She looked at Rhodes and Rosamond. "Your mother. I'm here now. My son has chosen his side." Tears filled her eyes. She blinked them away, looking more royal than I had ever seen her.

"Eitri is going to fight with his father, then?" Easton said, and she nodded. "Okay."

Her eyes widened fractionally. Then she returned to her cool composure. "You may do whatever tests you need to ensure that I'm not lying. I'm here to help." She pulled out a rolled paper from her robes and looked down at it. "This is all I could take. Nothing else. It's some of his strategy. Not all." She looked at me, hope in her eyes. "He doesn't know the true prophecy. He claims he does, but I know for a fact he's never heard it. Not even The Gray has."

"You've seen him?" Easton asked.

She gave a tight nod. "He's the one who helped my husband bind me. He only comes in shadows. He comes more often than usual lately, though. Ever since the king's brother died." She looked at Rhodes and Rosamond, and then turned back to us. "I'll do what I can, I'll fight by your side. I'm only sorry it took me so long."

Ridley was at her side then because it looked as if she had been deflated, her whole body sagging.

I didn't know what to say because it wasn't my place. I was only the one who was supposed to save the world, not rule it.

"Thank you," Easton said. "We'll take what you have, and we'll see what we can use. My uncle will go and help you rest. Heal up. Because we're going to fight. And we're going to need all the help we can get."

FROM SPIRIT AND BINDING

Warmth spread through me, and I reached out, gripping Easton's hand. He squeezed. There was no more time for hope or for anything else.

Instead, we needed to focus on what was in front of us.

The battle to come.

I wanted to believe in hope, so maybe I would hide it, but first...the truth of technicalities.

Later, when Easton went off to talk with the Lord of Fire and Teagan, I went back to my rooms, though not the ones I had slept in the night before.

I needed to wash my face and calm down. My head felt too full. I still had books to read. Knowledge to gather.

As soon as I tried to close the door, a hand stopped it, and I went on high alert. When I realized who it was, I took a step back as Wyn, Rosamond, Brae, and Emory in her cuffs walked into the room.

"What's wrong?" I asked.

"Maybe nothing," Wyn said, giving me a hug.

"We just wanted to check on you after last night," Rosamond said, taking a seat on the bed and looking through the book she had handed me.

"Oh."

Emory winked at me, then took a seat in the corner. She wasn't really part of the group, yet still in the room.

"You know?"

"Of course, we know," Wyn said, smiling. "You can see it all over your face. And Easton's, too. Even though we're all stressed out and worried and haven't been sleeping because we're trying to get this battle thing done, he looked relaxed. Not as high-strung as usual. You want to talk about it?" Wyn asked, and I shook my head even as Brae jumped into my arms. I scritched behind her ears, and then on her back between her wings.

"Well, you should," another voice said as a woman walked into the room.

I turned, and Brae spat fire. Alura just knocked it away, a small smile on her face.

"Alura?" I asked, and she smiled.

"I'm sorry it took me so long to get here. It took a while to get through the borders, and to ensure that those who were defecting from the Lumière had a path to get here."

"I knew we would see you again," Rosamond said, holding the other woman close.

I looked down at the bracelet on my wrist that had been so silent recently, and then back up at the other woman.

"Did you know I would need this?" I asked, shaking the bracelet a bit.

"Rosamond did, so I made sure you had it. Although you're right where you need to be, and with the borders fading as they are, it won't be much use to you now. It needed to get you to certain places at certain times. Now, it's merely there as a talisman. To remind you of where you came from, and where you need to go."

I looked down at the bracelet and nodded. "Okay, I can work with that."

"Since you're here, we were going to talk about what happened between Easton and Lyric last night," Wyn said, looking through the books with Rosamond.

"I never agreed to that," I said, blushing hard.

"Ah, so you've finally been with our king?"

"Maybe. I don't really need to talk about it. Everything's fine. He was nice. Gentle. And I really don't want to talk about it with you guys."

"Well, if you do, we're here."

"There's something I need to ask, though," Wyn said, and I looked over at her.

"Okay," I whispered.

"Did you guys do anything special?" she asked. My brows went straight up, blush staining my cheeks.

"Um, what on earth do you mean by that?" I asked, laughing nervously.

"Oh, I don't know, it could be the fact that I'm pretty sure that sleeping with Easton might have powered up the crystal."

I stared at her, confused, and so did the others.

Then Wyn stood up, stretched out her hands, and the earth shook around us.

"Your Wielding!"

"Yep. Apparently, sex magic is the thing."

"It is not," I said, putting my hand over her mouth.

"No, but I do think that the two of you together is powerful. The crystal clearly healed, at least a bit."

"That's not going to be how she heals the crystal completely," Rosamond said. And then she looked over at me. "But it is a nice touch."

"And, that's not all," Wyn said, and then she went over to the water basin and hovered her hand over it. Water slipped out, wrapping around her wrist before splashing back. She looked at us then, and I froze, my mouth gaping.

"Yeah, that was pretty much my reaction. I have no idea how to Wield Water. I've never had it before. It seems the crystal wanted me to have it. Now, somehow, I'm a dual Wielder, something I've never been. I have a touch of Lumière, and a touch of Obscurité. So, thank you. And maybe I should thank Easton, too. Because I am going to need a drink. Lots, and lots of wine."

"I think…I think I could use some wine, too," I said.

"Okay, that much I can help with," Alura said and then left the room, presumably to get some wine. Or food.

Something had happened last night. Something that had helped the crystal. I knew that sleeping with Easton wasn't the reason. No, it had been the power that flowed through me, the fact that I had felt closer to the five elements within my body because I trusted the person I was with.

So, sleeping with Easton wasn't going to save the world. Even as I thought it, my mouth quirked into a smile. I knew that everyone else knew what I was thinking.

If only that had been the answer. If it were, I would have gladly fallen into that outcome.

No, we would have to fight, blood would be spilled, and we would win.

For the moment, however, I would sit with my friends and talk about the things that I was supposed to talk about with girlfriends if I hadn't crossed the veil into this realm.

If I weren't the Spirit Priestess.

All those ifs.

One day, I would figure out what to do next.

CHAPTER 32

LYRIC

After all of our careful planning, all of our sleepless nights, and poring over maps and figures and trying to find out exactly how many people we had on our side now, we decided to take things on the offensive.

I had to pray it would work.

There would be no more trying to meet in so-called neutral territory. There would be no more hoping that the King of Lumière would see reason.

Though he hadn't been the true King of Lumière for a while. He had been a puppet of The Gray, something that could not stand. Not if we wanted our kingdoms to stay whole.

So, as I cinched the armor at my side, I looked over at Easton and tried to breathe.

"We're going to be fine," he growled out, and I had a feeling it had nothing to do with me. I didn't blame him for his frustration.

Dark circles shadowed his eyes, and I knew he hadn't been sleeping. The two of us had tried to take naps when we could, but there was no time for that. There was constant battle planning, and when we weren't doing that, we were making sure that we were trained, that our supplies were ready, and that those who couldn't fight were protected.

The wards could only protect so much, especially when the strong fighters would be on the defensive at the Lumière castle.

"Are you ready?" I asked, sliding my hands down the leather of my top, hoping it would stay. I wasn't used to fighting in this, and while my range of motion was still good, it wasn't perfect.

Easton came forward and put his hand directly over my heart. I blushed. He wasn't making contact just to be close. No, he was touching me where the tip of the knife had protruded from my chest, where it had pierced my heart, and he'd had to save me.

"I want you to wear like eight layers of this," he growled.

I raised a brow and then put my hand over his, giving it a squeeze before moving my hand to his chest.

"Then you should do the same."

"And then neither of us would be able to move our arms to Wield."

"Pretty much. We'll get to where we need to be."

"We'll have to make it work. I wish I could just lock you in here and make you safe."

He lowered his head and kissed me softly. I sighed before taking a step back. There was no time for that now. Only time for war and death. Something I'd never thought to say or think.

"You can't lock me up. Because I can't do the same to you."

"That just means I'll have your back like you'll have mine the whole trip. The entire fight."

"You don't even have to ask."

"I wish there was more time."

"There's never enough time. We're going to survive this. We have to believe that."

"I just don't know if everybody will. We've yet to come out of a battle unscathed. And I never want to see death in your eyes again. I never want to see my uncle scream because his husband is dying. I never want to see that look on Teagan's face because someone he loves is dead. I want none of that. However, I don't think we're going to have a choice. This is our life now. Or perhaps it's always been. After all, we were born into this."

"We'll make it through. We have to. Because if I think about any other outcome, then I won't leave this room. And I sure as hell won't let you leave."

"We'll survive. Because I'm not letting The Gray or the king or anyone else take you. If they try, I'll slice their heads from their necks, and I'll follow you into oblivion."

I looked at him then and shook my head.

"You're not allowed to die for me."

"I can say the same for you."

There was a knock at the door, and suddenly Wyn was there, her battle leathers on, and a sword on her back.

"Are you two ready?" she asked, and we nodded.

Easton frowned. "You never bring a sword to battle."

She shrugged and looked down at her hands.

"My Earth Wielding is as strong as ever, but I don't understand the Water in my veins. I don't know if I can trust it. Plus, what if this is only a temporary thing? What if I'm fighting and suddenly…it's gone again?" She shuddered, her face going pale. I didn't reach out to her, neither did Easton. She didn't want that.

And I didn't blame her.

She needed space. I knew Wyn well enough now that I knew she needed a fight to work through whatever she was thinking. And we would give that to her.

"I understand." Easton sighed. "We're going to fix this."

"Well, some of it might already be fixed."

"Then I guess we should go," I said, tugging at the bottom of my pleated leather top.

"Yes, let's get this over with."

Easton kissed me hard and then went to Wyn and kissed her on the cheek. And then, we were off.

Off to hopefully not die, to win this if we were lucky. Because if we could take the crystal, maybe I could use my elements to combine them.

I just didn't know if that would be enough.

However, if I kept thinking like that, it wouldn't be enough. We had to be stronger than this. So, I would be.

No matter what.

"We are going to survive this," Easton said to me as we made our way to the others.

We were going to use the crystal one last time to get through the wards and to where we needed to go.

Because the wards were so thin between the two courts, I wouldn't really have to use any of the crystal's power. Instead, it would be my power, along with that of the Lumière and the Obscurité to get us where we needed to go.

The crystal would only be the vessel. Hopefully, we would be able to leave some power behind when we did so.

Not enough to strip us of our own powers if we attached ourselves to the crystal for too long.

"We will," Rhodes said, coming up to Easton. He held out his arm in the way of a warrior, and Easton looked down at it for a bare fraction before gripping Rhodes' forearm and squeezing it.

"I trust you by my side, always," Easton said, and a hush filled the room.

I swallowed hard and looked over at the others. I knew that some of us were trying not to say goodbye, even though we were doing it.

We were going to fight, and I hoped to hell that we would win. Or, at the very least, survive.

"We must begin. If we don't, we'll be too late. It'll be too late for everything," Rosamond said, shaking her head. Her grandmother was there, rubbing Rosamond's temples, and then she kissed the top of her granddaughter's head.

We were ready to begin.

I closed my eyes as I stood by the crystal, and the others stood near me. Those of our inner circle tucked in close, including Lanya and Teagan's father.

The Lord and Lady of Earth were gone, but the Lord of Fire and the Lady of Air were with us. As was the Queen of Lumière, though I was sure she had lost her title by now. Regardless, she was still royalty, still a fierce fighter even if she had been forced to hide it for so long. Delphine was ready, and I wanted to trust her, wanted to believe that she wouldn't betray us. I knew that Lanya would be watching the other woman the entire time, but we had to trust a little. If we didn't, then no one would be on our side when we fought the enemy.

So, I pushed all those thoughts out of my head and tried not to think about the fact that I was going to bring hundreds of people through the crystal to the wards. Not just those in this room either, the people in the court, ready to fight. All forms of Wielders were ready to come to our side, ready to be a part of this, and I had to bring everybody through the crystal and the thin wards.

The magical barriers that were so translucent at this point, you could see the other castle far in the distance if you looked really hard on a sunny day.

The realm was fracturing, the kingdoms were crumbling, and we were running out of time.

So, I closed my eyes and thought of the crystal. I thought of the light crystal in the Lumière Kingdom and how I wanted them both to be whole. I didn't think there was a way to combine them completely.

Not as they were right now.

So, I pushed my energy into the dark crystal, used all five of my elements as they whirled around me and pulsated within my body, and I pushed.

Someone sucked in a breath, another gasped. Air moved over me, Water glided up my legs, and the Earth rumbled. Fire licked at my fingers, and warmth spread through me even as it chilled me to the bone. I knew that all five elements were there. And they were waiting.

As I opened my eyes, we were where we needed to be. Where the battle would be fought.

The King of Lumière was waiting.

I knew we had a traitor in our midst. Either that, or his spies were that good.

Easton had tried to find all of them, as had Justise over time, but there was only so much you could do in a court full of lies and whispers.

The King of Lumière and his people were waiting with some of ours until the battle was fought, right where Rosamond had Seen, right where it needed to happen.

The castle itself still looked whole, unblemished from all the taint of The Gray and the King of Lumerie's darkness.

It seemed odd to me that the Lumière, the kingdom of light, would be the one that became filled with perpetual darkness. Maybe that was just.

Because while the Obscurité might have been named for the dark, they were the ones who pulled through, that saw beneath the shadows and tried to protect their own.

Not all of their people, not all of those in charge.

Because I recognized some of ours on the front lines of the battlefield. Some of the warriors who had once fought for our side.

Two of them I knew. Two of them I had seen in the Spirit territory at some point.

I knew them, I had seen them, and they had looked at me with disgust and fear when they saw me almost lose control of my four elements at the time.

They had seen the darkness in me. Or maybe they recognized it in themselves and had fled to the King of Lumière.

The others with me muttered to each other beside me, and I knew that they could see the faces of their enemies now. Those who had, at one point, been their compatriots.

The betrayal stung, but we didn't have time for that.

I looked up, and even farther up, to where the King of Lumière sat upon a white winged horse, the regalness of the majestic beast bringing tears to my eyes. I didn't even know that Pegasus was real in this world—or in any other.

Its wings were pressed tightly against its side since the king was on the top of the hill and not using the creature to fly. I didn't want to hurt the beast. I wanted it to be free. It wasn't like I could actually save those fighting against me, though.

I could sense The Gray all around us. Could see the shadows billowing and snaking amongst the people who fought against us. Who stood in front of us, their Wieldings at the ready, anger on their faces.

They were doing what they thought was right.

They thought us evil, and they believed what the King of Lumière told them.

They put their faith in a false god and believed the lies of a traitor.

There would be no reasoning with them.

"You could have ended this, Spirit Priestess," the King of Lumière called out.

"As could you," I answered, the others letting me speak.

"If you had only come to us, had seen the side of good, you would not be responsible for so much bloodshed."

I ignored the hurt in my heart at that, even while Easton murmured that it wasn't my fault. Rhodes did the same.

I knew it wasn't *completely* my fault.

However, I also knew that if I wasn't strong enough, wasn't cunning enough to win this, more blood would be shed.

It wouldn't only stain my hands but that of the man who rode a Pegasus as if he were a god.

"So be it," the king snarled, and then there was no more talking. There didn't need to be. He had said his piece even before this. He had spewed his lies and egged on those who wanted to believe that nothing was wrong, that there wasn't a higher power orchestrating all of this.

They didn't want to give up what they had, and they wanted to put the fault on someone else.

So, they cast blame on Easton. And they blamed their beloved prince who had betrayed them in their eyes.

And they accused me, a prophecy come to life.

Because, in their estimation, I was the one stripping them of their powers.

Regardless of what they thought, I would protect them.

I would protect as many as I could, and then I would find a way to bring the crystals together.

It was the only way to make their plan work.

The shouts of the fight came at me all of a sudden, and I knelt on the ground, my hands shoving into the earth. I looked up and screamed.

I pushed all of my strength into the dirt, and a huge wave of Earth slammed into the men and women coming at me.

I stood up then and used my Air Wielding to soar into the air, landing on top of that wave and then using my Fire and Water as one, sliding my hands to the side, and then back together again. It created a spiral of Fire and Water that didn't douse. Instead, it burned hot, coalescing into a boiling mass.

It stormed the others, and the screams echoed in my ears.

I had to ignore the screams of those I couldn't help, and it killed me.

Teagan and his father were fighting together, each using their Fire in such manic ways that I knew they were feeling the loss of the Lady of Fire.

Despite the grief, they were still smart, still warriors to the end.

Teagan gripped his father's shoulder, and I could see the Lord of Fire become a funnel of sorts as Teagan shoved his power into his dad.

Twice the amount of Fire erupted from the lord, and it burned those in its path to a crisp.

I turned my head away from the screaming and focused on those I was trying to get past.

I needed to make a path, needed to get beyond the king and into the castle. If I could get to the crystal, maybe I could end this.

That was always a plan. Easton would take the king with Rhodes at his side, and I would take the crystal.

I just needed to get there.

Alura danced across the pile of Earth next to me, spinning out of the way of Air shards and Water crystals that tried to attack her.

I couldn't even see what type of Wielding she was using, but people were falling down, one after another as she shot her hands at them.

I still didn't know what type of Wielder Alura was. All I knew was that she was powerful and a little bit scary.

Rosamond was on her other side, using her Water and Air as one, trying to get through the combatants.

A Fire Wielder who had defected from us sprayed a torrent of Fire towards her, and she fell back screaming. I couldn't even reach her.

It didn't matter, Luken was there, Brae hovering by his side. She was larger than I'd ever seen her before, almost the size of a panther with large wings as she opened her mouth and growled flames.

Luken used his Air Wielding down his sword and shoved it at the Wielders who came at them. He held out one hand, and Rosamond took it. She shook off the dirt on her side and spat out blood before going back to using her Wielding.

Wyn stood off by herself, her Earth Wielding making the earth tremble around her.

People fell into crevices that opened up, and Water filled those holes, drowning them as they screamed and burbled.

There was such a manic expression on her face that it scared me a bit. I wanted to go to her and hold her. Tell her we would figure everything out.

Only there was no time for that.

Delphine stood at Wyn's side, using her Water Wielding in a way I had never seen before. She created soldiers out of Water, ones that moved in a marching pattern of wet slaps against the earth as they advanced on the other Wielders. They fought for her like an army or even pieces on a chessboard, battling those who came against her.

People she had trained, those who had been by her side.

I could see the moments of recognition when they noticed their former queen fighting on our side. That quickly turned to pure shock and then rage.

And then they came at her. But she was stronger.

When a Fire Wielder threw his Fire towards Wyn when she wasn't looking, I screamed, even as I attempted to shoot Air Wielding towards it to try and move it away.

Suddenly, Delphine was there and threw her body in front of that wave of Fire, her Water Wielding protecting most of her but not her eyes.

She screamed and fell back, and Wyn, who had almost died right then and there in front of my eyes, caught the Queen of Lumière as she toppled, holding her eyes as she screamed.

I wanted to help, but I couldn't. Instead, I stood between Rhodes and Easton as we fought back to back, combining our Wieldings as much as we could.

I still didn't know how to fight with Spirit, and I didn't know if it was actually an offensive element at all.

But, we were fighting. We were trying.

I looked up as Rhodes snarled under his breath, and I saw the Lord and Lady of Earth in front of us.

"We're not allowed to kill them," Rhodes growled out, and I looked at him, nodding.

"I am," Easton said with that smirk of his that I kind of liked.

He lifted up into the air, Fire licking at his feet, and then did something I'd never seen before. Fire erupted from his hair and moved down his body. He grinned.

"Lord and Lady of Earth," Easton shouted over the din of people. "I see you're late."

"You are a false king," Valor growled. "You have sent us to our deaths, brought destruction. You have corrupted the Spirit Priestess, and you have doomed us all."

I barely resisted the urge to roll my eyes.

"If that's what you think," Easton said, and then he shot Fire from his palms, the sound of it so loud, I almost clapped my hands over my ears.

It sounded as if I were in the middle of a tornado, and Rhodes reached out and gripped my arm, steadying me.

I trusted Easton not to hurt me. Just like I trusted Rhodes.

The Lady of Earth slid behind her husband. She didn't even bother to try and protect him.

I had always known she was hiding unknown depths of depravity. I hadn't known she would sacrifice her husband, however.

When Valor screamed as he burned alive, Zia screamed also, parts of her arms and legs that could not be hidden behind Valor burning, as well.

And then the Lord of Earth ceased screaming, and there was no sound from him as his corpse fell on top of Zia. I wanted to shout, wanted to do something.

Zia had to be alive. She had sacrificed her husband to save herself.

They had both sacrificed so much for their desires.

I was so busy watching what was happening in front of me that I almost missed the Air dagger coming at me. I cursed, trying to fling my way to the side. I knew I was probably going to be too late.

It was not going to end like this. I shot out my Air Wielding, but it wasn't at the right angle. A blink, and suddenly, someone was at my waist, pushing me down quickly. The Air dagger flew over my head.

I rolled to my back and looked up as Emory scrambled off me and held out her hand.

"What are you doing here?" I called.

"Apparently, saving your behind."

The shackles at her wrists lit up, and I knew that the energy within her that made her a siphon was calling out to the many people around her.

"You're going to get hurt, you're not trained," I said.

"No, I'm helping move the wounded. I just didn't want you to die."

She met my gaze, and I wanted to reach out and hug her. I wanted to go back for just a moment and pretend that everything was fine, and we were going off to college. I saw Braelynn off in the distance, protecting Luken and fighting for our side. I could feel the elements within me wanting to get out, needing to protect our kingdom.

With those realizations, I knew there was no going back. There never had been.

I gave Emory a tight nod, and then she ran off back to where someone was screaming for help.

She dragged them to the side, where Ridley and the other healers were helping.

She was doing what she could. She wasn't the same person she was before.

Neither was I.

I took a deep breath and felt the crystal within the castle calling to me.

It was so close. I could almost save it.

As I reached out, wings filled my vision, and I knew I wouldn't be able to get there anytime soon.

The King of Lumière swiped out, and I ducked, pushing Rhodes to the side as Brokk tried to kill his nephew. The king caught my braid and sliced down with his blade of Air.

My hair fell, the parts that were left lying in choppy waves around my face. It didn't matter.

He hadn't hurt me, he'd only taken my hair.

He could have it.

Because I was going to end him.

I had to.

I looked at Easton. He stood on the other side of the Pegasus and nodded at me.

This was the time. There would be no second chances. No surprise rescues.

We were it.

And the king was ready.

CHAPTER 33

EASTON

I slammed my Fire Wielding towards the king. He flew up, missing the band of Fire.

Lyric threw both hands into the air, creating a Water wall to protect her and Rhodes, and I cursed under my breath.

"Coward!" I called out.

"Are you okay?" Lyric asked as she came to my side.

"I should be asking you that. I almost killed you."

"No, I can protect myself. Now, we need to get the king."

I reached out and slid my hands through her now shorter hair.

"I kind of like it," I said, trying to lighten the mood.

She grinned at me, even though her eyes were a bit watery. And I knew it wasn't because of the hair.

"Okay, we're not done yet," Rhodes said, rolling his shoulders back. "The others can handle what we have in front of us and anything that comes after. We need to move forward. Get to the crystal."

"I bet you Eitri and the king are the ones protecting it."

"Is Delphine okay?" Lyric asked, and I shook my head.

"I can't tell. She's still breathing, so that counts for something."

Lyric nodded, squeezed my hand, and then we were off. The three of us used our Wielding together as if we had been born doing this, as if we hadn't been living in three separate worlds before this. Lyric was a mix of both Rhodes and I, and I relished it. She could use her Wielding with both of us, although I knew it was easier for her to do so with me.

That was fine. We were soulmates. It was what we were supposed to do.

The fact that she could use her magic with Rhodes didn't make me jealous. Maybe it should have, only not when we were at war. Not when I knew that if I were to fall, she would still be protected. There would be someone there to help her get through this, to help her survive and to fight on.

There would still be hope for our realm.

Because I didn't think I was going to survive the end of this war. I knew in my gut that The Gray had more plans for me.

He wouldn't let me go that easily. And he wouldn't be able to let Lyric go. If, somehow, we defeated him and we didn't survive, Rhodes would be there to protect our people. And knowing that calmed me enough that I could fight—even if it surprised me just as much.

The fact that the man had been my rival for my entire life and now was someone I relied on for so much should have shocked me.

But this was our destiny.

I shouldn't be surprised anymore that our lives were intertwined just like our fates were.

I slid my Fire Wielding up, mixing it with my Earth, and Lyric did the same, then used her left hand to mix in her Water and Air.

I had never seen someone do that, not that anyone in my life *had* all the elements.

The fact that Wyn had the two she now had was a revelation that I knew we would have to deal with.

First, we needed to survive this.

"The crystal should be over on the left."

"I can feel it," Lyric said, her voice shaky. "It's coming closer."

"The crystal?" I asked, confused.

She shook her head. "No, the tendrils from it. It's scared. It's sad. And we need to save it. We can't let it be used like this."

I frowned over her head at Rhodes. He shrugged.

We didn't know what she was talking about, but that was fine. We kept moving, kept fighting, and somehow, thanks to the others on our side, we were able to make it to the castle. The king was nowhere to be seen at the moment, and I growled out, wanting to scream or hit something.

One of the League came out of the castle, using Water Wielding to create sharp spikes of ice to fling at us.

Lyric slammed up her hands, and Air sliced off the tips of the spikes while I used my Fire Wielding and melted the rest.

Rhodes twisted his hands around, creating a vortex of Air that shoved the now-melted ice towards the League member.

The man didn't even scream as he drowned. We made it past another League warrior, and then two more Creed assassins, and then we were in the throne room. We worked on autopilot, working together as a unit so we could defeat anyone in our path. We needed to get to the crystal. Somehow, Lyric had to work with it to save our kingdoms.

The king had to be near. I could practically feel The Gray's presence, and that meant the king was around somewhere.

I didn't know if The Gray would bring his minions, but I wanted to face them. I wanted to kill them for what they did to Lyric.

I would end them all.

I just had to find Garrik and the rest of them. First, however, the crystal.

Rhodes kicked in the door to the crystal room, and I turned, protecting his flank as three more guards came at us, shooting daggers of Air and trying to lift us off our feet. Lyric slammed into the wall. I didn't reach out to her. If I did, it wouldn't be enough. The distraction would end us both. She slammed out Fire Wielding from her place on the floor, and the guards ducked out of the way. I used my Earth to slam a slab of stone from the castle right on top of them.

Sweat covered my brow, and I reached down to help Lyric up. Suddenly, she sent Water all around us, dousing the flame from a former soldier of mine. He had betrayed us, but even as I killed him, part of me broke.

My people were dying, and they were deserting.

All because of the king's lies. And there was nothing I could do to stop it. Nothing I could do to protect my people aside from getting Lyric into that room. Rhodes slammed into the door again, using all of his Wielding. And then, we were in the room. But we weren't alone.

Eitri was there, his slender body encased in leathers that I knew no blade could penetrate. Because I knew the scent of that magic.

The Gray.

Delphine's son, Rhodes' cousin, and perhaps the future of the Lumière Kingdom if we weren't careful, had also aligned with The Gray. We wouldn't be able to kill him easily.

Though we would.

Because there was no way to get to the crystal without going through him. Ending him.

"Traitor," Eitri snapped over at Rhodes.

"You've betrayed our entire race. For what? Power? No, I'm not the traitor."

"You are." Eitri snarled. "You couldn't have the girl, lost out, and yet you'll still kneel at the winner's feet. You never were a good loser, but it turns out you're just a supplicant."

"That's a big word for someone who hasn't actually fought on his own before," Lyric said, and I smirked.

That's my girl.

"You know, it would be easier if you just let us through," I said, trying to sound as reasonable as possible. "You're not going to beat us, not three against one."

Eitri puffed out his chest. "I'm not alone. I have your master at my beck and call. He'll protect me because I am the future of this realm. You never were, Easton. You were merely a pawn to get to her." The prince of the Lumière laughed. "And, look what happened? Her parents are dead, and it's all your fault," Eitri said, grinning.

Lyric shook between us, and then she slammed out her Fire Wielding. Gray smoke created a web between us and Eitri and doused her flames. We weren't done. We sent Water, Air, Earth, and more Fire at him.

It wasn't enough, not with The Gray battling us using Eitri as his puppet.

By himself, Eitri was nothing, not even a full-blooded warrior. But with The Gray practically stealing his soul, he was so much more.

And we were going to lose if we didn't find another way out of this.

"Hold me back if it becomes too much, if it overtakes me," Lyric whispered, and Rhodes and I looked at her, and then at each other.

"Don't sell your soul for this," I growled out.

"I won't. But he's already sold his."

And then her eyes went opaque, smoke reflecting in them. Not that of The Gray. It was white and beautiful and of the Spirit Priestess. The hair that now barely touched her shoulders billowed around her head as if caught in a magical wind.

She held out her hands, and a sense of magic swept over me. I knew this was Spirit Wielding.

Eitri's eyes widened, and then he gasped, clutching at his chest.

Lyric wasn't done.

No, she opened her mouth and screamed. However, I could hear no sound. Nothing.

But I knew she was screaming. She was in pain, whatever she was doing was hurting her, and there was nothing I could do about it. Eitri screamed, as well, and I could hear his voice, I heard his panic.

I felt no pity for him.

He had made his bed, and now he had to lie in it, a rotting corpse of the boy he had once been.

Maybe he'd never had a chance, not with the father and uncle he had.

Delphine had never had a chance to raise her son, and this was what happened because of it.

Eitri bent forward at the waist, and then backward. Then one leg after the other went out. Before Lyric could finish whatever she was doing, smoky chains wrapped around Eitri, pulling him into the abyss.

Lyric screeched and reached out. I gripped her waist, holding her back.

"He's gone."

"He was dead, I held his soul in my hand. The Gray took him, so I don't know what's going to happen to him now. I couldn't finish." She spit up blood and uttered a curse, wiping her chin after.

"Doing that almost killed you," I growled out.

"It was the only way. The Spirit Wielders came just now. Late as always, and they spoke to me. It was the only way."

"I'm beginning to hate those guys."

"You're not alone," she said and hugged me tightly before pulling back. Together, we faced the crystal.

"I can feel it calling to me. It's hurting. I think it's dying."

"It's alive?" Rhodes asked the question I had been thinking all along.

"It's not a true sentient being. However, it's more alive than we give it credit for, just like the dark crystal. It's been crying out for its brother this whole time. We need to fix this, I just don't know how."

"You'll never learn how." Suddenly, the king was there, gray smoke slithering in from every crack of every door and window. The power slammed into me, and my back hit the wall with bone-rattling force.

"The Gray sends his regards," the king whispered, and then I saw darkness.

CHAPTER 34

LYRIC

I shoved at The Gray's magic coming at us from King Brokk and screamed, pushing all five of my elements through my hands.

My body shook, and blood seeped out of my nose. I knew it was dripping down from my ears and my chin.

This was too much. I didn't have enough control, didn't have enough power. I wasn't about to die here. And I wouldn't let Easton and Rhodes die either. Both of them lay passed out at my feet, the blows from The Gray coming directly at them through Brokk rather than me.

The King of Lumière wanted me alive, and now he was going to have to face me.

Because I was the Spirit Priestess. The one who was supposed to save the world. Damn him for making me do this.

I shoved my Spirit Wielding out, threw the Fire and Air and Water and Earth. King Brokk screamed, going to his knees.

He clawed at his eyes, blood seeping from where his nails dug into his face. The Gray's shadows slithered around him like a snake, and then Brokk got to his feet, his Wielding ready to come at me.

Brokk slammed one Air dagger at me, and then iced it over with Water. I shoved Fire at him. It wasn't enough, so I ducked out of the way, the dagger piercing the stone behind me.

Both Rhodes and Easton started to wake up, shaking their heads as they pushed themselves out of whatever magics had slammed into them.

They were on their feet in the next instant, blood trickling out of their ears, as well. Rhodes had a bloody lip, and Easton had a shard of stone in his shoulder.

We were all bruised and bloody. But we were *not* broken.

The King of Lumière would not win.

"You will not prevail. The Gray will always win."

"He won't," I called out. "You are not The Gray. You are just his pawn." I slammed Fire into him, and it licked up his arm. He screamed, trying to shove at the flames, but it wouldn't go away. Especially because Easton had joined in, his Fire wrapping around the king's body. He screamed.

And then Rhodes shoved Air to mix with the Fire, egging it on, intensifying its heat.

The King of Lumière screamed again, his voice hoarse as his body burned. The Gray didn't come for him.

The Gray had clearly given up on him, just like he had given up on so many. Because, as I'd said, they were just pawns, they weren't worth the fight or the energy.

The king, however, had a little more energy to spare. He shoved out of the Fire, his left arm a charred thing. He threw blade after blade of Air and Water, still coming at us. The ground shook, and I was reminded that he was the King of Lumière, the most powerful Lumière Wielder of his generation.

Except, I knew Rhodes was stronger. He really should have been king. He hadn't wanted the throne, though, hadn't been ready to take the mantle.

I didn't think we would have much longer until we had to make the choice of who would rule—no matter that there might not be a realm left to rule at all.

The Spirit Wielders would want me to use my Spirit Wielding. I didn't have enough juice.

I was out of the last of my reserves, even though I had tried to hold back. Taking out Eitri and trying to save was too much.

I knew if I used my Spirit Wielding, I wouldn't have enough left to protect the crystals. And they were the most important part of this plan.

So, I shoved all four of my other elements at him, all at once. They created a sludge of Fire and Earth and Water and Air that slammed into the king. His body was thrown back, and he hit the throne made of gold and diamonds and crystals of beauty and light with a resounding thud.

A crystal shard from his own chair shot through his chest, and I held back a gasp. I hadn't meant to do that. But he had landed just right, so his own symbol of power pierced him clean through. Blood poured out of his mouth, and through the gaping hole in his chest. It wasn't enough, though. He wasn't dead.

We needed to end him. And it hurt me to admit that. It was too much. I didn't want to be this person, someone who killed without reservation.

Rhodes and Easton were at my side in the next breath, and I wasn't alone.

"You will never rule, you will die by his hand," the king gurgled out.

"*You* will never be able to hurt another person ever again," Rhodes said, his voice hard.

"You could have helped so many, could have brought us together. You chose not to," Easton growled out. There wasn't any anger in his voice, just sadness and utter disappointment.

Even though I didn't want to kill, maybe the good outweighed the bad. No, I knew I would have the deaths of those I ended marked on my soul until the end of my days.

I would no longer be whole because of what I had been forced to do.

I had already lost so much, but I needed to face my reality. That meant meeting his gaze and refusing to close my eyes as the King of Lumière let out one last shaky breath and then died.

Right in front of us, with no pomp or circumstance.

It was death at its cruelest, and I had been the Wielder.

So now, there was no King of Lumière. There was no sovereign of the enemy.

No one to help put the kingdom back together.

My hands shook, and I looked around. I knew the kingdom was still fracturing. As the king's soul left, and I watched it go to a place I could never reach, I let out another shaky breath and staggered to the crystal room. The light crystal, just like the one in the Obscurité Kingdom, pulsated, fractured light spearing out of it on the parapet like sun hitting a prism.

This crystal was the dark crystal's mirror image, its brother, and it was dying, too.

I staggered past the king's body on his throne and headed towards the crystal itself. And then I looked past that to where my home lay, to where the Obscurité waited for us, and tears slid down my cheeks.

"No!" Easton screamed.

"It can't be," Rhodes called out.

Others were screaming as spears of light slammed into the wards that separated the two courts.

The crystals themselves shook, and I knew that they were nearing their end, this was their last stand, their final moments.

And as people screamed, their magic being ripped from them as they became Danes right before our very eyes, the wards fell.

It was as if a curtain had fallen down from the heavens and slowly billowed away in silky sheets of magic and dust.

We could see the Obscurité Court clearly. We could see its people, the castle.

In the distance, a dragon or something like it trumpeted, and I knew that was Fire, and the earth rumbled from Earth.

The Air behind us swirled, and the Water sipped at the territory's dry shores.

The four elements were now one. In this instance, there were no kingdoms, only a realm taking its last breath.

I turned away and tried to face the crystal, attempted to help. It reached out to me, its spindly wispy fingers broken and tattered.

I knew this was the end.

"The crystals are fading fully," I whispered. Easton was at my side in a step, taking my hand.

"What can we do? If the crystals fade and fall completely, our realm is dead."

"Can we fuse them together?" Rhodes asked from my other side.

I took his hand and gave it a squeeze, and then let go of them both.

"I know what I have to do. I don't know how I know, but I know this is the next piece. We're going to find our way after this. However, right now, this is what must be done."

I looked at them, my heart breaking, and I knew they knew.

"Don't let this kill you, damn it," Easton snapped and kissed me hard on the mouth before taking a step back.

I touched the crystal once and then went to the end of the balcony to face where I knew the other crystal was.

I closed my eyes, and as the crystal shook, crying out to me, I held my hands out from my body in opposite directions to face each crystal.

The crystals screamed, their dying breaths ones of mania and pain.

So much corrupted magic had filtered through them over the years that they were now fragments of themselves, trying to protect. Not able to do anything right. At least in their minds.

I would have to rebuild them, to make them into what they once were. However, in order to do that, I needed the pieces.

So I shoved all the elements from my body, every ounce of my being that I had left, and I pushed it out towards the crystals.

Bright light beamed, and people stopped screaming as they looked on in awe at the colors and swirls of magic that bubbled and bounced all around us.

The crystals screeched, more light pouring from them before they shouted, *please, please!* in my head.

And then the crystals broke. One splinter after another, multiplying shards.

They shattered into a million pieces, into dust. Into virtually nothing.

More people shouted and screamed and called out. I didn't know who they were calling to. I didn't know anything.

I only knew that the dark crystal flew over the distance between us, its remnants swirling until they landed right on my skin, the light crystal's doing the same. The glittering dust swirled over my body as if tattooing me and etching my skin with its memories and power.

It sank into my flesh, and it burned, echoes of memories and of pain and histories long since dead and fallen seeped into my bones.

The crystals were no more, their power now within me. I would find a way to put them back together again.

They were home, even if this shelter was only for a moment.

I opened my eyes, and both Easton and Rhodes stared at me, their eyes wide, not able to say a thing.

I wasn't sure what I could say either.

I was the Spirit Priestess, the one who was supposed to save us all, and I had just destroyed the crystals.

Their energies flowed through my body as if trying to heal one another, and I knew this was only a step. Only a pause before the break, before the silence of death screamed into mercy and new beginnings.

Our people were safe, the realm was stable for now.

And once I figured out how to pull out this magic and form a new crystal or do something else that would protect everyone, we would be safe.

We would have a weapon against The Gray.

I just needed to survive the overwhelming power within my body first. We would find a way to come together—*all of us*. We would heal those who had given so much for us, and we would find a way to thrive in this realm. To heal it.

And as I looked at Easton, and he came forward to hold me close, I knew I wouldn't be doing it alone.

I would never be alone again.

CHAPTER 35

EASTON

I looked over at the wounded and then those helping others and tried to feel some semblance of warmth or confirmation that we'd won. It was hard to do with so many people on the ground, their eyes open and vacant. So many had died for this, to protect their realm, not their kingdom, not their territory, not their element. Their *realm*. And I wasn't sure we were done yet.

I looked over at Lyric, who stood by Rosamond, holding the other woman's hand as the Seer grunted. Ridley was currently pulling ice shards out of her back.

Apparently, one of the Wielders had learned how to make shrapnel from ice, and it carved into somebody's flesh. Especially if that person had covered a smaller person with their body, trying to protect them. I didn't even know which Wielder Rosamond had protected. I figured the only reason she'd even seen the ice coming was because of her visions.

She still had blood seeping from her nose, and I knew that was probably because of her Seer powers, as well.

People were helping her, just like others were helping everyone that was down for the count.

Our own men and women were even helping the Lumière soldiers who had fought against us.

A lot had fled when the king died. They took off into the mountains, and I knew that they would likely find a new leader. Probably The Gray himself. He was out of royalty to use as pawns, after all.

Other Lumière had shown up at our borders in need of aid, pledging their allegiance to freedom, rather than a kingdom. We needed everybody that we could get, and if we could prove that they weren't traitors, then we would use them.

At least, that was the plan.

Justise knew what he was doing, and between him and Rosamond using her Seeing, and Lady of Air with her secret ways I still didn't quite understand, we would be able to figure out exactly who was on our side when the time came.

As I thought of the vast amount of people who had perished, and those who were injured, or those who looked like they had lost everything because when the magic had stripped their Wielding from them, I knew that we would need *more*.

We would need those who had hidden themselves away, even those who had maybe been our enemies at one point.

We would need people like the pirate king, even though I had raised an eyebrow when Lyric mentioned it. Still, I wasn't above asking Slavik for help. And he would know the workings of the underbelly of our realm. He would know who might want to save our realm from fading away into extinction, even if they had questionable morals. Because that's what The Gray wanted. The Gray wanted the Shadow realm to rule.

And if the Shadow realm ruled, the Maison realm would die.

"Do you think Rosamond is the Queen of Lumière now?" Rhodes asked me as he came to my side. "Aunt Delphine abdicated when she left the realm."

I raised a brow as I looked at the other man who had fought by my side. He had put himself in front of Lyric and me to protect us.

It didn't matter that I had once hated him because of who his parents were. It didn't matter that I had fought against him for so many years. It didn't matter that I had hated him because he could love Lyric when I couldn't at the time.

He was my brother now. He was family. However, I could still be an asshole.

"So, it's either you or Rosamond, I would think. With your scrawny cousin dead and all."

"We don't know that Eitri is dead. Something happened right when he was pulled into The Gray," Rhodes said, shuddering a bit.

I joined him in that shudder. "Well, he's as good as dead, then. Rosamond is the next in line to rule in terms of age."

"I don't want to be the queen," Rosamond said.

"You might not have a choice," I said. "I didn't."

"I'm a Seer. Like the Spirit Priestess cannot be queen, neither can I. Leadership would go to Rhodes, I would think," she said, looking off into the distance. I didn't know if she was using a vision or just her hopes at that point.

Rhodes shook his head. "We don't have time for a King of Lumière, even King of Obscurité," he said sharply, and I nodded.

"We'll worry about the royal lines later. For right now, we're just generals, those who would fight for our Spirit Priestess and our realm."

"Don't fight for me," Lyric said, coming up to me. She wrapped her arms around my waist, and I held her close, kissing the top of her head. It was odd to be so affectionate with someone. To feel something so deep in my chest. This was my new normal. And I felt as if I'd been waiting my whole life for this.

I was so afraid that we were going to lose these precious moments, that we would only have a few of them left, so I didn't mind that everybody stared.

Because this could be the last time I held her, and I knew it.

I felt the power within her, knew the crystals etching their way into her skin had amplified it.

And I didn't think that her body would be able to handle it for long. It could barely hold her five elements as it was.

We had to get the extra magic out of her. No matter what.

"We'll deal. First, we must fortify our resources and work together," Rhodes said, and I nodded.

I looked around at those who'd survived and thought about the fact that we only had a small number of lords and ladies left, and that Delphine was now blind. I remembered that Wyn was dealing with a new element, and Teagan and his father were in mourning, still fighting yet scarred.

The Lady of Earth had disappeared. I knew she was alive, even though her husband was dead. There was so much to do, so much more to figure out. However, there was one thing we knew. We needed to defeat The Gray.

"We'll find what we need. We'll uncover our allies, and we'll go up against him. And then we'll bring back our realm."

Lyric looked up at my words and nodded tightly. "We'll bring back the crystals in any form we can." She looked down at her hands, at the fact that she glowed just a little bit in the light. The illumination was there for only an instant, but I had seen it, and so had the others.

"We'll find a way," I whispered, kissing her hand.

"I know." She leaned into me. And then Braelynn jumped into her arms, and Lyric let out an oomph before she laughed. Lyric wasn't small anymore by any means.

The fact that my Lyric could still laugh warmed me. She hadn't laughed as much lately.

She wasn't the same girl I met in the borderlands. Neither was I the same prince or king.

We had both changed, and I wasn't sure if it was for the better.

Braelynn nudged at Lyric's chin, and she smiled again, and then I just grinned at her. People were still milling about, doing what they needed to, yet I felt as if we were the only two people in the world.

Braelynn chirped.

Okay, two people and their cat.

"You did amazing, baby," I said softly.

"You weren't too bad yourself. We can do this. We are doing this. We can defeat The Gray. I know it."

And even as she said the words, something slithered over my skin, and my jaw tightened. I knew that sensation. I'd felt it every day I had the curse.

Something pulled at me, and Lyric's eyes widened.

The shadows descended along the borders and within their camps. People screamed, their voices stopping in an instant as the shadows enveloped them. Then the darkness skittered past, leaving them whole yet shaken. I threw myself in front of Lyric. I wasn't fast enough.

Lyric reached out to me, and I turned again, trying to hold her.

It was as if we were in a vacuum, as if something was dampening the sound, making everything disorienting, and pulsating within my ears.

It took too long for me to move my body, to speak, to do anything.

It was if I were a half-step behind, trying to come to terms with what was happening.

Finally, I was able to hold Lyric with Braelynn between us. Both of them had their eyes open, their mouths wide. Blood poured from Lyric's eyes and mouth and ears, and I could hear her scream in my head. Only I knew she wasn't actually making any sound.

I tried to keep her close, attempted to stop what was happening. Then, it was too late. I was holding air, and Lyric and Braelynn were gone.

And then the realm descended into silence.

THE END

Lyric's journey and the *Elements of Five*
series continues in …

FROM
SHADOW
AND
SILENCE

A NOTE FROM
CARRIE ANN

Thank you so much for reading FROM SPIRIT AND BINDING! I do hope if you liked this story, that you would please leave a review! Reviews help authors and readers.

This series is EVERYTHING to me. I'm honored with how many of you love it along with me and are following Lyric's journey. Thanks are intense and the world is breaking, and I cannot wait for you to read the next installment!

If you want to make sure you know what's coming next from me, you can sign up for my newsletter at www.CarrieAnnRyan.com; follow me on twitter at @CarrieAnnRyan, or like my Facebook page. I also have a Facebook Fan Club where we have trivia, chats, and other goodies. You guys are the reason I get to do what I do and I thank you.

Make sure you're signed up for my MAILING LIST so you can know when the next releases are available as well as find giveaways and FREE READS.

Happy Reading!

THE ELEMENTS OF FIVE SERIES:

Book 1: From Breath and Ruin

Book 2: From Flame and Ash

Book 3: From Spirit and Binding

Book 4: From Shadow and Silence

ABOUT
CARRIE ANN

Carrie Ann Ryan is the *New York Times* and *USA Today* bestselling author of contemporary, paranormal, and young adult romance. Her works include the Montgomery Ink, Redwood Pack, Fractured Connections, and Elements of Five series, which have sold over 3.0 million books worldwide. She started writing while in graduate school for her advanced degree in chemistry and hasn't stopped since. Carrie Ann has written over seventy-five novels and novellas with more in the works. When she's not losing herself in her emotional and action-packed worlds, she's reading as much as she can while wrangling her clowder of cats who have more followers than she does.

WWW.CARRIEANNRYAN.COM

MORE BOOKS FROM
CARRIE ANN

THE MONTGOMERY INK: BOULDER SERIES:
Book 1: Wrapped in Ink
Book 2: Sated in Ink
Book 3: Embraced in Ink
Book 4: Seduced in Ink
Book 4.5: Captured in Ink

THE MONTGOMERY INK: FORT COLLINS SERIES:
Book 1: Inked Persuasion

THE LESS THAN SERIES:
Book 1: Breathless With Her
Book 2: Reckless With You
Book 3: Shameless With Him

THE ELEMENTS OF FIVE SERIES:
Book 1: From Breath and Ruin
Book 2: From Flame and Ash
Book 3: From Spirit and Binding
Book 4: From Shadow and Silence

THE PROMISE ME SERIES:
Book 1: Forever Only Once
Book 2: From That Moment
Book 3: Far From Destined
Book 4: From Our First

THE GALLAGHER BROTHERS SERIES:
Book 1: Love Restored
Book 2: Passion Restored
Book 3: Hope Restored

THE WHISKEY AND LIES SERIES:
Book 1: Whiskey Secrets
Book 2: Whiskey Reveals
Book 3: Whiskey Undone

THE TALON PACK:
Book 1: Tattered Loyalties
Book 2: An Alpha's Choice
Book 3: Mated in Mist
Book 4: Wolf Betrayed
Book 5: Fractured Silence
Book 6: Destiny Disgraced
Book 7: Eternal Mourning
Book 8: Strength Enduring
Book 9: Forever Broken

REDWOOD PACK SERIES:
Book 1: An Alpha's Path
Book 2: A Taste for a Mate
Book 3: Trinity Bound
Book 3.5: A Night Away
Book 4: Enforcer's Redemption
Book 4.5: Blurred Expectations
Book 4.7: Forgiveness
Book 5: Shattered Emotions
Book 6: Hidden Destiny
Book 6.5: A Beta's Haven
Book 7: Fighting Fate
Book 7.5: Loving the Omega
Book 7.7: The Hunted Heart
Book 8: Wicked Wolf